# CAGED!

'You must have plenty of boyfriends, Isobel,' said Rollo Cragg, refilling her glass. Isobel allowed her eyes to fall once more to his bulge, inches from her own flesh. Her breasts heaved, thrusting up the creamy teat-flesh that Rollo made no pretence of ignoring.

'No,' she murmured. 'I'm rather shy.'

'Good heavens, why?'

'Are you sure Mrs Cragg didn't just mention *that*, too?' asked Isobel, with a thin smile. '*My special need*, sir?'

She swallowed, blushed and took a deep breath that thrust her breasts up; Rollo licked his teeth, flexed his whip.

*What are you waiting for, Isobel?*

'Gemma is a terrible gossip,' he replied, 'and sometimes it's a teacher who most needs to be taught a lesson . . .'

*It's now or never . . .*

'I'm a teacher, too, sir,' she blurted.

*By the same author:*

MEMOIRS OF A CORNISH GOVERNESS
THE GOVERNESS AT ST AGATHA'S
THE GOVERNESS ABROAD
THE HOUSE OF MALDONA
THE ISLAND OF MALDONA
THE CASTLE OF MALDONA
PRIVATE MEMOIRS OF A KENTISH
  HEADMISTRESS
THE CORRECTION OF AN ESSEX MAID
THE SCHOOLING OF STELLA
MISS RATTAN'S LESSON
THE DISCIPLINE OF NURSE RIDING
THE SUBMISSION OF STELLA
THE TRAINING OF AN ENGLISH GENTLEMAN
CONFESSION OF AN ENGLISH SLAVE
SANDRA'S NEW SCHOOL
POLICE LADIES
PEEPING AT PAMELA
SOLDIER GIRLS
NURSES ENSLAVED

# CAGED!

*Yolanda Celbridge*

This book is a work of fiction.
In real life, make sure you practise safe sex.

First published in 2001 by
Nexus
Thames Wharf Studios
Rainville Road
London W6 9HA



Typeset by TW Typesetting, Plymouth, Devon

Printed and bound by
Clays Ltd, St Ives PLC

ISBN 0 352 33650 1

# Contents

# Prologue

# Hauled and Strung

*There are two worlds, the cold and the hot. In the hot world, a wench's lust must be tamed, and in the cold world, it must be kindled. The instruments of both taming and kindling are the same: rod on bare arse, and tarse in coynte, or better, her nether hole most secret and sublime.*

Sir George Pollecutt, Universall Travels

'Fan harder, you wretch,' drawled the woman, reclining on her divan.

The male continued to wave the garland of goose feathers, his exertion as placid as his gaze, at the woman's half-dressed body, was stern.

'Bah! You don't understand a word,' she sighed. 'How I hate Tangier! The babble, the stink and fools who cannot speak the King's English. How I wish His Majesty had never gotten this place, nor given Pollecutt his post. Sometimes, I wonder if Dodd's tropic whippings weren't better than Pollecutt's neglect – at least I got regular swiving from him, with a tarse not so damnably big as to hurt my pouch.'

The windows were open on the balcony; below them, the noise of afternoon in the souk: donkeys, carts clattering, voices in Spanish, Berber and Arabic. The woman loosened an eyclet of the brocade corselet, which was all that covered her upper body, and allowed her maid and two male servants to view her white breast, straining against the heavy fabric. The ripe pears of her bottom were sheathed only in a voile negligée shift, its sweat-damp fabric clinging to the rippling contours of buttock and thigh, which were naked under the film of cloth. Her stockinged feet waggled the air, their curled Moroccan slippers discarded on the carpet beneath.

A second male filled her glass with mint tea, and proffered a dish of marshmallow. Both servants were muscular dark youths, Berber tribesmen, of the lady's own age, slightly over the twentieth year; like her, they were clothed for the heat, their upper bodies bare, with loose blue ankle-robes draped at their loins. Despite their ebony bodies, the young men had blue eyes. The barefoot, besmocked maidservant knelt by her mistress's feet, bathing her toes in scented water. Though tanned by the sun, she was European, of the same young age, ripe body and tresses as her lady. The lady sighed.

'So hot . . .' she gasped. 'Well, you are but heathens . . .'

She unfastened her corselet completely, allowing her bare breasts to spring free, with the strawberry nipples jutting and firmed. She shook her head, waving her long blond mane, so that its hairs caressed her nipples.

'*That's* better,' she murmured, sipping her mint tea.

'Yes, you damned hussy,' whispered a male, concealed behind a spyhole in a false wall, on the shaded side of the boudoir. His shirt was clinging wet to his torso, above cotton breeches and calfskin boots, with a brace of pistols, rope, donkey-crop and rapier at his belt. 'Messalina, Jezebel, the temptress Eve herself, were lambs compared to you!'

The lounging woman pulled up her negligée, baring her buttocks and pubis completely; her bush of tangled, golden pubic hair glistened with her sweat. She began to fan her loins with the voile negligée, parting her thighs, to show the rich ruby lips of her vulva and the wet, shining pouch within. The male servants continued at their tasks, each with a growing bulge at his crotch, while the maid lifted her smock and fanned her lady's feet, showing her own bare arse and loins, and a pubic jungle massive on the lithe, muscled basin of her quim.

'So,' said the lady, 'you are heathens, but men for all that! How I wish Sir George recognised my charms! I so rarely see him – prancing in the desert, in search of treasure, or, more like, goats to swive!'

'Foul harlot!' hissed the spying male.

'When he serves me, his tarse swives me so ill, I can scarcely move for the pain of it! More a horse's than an Englishman's, and too often put in the place unintended by nature! You have no English, so cannot understand my woman's plaints . . . but serve me well, and I shall reward you well.'

'Ah . . .' groaned the male. 'Calumny upon vileness!'

'Perhaps *this* you may understand,' she continued, licking her teeth and placing her fingers on the lips of her vulva.

She drew her lips back, and thrust three, then a fourth, finger inside her pouch, now gushing with copious juice.

'You see? My purse needs good meat for the filling – just as yours needs silver. Peruvian pieces, fresh snatched from the king of Spain . . . *piezas de plata peruviana!* – one for each of you, if you obey.'

She rose, casting off her negligée, and placed her hands upon her head, standing with one leg bent and raised, with the heel wedged in her open slit.

'I am as helpless,' she moaned, 'as a slave in your marketplace. The captain is away until tomorrow, and I have no one to protect me from your tools I see so monstrous, you lustful brutes.'

The two males had fully erect cocks, clearly outlined as they strained against the fabric of their robes. Her teeth and eyes sparkled in the shadowed chamber; a shaft of sunlight fell on her nipples, fully hardened and erect, like plums. Juice trickled from her quim down her thighs to the sole of her raised foot; her thigh trembled as it supported her. The two servants let fall their robes and the lady gasped, licking her lips. She reached out and touched each of the swollen, shiny helmets on the peehole.

'Your foreskins cut! Smooth horns, both, to give my husband horns! Truly, you are heathens, so I can commit no sin . . .'

'Knowing nothing else, you count sin as virtue, damned trollop!' snarled the watching male.

He continued to watch, as the lady took a marshmallow from her mouth and moistened it inside her wet quim. She bit the sweetmeat in half and put a piece in each of the servants' mouths; stretching herself belly down on the couch, she raised and parted her taut bare arse-melons. Both males chewed and swallowed their juiced sweetmeats. One stood at each end of the couch, while the maidservant drew up her smock, revealing her own naked loins and her tangled quim-hairs glistening. She mounted her lady like a pony, sitting on the small of her back, and began to rock back and forth.

'Ride me, Ghislaine, ride me . . .!' groaned her mistress.

The lady fastened her lips over the male's cock, and her tongue began to dance on the glans while her lips pressed and tickled the helmet's base, and her fingers dripped with her juice, as she frotted her swollen nubbin. She gasped as the second male's cock nuzzled the open lips of her gash, and grunted when the dark tool penetrated her wet crimson folds, right to the balls. Her mouth fastened completely on the cock at her lips, taking the whole shaft right to her throat. Her head bobbed up and down as she sucked one cock, while the second rammed her quim. The maidservant's own cunt was bared, seeping copious oil. She masturbated her swollen nubbin as she rode her mistress's back, slapping the lady's bare buttocks, quivering under the black tool's thrusts.

After several minutes of vigorous swiving and sucking, the lady moaned and gestured. Ghislaine remained in saddle; the males switched places, and she began to suck the cock slimed with her own cunt-juice, while its fellow penetrated her womb, fucking her vigorously for several seconds, before she grasped the member and transferred it to her opened anal pucker.

'Oh! I am the weaker vessel! Take me where you will!'

The cock sank deep into her arse-passage and she sighed, growling in her breast, and masturbated hard, using both hands to frot her clitoris and erect nipples, as the naked servant vigorously buggered her. She squealed, drooling, as she sucked, and her buttocks writhed under buggery, with the male's hips and belly slapping her bare arse-flesh.

'Do your worst, you Vandals!' growled the watcher.

Both males spunked in unison; she swallowed the sperm creaming her mouth, while the bugger's spunk bubbled at her jerking anus bud, and the lady masturbated her clitoris to a loud, long spasm. The maidservant's panting breath indicated that she, too, had masturbated to climax, attested by the stream of come flowing down her mistress's writhing bare back, Ghislaine's bucking mount.

'Ah – ah – *ahh* . . .' the lady squealed, her cries dying away to a sated gasp: '*Mmm* . . .'

The spy quit his cubbyhole. Moments later, he burst through the door of the chamber, clutching his pistols.

'You vile beasts!' he cried.

'George!' shrieked the lady, groping for her negligée.

The maidservant Ghislaine pushed down the front of her smock and curled herself in the corner of the room; the two males seized their robes and vaulted over the balustrade, to disappear into the throng a few feet below.

'Oh, Captain,' sobbed the buggered woman, clutching her bum-cleft. 'How thankful I am! You have rescued me from shame and agony! I gave those damned beggars a few coins, and they refused to leave me until they had earned my charity! Little did I know . . .'

Whap! Whap! Whap!

Her husband slapped her face three times.

'*Oh!*' she squealed, bursting into tears as he ripped her negligée from her, and wound her hair in his fist.

Holding her on tiptoe by her hair, he began to slap her naked breasts, until her strawberry nipples were bruised blue. She shrieked, sobbing, her mouth drooling spunk and her quim and bumhole dribbling. Her heavy teats shook under the slaps; her bare feet flapped helplessly, trying to kick her husband's calfskin boots; her bottom still glowed pink from her maidservant's spanks.

'You lie, slut!' he hissed. 'I saw you buggered. Your holes are still full of another's spunk! Little Ghislaine, your bawd, got those whelps to serve you.'

The maidservant emerged from the shadows.

'No, Sir George!' sobbed the lady.

'Though mute, Ghislaine speaks to me,' said her husband.

'Ghislaine!' shrieked the lady.

Ghislaine smiled coquettishly, and nodded. She expressed in swift, impish sign language the entire transaction: her procuring the males, and her mistress's promise of silver from the captain's treasure. Without command, she accepted the rope, uncoiled from the captain's belt, and bound her mistress by her wrists. The captain ripped her negligée in half and wound it around her ankles. Trussed, the lady was pushed on her belly, on the floor. The captain slid the point of his rapier under her pubic mound and touched her clitoris, obliging her to raise her buttocks and cunt basin; Ghislaine held the sword, while the captain unbuckled his belt. The lady sobbed, her sob turning to a scream as Sir George's cock penetrated her still-slimed anus, and began to bugger her, with hard, slamming thrusts.

'Take that, ma'am! And that!' he roared. 'Damn you for a strumpet!'

'*Ahh . . .!*' shrieked his wife.

'High office I have won, yet am still bound to a whore!'

'How *dare* you, sir!' she shrieked, her arse-globes writhing under her husband's buggery. 'God! The shame! *Oh! It hurts!* To be Lady Pollecutt, an *English* lady, *twice* ravished in the foul sin of buggery! *Ah! Ah!*'

'You were nothing but a bonded slut when Dodd sold you in the mart of Hispaniola, with your coynte the best travelled road in the Caribees, and the widest. Why, a man could get his camel to fill your chasm, and have room for himself and a squadron of hussars! Before your bondage, slut, you were Molly Coker, a whore from the alehouses of Hartlepool . . . my faithful Ghislaine, though heathen, is more a lady than you! Wait . . . yes . . . ah! A dirty job, but must be done! You'll have your punishment . . . ah!'

Sir George Pollecutt grunted as he spunked in her anus, his jet frothing over the lips of her squirming anal pucker, already slimed with arse-grease. His wife sobbed, quivering helplessly, as Ghislaine fixed her roped wrists to a pulley, which she drew up, until Lady Polecutt hung naked, with her bare feet wriggling inches from the floor. His member breeched, Sir George reclined on the couch, lit a cigar and accepted the bottle of port wine which bare-footed Ghislaine nimbly served. While she poured the wine, her master's fingers slipped under the girl's smock and began to play between her legs. He grinned at his trussed and suspended wife, who sobbed, staring aghast at Ghislaine's face of pleasure and the bouncing of her pert bubbies, as her loins swayed to Sir George's fingering. Leering at his helpless wife, the male withdrew his fingers from Ghislaine's basin, and showed them, oiled with her fluid. He licked his fingers, one after the other, of her come. His port wine drained and his lips and fingers well slimed by the pretty young maid, Sir George's cock was stiff.

'The tarse you affect to despise, dear,' he said to Lady Pollecutt, 'inspires your further chastisement.'

'No! Please! I beg you!' she squealed. 'I'm so sore! Oh, no, please!'

Sir George rose, and took his *tap*, the Berber crop of heavy braided leather used on the hides of asses and camels. Ghislaine knelt once more at her mistress's feet, this time to hold them still, pulling and stretching Lady Pollecutt's body, to present the quivering bare buttocks as a ripe, fleshy target for her husband's crop.

'No, sir! Please! Don't *flog* me!' she squealed.

'Whipping is the only language your whore's arse understands. Many's the time you were hauled and strung, to be lashed naked, as a bondservant.'

Vip! Vip! Vip!

His wife's bare buttocks clenched and squirmed as the crop bit her trembling skin.

'No!' she shrieked. 'It hurts so! *Oh, please, no!*'

Vip! Vip! Vip!

'*Ahh . . .!* You'll ruin my fesses!'

'On the contrary, madam! A pink arse is the tastiest.'

Vip! Vip! Vip!

'*Ahh! Ahh!*'

Her ankles firmly held by Ghislaine, Lady Pollecutt shuddered, wriggling, as the *tap* bruised the bare expanse of her fesses with livid stripes of crimson, darkening to purple. Sir George thrashed every exposed inch of her naked croup, from her haunches, which were soon black with welts, to the fleshy, quivering mid-fesse and the inner thighs below the croup, where the tip of the crop caught the jutting, swollen cunt lips amid her wet pubic jungle.

Vip! Vip! Vip!

'*Ah! Ah! Ahh . . .!*'

Vip! Vip! Vip!

'*OH! Stop . . .! Please stop . . .!*'

When Lady Pollecutt's flogged buttocks were a blotched, puffy mass of crimson and purple welts, her husband laid down his *tap*. The ridges, wealed in her thrashed bum-flans, were etched in shadow by the lowering sun.

'Now, dear lady, you shall see *real* pleasure,' said Sir George. 'I warn you – if you avert your gaze, your flogging shall begin anew.'

Sobbing and trembling, the trussed woman watched, as Ghislaine lifted her smock to reveal her heavily juicing slit and tangle of pube-hairs, exceeding her mistress's in richness; flat, muscled belly and hard, conic bare breasts, with domed nipples already stiff with excitement, as Sir George's cock penetrated her. Ghislaine lay beneath her dangling mistress, with her thighs wrapped around Sir George's back, clutching him to her, as he fucked the maid's copiously juicing cunt.

'I fuck in your arse for your pain, milady,' he panted, 'but in sweet Ghislaine's coynte, to give her pleasure! She is a true whore, as pure as the desert sands. Your lusts are cold and joyless, and only your arsehole has sentiment. You cannot feel pleasure without suffering pain, to remind you that pleasure is wrong.'

'*Mm! Mm! Mm!*' Ghislaine cried, rocking back and forth, as her belly threshed under the male's pounding.

Sir George began to fuck her very slowly, withdrawing his cock to its full length from the wet, squeezing gash, before plunging into her again, each stroke right to the hilt.

'See how Ghislaine enjoys, my dear! As she will enjoy our bed tonight, while *you* hang, to meditate on your sins.'

'*No . . .!*' wailed Lady Pollecutt.

'There are many like Ghislaine here in Barbary,' said Sir George. 'Pity a slut like you cannot share my philosophical interests. What can *you* understand of the goddess *Flagella*, worshipped by Roman and barbarian alike? Nature repeats herself, in strange harmonies and strange places. How many tribes have seeded the desert sands! Greeks, Goths, Romans – Vandals, like Ghislaine here, blue of eye and blond of tress. Our English race itself is nourished by divers roots. I feel it my duty as an Englishman to reacquaint *these* beauties with the joys of an unskinned tarse . . . and a well-pickled rod for their fesses!'

'*Ah! Ah . . .!*' shrieked Ghislaine, her body lathered in sweat and her cunt pouring come, as Sir George, fucking vigorously, spunked at the neck of her womb; his cream spurted from her gash flaps, over her thighs, and the maid writhed in whimpering orgasm. '*Mm! Mm! Mmm . . .*'

As the room dimmed, with the setting sun's rays a departing red glow, Sir George Pollecutt followed Ghislaine downstairs, where the two blue-robed youths waited in the shadows of the courtyard. Sir George handed each a silver coin.

'Guiseric and Alaric . . . fine names, my lusties,' Sir George said, clapping the backs of both the males who had served his wife.

He reascended the stairs, and took port wine and biscuits as he watched Ghislaine at her toilet. The lithe brown girl stripped naked, then pissed and stooled into a rose-tapterned English chamberpot, which she emptied into the street. She wiped and perfumed her loins with her fingers, before climbing into his four-poster bed. Sir George crept into the salon, where his trussed wife hung, snuffling and sobbing. He picked up her brocade corselet from the floor.

'An English lady mustn't catch cold, my dear,' he said, pressing the brocade to her bare bottom.

The brocade stuck.

# 1

# Scene

Afternoon wind breathed softly across the baked rock of the desert, bathed in pink light from the lowering sun. Not a shrub, nor blade of grass, shivered under the azure sky; whorls of dust spurted briefly, to float, glittering in the haze, beneath jagged red mountains, with the fort and its cluster of humans no more than shards in the moonscape. A pennant of pink brocade fluttered atop the ochre fort, topping clusters of bougainvillea, honeysuckle, date palms and hibiscus fringing a limpid oasis pool.

Tears streamed down the fair girl's cheeks, as her body jolted against the bars of her cage. Her T-shirt, once white, was smudged and ripped, as were the filthy panties wrenched to her crotch and scarcely covering her bare tan thighs. Ragged and sweat-soaked fronds of pubic hair glistened beneath the fabric, riding up over their tufts, and her shirt, translucent with moisture, clung to the massive breasts, their nipples stiff, squashed against her ribcage by her jolting. Her head was bent, and her back and buttocks pressed against the rusty cage bars, better for an animal smaller than a woman. Her eyes were wide and frightened, yet she did not emit any sound of protest other than a whimper. The toes of her left foot were jammed into her mouth, held there by a rope, which bound her right ankle around her neck, parting her thighs and extruding the glistening lips of her quim from her panties.

Metal cuffs, looped to a pin-studded rubber punishment corselet under her breasts, clamped her wrists high up her back. Her mane of yellow hair was plastered to her skull, dripping with sweat that sparkled in the sun. A garland of honeysuckle in her hair shaded her brow. Her eyes were wide, as her two male bearers, each swathed in sky-blue robes, padded on bare feet across the rocks, towards the flogging frame. They held the cage on poles, balanced on their shoulders, so that the girl's shame was fully exposed to the audience of captives.

Nine sullen, fearful, wide-eyed European girls crouched barefoot on the desert rock, their wrists cuffed at the small of the back, and shackled to a chain, whose end rested with a third blue-robed guard, his free hand holding a coiled leather whip. The chained girls were nude. They crouched with their bellies positioned over spikes driven into the rock, the points almost touching their pubic mounds and keeping their bottoms high in the air. All wore pairs of nipple clamps, each pair of clamps threaded by a short chain to a spike driven into the rock, obliging the girls to hold their heads as high as their croups. The girls were bare-headed under the sun's glare, broken only by the shadow of the ochre fortress and by human figures, stark against the desert, and by the gaunt oblong of the flogging-frame. Eddies of sand blew over their footprints from the fort to flogging-frame. From the oasis pool, beside the fort, a single track snaked through a pass in the jagged mountain; in the far heat haze, the same high peaks ringed the fortress, adding nature's confinement to that fashioned by humans.

The blue-robed guards were ebony; two Europeans were present at the scene of punishment, and both dressed in white. One, a young, hard-muscled male, sweated in a cotton suit, with his striped silk tie tight beneath his jaw, shaded by a panama hat. The second, a woman his junior, stood with arms folded, holding two coiled whips. She wore a thin cotton *peplos*, hanging to just below her vulva from two knotted shoulder-strings, and cut deep at the breasts, rippling on her body free of underclothing. Her long brown legs were roped in high sandals that covered her calves. The tip of a slender cane, worn on a leather thong at her waist, slapped the ribbons of her sandals. The contours of her proudly jutting breasts and full, taut buttocks were plainly visible to the guards and audience alike, with the crimson plums of her nipples already erect in excitement as she watched the caged girl advance to her. She was bare-headed, like the other females, but with her long honey tresses smooth and a parasol held over them by another blue-robed guard. The guards approached her, stopped and, without a sound, dropped the cage with the girl inside it.

The woman in the white skirtlet walked around the cage, inspecting her prisoner. The dozen chained girls stared at the caged girl and at the woman, who smiled as her prisoner sobbed. She nodded and the blue-robed guards unlocked the cage door, dragged the girl out and untied the rope that gagged her with her toes. They wrenched her erect and forced her to stand, wailing in a choked sob, her wrists straining against the cuffs that furrowed them. Her head hung low in shame. The woman kicked her legs apart, revealing yellow liquid streaking her inner thighs.

'Frightened, Edwige?' she said softly.

Sniffling, but without looking up, the girl nodded.

'Yes, Mistress,' she sobbed.

'Your bottom is no stranger to my cane, Edwige,' said the blond woman. 'But this is your first proper whipping.'

Edwige snuffled.

Without letting go of her whips, the blond woman cracked her palm full across Edwige's cheek.

'Oh . . .!'

'*Isn't* it, Edwige? Your first flogging?'

'Yes, Mistress . . .'

'So – this time, not dusted a few dozen stingers with my dainty woman's cane on your bottom, but flogged by the strongest of *males*, on the bare back, in front of your comrades in filth . . . what you *really* came here for. Isn't it?'

'Oh! No, Miss Habren, I swear!'

Habren slapped her face twice more, then her bare breasts, several times, so hard that the nipples slapped one against the other.

'Miss Edwige Joule, so prim and proper and submissive!' she spat. 'Is this honestly your first real flogging?'

'You *know* it is! I've never taken a back-whipping before, only bare-bum caning! *Oh, God . . .!*'

She stooped suddenly, parting her thighs, and a jet of golden fluid hissed from her crotch, splashing her feet and the rock between them. The domina turned to her crouching prisoners.

'Edwige disgusts me. You *all* disgust me,' she spat. 'Girls who should be the decent property of their males, allowed to roam Africa, in search of forbidden, or fancied, excitements. And you end up here, in the women's prison. The Berber are a proud and pure people. By your immodesty, you have forfeited the right to be considered human, and are chained like bitches. Every single one of you has screamed as her bottom reddens under my cane, and *still* you will not learn! Perhaps Edwige's whipping, and loss of remission, shall be a lesson. You, Edwige, shall serve your full year. It shall go easier, if you explain why you are to be flogged.'

'I looked through the bars, Mistress, and watched a male bathing in the oasis at night,' stammered the girl.

'Knowing full well that a Berber male may not be seen disrobed by any woman not his wife. That was the crime that sent you to the women's cage, wasn't it? The male found with you went unpunished, of course – to the Berbers, the female is the temptress, the lustful beast, who must be tamed by corporal punishment. That is why canings on the bare are part of all your sentences. Any objections?'

It was not a question.

'N-none, Mistress.'

'Go on. Why do you merit whipping?'

'It was the heat . . . this dreadful, scorching heat, night and day . . . I couldn't help myself! I . . . I masturbated as I watched.'

'I have caned you on the bare, several times for masturbating, Edwige. What is the tariff?'

'Twenty-one strokes for solitary pleasure, forty-two each for girls caught together, or sixty-three each for triads . . .' Edwige blurted. 'But this *heat* . . .!'

'On four occasions, you and two companions have taken sixty-three strokes on the naked buttocks,' said Miss Habren crisply. 'This time, your eyes gleamed at your cell window, and were observed by the guard, who shall now flog your back to the bone. It shall hurt much more, and much longer, and you shall bear your stripes home – if your perverse nature ever lets me release you.'

'*Oh . . . no! Please!*' Edwige wailed, convulsing in sobs.

At a nod from Habren, the guards ripped her T-shirt and shorts from her, and she stood revealed in her nudity, breasts and belly trembling, and with her massive pubic bush drenched in her sweat and the pee, which still dribbled from her shining red gash. They undid her corselet and handcuffs, showing her tan flesh bruised from the studs inside the corselet. The flogging frame was a simple wooden oblong, embedded in a basalt plinth, with cuffs for the wrists and ankles, at each of its corners. The cuffs hung on cords, adjustable to the victim's height. Dangling from the centre of the crossbar, was a headcage of metal strips: a brank, or scold's bridle, with a tongue depressor. One berobed guard cuffed Edwige's wrists and the other her ankles, taking only seconds as her height made no adjustment necessary.

When her naked body was stretched, hanging in a cross, between the posts of the frame, each guard disrobed and stood nude, save for a blue loin-thong. One held the girl's head, while the other fitted her into the brank, with the tongue depressor clamped in her mouth. Although the chain was left slack, the wide collar of the brank would oblige its occupant to hold her head high throughout her punishment. Edwige faced her sister prisoners, whose eyes fixed on her nude body, already trembling and with pee dribbling from her bush. Habren handed a whip to each of the guards.

'*Two* males shall whip you, Edwige –' she said.

'*Two*, Mistress? *Oh . . .!*'

'– and naked, for their greater comfort and power. There is no taboo broken, for chained women are mere animals. They shall feast on every shudder of your whipped body, and every tear that falls from your eyes, and, when your whipping is complete, you shall not dress, so that your welts may urge your sister sluts to behave.'

She murmured in Berber dialect and both males raised their whips behind the naked prisoner. The young European male in the panama hat stared, licking his lips, at the nude body of Edwige, glazed with her sweat.

'Satisfied?' said Habren, and he nodded.

'I don't expect you to stay still, Edwige,' said Habren, 'or to be silent. Your brank should help muffle your screams and save you from total shame, but, I warn you, I shall extend your tariff if you blub overmuch. As it stands, your tariff is one hundred lashes. As for you, young ladies, you saw Edwige at the dormitory window, and your complicity in her crime has earned each of you a dozen strokes from my cane. You are not branked, so that if there is the slightest squeal from any girl, her set shall be repeated right from the first stroke. If it happens that I have not completed your canings by the end of Edwige's flogging, then Edwige shall be whipped on, until your canings are complete.'

She murmured again, in Berber, and leather flashed.

*Crack! Crack!*

Each whip lashed Edwige's naked back, the first striping the shoulders and the second her mid-back. Edwige's nude body shuddered violently, her face twisted, and her gorge trembled.

*Crack! Crack!*

'*Mmm . . .!*'

Habren strolled to the first of the nine pegged girls and raised her cane.

Vap!

The girl shivered, as a pink weal appeared on her bare bum-flesh.

Vap! Vap! Vap! Vap!

Her buttocks began to clench as Habren's strokes became faster. The dry tapping of the cane was drowned by the crack of the two whips on Edwige's naked back, the strokes now slamming her body against her restraints, as her head bobbed in its metal prison. There was no pause between the strokes, the whips dancing like twin pistons.

*Crack! Crack! Crack! Crack!*

'*Mmm! Mmm! . . . Mmm . . .*' came Edwige's gurgling cry, her body shaken like a doll's.

Habren completed the dozen strokes to the shivering jellies of her victim's bare buttocks, red as her face, straining not to blub under punishment. As Habren delivered the last stroke, the girl shook desperately and a stream of pee flooded her clamped thighs. Habren smiled, lifted her skirt well above the jungle of her pubis, and looked at the young man in the panama hat, sitting forward in his chair, with his eyes darting from the flogged girl in her brank to the shuddering bare bum caned by the sandalled woman, her flimsy *peplos* swirling as she caned. His crotch bulged in erection as he fanned himself with a newspaper. Habren's eyes flitted to the naked whippers, and her smile widened as she looked on their own bulging cocks beneath their blue loinstrings.

Habren raised her cane above the tensed buttocks of the second crouching girl, and placed her fingers at the wet slit under her pubic jungle. The girl's clitoris peeped hard and swollen from the moist folds of her labia. Habren brushed her hair back from her brow, and looked at the guard who held her parasol. His robe bulged at the crotch and Habren flicked his erection with her cane tip, pursing her lips in a pout of mock surprise. She nodded and the guard grasped the hem of her dress, raising it over her swollen nipples and holding it at her collar-bone, but without touching her skin. Habren placed her free hand at the jutting peach of her croup and slipped her fingers into her bum-cleft. She lifted her right leg and placed it on her left calf, widening her cunt basin, so that her palm and fingers could embrace both anus and vulva.

Vip!

As she caned her second girl, Habren began to masturbate. She reached between her thighs, stroking her wet vulva and thumbing the bud of her anus pucker as she applied even strokes of her cane to the girl's bare.

Vip! Vip! Vip!

'*Ahh . . .!*' the girl moaned.

'Blubbing! Wc bcgin again,' hissed Habren, her fingers probing deep into her dripping slit.

The girl stifled a sob as Habren reapplied the cane to her fresh welts, deepening them to crimson and making the buttocks clench white around the dark red stripes. Each stroke slammed the girl's clamped nipples against their fastening and jerked her belly close to the raised spike, close beneath her opened buttocks. Habren took her to her dozen; the girl's body quivered helplessly, her face red and her buttocks squirming, clenching flans of crimson. Come dripped on the spike, inches below her moist gash flaps.

As she caned the next girl, Habren's eyes fixed on the whip-jolted body of Edwige, flogged on her bare back and jerking in the frame as each lash of the twin thongs scarred her. Habren's aim to the buttocks, bared below her, was swift and accurate, and no sound accompanied the caning, save for her victim's faster and faster panting and the slam of her nipple-clamps against their tethering spike. Habren's fingers were slopped with juice from her own swollen red gash and, without pausing in her caning, she slid her hand from her anal cleft, to lick her fingers clean.

*Crack! Crack! Crack!*

Edwige's body dripped tears and sweat, as each whip-stroke sliced her. Deep in her throat, a harsh gurgling whimper vibrated, her clamped tongue unable to form words. Her whippers glistened with sweat, their muscles rippling over their massively swollen loin-pouches, as they striped Edwige's writhing golden back, her ribs pulsing into relief at each shuddering breath between strokes. Her breasts bounced like balls beneath the collar of her brank at each crack of leather on spine and shoulders. As Habren caned the last girl, Edwige's gurgle of agony was a long, single mewl. Her vulva dribbled pee without ceasing, yet the yellow fluid glistened with pouch-oil. Whipped so hard, the girl was juicing at her gash.

Habren paused as the last girl raised her bottom a fraction and parted the cheeks, to show the hairy wet mass of her pouch and perineum. Her auburn hair was cropped to sleek fleece but her mound boasted a jungle rivalling Habren's; the breasts, massive as Habren's own, pressed around their spike, unstrained by the nipple clamps, and her pencil waist ripened into tan buttocks like bursting calfskin, lined with canemarks, with her cunt dripping come over the menacing belly-spike.

'One would think your bottom invited my cane,' Habren murmured. 'And your gash, too, so insolently displayed. English, aren't you? Susan Race . . . cheeky bitch.'

The girl did not respond but stared at Edwige's squirming body.

Vip!

Habren slashed her cane hard between the arse-cheeks, deep in Susan's befurred slit. Susan shuddered but did not squeal.

Vip! Vip! Vip!

Habren lashed her again on the open vulva, and twice more. Her fingernails were a blur as she masturbated.

'Those strokes don't count to your caning,' she panted, and Susan nodded, smiling as she gasped.

Vip!

The cane lashed Susan's bared buttocks full in mid-fesse. The hard, muscled flesh quivered as a pink weal appeared amid the hardened dark skin of previous canings.

Vip! Vip!

Two strokes took her on the tender skin of the upper fesses.

Vip! Vip!

Two more followed, one to each haunch, raising livid welts. Susan's cheeks began to clench, rapidly and involuntarily, as the wood reddened her skin. Her back remained straight and her breasts quivered only slightly at each impact. Juice flowed from her swollen pouch flaps. Suddenly, Edwige's mewling became a muffled howl. The whips continued to stroke her back, but she threw herself against the flogging-frame, instead of allowing the whips to jolt her, and began to jerk her branked head from side to side, her eyes wide, staring at Habren. Habren paused in caning Susan's bare.

'*Mm! Mm! Mm!*' moaned Edwige, shaking her head frantically.

'How many strokes left?' Habren barked.

'Sixteen, Mistress,' said the first whipper.

'*Mm! Mm!*' sobbed the flogged girl, shaking her head.

'Can't take it, Edwige?' said Habren. 'Had enough?'

Edwige nodded yes, her moans fainter.

'Give the girl her sixteen, and continue to whip her until I have finished this one,' Habren rapped, and recommenced her caning of Susan.

*Crack! Crack!*

The whips streaked across Edwige's writhing bare back.

Vip! Vip! Vip! Vip!

Four strokes bruised Susan right on the softest skin of her top buttocks, and her back and buttocks began to shudder.

Vip! Vip! Vip! Vip!

'*Ahh . . .!*'

After four cuts to her gash, Susan yelped, and Habren murmured that she must begin her dozen over again. Susan's punishment was continued three times, while Edwige's body stiffened and jerked at each whiplash, carrying her well past her hundred. When Susan Race's bare fesses were two puffy crimson gourds, Habren delivered a final cut to the arse-cleft and vulval lips, and her thumb pressed her own stiff clitoris into her pubic bone.

'*Ah! Ahh . . .*'

Habren sighed in climax as her come flowed down her quivering thighs, puddling the rock beneath her and staining her sandal-leather.

'Enough,' she ordered. 'Cut her down.'

'*Ohh . . .*'

Edwige collapsed, sobbing, on the sand at Habren's feet; she ripped the honeysuckle garland from her mane and threw it to Habren's juiced pubis.

'*You bitch!*' she wailed. '*You fucking bitch!* I begged you to stop . . .! *I couldn't take it!*'

'But you did,' said Habren, 'and deserved it, too, you submissive bitch.'

She lifted Edwige on to the chair beside the young male, and began to bathe the wounds of her back with scented salve. Habren stood at the chair back, leaning over, so that her nipples brushed Edwige's forehead. Her fingers ran up and down the girl's spine, covering every inch of her flogged skin, then descended into the buttock cleft and massaged Edwige's anus. Edwige moaned. Habren parted her legs and Edwige lifted her head.

Hesitantly, her tongue slipped out of her slack lips and penetrated the swollen folds of Habren's gash. As Habren rubbed her anus, twisting to get her fingers in the flogged girl's quim, Edwige began to press Habren's erect clitoris with her teeth, then penetrated the slit with her whole tongue, swallowing the juices that seeped from the swollen cunt. The young male watched, face red and crotch bulging, but he did not move. When Edwige's scarred back was thick with salve, Habren ordered her to kneel while continuing to tongue her mistress's gash. With the blond girl kneeling and her mouth slopped in Habren's come as she nosed and tongued the proffered vulva, the girl masturbated her own clitoris and her come juices joined her mistress's in an oily pool on the rock. The first whipping-guard lowered his loinstring and stood nude behind Habren's buttocks.

She lifted her left thigh and, at once, he reached to her vulva to retrieve a palmful of her come oil. With her own fluid, he lubricated her anal pucker and shaft, putting an index finger in, while oiling the bulb of his own giant cock, before nuzzling her exposed anus with his peehole. A swift jerk of his loins and his massive black tool was halfway embedded; a second and he impaled her anus, right to his balls. The young man in the panama hat gazed, transfixed.

With Edwige still licking her clitoris, Habren began to respond to the black tool's thrusts as it buggered her vigorously, withdrawing to the crest of the glans before each new penetration and soon slimed with Habren's arse-grease as well as the come from her slit. The black guard buggered Habren for several minutes before he groaned, and bubbles of sperm frothed at her anal mouth, stretched by the cock to many times its pucker.

His place was at once taken by the second whipper, his cock as massive as the first and his buggery as hard. The guard who had shaded Habren laid down his parasol and grasped Edwige by the belly. He pushed aside her masturbating fingers and took her from behind, thrusting his cock into her wet vulva and tooling her at the crouch, with his belly slapping her squirming buttocks, while she continued to tongue Habren's clit. Habren's fresh bugger gasped as he spunked in her anus and his sperm dripped to a creamy pudding on her thighs.

The guard, holding the shackle of the nine caned girls, dropped the chain and removed his own robe. Four guards were now nude; the two already spunked put their cocks turnabout in Habren's mouth while she tongued the helmets, raising the cocks to new stiffness. Grunting, the male fucking Edwige spermed in her cunt, and at once presented his slimed cock for sucking by his mistress, while she climbed on to the chair, parted her buttocks, and was anally impaled by the first guard who had buggered her, his cock sucked to new hardness. She pushed the chair away, and swayed, her full weight taken by his impaling cock, with her feet cradling her face, and calves squashing her breasts, so that her erect nipples jutted like pears.

The second guard thrust his own erect tool into her soaked gash. Both men fucked her, one anally and the other in the cunt, squeezing her slippery body between them, while Edwige, masturbating her clitty, clawed Habren's exposed nipples, and Habren's mouth took the cocks of the other two guards turnabout, sucking them to orgasm, swallowing their spurts and licking her lips clean of their copious creamy spunks. She moaned in constant orgasm, and the dripped come under her loins grew to a pool. When the males were gasping and spunked dry, Habren turned to the rear of the scene where a film camera whirred.

'Cut and print!' she cried. 'I only meant it as a rehearsal, but I think it's good enough to use.'

The guards released the tethered girls from their fastenings; all, rubbing their caned bums, clustered around Habren.

'You didn't have to leave us trussed quite so long, Mistress!'

'Nor cane us quite so hard!'

'Verisimilitude, my dears,' said Habren. 'I make a film about caned sluts in a Moroccan prison fort, *in* a Moroccan prison fort.'

'I begged you to *stop*!' Edwige wailed. 'Shaking my head was a *sign*! I really meant it, Habren! God, that whipping hurt!'

'When does *acted* penance become *real* penance? You are glad it didn't stop,' purred Habren, staring Edwige down.

'Yes,' sobbed Edwige. 'I deserved it. I've never hurt so hard, or come so much . . .'

Habren slapped a square of pink brocade into Edwige's bum-cleft, and it clung to the bruised skin. Edwige patted her flogged bottom and smiled.

'Any girl who tires of being paid to do what she *likes* doing, is free to go back to Marrakesh,' said Habren.

She turned to the gaping male in the panama hat, his crotch still bulging, as he ogled the nude, fully suntanned girls rubbing their flogged bottoms.

'Have you no shame?' Habren snapped. 'You're stiff, you dirty little creep. How can a husband watch, drooling like a pervert, as his *own wife* is abused?'

'But, darling – you *know* I am your *most* devoted fan. That is how we met – oh, the glory that you noticed me! – and . . . and let me produce your films! I *love* your acting!'

'A girl buggered is *never* acting, dear Joss. As for producing my very money-making films, you still haven't the nerve to sell them in your beastly supermarkets.'

'But Abby, you know . . . the uninformed public might think them lewd,' he blurted.

'Miss Habren, to you,' she drawled. 'Lewd, eh? Not like the big tits on your checkout girls.'

'Darling Abby – I mean, Miss Habren –'

'No, I think, "Mistress" . . .'

'Mistress, you know I've nothing to do with actual hiring at Gauntco . . . I merely approve.'

'And afterwards?'

Joss Gaunt squirmed in his chair.

'We have already established your regime of correction,' she said. 'How lucky you are that I permitted you to marry me, before you wasted all Papa's money on filthiness.'

'Am I to be caned, for watching you *act*?'

'Why, yes,' she murmured.

'How many, Mistress?'

'A good three dozen. No, four.'

'On the bare?'

'Of course.'

'Oh, Habren . . . Mistress . . .'

'Not *yet* . . . you must wait.'

'*Ohh!* You are *awfully* cruel,' he gasped.

'Yes,' said Habren.

# 2

# Payback

Angarad Stark shivered in her woollen pullover, skirt and tights, all navy blue, with the company logo at her breast, and her clothing thick enough to keep out the English winter. Below, on the Earl's Court Road, vehicles made swishing noises as they ploughed the sleet.

'I'd rather you sat down, Angie,' said her boss.

'But I prefer to stand, Will,' she replied. 'I'm scarcely here for a bonus, am I? If you're going to sack me, I'd rather leave fast, and with dignity.'

'*Sack* you . . .!'

The young man, also wearing blue, but in jeans and sweater, rose from his desk, where his computer monitor glowed with the lurid colours of a maze. He looked at the tangle and smiled.

'Our interactive games are almost as important as your interactive fashion,' he said. 'With "Labyrinth", we might even outstrip you . . . players creating their own maze as they go through it! It's impossible to win, yet impossible to lose. People like mazes. They're trapped, but safe, just as girls like tight knickers. Heavens, I'm not going to *sack* you, Angie! You're the best! If only . . .'

He perched on the side of the desk, frowning.

'You make me feel *I'm* the one who's done wrong,' he blurted. '*No!* Nobody's done wrong, it's just . . .'

'I *have* done wrong, Will, and I feel awful,' Angie whispered. 'I've let you and the team down, and the customers . . . perhaps I deserve the sack.'

She hung her head, the long blond tresses caressing the tips of her breasts, jutting under the fluffy sweater. Her hands were clasped at the small of her back.

'I accept I have to make amends, or . . . or be punished, somehow,' she added. 'It's only fair.'

'*Punished?*'

'It's an old-fashioned notion, but I *am* old-fashioned. You could dock my salary . . . though I don't know how much my sloppiness was worth, in money.'

'Oh, come *on*!'

Will sighed.

'It's ironic . . . a paradox. How do you punish someone who *wants* to be punished? Sloppiness is no crime, but we still feel it deserves a lesson, to encourage the others.'

'Then we agree,' said Angie, lowering her head. 'Thank you.'

'This is ridiculous!' Will exclaimed. 'I'm not Sergeant-Major Cragg, I'm a computer graphics artist! All I know is, if our backers think anything in Metawear.com is less than perfect, we're done in. Interactive fashion over the net . . .! Such potential, Angie, yet so open to piracy. I've sold it on my staff, my business plan, my *creative* plan – any flaw would take us down. We are talking many millions here, Angie, and you've accidentally downloaded thousands of personal files, who knows where? So a girl struts out in her new Metawear designer kit, because everything – fabric, design, cut – is her own exclusive, then sees half a dozen lookalikes in the High Street! God, I'm being a bastard.'

'No, Will,' said Angie. 'You're proving my point. I've done wrong and must make amends. The team knows my mistake and no payback is bad for morale.'

'*Any* payback is bad for *someone's* morale – like yours.'

Will put his arm around her trembling shoulders.

'Is there something you want to tell me? Boyfriend?' he said, gently.

She shook her head, then grinned.

'Derek, isn't it? From our outsource accounting?'

'Darren . . .'

'None of my business, damn it!'

'It's hardly a secret.'

'Look, I'm not angry at you, Angie. I just want to work the problem. Don't be hard on yourself – you're preoccupied, that's all.'

'That *is* the problem, Will. I haven't been hard on myself. I don't want to think I've just had a bad hair day. I *want* to make amends . . . to feel better.'

Will sighed again.

'A paradox,' he said. 'If you walk out of here miserable, morale suffers. If you wear a cheeky grin, you've got away with it, and morale suffers.'

Angie swallowed, and spoke rapidly in one breath:

'It . . . it needn't be a cheeky grin, Will. There are tearful ones, too,' Angarad whispered. 'Oh, God, forget I said anything. I'll resign . . .'

'No!' cried Will. '*Tell* me.'

'It would be one way of solving the problem.'

'Problem-solving is our business.'

'I mean, I would be punished . . . but not discouraged.'

'Enough riddles,' said Will. 'I want you back at work.'

Angarad took a deep breath.

'Promise you won't think I'm being funny, or teasing?'

'I promise,' said Will. 'Just tell me.'

'You . . . you could give me a spanking,' Angarad blurted.

'*What?*'

'I knew I'd make a fool of myself,' she said. 'I'll go.'

'Wait!' Will rapped.

Angarad halted and hung her head again. He looked her up and down, stroking his chin. She crossed her legs, the slither of her nylons revealing a flash of panties, and shifted in her seat to cover a damp patch on the leather beneath her gusset. Angarad blushed.

'It's an idea,' he said finally. 'Pretty corny – kinky, too. People do it for fun.'

'I didn't say it was for *fun*!' Angarad spat. 'I'll *hate* it. There is nothing, absolutely nothing, in the way of pleasure from it, I promise you. It will be a short, painful lesson, and I'll feel better when my tears have dried, knowing I've made amends. That's *all.* Payback.'

'Look, Angie, if you're into some kinky scene –'

'*No!*'

'At least give me some explanation,' Will said. 'Your parents – were they, you know, strict?'

'My *foster*-parents are gentle innocents,' said Angarad. 'Dad can't even fight to stop Gauntco supermarkets putting his shop out of business.'

'I'm sorry. But this spanking . . .'

'*I was spanked at school!*' Angarad blurted, her eyes moistening. 'That's the way things are done in the sixth form at Ditton Girls' Grammar, and it's all you need know. Lower forms got detention, or lines, but when you were a sixth-former, it was spanking. That way, teachers didn't waste their own time. Spanked or slippered, on panties or on the full bare! I hated it, and it smarted, and I wept, and I thought two years ago that I'd never have to endure the pain and shame ever, ever again, but it's the only way I *know* to atone for my mistake, so please, Will, *spank my bottom and get it over with.*'

Will shook his head, frowning.

'I can't just . . .'

'*Please!*'

Will sighed.

'OK, Angie,' he said, 'I'll spank you. I've never done anything like it before. Won't people hear?'

Angarad's face was pale.

'*That's the point,*' she whispered. 'They'll know. Girls *always* know when another girl's been spanked.'

'I suppose I'd better sit, with you bent over my knee,' Will said. 'Isn't that the way? It seems weird.'

'Or over the desk,' she said. 'It's up to you. Over your knee, I suppose, is more comfortable for you. And it's not weird, Will, it *hurts.* There's no point if you *don't* hurt me, or if I feel you're just going through the motions. I have to be wriggling and my bum smarting. Oh, God!'

'OK then,' he said, looking at his watch.

His blue leather armchair squeaked as he sat, heavily.

'I'm ready,' he said, his voice cold. 'Bend over my knee, Angie. I *am* a bit angry with you, for putting me through this weird game. So I do feel like hurting you. Satisfied?'

'It's no game,' Angarad hissed, as she positioned her belly on his knees, her toes and fingers on the carpet.

She lifted her skirt and tucked the hem under her belly, revealing her buttocks thrust upwards and clothed in thick blue wool of her tights.

'I'm going to spank you till I think you have made amends, Angie,' said Will. 'OK?'

'Yes. You'll know when to stop. That's when you mustn't, I'm afraid . . .'

Will pinioned the back of her neck and his fingers pulled down her tights.

'I *am* afraid,' she whispered.

'There, there,' he soothed. 'No point in spanking you with all that cladding. You mentioned the full bare . . .'

'Yes,' she said, her voice muffled in the blue leather.

He pulled down the tights, until the globes of her croup trembled under yellow satin panties cut high and clinging wetly to her skin, with the slightly stained fabric stuck in her cleft.

'Not company knickers, eh?' he whistled. 'That *does* deserve spanking.'

'Please don't make fun, Will.'

'I'm not. I'm serious. Maybe you've unleashed my inner beast.'

He pulled the panties up high so that the cloth stretched fully on her taut buttocks and left a generous expanse of naked skin at each haunch. Still pulling the waist elastic, he worked the satin into her cleft, until the buttocks were covered by little more than a sliver of cloth and presented two orbs of bare smooth skin for the spanking.

'I'm going to lay it on hard, Angie. I am quite serious. The yellow panties are kind of cheeky. I suppose you girls compare undies in the loo and think how clever you are not to wear company blue. Some team spirit . . .!'

'*No! It's not true!* Oh, please don't be cross with me!'

Crack!

'Ah . . .!'

Crack!

'Oh!'

Crack!

'*Ouch*, Will!'

Crack!

'*Mmm*!'

Will spanked Angarad's almost fully-bared buttocks with crisp slaps that covered the full expanse of her mid-fesses.

'Are you sure it's not true, Angie?' Will murmured.

Crack! Crack! Crack!

'*Ouch!* Oh, God!'

Angarad's buttocks clenched frantically, their flesh pinking, with Will's fingerprints etched in crimson on the quivering naked fesses.

Crack! Crack! Crack!

'About the panties, I mean. Come on, Angie, you can tell me. I bet you all giggle when you wear sexy colours.'

Crack! Crack! Crack!

'*Oh! Ah! Ohh . . .!* Don't be crude!'

Crack! Crack! Crack!

Angarad's bare fesses clenched so hard that the thin pink strip of her panties was engulfed in the quivering mass of her bruised bare buttocks.

'Oh, God! It's awful!' she sobbed. 'I've never been spanked so hard! Oh, God, Will, *stop*! I didn't mean what I said! Please *stop*!'

'You haven't answered my question. I like the panties, Angie, honestly. Design them yourself?'

Crack! Crack! Crack!

Her naked fesses, spanked darker than the pink panties, clenched uncontrollably.

'*Ouch!* Yes . . .'

'On company time, I imagine?'

Crack! Crack! Crack!

'*Yes, damn you!*'

Each slap made Angarad's buttocks jerk as though invisible fists were poking inside her skin. Will's palm spread its impact evenly over the lower fesses and, with spanks to the bare haunches, which wealed a darker crimson than the fleshy mid-fesse, the entire croup was marbled in blotchy crimson, with some bruises, spanked over, darkening to purple.

Crack! Crack! Crack!

'*Ohh . . .!*'

'And you girls like to show off your Metawear creations in the bathroom, don't you? Knickers, bras, corsets, basques . . . all sorts of frillies, I dare say. I'm well aware that many of our customers are shy of their own fantasies . . . which my team likes to plunder, eh?'

Crack! Crack! Crack!

'*Ahh!*'

Crack! Crack! Crack!

'Oh! Oh! *Don't!* Please . . . please stop . . .'

'It's true, isn't it? My team, their own best customers . . .'

Will continued spanking, his palm rigid. At each impact, her flesh cringed, clenching and squirming, but despite the shuddering of her spanked flesh, she was helpless to escape his pinioning hand on her neck, and his leg trapping her ankles.

Crack! Crack! Crack!

'*Oh, God!* Yes, it's true! Just a bit . . .! But I hardly ever . . . I mean, you should see Roz Cardus's . . .'

Crack!

'Ahh . . .!'

'A thing . . .'

Crack!

'*Mmm!*'

'Cannot be . . .'

Crack!

'*Ah! Ah! Ah!*'

'Just a *bit* true . . .! How interesting that Roz, too, is a malefactress! Don't you like that old-fashioned word, for an old-fashioned spanking?'

Crack! Crack! Crack!

'Oh, God! Enough! Please, please stop! *Oh! Please, please, please stop, I beg you!* Oh God, it hurts so much! *I can't stand it! What can I do to make you stop?*'

'Absolutely nothing,' said Will. 'I have twenty minutes until my next meeting, and I am going to spank you for those twenty minutes, Angie.'

'*Oh, no . . .!*' Angarad screamed.

Crack! Crack! Crack!

Angarad's voice broke to a whimper; her spanking continued quietly, except for the rhythmic thwack on her bared croup, and her constant snuffling moan broke into a little yelp of agony at each spank, before subsiding into choked sobs. Though her entire body shook at each slap to her fesses, she no longer struggled to free herself from Will's grip. Her skin was mottled a dark crimson, with purple finger-shaped gashes, and the extent of the bruising was from the soft upper thighs, across the underfesses and in a crescent across the haunches and the top buttocks, where the spank marks were darkest. The stretched yellow satin of Angarad's panties was also darkening with a stain of moisture from her writhing bare slit. Will looked at his watch and delivered a final, hard slap in the cleft of her buttocks. He wiped his hand on her tights, then released the sobbing, quivering girl.

'I can't say I enjoyed that,' he said easily, 'but the creative interface was instructive.'

'Don't mock, Will!' she sobbed, pulling her tights back on. 'God! You didn't have to be *so* cruel. My skin'll be hard as leather for days, I know it! It was my own fault, I was such a fool for asking to be spanked, but I've learned my lesson. I never ever want to go through that sort of hell again, *not ever*!'

He picked up the phone and spoke rapidly.

'That's right . . . say I'm running late with a new design team. And I want to see Roz Cardus, right away.'

Angarad frowned.

'Roz?' she said, wiping tears from her face.

Will smiled, stroking his chin.

'I never joke about the creative interface,' he said. 'I want you back here in one hour. By that time, I plan to have spanked Roz Cardus, for *her* cheek, and then the three of us are going to work on a brand-new hot lingerie programme, with you and Roz up front.'

Still sobbing, Angarad left the office without a backward glance.

'One hour!' Will cried.

Angarad brushed against the svelte figure of Roz Cardus on her way in.

'Heavens, what happened to you?' asked Roz.

'You'll find out,' hissed Angarad.

Angarad half ran, half stumbled, to the lavatory and locked herself in a cubicle. The place was deserted. She allowed her sobbing to reach a crescendo as she lowered her yellow panties and felt her spanked buttocks. She peed long and noisily, the hiss of her fluid masking her sobs. She took a mirror from her purse and twisted to inspect the bruises that darkened her bare fesses. Her fingers stroked the hardening skin of the buttocks, with the index fingernail running up and down her inner cleft, the only portion of her bottom left unmarked. She brushed her anal pucker and the moist lips of her vulva. Then she reached into the wet pouch underneath her thatch. Angarad's sobs turned to moaning, staccato gasps as she masturbated.

Angarad's face was turned to the ground as she walked through the freezing slush, all along the Old Brompton Road, carrying a briefcase and a shoulderbag. She paused to visit a store with an array of frilly underthings in the window, spending less than five minutes inside. She continued through the snow and sleet to Onslow Square. She unpacked her purchase and slipped it into her shoulderbag, throwing the wrapper into a bin. She rang the middle doorbell of a white terraced house, was admitted and climbed to the first floor.

'I'm sorry, Darren,' she said. 'I must look a mess.'

'You're freezing!' he cried, hugging her. 'It can't be snowing that hard.'

'I didn't take the tube,' she said.

'A taxi, surely.'

'No, I walked. I felt bad. I don't really feel like going out for dinner . . . I'm not going to be good company tonight.'

She put down her briefcase. The young man took her shoulderbag and steered her towards the bathroom.

'Rubbish,' he said. 'I don't choose bad company. Soak in a hot bath and I'll bring you a drink. Why didn't you call and I'd have picked you up in the Porsche?'

'Showiness isn't my thing,' she said.

He turned the hot water on and poured bath salts and scented oils, then placed her suitbag on the floor.

'Can't think why you don't leave a stash of clothes here, Ange. I'm not asking you to move in with me.'

'No, you're not, are you?' she said. 'I don't want my things hanging beside . . . your other women's.'

Darren raised his eyebrows.

'Other women? *Moi?*' he said, gesturing at the armoire. 'You're free to look, lady.'

'You know I won't,' she replied. 'I've no illusions, Darren, even though I hate sharing you. *You*, at one time, in one place, is all I want. I want to *know* you, Darren, but I won't have part of me . . . caged here.'

'Anyway, you must be clairvoyant,' said Darren, 'because we're eating in tonight. I've ordered us Italian from Portofino's. I don't want to freeze, waiting for cabs, and anyway I've got some phone stuff to do. Surprise for you, too. Food's due about eight. Hurry up and get naked, and I'll bring you that drink.'

Angarad made no move to strip.

'What's the surprise?' she said.

'Tell you when. Otherwise it wouldn't be a surprise. You're staying tonight, OK.'

'I don't know . . .'

'Last bleeding tube all the way to Richmond? I'm certainly not driving that far. You're staying tonight.'

Darren took her by the shoulders and his eyes pierced hers until she lowered her head. She smiled briefly.

'OK,' she whispered.

'That's a good girl. Now get in the bath.'

'I'll take the bath, Darren, but . . . I'd rather you didn't see all of me just now. I need to unwind. I did a bad thing at the office, you see.'

She blurted the story of her carelessness, adding that she had been reprimanded.

'That's not bad, just unfortunate!' he said.

'That wasn't the bad thing. Leave me alone for my bath. A soak and a ponder and I'll be fine.'

The telephone rang and Darren swore, then left her to answer it. Angarad closed the bathroom door and slowly, mechanically, began to undress, folding her things, including her bra, stockings and panties, and placing them in her shoulderbag after removing her evening wear. She gazed at the reflection of her bare bottom in the mirror, until she was misted by steam. Then she turned off the hot water and slipped into the bath with a sigh. Darren's voice rasped into the phone: 'Yah . . . uh-uh . . . you got it . . .'

The two young men from Portofino's deftly laid the table: fresh linen, crystal; French, not Italian wines; puddings in the fridge, candles lit.

'Can't go in the bathroom, guys,' said Darren, 'there's a naked bird in it. Even I can't go in, and I'm bursting.'

The caterers dutifully laughed, were paid and went. Angarad emerged from the bathroom in full make-up, with a silver ringlet pinning her blond tresses back on the left side, and a black voile evening dress with its single strap on her left shoulder, hemmed at mid-thigh, over black sheen nylon stockings and stiletto shoes. The black panties, garter belt and straps, and low, scalloped bra were phantoms, visible under the voile dress. Darren was on the phone again, looking at his computer monitor.

'Do you like me?' Angarad said after several moments. 'I'm wearing . . . *those* panties.'

She blushed.

Darren glanced at her.

'Split crotch? Very tasty,' he said, smacking his lips.

'It's what you bought for me,' she replied.

With one hand, Darren poured her a generous measure of Campari, adding soda and ice.

'Thank you,' said Angarad, and sat in her place at the dinner table.

She sipped her drink, occasionally crossing and uncrossing her legs, with a slither of stockings that made Darren look up. He finished his phone call and grandly switched off his computer. Excusing himself, he went into the bedroom and after only a minute, emerged in crisp dinner attire and bow tie. Angarad smiled and clapped her hands.

'Right, darling,' said Darren, pouring her a glass of red wine. 'Let's nosh.'

Angarad had downed two glasses of wine while Darren had only sipped his first. He wolfed his pasta, while she wound the strands round her fork, then unwound them.

'You never drink much,' she said.

'Keeps a clear head. I like seeing other people drink, though,' he answered.

The phone warbled and he stuck it to his neck, talking as he ate: 'Yah . . . OK . . . buy.'

'You've a finger in every pie,' Angarad said.

'Got ten fingers, might as well have 'em in ten pies.'

'After two months, I don't know much about you at all.'

'Let's keep it that way.'

Angarad gulped more wine.

'Why did you buy me the panties I'm wearing?'

'Don't you think you're going to find out . . . pretty soon?'

Angarad blushed.

'I could ask why you've chosen to wear them at last,' he said. 'Except I know. Female curiosity. You know they turn me on, but you want to find out why.'

'It's a sort of power fantasy, I suppose?' she said. 'Taking a woman through her clothing, piercing the carapace that both shields and identifies her.'

Angarad gasped and crossed her legs with a slither of her nylon stockings.

'Does the fantasy work both ways, Ange?'

She smiled as Darren reached under the table, slid his hand up her dress and touched her vulva.

'Don't . . .' she said faintly.

He withdrew his finger and licked it.

'Seems to,' he said.

She shivered, mouth open and tongue licking her teeth. She gulped wine as Darren touched her again, and began to moan. He probed the inside of her pouch as he ate, seemingly unconcerned, but shifted to show the girl his erection.

'Mm . . .' she gasped, her bottom and haunches writhing.

'I've always wondered about you, Ange . . . You've the tightest, wettest pussy, but so prim and proper, lights out, missionary position and that. It's part of your charm. But maybe there's a beast inside you waiting to be unleashed.'

'Don't say that. Somebody said that, today . . .'

'I've never probed your secret fantasies, Ange, because I prefer you as my porcelain goddess. Surprising what a bit of money can do to unleash beasts, and that brings me to your surprise.'

Darren abruptly withdrew his fingers from her juicing vulva, reached to his desk, and showed her a document of several pages. He folded over the last page where there was a space vacant for a signature. His thumb left an imprint of her cunt slime.

'A nice little earner, just for signing your name. Ten grand for you up front, and ten grand every month after that. Suddenly, little porcelain Ange is a golden goddess, and who knows what tricks she'll think of?'

Darren explained that it was a shell company for offshore investments online. It needed himself as executive director and Angarad as company secretary.

'You don't have to do anything at all, except sign the company report every half-year. Before you sign, I insist you read every line of the small print.'

'I didn't say I'd sign. It sounds illegal.'

'Not in the Cayman Islands, it's not. Go on, read the small print.'

'No, Darren,' she said, 'I'll sign it because I trust you. I *want* to trust you. Give me a pen and I'll sign.'

Darren pierced her eyes with his, saying nothing. Angarad lowered her gaze.

'I'll sign first, *then* read it,' she whispered.

Darren handed her a pen and she signed, then turned to look at the first page. Suddenly, she dropped the papers into the bowl of spaghetti sauce steaming on the table. All the pages except the last were soiled. Darren cursed.

'Send *this* in, and what do I look like?' he spat.

'Oh! I'm sorry,' she cried. 'It'll be OK in a day or two when it's dry, but I can't read it now. Please don't be cross, Darren. Don't take it out on me!'

'You're devious, you are,' Darren said, with a leer. 'It's as if you're *daring* me to punish you. What would be really naughty, something you'd hate, eh? This, for starters?'

He picked the dish of sauce, and flung its contents over Angarad. Her hair, breasts and thighs were soaked red, the voile dress clinging to her and showing her underthings.

'*Oh!*' she gasped, and began to cry.

Darren took the wet contract from her and locked it in his drawer.

'There's a downside to prim and proper. You want to *know* me, do you?' he sneered, mimicking her.

He grasped Angarad by the hair and swept the dinner things from the table with a clatter. Her bottom squirmed on the wet table-cloth as Darren pinned her head below the table's rim, while stripping himself. He thrust a hand between the lips of her vulva and began a brutal probing of her wet pouch, then took his fingers from the quim and rubbed them across her lips and nose.

'Darren!' she sobbed. '*Stop* . . . I want to go!'

'Taste yourself, Ange,' he hissed. 'You're hot for it.'

He stuck his fingers in her mouth and she licked her own cunt oil, then bit hard on his fingernails.

'You fucking bitch,' Darren snarled, mounting her.

'*Ah . . .!*'

Angarad screamed as Darren's cock penetrated her wet cunt in a single thrust. He began to fuck vigorously, his body pinning her to the table, and her thighs parted automatically to grasp him, with her shoes trembling as her heels dug the cleft of his pumping buttocks.

Slap! Slap! Slap!

There was a rhythmic, liquid thud as his hips slammed against her belly. Her garter straps and stocking tops were filmed with oil that flowed from her fucked gash. He pulled the dress from her quivering teats to expose her brassiere, then ripped that from her, lowering his head to bite and chew each of her erect bare nipples in turn.

'Oh, God . . . *Ahh* . . .!' she groaned. '*Don't stop* . . .'

Panting, Darren withdrew his dripping cock from her pouch and heaved her body over. She flopped on her belly as he mounted her from the rear, and her buttocks rose, parted for penetration. Her gash was a shining pink oyster, trapped by the pinching shell of the crotchless panties.

'These aren't the panties I gave you!' he gasped. 'Mine were rose pattern, and low. These cover your arse, and the design's honeysuckle or something! What the fuck are you up to?'

'Oh, Darren,' whimpered Angarad. 'Don't stop. Come inside . . . fuck me, I'm almost there . . .!'

'I wonder who else has fucked you in these panties,' he rasped.

'No one! I swear!'

'I'll fuck you bare arse,' he grunted, and tore away the flimsy garment, to reveal the bruises of her office spanking.

'*What* . . .!' he cried.

Angarad wriggled her bottom and, delving under the panties, began to masturbate.

'Darren, I'll explain! I'm almost coming! Oh, finish me, please! Take me! *Fuck me!*'

He slapped her fingers away from her stiff clitoris.

'I'll fuck you, all right,' he said. 'You never told me you were fond of spanking.'

'I'm not! I hate it! Oh, God! Will – that's my boss – he spanked me to make up for my mistakes, that's all! It was my suggestion! My dress is ruined . . .' she wailed.

'So it's "Will", eh? And what does *Will* do after he's spanked you?'

'Nothing! It was the first time! Oh, don't be so cruel!'

Darren tore the shoe from her left stockinged foot.

Vap!

'*AHH! Stop!*'

Angarad's left fesse glowed a new pink where he had thrashed her with the sole of her shoe.

Vap! Vap! Vap! Vap!

'*Oh!* Oh, God, it *hurts*! Please stop!' she sobbed.

He lathered each bare buttock with fierce whops from the shoe leather as her bottom began to clench, squirming and splashing in the pool of red meat sauce.

Vap! Vap! Vap!

'*AHH! No, Darren! Please . . .!*'

Vap! Vap! Vap!

'Oh, God . . . no . . . *no . . .!*'

Angarad's buttocks flamed scarlet as her shoe worked on the existing weals of her hand-spanking, opening and deepening them. After fifty slaps, her bottom was fiery dark, and the squirming of the thrashed bare fesses as uncontrollable as her choking sobs.

Vap! Vap! Vap!

'*Ahh! Oh . . .!* Darren, I can't stand it! You're hurting me! It's agony, my bum's so sore from my spanking!'

'It's supposed to be agony,' he snarled.

Vap! Vap! Vap!

'*AHH!*'

Angarad's body convulsed, as a long stream of golden piss steamed from her quivering cunt, soaking her dress and dripping down her torn stockings. Darren's fingers poked between her quim lips and emerged, shining with her mingled cunt slime and pee. He wedged her buttocks apart and rubbed the liquid into her anal pucker.

'Darren, what are you *doing*?'

'You told me to fuck you.'

He pushed the crinkled anal pucker open with the cunt-slimed glans of his cock.

'Not there! *NO!* I've never – *AHH!*'

'But you want it . . . don't you, bitch? Like the rest . . .'

'Please! *Please!*'

Angie howled, and a second jet of piss spurted from her quim as Darren plunged his cock fully into her anal shaft.

'Oh, God! No! Don't! It hurts! It hurts ! It –'

Vap! Vap! Vap!

'Oh! Oh! *AHH!*'

As he began to bugger her, Darren resumed his slippering of her scarlet bare fesses. He held both her shoes, his cock impaling her body, which quivered, helpless to move. As he rammed her anal shaft, his cock sank right to his balls, withdrawing fully before each thrust, and baring the whole of her buttocks for a flurry of spanks. When he penetrated her, he remained in place for seconds, writhing his hips as his cock-tip probed and teased the root of her anus. During buggery, when his loins covered her central fesses, he thrashed her haunches, which were already bruised blue, the skin puffy and mottled in deep ridges.

Vap! Vap! Vap!

'*Oh! Oh!* It hurts! It's shameful! Oh, *I hate you*! Oh, do me . . . *Yes . . .!*'

Darren buggered her harder as his spanks increased in savagery; her squirming bare bottom was darker than the meat sauce in which she splashed, and the flow of come from her cunt was so copious that only its limpid oiliness distinguished it from any further spray of girl-piss. Darren grunted as he began to climax and sank his cock right to her root, bouncing on top of her, while leaving the glans pressed to her anal womb for his ejaculate. Bubbles of his creamy froth surged from her impaled anal hole and Angarad's come flowed faster as her cunt gaped and wriggled; her whole body shuddered, and her belly was sucked in by the intensity of her own orgasm.

Darren grunted and withdrew his cock from her anus with a sucking sound as the pucker closed. He snapped the heel off each of Angarad's shoes, reopened her bruised pucker with his thumb, then slid each stiletto heel fully inside her anus; oiled by his sperm and her arse-grease, they slid in smoothly to her root, while she squealed and wriggled, sobbing. He held them in place, churning her anus for some minutes, while he continued to spank her writhing bare fesses with the shoe flats. Angarad masturbated her dripping cunt, as she was arse-reamed and spanked; her sobbing became panting gasp, then a squeal.

'*Oh . . . oh . . .* I'm there! I'm coming . . . *do it to me . . .!*' she wailed, her belly and teats heaving as she spasmed once more, with her come a torrent from her swollen cunt.

Darren ceased spanking, grasped a hank of her hair and wiped his cock clean before releasing her soiled mane.

Angarad sobbed in the bathroom as she removed the shoeheels from her anus, her whimpers louder than the running water; she emerged in her street clothes.

'Don't offer to drive me home,' she said. 'I'm in time for the last tube. Darren . . . I think it's better we don't see each other again.'

'Suit yourself,' he said. 'Bye, now. You know my number, darling.'

Angarad sobbed louder.

'I'm sorry,' she said. 'I'll throw away your number, because I *won't* be seeing you again. *Oh, Darren* . . . how *could* you?'

'You can keep the panties,' he said, without opening the door for her. 'I mean, they were yours anyway. And wipe your arse and cunt with this. I promise it's been cleaned since the last user.'

He pulled up her skirt and clapped a square of pink brocade cloth to stick to her welted fesses.

'*Oh! God! You animal!*'

Angarad stumbled down the stairs and ran across the snow-covered square towards the tube station. Only when seated in the last District Line to Richmond did she control her sobbing and open her purse. Her hand fastened on a piece of paper. Made out to Angarad Stark and signed by Darren Dodd, was a cheque for ten thousand, on the bank of Cragg, Joule and Co, Grand Cayman. Beside it were the split-crotch panties, still soaked in her cunt's fluids, which had abetted Angarad's first buggery. Her cunt and bum-hole still seeped: she slipped her hand under her skirt, withdrew the square of pink brocade, and wiped herself, until the brocade was soaking, all the way to Richmond.

# 3

# Gymslip Mistress

Isobel Coker looked at her watch, before taking it off and slipping it into the waist-pouch strapped over her gymslip. It was twenty-five minutes past three. She pursed her lips, pausing before the door to the gymnasium. The sixth-formers were always difficult, especially the last class of Friday afternoon. The younger girls gave no problem, scaling the bars, jumping, doing their bends, squats and somersaults obediently, but the sulky young ladies, ready to leave Wearbridge Girls' Grammar for ever, were another and quite rebellious matter. *They* didn't see why they should waste energy more profitably saved for the night's clubbing. Worse, this was the very last class of the winter term. Other teachers let their classes mess about on the last day, but Isobel Coker insisted on the last drop of sweat from the bodies of her charges.

Isobel entered the empty gymnasium and stood by a vaulting-horse, ready to welcome the sixth-formers. The room still smelled of the girls' sweat from her last class an hour before, since when she had taught a period of elementary geography. Three-quarters of her work was athletic, and her title was gym mistress. Only a few years before, Isobel herself had been one of those sixth-formers, though already devoted to the gym: the three years at college, to earn her teaching certificate were merely an interruption of her beloved Wearbridge and its ancient school.

Wearbridge Girls' Grammar was a rare survivor, remaining independent of the state, thanks to its founder,

Lady Gertrude of Spennymoor, whose husband, of Frisian marauder ancestry, had brought back a fortune from the Fourth Crusade. The towers and crenellations of the school had, for centuries, provided 'board, instruction and discipline' for deserving girls of marriageable age who were orphans or of lowly rank. Nowadays, only a few girls boarded, there were as few orphans, and the discipline was a shadow of its former self, but the school still smelled of tradition, of history . . . of *England*; as did Wearbridge itself, untouched by the industrial or any other revolution.

When Isobel had been head girl a few years before, the headmistress, Mrs Cragg, had allowed her to read a rare copy of a privately published school history, written by a twentieth-century alumnus, identified only as 'G.D.'. Isobel had searched in vain for any mention of athletic pursuits, for, until the beginning of the twentieth century, Wearbridge girls were permitted nothing more strenuous than crochet; the girls of olden times must, however, have been sturdy beasts, for the writer dwelt at some length on the 'discipline' designed to make them English ladies, and their uncomplaining acceptance of punishments latterly unacceptable, or downright illegal.

Isobel was at first shocked, but, as she read through the centuries, marvelled at the praise of her school and its disciplinary methods, by each alumna who had written of her education at Wearbridge. The slightest failure in manners, handwriting, grammar or deportment brought punishment which the miscreant not only accepted but welcomed, and no punishment was inflicted without the approval of the miscreant, conscious of her error.

Isobel had imagined that beating on the buttocks was the gruesome privilege of boys' schools, but she learned that had never been the case. English girls were flogged just as enthusiastically by their mistresses as English boys by their masters. Isobel found herself skipping the lists of ennobled or successfully married alumnae, and following the disciplinary history of Wearbridge, threading through the ages as a story in itself. The annals of Wearbridge detailed severe floggings, and even birchings, often on the buttocks covered only in a 'flogging-cloth' of thin brocade, or, in some cases, actually on the bare. A girl caned would usually be held down by two other girls, and bent over a rail, with a third holding the brocade cloth over her bared buttocks and, sometimes, her skirt lifted to hood her head. She had her flogging-brocade as a keepsake and, if birched naked, was permitted to keep her denuded birch.

Each age had its own coquetries of beating: in mediaeval times, birchings were administered on the 'throne of error', a chair built just like a royal throne, upon which a miscreant sat, with her wrists strapped to the armrests. The chair had no seat, and the girl's croup was bare, birched from beneath in an uppercut flogging, while she recited prayers in Latin. Twenty cuts of the birch, on the full bare, was not an uncommon punishment. The girl might wear a brank and tongue-depressor for a 'grand birching' of more strokes for she was considered unable to restrain her screams, than which no deportment could be less ladylike. 'Whipt in a cage', without further detail, was another antique practice.

Sometimes, girls were beaten wearing shameful head-gear, such as a crown of thistles or goose-feathers, or were ducked naked in the River Wear, then flogged on bare wet skin, for extra pain. Naked beatings were, in fact, often at the miscreant's own request: preferring to be whipped nude than risk damage to her garments from the instrument of chastisement. Throughout, the book hinted that northern English girls, and those of Co Durham in particular, were a tougher and more truly English breed than any others. As she read on, Isobel suspected that G.D.'s real theme was not so much the success of Wearbridge alumnae in high society, as the beatings that had got them there.

The Elizabethan age saw beatings taken in the pillory, or stocks; in the former, the girl's skirts were pinned up to reveal her bare bottom; in the latter, her wrists were roped to her ankles and her chemise lifted for a whipping on the naked back. In the eighteenth century, whippings were delivered in the upright position: either at the whipping-post, with the girl's arms wrapped around the post and her legs free; or, for a 'grand beating', with her arms and legs splayed, and the wrists, or sometimes both wrists and ankles, roped to the corners of a whipping-frame.

Nineteenth-century Wearbridge aped the newly popular boys' boarding schools, with young female miscreants being invited to bend over a chair back, or touching their toes, for a caning, which, by that time, was almost always on the bare; the full brocade of previous centuries had given way to a token square of the fabric, placed on the cleft of the buttocks, and soon sliced away by cane or birch, leaving the buttocks naked – although the punished miscreant was still awarded her flogging brocade as keepsake. Birching was carried out at a block, at which the offender knelt, having her waist strapped by a rubber thong two feet in width, and then her skirts pinned to her collar, she having previously removed her undergarments.

Caning or birching on the buttocks was always more popular than public whipping, rare in the nineteenth century, although in the early twentieth, there was a vogue for 'full bare flogging' of both back and bottom, the front portion of the body draped, but the rear completely naked – using twelve-thonged quirts of Malayan rubber. G.D. concluded that throughout Wearbridge's history, caning and birching of the female fesses were more popular, because speedier, and less formal, than the more shameful public whipping, although private chastisement of the buttocks was generally accepted to be more painful.

Caning continued throughout the twentieth centuury, although birching became a rarity, and was discontinued in mid-century. The tradition of the token brocade flogging-cloth was maintained, even in the nineteen-twenties, G.D.'s 'golden age' of discipline, when modesty had weakened sufficiently to let girls take their floggings completely nude, yet 'namby-pambyism' had not yet tried to outlaw the practice. As well as the formal punishments detailed in the punishment annals, Wearbridge had a tradition – a healthy one, G.D. suggested – of informal spankings taken privately, on knickers, nighties, petticoats, or on full bare, with the undergarments lifted, lowered or discarded.

Isobel learned that punishment annals, dating back to the school's foundation, were kept locked away. Mrs Cragg had assured her that if she excelled at college and returned to Wearbridge qualified to take the post which awaited her, then she might see the punishment books. When Isobel at last saw them, she gasped at the formal, yet matter-of-fact descriptions, in the quaint lettering:

*Beth Shadwell, to be held down for fifteen strokes of the cane on the bare nates, with shift at her ears, for impious thoughts;*

*Elizabeth Joule, to be whipt thirty lashes on bare back at the pillorie, for failure in grammar and catechism;*

*Sarah Dunton, to be birched on naked posterior twenty strokes, in the throne of pleasure, for swearing; to be whipt straight thereafter twenty lashes on bare back in the pillorie, for opening her eyes during prayer; to remain pilloried with skirts pinned up and back bared, for three hours, for the sport of her collegians . . .*

'Sometimes,' said Mrs Cragg, 'I wonder if things weren't healthier in the old days. Punishments were given and forgiven, free of modern do-gooder nonsense, which just causes anxiety. I hate writing reports in jargon, when sometimes all the girl needs is a good spanking! Girls at gym sometimes get rowdy, and if *you* decided a whopping would clear the air, it would save me paperwork, and I would look the other way, as it were . . .'

'I'm not sure I *could,* Mrs Cragg, but I'll remember . . .'

Although Mrs Cragg was in her mid-thirties, her almost girlish vitality and trim figure encouraged Isobel to confide in her as a sister.

'I don't seem to make friends easily,' Isobel admitted.

'Your trouble is, you are too attractive,' said Mrs Cragg. 'Your height and, frankly, *superb* body make women jealous, and men afraid. I take it you include boyfriends.'

'Well, yes,' said Isobel, blushing, and tossing her long blond mane back from her breasts. 'I've had boyfriends, and – you know – but it never seems to work out. I . . . I don't know how to put it . . . they don't seem to satisfy me.'

'You're a healthy young woman,' said Mrs Cragg. 'Forgive me for prying, but I think I know what you mean. Some men aren't very . . . well, *manly*, where it counts – in the *size* department. I take it we are talking about size.'

'Yes,' said Isobel, blushing furiously.

'Until the right one comes along, there's nothing wrong with a jolly good manual workout,' said Mrs Cragg, and both women laughed.

Finally, when settled and confident as gym mistress, Isobel confided to Mrs Cragg that when a sixth-former was 'being *really* obnoxious – *you* know', the girl could choose to go on report, or settle matters with a spanking by ping-pong bat on her knickers – 'only with girls of proper age and never touching skin. As a gym mistress, I have to be very careful. I shower separately, and only after supervising their own showers, together with a prefect. Spanking has to be done fast, hard and by surprise, in front of the others.'

'I imagine so,' said Mrs Cragg.

'I hope I'm not too awful . . .'

Mrs Cragg smiled, clapped her hands, and said she hadn't heard a word.

'Sometimes, a girl's skin is all the better for being touched,' she added. 'Do keep me informed.'

Isobel's commanding physique made such occasions rare, but when she did have to spank a sixth-form girl, Mrs Cragg took a lively interest in the punishment – how the girl took it, did she cry, or wriggle, or say anything rude, whether the beating was on knickers, or bare bum. Mrs Cragg's eyes lit up whenever Isobel said she was so cross, she had spanked the girl on the bare.

'It seems wrong to hurt,' she said, 'although I see it as my duty to the school, and to save *you* trouble.'

'There are people who do that sort of thing for pleasure,' said Mrs Cragg. 'One reads about them in the Sunday newspapers, at least the sort I hope you *don't* read.'

'Ugh,' Isobel said. 'How vile!'

'You've never been spanked, Isobel?' said Mrs Cragg.

'Of course not!'

'I'm glad to hear it. Although I dare say a spanked bottom looks more dramatic than it feels. How many do you give them?'

'Oh, only about a dozen whops. Not too many.'

'About a dozen? It's better to count exactly, Isobel – they take it more seriously that way. A dozen whops certainly isn't too many. Use your discretion . . .'

Now, awaiting three-thirty gym class, her heart sank, as she *knew* Helen Dummett would be obnoxious. The last few classes, she had been less and less obedient. This one, Isobel felt, would take her across the line. She had never spanked Helen, but reported her twice; she knew that Mrs Cragg would regard further reporting as failure; knew, too, that Helen cursed her for reporting her, but did not wish to have three report marks, with permanent loss of privilege. Further goading by Helen would require spanking: another report would suit nobody. Isobel was invited to a term's end drinks party at the Craggs' that evening – no use being in foul mood. The class arrived, giggling and in no mood for seriousness on this, the last class of term. They wore gym uniform of short blue skirt, fluffy white socks, tennis shoes and blue T-shirt, with optional bra. A few firm-titted girls loved to wear an extra-skimpy T-shirt to show they were braless, and Helen was one.

Isobel told them that they should be glad to warm up, as further snow was forecast to add to the inch already slushing the ground outside. First exercise was climbing the wall bars, hanging upside down, then descending. Helen Dummett made a face, then, turning directly to Isobel, expelled a cloud of blue cigarette smoke from her mouth. The others laughed; Isobel flushed, knowing she must meet the challenge.

'Helen!' she rapped. 'You have been *smoking*!'

'Oh, it's just steam from the cold air, Miss Coker,' whined Helen.

Isobel took her pingpong bat from its drawer.

'Don't lie,' she said evenly, 'and don't tell me you'd prefer a third report to a spanking.'

'Oh, *Miss*,' Helen moaned, 'it's the last day of *term* . . .'

Helen, five inches shorter than Isobel, was lithe and wiry, and one of Isobel's best gymnasts. Isobel bit her lip.

'Well?' she said. 'It's up to you.'

'Oh, Miss, it's not *fair* . . .' Helen moaned, rolling her eyes and playing to her audience.

'Spanking or report?' Isobel snapped. 'Make up your mind, *now*, young lady!'

Her tone wiped the grin from Helen's face.

'Spanking, Miss,' she muttered, then, her lips only half shielded from Isobel's gaze, she mouthed 'fucking cow'. The girls tittered. Flushed, Isobel grabbed Helen by the hair and bent her over a vaulting-horse.

'Get your skirt up and your knickers down!' she said.

'*What?*'

'I'm spanking you on the bare! You know why.'

'I . . . I . . .'

'*Bare bum, girl!*' blurted Isobel. '*At once!*'

Helen sullenly lifted her gymslip and lowered her blue knickers to her knees. Isobel kicked them down to her ankles. She lifted the bat, bringing it smartly down across the full expanse of the girl's bare, muscled fesses.

Crack! Crack! Crack!

'*Ouch!* That *hurts*!'

'You'll take your beating in silence, Helen. I'm going to start again, now – any noise means an extra whop.'

'How many am I getting, then?' Helen stammered.

Isobel took a deep breath.

'Two dozen, Helen,' she said, trembling.

'Two dozen?'

'Now, it's *three*!' Isobel blurted.

Crack! Crack! Crack!

'Mm! Mm! *Ahh . . .!*'

Thereafter, Helen took her whopping in silence, but gasping harshly, and with her bare bum wriggling more and more frantically, as Isobel's whops, delivered on the two seconds, quickly reddened the naked buttocks to scarlet. Beads of sweat formed at the cleft of the girl's clenching buttocks and dripped into her tangle of pubic hair. The class watched in awed silence; Isobel's panting, as she spanked the girl, was as harsh as her victim's.

Crack!

'*There!*'

The beating had taken less than two minutes, and Isobel had gone one over the three dozen. Helen was unable to control the frantic clenching of her bare buttocks, or her grimace and tears.

'Oh! I'm sorry, Helen . . .' Isobel blurted.

Helen's face was as scarlet as her whopped bare bottom. Slowly, she pulled up her knickers and lowered her skirt.

'How *dare* you, Miss?' she sobbed, her cheeks moist.

'I'm sorry . . .' said Isobel, shifting nervously to ease her crotch in her dampened knickers.

'I'll *get you*!' spat the thrashed girl.

Isobel hurried home, through eddies of snow, to her cottage by the school gate. Once inside, she ran a hot bath, set a pan to boil and opened the refrigerator. She removed a dish of butter and one of three massive corn cobs, a foot in length and a hand's span, which stood like sentries in the fridge door. The cob went into the bubbling water, and Isobel went to her bedroom to strip off the gym clothes she still wore. Nude, she inspected herself in the mirror: the full, jutting breasts, alabaster, body rippling with curved muscle; the huge tangle of pubic thatch, which crawled halfway to her navel and hung in fronds beneath the thick red lips of her quim. She half-turned and stroked the unblemished firm skin of her ripe buttocks.

*I've never been spanked. How awful it must be! Yet, I lost my temper with Helen. Perhaps I should know what I'm dishing out . . . perhaps I deserve it . . .*

She returned to the kitchen and took the corn cob from the pan; it was hot, but scarcely softened. She placed it in a dish and covered it with butter. Then she took the dish to the bathroom, shutting the hot tap. The bath was full; Isobel perched with one foot on either side of the tub, her thighs parted and her quim open to inspection, a vivid red slash in the misted mirror. Isobel touched her clitoris, moaned, trembled, then began to rub. The corn cob, lathered in butter, approached the open folds of her gash, now dripping with oily come. The mist was clearing from the mirror and Isobel watched her vulva, as the tip of the corn cob hovered between the fleshy, swollen lips. She yelped as the hot buttered cob sank all the way into her cunt, until only an inch was left for her nails to grasp. As the fingers of one hand masturbated her clitoris, Isobel cunt-fucked herself with the giant cob, twisting and reaming and thrusting its hot tip right up to the neck of her womb. In less than a minute she brought herself to orgasm, squealing, and her belly spasming, as the heel of her fist rammed the tool to fill her wet pouch. She sank into the bath, holding the cob inside her and pressing her clitty.

'Ahh . . .' she sighed.

*That's better. That's always better.*

Isobel pedalled cautiously through the drifting snow to the priory, or headmistress's house, half a mile away across Wearbridge estate. She propped her bicycle and entered the brightly lit house where the noise of the party was already spirited. Mrs Cragg, flushed and wearing a strapless silk gown of startling décolletage, greeted her.

'Be of good cheer, Isobel,' she murmured, her eyes twinkling.

In the cloakroom, Isobel hung her overcoat, mittens and woolly hat, and swapped her rubber boots for a pair of low slingbacks from her handbag; a quick visit to the loo, where she squatted, combing her hair in her pocket mirror as she peed. The drawing-room held a large crowd, of faces mostly unfamiliar, and Isobel drew glances as the tallest and most striking female in the room. She wore a black evening frock, tightly clinging and with string straps that left a generous portion of breast-flesh bared, the breasts themselves thrust upwards in a black scalloped bra, to match her panties; the dress had a four-flounced hem a few inches above her knees; seamed black stockings; a single choker of fake pearls at her throat.

Equipped with a glass of punch, Isobel stood by the door, looking around for someone to talk to. There was a clattering outside and Mrs Cragg broke away from her own conversation to go to the front door.

'Rollo!' her voice carried. 'Go and change!'

'All in good time, gel!'

There was a slap and Mrs Cragg giggled.

'You're dreadful,' she said.

In the doorway, Rollo Cragg appeared in riding apparel, with skin-tight jodhpurs, muddy boots and a cutaway riding coat. Isobel gazed, at once. He was perhaps the same age as his wife, but his aquiline face did not draw Isobel's attention. The cutaway coat fully exposed the crotch and the skin-tight breeches outlined, so clearly that it seemed almost naked, a penis bigger than any corn cob. His bulge was massive, even though the organ was not erect. Isobel, and every woman in the room, stared at Rollo Cragg's cock, across which he held his riding crop.

'Hello, all! Had to take the nag for a canter, to quiet her. Mare on heat, in this weather!'

It was the first time Isobel had seen Mr Cragg close up. The founder's statutes, often amended, now permitted mistresses to be married and cohabit with their husbands; yet, by unspoken consent, males stayed in the background, school affairs being strictly female. Isobel had only seen Rollo Cragg in his car from a distance. Rollo gazed on Isobel.

'With you in a jiffy,' he said, his eyes piercing hers.

'Yes,' said Isobel. 'Yes . . .'

Returned, and in casual attire, Rollo's eyes transfixed Isobel as Mrs Cragg introduced him.

'So this is your notorious spanking gym mistress, eh, Gemma?' murmured Rollo.

Isobel blushed a fiery red, and Mrs Cragg grinned.

'Don't be cross, Isobel,' she said. 'I only *mentioned* it.'

'Girl with spirit,' drawled Rollo. 'I like that in a filly.'

He had changed into designer jeans, almost as clinging as his jodhpurs and which showed his bulge as vividly. He joined his wife in a grin, as Isobel lifted her eyes.

'I'll leave you two to get to know each other,' said Gemma Cragg.

'You must have plenty of boyfriends, Isobel,' said Rollo, refilling her glass.

His hook nose seemed to tremble and the nostrils dilate, like a horse's. Isobel allowed her eyes to fall once more to his bulge, now swelling, quivering and inches from her own cunt basin. Her breasts heaved, thrusting up the creamy teat-flesh that Rollo made no pretence of ignoring. She hung her head, staring at the growing penis.

'No,' she murmured. 'I'm rather shy.'

'Good heavens, why . . .?'

'Are you sure Mrs Cragg didn't just mention *that*, too?' asked Isobel, with a thin smile. 'My *special need*, sir?'

She swallowed, blushed, and took a deep breath that thrust her breasts up; Rollo licked his teeth, as his cock-bulge grew.

*What are you waiting for, Isobel?*

'Gemma is a terrible gossip,' he replied, 'and sometimes it's a teacher who most needs to be taught a lesson . . .'

*It's now or never . . .*

'I'm a teacher, too, sir,' she blurted.

'Now the bra and panties,' purred Rollo Cragg.

The shadow of his erect cock fell across Isobel's breasts as she knelt before him. His peehole and glans were wet with her saliva; the crotch of her black panties, furrowing her cunt, glistened with her copious come that doused the pubic forest sprouting outside the panties thong.

'Please . . .' she whimpered.

'Do it!' he snapped. 'I want you nude. Then you can watch me teach my wife a lesson. And then . . .'

'Please . . .' Isobel sobbed.

'Please, *what*?'

Vip!

'*Ah!*'

He cracked the riding crop on her bare haunch. Her eyelids were heavy, her lips slack; drool slimed her chin.

'Oh! *Please, yes . . .*' she gasped.

'You'd do *anything* for my husband's cock,' said Gemma Cragg, daintily stepping out of her panties.

Isobel whimpered.

'My wife tells me you've never been properly swived,' said the male. 'Something of a loose box, eh?'

Isobel shuddered.

*What am I doing here? My ankles roped, kneeling in the filth of a stable, ready to be whipped! They said it was just a game . . .*

'I . . . I've never met a man big enough for me,' she wailed.

'So you wank off a lot,' said Gemma Cragg. 'What with? A cucumber? Or some fancy electric vibrator . . .?'

'*Please!*'

With numb fingers, Isobel unhooked her bra, letting her bare breasts spring free. The bra fell into the manure-flecked straw. She began to wriggle out of her panties.

'You'll have to untie me,' she said, 'or I can't get them off.'

'No,' said Mrs Cragg. 'Rollo likes the panties at the ankles. It is so fetchingly helpless. But you haven't answered! *How* do you masturbate, girl? Thumb and fingers, or some phallic toy?'

'A corn cob,' Isobel wailed.

'And you *do* masturbate a lot.'

'Every day,' whimpered the gym mistress. 'I can't help it! I just need to . . . oh! I don't know!'

'Do you think of girls' bare bums, red from spanking, and squirming, while you wank off?'

'*No!* I mean, yes, I do . . . oh, *please*!'

Isobel squirmed until the panties clung to her roped ankles. Rollo, nude but for his boots, placed a heel on her neck and forced her face down into the muck.

Vip!

'*Ahh!*'

Isobel screamed as the crop took her full across the bare buttocks.

'Please, don't!'

'To take a horseman's cock, you must be thrashed like a filly,' said Mrs Cragg. 'Look, Isobel!'

She thrust her naked buttocks, framed by satin sussies and sheer stocking-tops, into Isobel's upturned face. Isobel gasped, sobbing, but unable to avert her gaze from the crisscross of weals etched into the headmistress's bare buttocks.

'We are the sort of people you read about in the Sunday newspapers,' she said. 'Rollo beats me two dozen with the crop after his breakfast, and three dozen after supper, every day, with an extra four dozen at Sunday teatime. We call ourselves the scene, and there are more of us than you'd think, devoted to practising what most only dream of.'

'*Caned to three or four dozen?*' Isobel cried.

'To twelve, on special occasions,' said the male. 'Rise, Isobel, and help rope my wife to the post, and then you may witness how you should take your own beating.'

'Don't tickle her,' said Mrs Cragg. 'Thrash her properly. She's spanked plenty of girls, and masturbated thinking of their bums, so this is her due initiation.'

'I'm scared!' Isobel sobbed.

Vip!

The crop lashed her naked breasts, full on her erect nipples.

'*Ah! God . . .!*'

Hobbled, she staggered to her feet and roped each of the nude headmistress's wrists to a vertical pole. Mrs Cragg's waist was bent on a rail, which thrust her buttocks up and left her toes dangling inches from the ground, with her back slanted at a forty-five-degree angle. When his wife was bound to his satisfaction, Rollo tied Isobel's own wrists at the small of her back and kicked her on to the dirt, where she lay, trussed and sobbing.

'A small price to pay, for your first *proper fuck*,' sneered the trussed headmistress of Wearbridge Girls' Grammar.

Vip! Vip! Vip!

'Ahh . . . *yes*!' she sighed, her face creased in a rictus of delight. 'Harder, Rollo . . .'

Vip! Vip! Vip!

Her naked bottom danced, slashed by the crop, with new pink weals blossoming on older growths.

Vip! Vip! Vip!

'*Ouch!* God, I need that!'

The headmistress's flogging continued, until her bare, clenching buttocks were striped and bruised with livid purple welts. Rollo panted, his monstrous cock swaying with each lash of the crop on his wife's bottom. Isobel gazed, squashed in the muck by his boot, as the flogged woman's bum-jellies shivered.

Vip! Vip! Vip!

'*Ohh!*' Mrs Cragg squealed. 'They're getting tight, Rollo. Save your strength for the bitch! You see, Isobel, I wouldn't have enlisted you quite so soon, if you hadn't lost your temper with Helen Dummett this afternoon. She's threatened me with social services, the newspapers . . . her family has influence on Wearside. I'm afraid you'll have to be sacrificed, for the good of the school – a discreet departure, Isobel.'

After forty-eight strokes to his wife's bare arse, Rollo laid aside his crop and lifted Isobel by her belly. He thrust a metal pole between the lips of her dripping cunt, and set the rail's ends on two standing T brackets, six feet apart. Isobel was balanced on the pole in her cunt, with her roped torso squashed to the rail and her legs dangling underneath her. She squealed, as the pole bit into her gash. Her feet wriggled, helpless to find a foothold. Rollo untied his wife, who held Isobel's head down by twisted tresses, while her husband commenced the girl's bare-bum thrashing. As the crop hovered above her trembling fesses, Mrs Cragg poked a square of brocade cloth into Isobel's anus, where it lodged like a pennant.

Vip! Vip! Vip!

'*Ahh!*' Isobel screamed, as the crop lashed the pale melons of her buttocks, clenching and squirming, as her supporting rod bit into her cunt. '*No, please!*'

Vip! Vip! Vip!

'*Ah! Ah! Ah!* Oh, God . . .'

Rollo paused, and moved to place his erect cock before her face, as his wife pulled her head up by the hair.

'Only four dozen, slut, and then you get *that* in you! Isn't that what you've dreamed of? Isn't it worth any pain?'

'*No! No!* . . .'

The erect cock danced before her eyes, like a python.

Vip! Vip! Vip!

Her bare bum reddened, clenching and squirming on the rail poking between her cunt flaps, and wet with her come.

'*Ahh!*'

'I believe she's juicing,' said Mrs Cragg, and thrust her hand inside Isobel's pouch. 'Yes, the slut's wet!'

'I'll have nowhere to go,' Isobel wailed.

'There are possibilities,' panted Rollo.

Vip! Vip! Vip!

'*Ahh! Ahh! No! Please stop!*'

Isobel's bare croup was blotched a heavy mottled crimson, with puffy welts and ridges where the crop had bitten twice or three times. The dark glow suffused her entire bare, with Rollo's crop slicing the whole area of haunches, top buttock and underfesses, as well as the fleshy central melons. Her fesses quivered, clenching like automata, and her choked, sobbing squeals were uncontrolled. Mrs Cragg began to masturbate the girl as she was flogged, and her wrist soon glistened with Isobel's come. The beaten girl's screams turned to whimpers.

At the final stroke of four dozen, she drooled and sobbed, eyes tight shut, and allowed Rollo to release her and drape her over the shoulders of his wife, crouching bare-breasted with her back raised, her stockings filthy from the stable floor and shredded from her own beating. Rollo lowered himself, with his body straight, and supported himself with one hand on his wife's neck. His massive cock tickled the wet gash between Isobel's thighs, and she whimpered, gasping over and over, '*Please fuck me, fuck me, fuck me* . . .' Rollo slammed his massive tool right to the neck of her womb, as she rode his wife bareback.

'God, she's wet!' he cried.

'Whipping is sweeter fucking, Isobel,' said Gemma Cragg.

Vip! Vip! Vip!

As he fucked Isobel's cunt from the rear, Rollo applied the crop to his wife's haunches, and she began to masturbate her clitoris and copiously juicing gash.

'*Ahhh . . . yes . . . Ohh . . .*' moaned Isobel, her wealed bare bum squirming to clasp and squeeze the monstrous cock that penetrated her. '*Oh, fuck me, yes, fuck me . . . oh! oh!*'

Isobel gasped in her onrush of orgasm. Rollo fucked her with ramming thrusts, his belly slapping her bum-weals, for a good half hour, his cock bringing her twice more to climax. Only then did he release his own sperm, which jetted copiously, overflowing Isobel's cunt, and dripped on his wife's haunches. Gemma groaned as she wanked off to a shuddering, belly-heaving climax. Isobel was left to slump on to the dunged straw, whimpering, gasping and sobbing, while rubbing her welted arse.

'God!' she cried. 'If I have to leave Wearbridge, I shan't have a chance of . . . of that *filthy thing*, ever again! I've never had a proper cock inside me before, and now I've tasted it . . . oh, that's cruel!'

'You have devoted your life to caring and teaching,' said Mrs Cragg. 'What better profession than the prison service? HMP Wrigley Scrubs, a specialised female unit in Yorkshire, has vacancies for wardens, and I shall give you a glowing reference.'

'Yorkshire?' said Isobel.

'It is not the end of the world,' said Mrs Cragg, 'and being privatised, Wrigley Scrubs is managed by SPV Security, a firm of which Rollo is a director. You may take a copy of my school history with you,' said Mrs Cragg. 'It may be useful for duties in a *specialised* female unit. Keep your flogging-brocade, too. It is fifteenth century, from my collection. A secret, now you're going – G.D. is Gemma Dodd, my maiden name . . . I wrote the history.'

Isobel pulled the flogging-brocade from her anus and pressed it, smeared with her arse-grease, to her raw weals; then to both her nipples, bruised by the crop.

'There's one other thing,' said Mrs Cragg. 'I should like a wax model of your vulva for my other collection . . . you can easily bear the pain, if you want that job.'

'What? Oh, God! That's disgusting . . . shameful!'

'Like coming after caning, with a big cock fucking your gash. *Don't you want to be shamed, bitch?*'

'*Ohh . . . you made me come, and come . . .*'

Sobbing, Isobel parted her thighs and lay on her back, while hot candle wax dripped into her cunt. She began to groan, then cry, as the melted wax filled her wet pouch.

'*Why . . .?*' Isobel sobbed.

'A Wearbridge tradition. I am sure you have quite the largest cunt in our history. Some of our alumnae pleasure themselves, using toys with historical provenance.'

Isobel whimpered but kept still until the wax solidified inside her pouch, and Rollo removed the hot dildo.

'Must I go for interview?' said Isobel. 'I've no training . . .'

'Oh,' said Rollo Cragg, 'you've just had your interview, and your training.'

# 4

# Whipping Fort

Whop! Whop! Whop!

'Oh! Ouch!'

'Be quiet, slut,' snapped Habren Gaunt, turning from her reflection in the mirror. 'It's only an afternoon slippering.'

'But, Mistress,' sobbed Edwige, 'on top of yesterday's weals . . .'

Whop! Whop! Whop!

'*Ahh!*'

'Why are you here, then, you *dirty submissive*?' Habren spat.

Habren licked her teeth as she gazed at her nude body in the looking-glass. Behind her was the reflection of the crouching Edwige, head hanging low, with her hands bound to her ankles under her arse-cheeks, held apart by a surgical speculum anchored to the floor. A cord looped two copper rings, pierced through her nipples, to a wooden cunt-hobble, clamping her quim lips shut and disabling her from rising. Edwige wore only a ragged T-shirt, pulled to her neck, leaving the ringed titties stretched to pale bare pouches. Susan Race stood over the orbs of her bum, bared for whopping: herself bare-breasted, in a crumpled cotton slip, and wielding a long Moorish leather slipper, curving at the toe and with copper studs at its tip.

Whop! Whop! Whop!

'Oof!'

At each thwack to Edwige's scarlet bare buttocks, Susan's bare teats trembled. Her auburn head-fleece was streaked with grime and sweat; the skirtlet danced up as she whopped the crouching girl's arse, revealing a matted tangle of pubic jungle trailing beneath her cunt lips, which peeped through its mass of curls. Habren stood with her legs planted apart on the flagstones of the vaulted living chamber. Slit windows in the heavy limestone allowed slivers of light to dapple her nude body, and to illumine briefly the squirming figure of the slippered girl; Susan's breasts bounced in the light, showing nipples fully erect.

Whop! Whop! Whop!

'*Ohh!* How much more, Mistress?' wailed Edwige.

'More than I had intended, for such an impertinent question,' said Habren. '*Mmm . . .*'

As she watched both her own sweat-dewed flesh and the shivering bottom of Edwige, Habren masturbated, slowly and luxuriously, her fingers bathed in the slime dripping from her gash, and her thumb drubbing the stiff pinnacle of her clitoris; her other hand squeezed her breasts together, flicking upwards and pinching the erect nipples. In the shadows of Habren's penthouse chamber, a camera whirred. Behind it, an impassive black male, in blue loincloth, pointed the camera; out of its range was the seated, white-suited figure of Joss Gaunt, his eyes swivelling from the figure of his masturbating wife to the helpless roped girl crouching on a reed mat.

'Continue to whop the slut, Susan,' Habren murmured, flicking her engorged clitoris. '*Mm . . .* this will make an adorable dream sequence.'

Whop! Whop! Whop!

'*Mm . . .*' Habren gasped, as come flowed from her wanked cunt. '*Yes . . .!* Redden her arse, Susan. I like the way your boobs wobble as you whop.'

Whop! Whop! Whop!

'*Ahh!*'

Three sharp undercuts in quick succession took Edwige in the parted bum-cleft, slapping her swollen cunt lips and clitoris. Susan turned the slipper face up for the cunt strokes, so that the copper-studded tip sliced Edwige's nubbin and gash, dripping with her cunt slime.

Whop! Whop! Whop!

'Oh! Oh! *Ohh . . .!*'

Edwige wailed as three more tip-strokes thrashed her open slit, and a hard jet of piss sprang from the swollen quim lips, its golden fluid shining oily with come. Habren's masturbation grew more vigorous, and she smiled.

'*Yes!* You'll lick up every drop of your piss, of course,' she purred.

'Oh, Mistress . . .!'

'. . . while Aggar buggers you.'

The cameraman leered from the shadows.

Whop! Whop! Whop!

'*Ah! No! Please!*'

'All part of acting, Edwige. And the mat will be your clothing, stinking of your piss. You may walk the camp rolled in it, like an Egyptian priestess. Most cinematic.'

Edwige's head sank, her eyes dripping sweat and tears, and her voice a choked sob.

'If it please you, Mistress . . .' she stammered.

Whop! Whop! Whop!

'*Ah! Oh! Oh!*'

'*That's* better. Remember why you came to Gaunt Studios, Edwige? You had bit parts in sword and sorcery epics – when some slave girl had to be whipped, it was *your* back they striped, because you could take it – *wanted* to – in real time, without special effects.'

'It was part of realistic acting, Mistress. If I played a girl whipped, then I should genuinely be whipped.'

'And thus discovered your submissive nature! *Flagellant realism* shall make you a star.'

Whop! Whop! Whop!

'*Ahh!* Oh! Thank you, Mistress.'

'Continue to whop the bitch, Susan,' murmured Habren, her nude body dancing softly; her teats swayed, her quim flowed come, and her belly sucked in, heaving.

Her climax signalled itself, not by squeals, but by a heavy, almost mannish, grunting. Come flowed over her probing fist, deep in her cunt, while her thumb pummelled the clitoris, bringing her off.

Whop! Whop! Whop!

'*Ahh! Ooh!*'

Susan made her blows harder on the sobbing Edwige's own juicing cunt, and Edwige's squeals accompanied Habren's hoarse rasp as she orgasmed, her eyes fixed on the red whopped meat of the girl's cunt and the shivering scarlet jellies of her arse. Habren's cunt juces slimed her quivering thighs and dripped over her calves to her ankles and feet, clutching the floor beneath her twitching gash, mirrored in the flagstones.

'You, Susan, are a different kind of slut. A jailbird, no less. How utterly exotic . . .'

'Wrigley Scrubs wasn't exotic, begging your pardon, Mistress,' Susan panted. 'It was tough. They aren't supposed to flog prisoners. Not girl prisoners, anyway.'

'And yet you enjoyed it, for the same reasons the slut Edwige enjoyed her whipping scenes.'

'Can't say I didn't, Mistress. Something awoke in me . . . in all of us. Girls know how to punish girls best, just as they know how to pleasure them. Not that we went without proper fucking at Wrigley Scrubs . . . but men are brutes.'

'So you are now of *my* brutish cast . . .' purred Habren. 'You enjoy beating Edwige, don't you?'

'Can't say I don't, Mistress.'

'Because you'll get the reward of a smoke – how quaint and jailbirdish. Or perhaps because she reminds you of me? We are so alike – almost twins.'

'If you say so, Mistress.'

'I do say so. I like watching *her*, especially, beaten.'

Having climaxed, Habren did not cease to masturbate; she paid attention to her bulbous hard nipples, while stroking the rim of her cunt and brushing the still-erect clit; her pouch continued to puddle the floor. Shafts of sunlight struck the pool of her come.

'How many whops has Edwige taken, Susan?' she said.

'I lost count at two hundred, Mistress. Oh! I mean . . .'

Susan's hand flew to her lips.

'You lost count? Luckily, the camera records all. But *losing count*, Susan . . .?'

Habren Gaunt clicked her tongue. Sitting in his canvas chair, her husband, cock bulging, licked his lips. He watched his wife masturbate, his eyes darting to the buttocks of the roped girl and the pendulous bare titties of her chastiser. Habren signalled into the shadows; the camera continued to roll on automatic as Aggar strode forward, unfastening and, in the same practised flourish, dropping his loincloth.

Below, another camera filmed in the pink afternoon sun. Habren, fingers in her slit, gazed through a window at a prisoner caned on the bare buttocks. The girl wriggled, roped at the ankles and suspended from the flogging frame by a pulley held by six girls strung together at the waist; their victim made no sound, for she hung upside down, her head submerged in a tub of water, from which bubbles emerged. The caning was brief: a dozen, bare-bum, delivered on the half-second, after which the girl was hoisted into the air, sobbing, wheezing and her face as red as her naked croup. Habren gestured from her window, and the black caner tipped his instrument in salute. He nodded to the tethered girls, and they lowered their victim once more into the water. The nude body squirmed, the water threshed, as a dozen strokes lashed the bare buttocks, now a dark crimson in the lowering sun. The pulley raised her and Habren signalled another dozen.

'*Ah! No! Oh, God, please no . . .!*'

At Edwige's scream behind her, Habren turned her head back to her salon. Nude, the giant Aggar smacked his hips against Edwige's scarlet buttocks as he squatted behind the roped girl. She wailed and squirmed as his black glans nuzzled her pink arse bud, and then he was inside her to an inch – two, three inches – and his massive cock-shaft slid all the way to the girl's anal root as he commenced buggering her. Habren clapped her hands, oily with her come, and smeared her cunt slime across her breasts before resuming a vigorous masturbation of both nipples and clitoris. Susan Race lifted her skirt and began to wank off, kneeling behind the black man and getting her tongue half an inch into his anus. She moaned as she wanked off her swollen clitoris, and her tongue penetrated deeper into the black man's anus.

'*Ah . . . ah . . . ah . . .*' groaned Edwige, her buttocks squirming as the tool impaled her bumhole.

Come dripped from her writhing cunt; the giant cock, slimed with her arse-grease, rammed the blond girl's anal shaft, its pucker stretched like a pink balloon. Habren rapped an order to the male: he was to bugger Edwige to orgasm, but retain his own spunk for his mistress. For the first time, Habren cast a disdainful eye at her husband.

'You filthy peeper!' she cried.

'Are you going to cane me, darling?' blurted Joss Gaunt.

'You have known since yesterday.'

'I couldn't sleep, for fear,' he mumbled. 'And my cock-harness chafes so abominably.'

'I'll chastise you, but need another man's spunk in *my* arse before I can cane *yours*, worm,' she drawled.

'Oh, please, darling! You know how it hurts me, to see my own wife . . . *abused* . . . by another man's cock!'

'Yes,' said Habren.

She approached within inches of his face, writhing her hips as she wanked off. His tongue darted to lick come from her inner thigh and the dangling forest of pube-curls, sodden with her exuded cunt slime, but she slapped his head away with a flick of her hips, striking his cheek with her pubic bone.

'Don't you *dare* touch me!' she hissed. 'Only a *real* man may do that . . .'

She slapped the bulge of his erection, the penis fully equal to Aggar's, and he yelped, his face glowing. Aggar's buggery had slowed, and he withdrew his cock to the peehole at each stroke, before plunging it slowly, right to his balls, inside Edwige's anus. Susan Race used thumb and forefinger to hold his buttocks apart, and had almost the whole length of her tongue embedded in his anus while her free hand wanked her swollen cunt, in rapid, blurred frottage. Come dripped from Susan's slit onto the floor. Edwige's breath came in frantic gulps, until her body shuddered and she squealed in climax.

'*Ah! Ah! Ah! AHH . . .*'

Copious come flowed from her cunt as she struggled against her restraining ropes.

'Noisy bitch,' Habren murmured.

The black man withdrew from Edwige's stretched anus, his cock making a plopping sound, leaving Edwige still crouching, sobbing and rubbing her buggered bottom. He reached behind him and grasped Susan by her cropped hair, just above her ear. Susan howled. Aggar drew her upright and slapped her face, twice. She raised her fist to strike, but he clamped his fingers on her wrist, and drew both wrists above her head, lifting her body to twirl helplessly a few inches from the floor. Her naked teats wobbled violently, as though expressing rage for which her red face, and squeals of protest, were not enough.

'*Ohh . . . stop!*' she wailed.

Aggar began a rhythmic hard slapping of her bare breasts, using the palm and back of his hand, and striking her erect nipples with the heel of his fist. Susan wept at her breast-spanking; Aggar paused and ripped the skirt from her haunches. Susan swayed helplessly as her bare teats were thrashed, her nude body shuddering. Droplets of come sprayed from Susan's writhing cunt; smiling, Habren masturbated.

Thwack! Thwack! Thwack!

'*Ahh . . .!*'

Susan's breasts darkened rapidly, bruised blue by the black man's hand. At each swivel of her body, the jungle of her pubis, dripping come, brushed the glans of his erect cock, slimed from Edwige's anus.

'Oh! Please stop . . .! *Please!*'

Thwack! Thwack! Thwack!

'*Ahh! No . . .!*'

Habren took a long, coiled rope and began to wind it, beginning at Susan's feet. At first, the girl resisted, kicking, but Habren's slicing claws to her clitoris reduced her to moaning submission. Susan's cunt writhed, dripping come, as Habren's fingernails bit her nubbin, and she whimpered.

'This was called "playing the lute" at the hareem of Marrakesh,' Habren said. 'The trick is to bind two sluts, preferably lesbian lovers, so that if either one jerks or wriggles under punishment, she hurts the other – and, of course, you'll both jerk and wriggle.'

'We're not lovers, Mistress!' Susan shrieked. 'We wank off, but so do all the girls . . .!'

'Then you won't mind.'

When Susan's legs were bandaged mummy-tight in the coarse hempen rope, Habren knotted her sheath in place, leaving the cunt and buttocks bare, then took a second coil and began to rope her belly. Soon, Susan Race was swaddled completely, with only her breasts, cunt and buttocks bare, and tiny holes at nose and mouth. Already, the ropes swaddling her upper thighs were wet with seeping come. Her bare arms still dangled from Aggar's wrist; he parted them, allowing his mistress to fasten each wrist wide apart, to pulleys from the ceiling hooks.

Susan dangled, swaying, as Habren wrenched the sobbing Edwige by her long blond tresses, and placed her, face upwards, on the floor beneath Susan's juicing cunt, so that the swaddled girl's come dripped into Edwige's mouth. Habren roped a third fastening around Susan's bound feet, knotting them to the cord stretched between Edwige's nipple and quim clamps, and gradually lifting that cord up, quivering like a violin string.

'*Oh . . . Oh . . . Oh . . .*' Edwige sobbed, as her nipples and gash flaps were wrenched upwards.

She lay, helpless to make the slightest movement without pulling her flaps of flesh tighter, just as any twitch of Susan's feet would jar Edwige's nipple and gash bonds. Habren clapped her hands and Aggar handed her a cane, four feet in length and half an inch thick. Habren stood well back from Susan's bound body and lifted her cane above her head.

Vip!

She sliced down, in a slanting motion that laid a crisp pink weal on Susan's upper bare buttocks.

'*Ahh!*' the bound and hung girl squealed, jerking in the rope swaddle.

Her scream was echoed by Edwige, her belly string twanged taut by Susan's shudder, and her nipples and cunt flaps wrenched.

'*Oh! God! It hurts so . . .!*'

Vip!

'*Ah! No!*'

Vip!

'*Mm! Oh, please, Mistress . . . Oh!*'

Both girls screamed, sobbing, until Aggar silenced Susan. Lifting himself by the pulley that held her, he thrust his cock to her lips. The glans, slimed from Edwige's arse, nuzzled Susan's teeth.

'No . . .' she moaned.

As her lips parted, Aggar thrust: his shaft penetrated her mouth to the base of his helmet, forcing her mouth wide. Susan gurgled, sobbing, as her lips pressed on the black cock-meat.

'Mmm . . . mmm . . .' she wailed, shaking her head.

Aggar's buttocks twitched, and his cock plunged to the back of her throat.

Vip!

Habren's cane lashed Susan's naked arse.

'*Ah . . .! MMM!*' the girl squealed, choking on the huge black cock that vigorously throat-fucked her, and sucking in time with Aggar's thrusts.

Vip! Vip! Vip!

At each stroke to her bare, Susan jerked up, pulling at the belly-cord tethering Edwige's cunt and nipple flaps.

'*Ohh . . .!*'

'*AHH!*'

Both girls screamed together as their bound bodies shuddered. When Susan had taken fifteen strokes to the buttocks, Habren padded around her and began to cane the tip of her erect clitoris.

Vip!

'*Ahh!*'

At the first cunt-slice, Susan pissed herself, the powerful jet of golden fluid hissing over Edwige's jerking bare body and drenching her. Habren stood directly under Aggar's pumping arse; as she continued to cane Susan's cunt, getting her strokes right inside the come-gushing pink slit, she began to lick Aggar's balls. Joss stared in dismay, as his wife took the black man's ball-sac fully into her mouth, while continuing to cane Susan's red wet gash. Susan twirled, spraying her come over the piss-soaked Edwige, who jerked and screamed as each convulsion of Susan's body pulled her binding cord. Susan's screams rose to a shrill, staccato whimper, and suddenly her belly heaved, as she squealed in orgasm. Habren pressed her lips on Aggar's balls, and he withdrew his cock from Susan's mouth, leaving her lips flapping and her tongue probing the air. Carrying Aggar on her shoulders, with his cock at her nape and feet probing her breasts, Habren snapped the clamps from Edwige's nipples and cunt.

'Susan has taken enough for the moment,' she said. 'You may free the slut, Edwige.'

She bent, allowing Aggar to dismount, and turned to her husband, while grasping the black man's slimy stiff tool and playing with his balls between finger and thumb.

'Now it's your turn, you worm,' she spat. 'Get out of your chair and bare up below.'

'*What . . .?*'

Habren laughed and prodded his erection with her cane.

'Everything off beneath your waist,' she rapped. 'Then, bend over for your caning. We'd better cane that disgusting erection away.'

Joss Gaunt touched his toes, his arse bare for his wife's cane, and his head hanging, with his face beetroot red. She unlocked the buckles of his rubber cock-restraint and his huge stiff shaft leapt up.

'Face sideways!' she commanded.

Joss did so, and gasped.

Habren's cane hovered, a foot above his bare arse. His wife stood bent at an angle, with thighs parted. She reached one hand behind her and spread her bum-cheeks. Aggar's erect penis brushed her anal pucker, then slid inside the shaft, to a depth of an inch. Habren squirmed, pulling her fesses further apart; the black man thrust, grunting, as his cock penetrated her anus right to his balls.

'No . . .!' wailed her husband.

Vip!

'*Ah!*' he squealed, as a livid pink welt coloured his croup.

'Mm! *Yes!*' Habren groaned, her body quivering, as Aggar's hips smacked her naked buttocks, and his cock rammed her bumhole. '*Yes . . .!*'

Vip! Vip! Vip!

'Ah! God! That's too hard!' cried her husband as Habren's cane wealed his buttocks.

Vip! Vip! Vip!

'Ah! Darling . . . *Ahh!*'

'Watch, you filthy little pig!' Habren hissed. 'Watch me buggered!'

Vip!

'*Oh!* I can't stand it . . .' he sobbed.

Her husband's arse clenched and squirmed, as each cut of her cane sliced the quivering bare buttocks, but his cock still stood, massively erect.

'Watch, I command you! Look at Aggar's big black tool pig-sticking your wife's arse! Buggering your own wife's hole, while *she* . . .'

Vip Vip! Vip!

'*AHH!*'

'. . . *thrashes* you!'

Habren's bare, dangling titties quivered like melons at each ram of the cock in her anus. Her buttocks clenched, gripping the black tool as it slid out of her squirming hole, right to the glans tip, before spearing her again. Each new penetration drew a grunt from the bugger's victim.

'God, yes, that's good!' Habren gasped. 'Fuck my hole, Aggar! Make me wriggle! Poke me! Give me every drop of spunk! I want Joss to see a real man's spunk bubbling from my bumhole!'

Vip! Vip! Vip!

Her husband took his beating, choking back his sobs and whimpering, but with his eyes glued to the flow of come from his wife's cunt lips, and the slamming of the tool between her naked fesses.

'I wish you could have been there, when I took a whole Foreign Legion platoon, during our honeymoon in Corsica,' she said. 'Buggered and cunt-fucked and sucking cock, for three and a half hours . . .'

Joss wailed.

Vip! Vip! Vip!

'And you thought it was all acting . . .' Habren hissed. 'I've had a *thousand* cocks in my arse, never mind my cunt.'

'You punish yourself . . . too hard . . .' Joss gasped.

Vip! Vip! Vip!

Whop!

'*Ahh . . .!*'

Susan's voice shrilled above Joss's wails. Edwige had managed to uncoil the rope from Susan's torso, so that the girl hung, still helpless, but with her legs still sheathed in rope. Edwige wound the discarded rope into a flail of five thongs and delivered a strong whop, that covered the whole expanse of Susan's flaming red bum.

'*Edwige! Why . . .*' Susan squealed, her whipped buttocks clenching under the rope's lash.

Whop! Whop!

'That's for hurting my quim and titties, you bitch!' Edwige cried.

She whipped Susan alternately on naked buttocks and breasts, with the teat-flesh soon a mass of purple bruises from the five thongs, covering the whole breast and targeting the nipples.

Whop! Whop! Whop!

'Oh . . . don't . . .'

'Piss on me, you slut?' cried Edwige.

Whop! Whop! Whop!

'Edwige . . . no . . . I'm sorry!'

'Is that what you learned in jail, you fucking jailbird?'

Susan's body spun, unravelling the rope from her legs.

Whop! Whop! Whop!

'*Ah!* You wouldn't last ten minutes at Wrigley Scrubs, you fucking slag! *Ah . . .!* Stop! Oh, *please* stop . . .'

Edwige flogged the girl's bare bum and torso until Susan's skin was a mass of mottled bruises and puffy ridged welts, her titties like bright red canteloupes. The last strand of rope slithered from her shuddering feet. At once, she jack-knifed her legs and got Edwige's neck in a scissor lock, forcing her whipper to the floor. Edwige gasped for air.

Vip! Vip! Vip!

'Oh!' Joss gasped, his bare flogged arse a quivering patchwork of welts. 'How many more . . .?'

'I shan't stop caning you until Aggar spunks in me,' panted his wife, 'and he shan't spunk until I tell him to.'

Susan's thighs rippled as she dragged Edwige's head up towards the dripping jungle of her crotch hair. When Edwige's tongue was level with her slit, Susan whispered, 'Now, eat me, slut.'

Edwige's tongue darted forwards and penetrated Susan's gaping wet cunt, while her nose pressed the stiff clitty. Susan gasped.

'*That's* better . . . that's one of the things a girl learns at the Scrubs . . .'

Habren looked over her shoulder, laughing as Susan moaned, her cunt basin jerking at the blond girl's expert cunt-licks. Edwige had her jaw clamped around Susan's whole pubis, and chewed rhythmically, up and down, with her tongue flicking the erect nubbin, then poking into the gushing slit and the anus bud. Edwige's face shone as Susan's cunt slimed it with her come. Aggar grunted, buggering his mistress faster; Habren began to cane her husband's buttocks with forehand and backhand strokes, two or three to a second, her torso swaying. Her teats bounced as the black man shafted her bumhole.

'Oh, God, enough!' Joss wailed.

'Wrigley Scrubs? Tell me,' purred Habren.

'It's a whipping prison,' gasped Susan. 'You opt for a light sentence, but get hard caning and whipping. The screws are all girls, some of them former slags, and they are the toughest . . . *Oh!* Yes! Don't stop!'

Edwige chewed the erect nubbin, while masturbating her own clitty. Susan's come flowed between Edwige's bare breasts, over her heaving belly, and into her bush, where it joined Edwige's sweat and the piss Susan had showered, until the commingled fluid dripped copiously from the lush tendrils of Edwige's own cunt jungle.

'They are always showing the scrubs on TV, as a model privatised prison,' Susan gasped, 'but it's fucking bullshit. They show the sanitised version, not the real Scrubs, with the whips and the screams and licking the toilets clean, and girls caned on their bare bums till they beg for mercy . . . *Ahh!*'

Susan's belly sucked in as her come splattered Edwige's mouth in her fierce squeals of orgasm. Aggar, buggering Habren, grunted, and Habren's bum tightened on his cock, trapping it at the root of her anus as he spermed inside her. Spunk bubbled from the tightly clamped anal pucker and dribbled on her inner thighs. She dropped her cane, flicking her clitoris hard, until she gasped in her own climax.

As Habren's belly heaved, Edwige wanked herself off, joining Susan in her cries of pleasure. Habren touched the peehole of her husband's erect cock. She slid her fingernail into his peehole and clawed. His caned arse still trembling, Joss yelped and a jet of spunk spurted from his cock over his wife's hand. Habren ordered Aggar to release Susan and take the cane, while the two girls crouched to lick up the come, pee and spunk bedewing the floor. Whimpering, the two nude girls obeyed, their bare bums high and clefts wide open for Aggar's cane as they licked the floor clean of fluid, swallowing on command of his canestrokes.

'A whipping prison. Well, well,' Habren said, as she fastened the restrainer over her husband's cock, 'and privatised?' That means it's for sale . . .'

'Shall I speak to our acquisitions director, darling?' said Joss. '*Ouch!*'

'Yes, do.'

# 5

# The Full Bare

'You're the nearest person I have to a friend, Tamsin,' Angarad murmured.

'Wow! Thanks a million,' said Tamsin Pollecutt, blowing the steam from her cappucino.

Outside, snowflakes drifted on Richmond Green.

'No! I didn't mean . . . I mean, you're my best friend, really,' Angarad stammered, blushing.

'We English aren't good at expressing our feelings, are we?' said Tamsin. 'Verbally, at any rate . . .'

She tossed her raven mane, which made her heavy, jutting breasts swell in her clinging green cashmere sweater.

Angarad sipped her own coffee, stared out at the trees, the snow-shrouded grass, and shivered.

'I sense some revelation,' said Tamsin. 'Do tell . . .'

She crossed her sheer-stockinged legs with deliberate slowness, revealing a sliver of thigh and garter strap that drew glances in the tiny tea shop. Tamsin smiled.

'Oh, it's nothing, really,' said Angarad.

'That means it's everything. Let's take the fidgeting for granted, Angie, and get to the beans, spillage of.'

'It's a bit . . . embarrassing, I suppose.'

When Angarad had completed her account of the events three days before, Tamsin stared at her friend with a smile playing on her lips and the tip of her tongue flickering.

'And how do you feel now?' she said. 'I mean, about this new assignment with Roz Cardus.'

'Oh, *that*? It's going very well, actually. Roz and I seem to get along. We've some fabulous new lingerie designs, awfully kinky, actually. I blame *her* . . .'

'Don't,' said Tamsin, putting her hand on Angarad's. 'Rockingham's have promoted me to fashion buyer for their London shops, and I've every intention of pushing their envelope in direction outrageous! So, let's network. And after what you've told me about Darren . . .'

'Tammy, I feel worse about *that* than ever. I mean, confessing has helped, I suppose . . .'

'You'd never been bummed before?'

'*No!*'

'Spanked?'

'You *know* I was a Ditton girl.'

'Of course. Same regime as at Sunbury Reginae, where they favoured the Scots tawse, as if I could ever forget. Skirt up, knickers down, a dozen whops on the bare . . .'

Tamsin licked her teeth.

'I hated it!' Angarad cried. 'Spanked, I mean, on my *bare bum*, by Will, then that unspeakable thing with Darren . . . I haven't stopped thinking about – *you* know. It makes me feel awful, as if I'm a really bad person.'

'Buggery, unspeakable? Yet, you *have* spoken.'

'Oh, *don't*! You can't imagine how it hurts, and how shameful it is . . .'

'Actually, I don't have to,' said Tamsin, with an impish grin, stroking Angarad's wrist. '*Why* haven't you stopped thinking about it? Because it hurt and shamed you? Or because you'd already thought about it before . . .?'

'I told you, I haven't been spanked since I left school!' Angarad cried. 'Ouch! You're hurting!'

Tamsin's fingernails had tightened on Angarad's wrist, pinching the skin to white. She relaxed her grip, slowly.

'I didn't mean just the spanking,' she said. 'Does your arse still smart? Your bumhole still hurt?'

'Sort of,' replied Angarad cautiously.

'What kind of sort of?' Tamsin demanded. 'You mean, it feels *nice*?'

Angarad blushed.

'I shouldn't have mentioned it at all!' she blurted.

'Oh, yes, you should. I'm your best friend, remember? Angie, have you ever been to Morocco?'

'No,' Angarad replied.

'Visit the English churchyard in Tangier, right in the middle of the *souk*,' she said. 'You'll find the grave of Captain George Pollecutt, an ancestor of mine, from Yorkshire, and a noted, umm, *polygamist*, with two of his wives being identical twins. Colourful lad, so colourful, in fact, that he isn't actually buried in his own grave. For twenty-two years, Tangier was part of the British Empire, as the dowry of King Charles II's Portuguese bride. Off Cadiz, Captain Pollecutt captured a Spanish ship, full of Peruvian silver, and landed in Tangier, to avoid a Spanish revenge party. He presented the galleon and treasure to the King, of course – apart from half the silver, which he had hidden along the Atlantic coast of Africa. His men got paid off, while he was given a sinecure, as adjutant to the governor of Tangier.'

Tamsin paused to sip her coffee and shift in her seat, not bothering to smooth her skirt, ridden up to show her stocking-tops.

'Captain George didn't have much to do, except indulge in four of his passions,' she said. 'One of them was exploring; the other was gold. He spent months away from Tangier, exploring the south, to try and find a safe overland route to the hinterland of the Gold Coast, to avoid buccaneers like himself. The Berbers considered silver and salt as more valuable than gold; equipped with those, he would venture far into the Sahara, amongst the Berbers. I should mention that part of his treasure was a brace of identical girl twins, natives of Hispaniola, which the Spanish were intending to present at court. Captain George preferred to keep them as slaves, in a desert hideaway far from his wife, Molly, who was no better than she should have been. Their beauty intrigued him, neither Spanish, African, nor Asiatic, but with long skulls, straight noses and high cheekbones, as well as figures . . . well, the sort of thing men like – you, for instance. They were docile and "fond of the arts of love". He found that they resembled the Berbers, when the Berbers knew him well enough to bare their faces, and sell him their unmarried daughters as slaves. As he ventured further and further south, he set up a chain of forts as supply stations, garrisoned by his obedient wives, or slave women. He was convinced that his Hispaniolan twins were the same stock as the Berbers, and long ago formed a seafaring nation, bridging the Atlantic, in the days when the Sahara was not a desert. That is by the by – there was another reason Captain George got on so well with the Berbers. He called his victualling stations *whipping forts.* The Berbers liked to watch an Englishman administering expert chastisement to naked slaves and eventually brought their own miscreant womenfolk to him, for whipping, beneath their own dignity to give.'

'I . . . I don't understand,' said Angarad.

'*Yes, you do,*' said Tamsin. 'Captain George's third passion was whipping women on the bare.'

'God! How awful . . .' Angarad whispered. 'And the fourth passion? I'm almost afraid to ask.'

'Buggering the women, afterwards.'

Angarad shivered; even with the heating on full, it was freezing in Tamsin's car. Headlights lit gleaming compacted snow, and her wheels hissed through slush.

'Not far now,' said Tamsin.

'Teddington seems such a funny place for . . .'

'Pinkar's Club? Everywhere's a funny place, and nowhere is. *Pinkarse* was the rollicking seventeenth-century nickname, though Oswald Pinkar, Earl of Wrigley, named it for himself, and it's said *he* was really Captain Pollecutt. He had mysterious wealth and spent it on exotic imported *flagellabilia*. The club was incorporated in the less rollicking nineteenth century as the "Society for the Punishment of Vice". Call it the SPV if it sounds better – or I'll stop and you can get the bus home, if you want.'

'No! As long as I don't actually have to *do* anything.'

'A beautiful girl *never* has to do anything,' said Tamsin.

'I still can't believe that *you* . . .'

'I never told you I was part of the scene, because the subject never came up. I've never told you what sort of cereal I eat for breakfast, either. It's just what I do, except pain and pleasure are more absorbing than breakfast cereal. It's about finding your real self, which is why *you* are here, after claiming you *hated* being spanked and buggered.'

'I still wonder what mysterious part you play in the . . . the Pinkarse Club!' Angarad said, with a sudden smile. 'Such a quaint, innocent name . . .'

'Mysteries are absorbing,' Tamsin said. 'So is innocence. Remember being spanked at school, and how waiting was part of it? Heavens, Angie, admit the truth about yourself. You have perve's eyes!'

'What?'

'An innocent dreamy look, sort of faraway, but deeply knowing, of something we all envy, which is why dominants can be beastly to subs . . . like you.'

Angarad swallowed, looking nervously with wide eyes at her friend. They drove south with the somnolent Thames to their left, past rich villas and terraces. Tamsin slowed before a detached villa, set back from the roadway, and cruised until she could slip into a parking space.

'You didn't tell me why Captain George's grave in Tangier is empty,' Angarad said, as they approached the house, dark, save for chinks of light peeping from drapes.

Both girls wore long coats and scarves; Angarad, a bottle-green velvet dress, strapless, with a high hemline; seamed sockings, a pubic string, and full sussies in green lace; which Tamsin assured her was sufficiently outrageous, for a beginner. Tamsin herself had refused to let Angarad see under her clinging coat, which had a dull, metallic sheen and an aroma that Angarad recognised as rubber. It swung halfway down sheer, spike-heeled and pointed boots, also of rubber, but shiny.

'It's not empty. He fought a duel with another rogue named Cragg, about a woman they had both buggered, and left him wounded in the arse. He went through Cragg's pockets and found stolen letters of credit on a Portuguese bank worth a fortune. So he swapped coats with Cragg and bribed the servants to say Captain George had lost the duel, then bury a coffin full of stones. He took the goodies and disappeared.'

Tamsin gave the doorbell three long rings, then two short ones. The door opened, to the bright light and chatter of a party in full swing. No face appeared to greet them. There was a click as the door latch sprang back into place. Below them crouched a girl with long, flowing blond tresses. The girl was nude and had her wrists handcuffed behind her back. Her upraised bare bottom was marked with raw crimson weals; an unseen hand held a rope leash tautly fastened to a spiked chain around her neck and her ankles were encased in a metal hobble bar. She had opened the door with her teeth.

Tamsin did not enter but unbelted her greatcoat and let the flaps fall open, revealing herself to the girl. The girl gasped. Angarad followed Tamsin into the hallway and put her hand to her mouth when her eyes fell on Tamsin's body. Her friend wore a brassiere of rubber cords, holding conical silver cups, to cover no more of her massively jutting breasts than the swollen, strawberry nipples. She wore rubber sussies and stockings, woven in close fishnet, but no knickers. Hanging from her silver waist-chain was a riding crop of braided leather; strapped at her crotch, in erect position, was a rubber penis of fifteen or more inches, and the girth of a girl's fist. Jutting at its base, and parallel to the rubber cock, was a smaller dildo seven or eight inches long, and the thickness of an erect cock.

'Hello, Bee,' said Tamsin. 'Have you been a good girl?'

'Welcome to Pinkarse, Mistress,' said the girl's voice. 'No, I'm rather afraid I haven't . . .'

The person holding Bee's rope handed the leash, with a smile, to Tamsin. He was a man in early middle-age, wearing a grey business suit, collar and tie, and black shoes, but with a leather mask covering his cheeks, chin, and lower brow.

'Tamsin! Delightful! Just in time to take charge of this brat. Bee has been awfully whiny awaiting you. And your friend, Angarad? I am enchanted. She is even lovelier than you painted her.'

His voice was a purring baritone.

'Hello, Marcus,' Tamsin replied.

Marcus bent to brush Angarad's hand with his lips.

'Do join the throng,' he said, his eyes fixed on Angarad's breasts. 'You'll find us eccentric, but lovable . . .'

Both girls deposited their coats in the cloakroom and Angarad followed Tamsin into the drawing room, which looked out through closed French windows on to a broad, snow-shrouded lawn sweeping down to the sluggish river. The room was hung with velvet drapes, four or five feet from the wall, as if they were in a dressing-room or stage set. It rang with party chatter, and Angarad whispered to Tamsin that she was sure she recognised some voices.

'Marcus's voice is familiar, too,' she said.

'The TV studios are nearby,' Tamsin answered. 'You might meet some celeb like Max Ogule. Nervous?'

'Yes.'

'Don't be. Nothing will happen to you unless you want it to. We perves are the nicest souls.'

'It seems so casual. Apart from . . . well, you and Bee.'

Bee crawled behind Tamsin, who held her riding crop and absent-mindedly flicked Bee's bare buttocks, making the girl squeal like a piglet. Bemetalled women posed in rubber costumes or black leather; whips and canes dangled from studded belts as casually as handbags. Others had clothes everyday to the point of aggression, with men and women in business suits, but each with a fetish sign – a rip, a knotted kerchief, an angled brooch.

Four girls wore frilly French maid's outfits, their tutus and bodices, or corselets, leaving breasts, buttocks or both artfully bare. Other girls were pink sugarplum fairies, with diaphanous gossamer costumes that showed breasts thrust up by bras many sizes too small, or with perforated cups that squeezed the nipples to gooseberries; bellies strapped in rubber waspie corsets, loins swaddled in lattices of knotted rope or fastened in heavy rubber clamps; some wore nothing at all beneath gauze. Chat hummed.

'Haven't seen you since I gave you a seven dozen on the bare with my rattan – no, it was eight, I think.'

'Darling, how can you *take* so many hours with a studded corset, brank and butt-plug? And tit-caned *as well*!'

There was a buffet with plenty of wine and food. Tamsin was greeted with embraces, kisses, cries of delight, but her greeters focused on Angarad, who trailed behind her, alongside the petite blond Bee, snuffling in her cords, and sobbing every time Tamsin punctuated her conversation with a flick of her crop to Bee's bare arse, or sometimes undercutting her pendulous bubs. Bee was blond, like Angarad, and her hourglass figure a petite replica of Angarad's. She alone had nothing to eat or drink – until Angarad saw a saucer of water in the corner, which Tamsin permitted her to drink, occasionally throwing her a scrap of food, at which the roped girl twisted her nude body, to gnaw voraciously.

'Tamsin,' Angarad whispered, 'why does she do it? Bee, I mean. Abase herself so?'

Tamsin delivered a particularly vicious slice to the cleft of Bee's bum, catching her on the anus pucker, and her crop tip flicking the swollen cunt lips, moist with fluid.

'It is her nature,' she replied. 'She's a sub, and a wretched little squirt, like all subs. Aren't you, Bee?'

Vip!

The crop lashed Bee in a fierce undercut, slashing both her erect nipples. The sub's come dripped copiously.

'Yes, Mistress,' she whimpered.

Gradually, plates were cleared by the girls dressed as French maids, and the light slowly dimmed to a red, incandescent glow. Behind each French maid's croup sparkled a filigree chain, reaching between the pleats of her skirt into her arse-cleft. The maids were bound together by this most delicate shackle, yet managed to weave their way about their tasks without entanglement. Each wore her hair ironed perfectly smooth, and had identical fishnet stockings with teetering high stilettos, although the arrangement of their skirts and corselets varied, to tease with an exact amount of exposed flesh. Drinks were replenished to the full, but the food table disappeared. Those whose dinner plates still held food twanged the French maids' waistbands, and dropped leftovers down her rubber knickers; at which the maids curtsied, bowing low, to reveal their expanse of tethered teat-flesh. The air was heavy with cigar smoke: those wishing to tip ash, did so down the cups of a maid's brassiere. One maid served as a receptacle for finished tobacco stubs; her skirt had a tin cup, pressed close to her knickerless pubis, and guests summoned her to stub out their smokes in this metal cunt-pouch. She grimaced as she curtsied, then smiled, as the hot metal singed her cunt hairs.

'I am so glad you could make it, Tamsin,' Marcus said. 'Bee has been an absolute bitch, whining for you. No amount of whopping seems to keep the slut quiet.'

'Mm!' Bee protested, with sob.

Vip! Vip!

Tamsin gave her two cuts to the full bare, already laced with cane marks.

'*Mmm . . .!*'

Drool dribbled from Bee's slack lips, like the droplets of fluid dripping from her cunt and her bushy, untrimmed jungle of pubic fronds. Tamsin wrinkled her nose.

'The slut needs a bath,' she murmured.

'I'm sure you can give her an imaginative one, my dear,' said Marcus.

He melted into the shimmering red half-light, touching a switch; the drapes rose to the ceiling. Angarad gasped; festooning the walls, sullen in gunmetal, stood clamps, irons, whipping frames, racks and apparatus of supplice. Whips hung, oiled and gleaming; canes, as crisp in their racks as fresh young schoolgirls. Five rope nooses dangled from the ceiling, with the same at ankle level; buckled rubber waist cinchers, heavy flanges two feet thick, were hinged to the wall.

'Welcome to my dungeon, friends,' said Marcus. 'Enjoy, and thank Pinkarse.'

'I just can't believe people use these things for *fun*,' said Angarad.

'It's not fun,' said Tamsin. 'That's the point.'
Vip! Vip!
Her crop striped the bare buttocks of the snivelling Bee.
'Is it, slave?'
'N . . . no, Mistress,' Bee whimpered.
Vip! Vip!
'*Ah!* Ouch!'
'You hate it, don't you, Bee?'
'Yes, Mistress.'
Vip! Vip!
'Wrong answer. I'll have to punish you for that, you realise.'
Vip! Vip! Vip!
Bee's bare bum glowed violet in the half-light.
'*Ohh . . .!* Yes, Mistress!' she sobbed.
Angarad watched as business suits came off, to reveal a variety of costumes as bizarre as Tamsin's; or otherwise nude bodies, corseted, sheathed and strapped, or pinned and ringed, at breast or genitals. Everyone donned mask or pixy hood, except for Tamsin, Angarad, Bee, and the four French maids.
'This is where your saucy designer lingerie leads, Angie,' said Tamsin, 'only, the scene got there first. In a few years, this stuff will be in every Rockingham's shop window . . .'
Vip!
The first canestroke pierced the air.
'*Uhh . . .*'
A woman, nude, straddled a spanking stool like a milkmaid's, her bare bum held high, with her head and arms pinioned by the masked man, introduced only minutes before as her husband. Her caner was a female, nude but for a pixy hood and rubber boots, extending almost to the jungle of pubic curls that dangled well below her red, swollen cunt lips, each of them pierced with a silver ring. The domina's clinging boot rubber glistened with come, dripping from her cunt rings, as she raised her cane. Behind her, a black male, nude but for a leather mask, spread her pale, quivering bum-flans, and penetrated the domina's open anus with a massively swollen cock.

Vip! Vip!

Her titties trembled as she flogged; her victim's bare buttocks clenched, as pink stripes etched across the quivering skin. The black male fucked the caner's arse in powerful thrusts, his slimed cock withdrawing from her cleft, to pierce the caner's anus, in time with her strokes to the helpless bare female.

'*Uhh . . .! Yes . . .!*'

Tamsin's cane sliced Bee's anus bud, directing her towards the erect cock of the flogged woman's husband. Obediently, Bee got her lips around the swollen crimson glans, and her tongue began to flicker on the peehole.

Vip! Vip!

Tamsin began a rhythmic caning of Bee's croup, as her slave's throat accepted the man's cock.

Vip! Vip! Vip!

Tamsin thrashed Bee's naked arse with strokes at one-second intervals; she reached between her legs, getting her fingers between the strap-on tool and her massive wet cunt bush, her nails right down to the slit lips. She touched her distended clitty, poking at her rubber dildo, and began to masturbate as she caned Bee's quivering bare fesses. Bee took her punishment in silence, except for a gurgling noises as she fellated the man, whose caned wife seemed to enjoy responding to the cane of the buggered woman, with a drama of strangled gasps.

Vip! Vip! Vip! Vip!

'*Ouch!* Ooh! Uhh . . . *Ahhh . . .!*'

Her naked buttocks, bruised with a crisscross of darkening weals, performed a sinuous, writhing dance as the naked arse-globes squirmed under the cane's welt. The flogging-stool was well slimed with her come, seeping from the gash lips that fluttered in time with her caning.

Vip! Vip! Vip!

'Oh! Yes! *Ohh* . . .'

She began to rub her pubis on the wood, smearing it with come, as the caning passed twenty-five strokes. Another ten and the woman was scarlet in the face, her cunt gushing fluid, and she sobbed to her husband.

'*God, it's so good!* Just one touch, darling! Bring . . .'

Vip!

'. . . me . . .'

Vip!

'. . . *off . . .! Oh! Oh!*'

'At the fifty, bitch.'

Vip! Vip! Vip!

'I do think she needs more discipline at home,' Marcus murmured to the husband of the caned female. 'My sister would never listen to *my* advice . . .'

The strokes continued towards the fifty. At the fiftieth slice of the buggered woman's cane on his wife's frenzied, quivering arse-jellies, and with Bee continuing to suck his cock, the male pinched his wife's swollen clitty between thumb and forefinger; she squealed, heaving in orgasm. Her husband released her and grasped Bee's titties, squeezing and clawing them as her bum continued to writhe under Tamsin's cane. He pressed the nipples until they stood white; Bee groaned, with her head bobbing like a pigeon's, as she fellated his stiff tool, until her groans turned to a gurgling and her throat bobbed as the male spunked in her mouth. She swallowed his spunk, but a little of the powerful jet dribbled from her lips to splash her squeezed bubs. Tamsin began to lash Bee's titties with hard, rapid strokes, concentrating on the spunk-slimed nipples. The male withdrew his cock, leaving Bee's mouth drooling the remnants of his sperm. Her bare bum still clenched, even when Tamsin varied her caning, with strokes to her quivering bare breasts; Bee's rosebud cunt juiced with heavy come.

'Filthy little beast,' said Tamsin. 'I think it's bathtime . . .'

Female bottoms were bare, for spanking, slippering or the loud thwack of the tawse or cane. The pink sugar-plum fairies had their gauzy dresses torn from them and were held helpless and squealing, to be thrashed by females in rubber; others meekly, or teasingly, bared their bums, daring their thrashers to hurt them. The black cock pumped between the domina's arse-cheeks, while she frotted her clitty to orgasm; he cried out, a froth of spunk bubbling from her anal pucker, between her buttocks, to drip down her perineum into her luxuriant cunt bush. Tamsin directed Bee to suck the domina's cunt hair dry, before proceeding to her own cleansing. When Bee had drunk come from the domina's cunt as the domina masturbated her still erect clitty, then sucked the black male's spunk from the soaked pubic bush, Tamsin jerked her rope, and ordered her to open the handles of the French windows with her mouth, then go into the garden.

Bee obeyed; there was a gust of cold air before the windows closed again. Tamsin ordered Bee to roll naked in the snow, as Angarad watched, mouth agape. She looked further and saw a shadow over the river, like a gibbet, with a chair beneath it: a mediaeval ducking stool. Bee rolled herself into a snowball, then came to a halt, with only her head exposed from the hillock of snow and tears streaming from her pale, shivering face. Tamsin grinned, looking down at Angarad's crotch; Angarad followed her gaze and blushed a fiery red. Her hose tops were slimed with come, seeping from her cunt string.

The French maids flattened themselves against the wall, each patting her ironed hair straight. Their faces were unsmiling, as they spread their legs and raised their wrists to the rope nooses hung at the ceiling. Marcus's sister, still rubbing her own caned bottom, helped fasten the first maid in her wrist and ankle ropes, then stripped her of her maid's uniform, all except her stockings and shoes.

'The full bare,' said Marcus to Angarad, who trembled.

He eyed her moist stocking-tops and smiled at her. Angarad shifted in her tight dress; no shifting could conceal her upthrust bare teat-flesh, nor the thighs and stocking-top, gleaming with tell-tale come. The sister fastened her maid in the rubber waist cincher, wrenching the slab of latex until it strained to bursting and the girl's flesh was pinched in tight, serrated folds, beneath her rib cage. The three other maids accepted the same fate at the hands of males: the recently spunked black man, whose cock was already trembling half-erect, and Marcus's brother-in-law, seeing to the girl beside his wife, and Marcus himself. Four of the five whipping-emplacements were occupied by shivering girls, bared for whipping, and each with a steady drip of come from her cunt into her sussies and stocking tops. Marcus folded each girl's long tresses over her titties, squashed to the wall, thus leaving her shoulders bared.

'The full bare,' Marcus said to Angarad, 'means chastisement of both buttocks and back. Whip or cane may be used on either portion, or both.'

Marcus stripped completely; Angarad shivered, unable to take her eyes off the bodies of the four naked victims. Marcus's sister took position, holding a cat-o'-nine-tails above the fully bared back and arse of the first, shivering maid, now helpless in her bonds.

Crack!

The first whipstroke fell, the cat leaving a vivid pattern of dark red stripes on the girl's upper back. She shuddered but did not cry.

Vip!

A four-foot rattan cane took the second girl clean across both buttocks, leaving a pink weal.

Thwap!

A three-tongued tawse began the punishment of the third, leaving a dull bruise across the whole bare croup.

Vap!

A second rattan cracked across the fourth maid's naked shoulders. All four girls shuddered, their arses and backs squirming. A pattern emerged of ten strokes to back, followed by ten to fesses, and vice versa, so that no portion of the girl's rear body went unbeaten. Strokes fell on the naked thigh backs, ripping come-wet stockings. As the punishments continued, with the whipped victims squirming against their ropes, the spectators accompanied the groans of the flogged girls with their own cries, as bare bottoms reddened under strap or spank, females bared their anal puckers to serial buggery, and sucked tool after arse-slimed tool. Angarad shivered.

'I can't believe this . . .' she gasped, ashen-faced.

Marcus paused, and turned, his cock massively erect.

'Your *cunt* believes it, Miss,' he rasped. 'Don't you want to masturbate, at least? You are here to *enjoy* . . .'

The French windows opened, admitting a gust of freezing air; Tamsin reentered, dragging Bee by her hair. Bee's body was a faint blue with cold and her teeth chattered. Tamsin placed her at the fifth, empty, flogging emplacement. She looked at Angarad and leered as Angarad's fingers flew away from her crotch.

'Slight change of timetable,' she hissed, forcing Bee to crouch, with her bare buttocks spread high.

Tamsin plunged her fist into Bee's cunt, lifting her, so that Bee was supported by Tamsin's forearm. With her weight taken by her cunt, Bee wriggled and squealed; Tamsin put her back on the floor and withdrew her fist, dripping with cunt-slime. Tamsin applied the come to Bee's anal pucker, poking well inside with two fingers, until the mouth of the arse bud gaped open. Tamsin took the girl again by the hair, pulling her on to her back, with her legs spread, straight in the air. She waggled her bum and hips, so that her rubber strap-on tools quivered. Bee moaned; Tamsin swooped on her like a hawk, plunging the two shafts deep inside her gash and anus, in a single, brutal movement. A second thrust drove the dildos right to Bee's womb and arse-root, and she sobbed, her arse writhing, but unable to escape the impaling prongs. Tamsin's bum began to jerk, as she cunt-fucked and buggered her sobbing slave. Caning the bare nates of his own victim, Marcus licked his teeth.

'Make Bee howl,' he hissed. 'She won't be truly subdued, until she *hates* me for marrying her.'

'*Oh . . . no . . .*' Angarad moaned. 'I didn't *want* to . . .'

Her fingers delved beneath the hem of her skirt, found her sopping cunt-string and slid beneath it to the swollen wet flaps of her slit. She got two fingers inside herself, then a third, while her thumb pressed her erect clitty. Her other hand stroked her bare bum, still leathery from her spankings, and her index poked her anus bud. Come flowed down her wrist and stockings, and soaked the hem of her dress. Angarad's eyes darted from her friend, gamahuching her squealing slave, to the naked bodies of the whipped girls, jerking like marionettes. She lifted her dress to her bubbies, with a trembling sob, as she exposed herself. Angarad masturbated, her hand slippery with gushing come, and her nubbin and cunt flaps swollen, but did not close her eyes when she squealed in orgasm. She did not resist when several hands fastened her, and drew her by wrists and ankles to the nooses of the fifth flogging-place.

'Let the bitch have what she *really* wants,' hissed Tamsin. '*The full bare . . .*'

'No! No! *God, no!*' Angarad screamed.

Thwap! Thwap! Thwap!

'*AHH!*'

The cat-o'-nine-tails flogged Angarad's naked shoulders, its thongs wrapping themselves to her breasts, and lingering, before slithering across her welts for the next stroke; the whipping jolted her teats against the wall, wrenching her wrists and ankles, already tight in their drawn nooses. Her fesses bulged, jerking helplessly beneath her vicious rubber corset. Her head sagged, drool dripping from her mouth.

Thwap! Thwap! Thwap!

'*Ohh!* Bee, stop! *Stop . . .!*'

Thwap! Thwap! Thwap!

'*Ahh . . .!* Ahh . . .! God, it *hurts*!'

'It's meant to hurt,' snarled Bee, flourishing the scourge. 'Haven't you learned to say please, bitch? This is my *treat*, and you are going to *enjoy* it . . .'

As she flogged Angarad, Bee's striped bare bum squirmed under buggery from the black male.

Thwap! Thwap! Thwap!

'*Uhh . . .! Oh, Tamsin, make her stop!*'

'Perhaps you *should* say please,' panted Tamsin, making Marcus's sister shriek with a double-dildo fucking.

Petite Bee, nude, delivered twenty strokes with the cat, until Angarad's bare shoulders and upper back were bruised livid. Angarad shuddered, moaned and squirmed at each slap of the quirt on her reddening naked skin, her eyes opening to roll, then closing tight again. The black man's belly slapped Bee's buttocks until he grunted and spunked in Bee's anus, with the cream bubbling at her anal lips. She lowered her whip, masturbating herself to orgasm with her fingers on her clit and cunt flaps, and the whip's handle a dildo pumping inside her soaked gash. As Angarad sagged limp in her bonds, Marcus wielded a cane and began to flog her naked buttocks. At his first stroke, Angarad's buttocks clenched and she screamed, as a livid blue welt striped her bare bum-flesh. Bee crouched; Tamsin, after fucking and wanking Marcus's sister to climax, lashed Bee's naked croup, while the crouching submissive sucked cocks *en série*, with canestrokes to her cunt if she failed to swallow every drop of their spunkings.

Vip! Vip! Vip!

'*Ohh . . .!*'

The rattan seared Angarad's squirming bare bottom, helpless under the restraining rubber corset. Beneath her, Bee's chin drooled with spunk, while her shoulders and hair glistened with come from Angarad's twitching cunt flaps.

'My dear wife,' said Marcus, 'think what you look like! It'll have to be a whipping and a ducking at the very least, when our guests have gone . . .'

Bee was unable to reply, with a cock discharging its load of sperm in her eager throat, but she masturbated more vigorously, her fist pulsing inside her flowing cunt.

'*You want it, don't you, Angie?*' hissed Tamsin.

Vip! Vip! Vip!

'*Ah! No!* Make him stop! . . . *Stop . . .*'

Vip! Vip! Vip!

'*Oh! God . . .*'

'You're dripping come, Angie. Your cunt is a river and your clit's monstrous. Are you going to come, under cane?'

'*No . . .!*'

Vip! Vip! Vip!

'I think you are.'

Vip! Vip! Vip!

Angarad's full bare was puffy with bruises and welts, her mottled buttocks ridged in coruscated furrows. Each stroke slammed her against the wall, bruising her titties; squirm as she might, her bonds held her, rocking helplessly.

Vip! Vip! Vip!

'*No! No! AHH! Yes . . . oh, God! Yes . . .!*'

At the fortieth stroke of the rattan, her belly heaved as she wailed in climax, rubbing her distended clitty against the wall. The caning ceased; Tamsin's fingers prised apart her clenched buttocks for Marcus's cock to penetrate her anus. He drove into her powerfully, plunging to her root with a single thrust, his cock oiled with Angarad's own cunt-slime, and buggered her for minutes, before spurting his spunk. Marcus withdrew, and his brother-in-law mounted Angarad, buggering her greased bumhole with only a few hard strokes, before his sperm frothed at her anal lips. Angarad's anal shaft was filled to the brim with spunk, her belly slammed against the wall, and her flogged arse wriggling under continuous buggery, as each new ejaculate spurted to dribble down her thighs. She wailed.

'It's what you *want*, *isn't it*, Angie?' purred Tamsin. 'A proper whipping and bumming, like Bee's? You never said *please* stop, you bad, bad girl . . . Do you want to say it now?'

Angarad shuddered, helpless in orgasm, as the black male buggered her; mouth agape and drooling, she shook her head. Sweat, perfume, spunk, lashes and screams: her world melted to the whip, the cock and her buggered anus. Only with the pinking of dawn did the Pinkarse scene, and Angarad's humiliance, cease. Hand in hand with Tamsin, she walked stiffly to Tamsin's car, her anus still creamy with spunk and her cunt dribbling come into the gusset of pee-soaked panties. She shivered under grey clouds and a chill, presaging snow.

'Oh, God,' she snuffled. 'I can't believe it . . . I just came and came and *came* . . .! Have *you* had your bum caned at Pinkarse, Tamsin?'

'Never!' Tamsin spat. 'That's for subs, the dirty little sluts.'

'Is *that* what you think of me?' Angarad gasped.
'Yes,' said Tamsin. 'Be happy! There are worse things.'
'Name one!' blurted Angarad, sobbing.
'You could go to prison . . .'

# 6

# Done and Dusted

Angarad sat trembling in the leather chair, before the desk of Mr Shadwell, junior partner of Shadwell and Cragg. She crossed and uncrossed her grey nylons, beneath a grey woollen business suit; her black shoes were brightly polished. Below, traffic snarled in the slush of Theobalds Road; in the oak-panelled lawyers' chambers, all was serene, save for Angarad's face. Rex Shadwell swivelled in his chair, fingertips under his chin, and stared down at the cars and the denuded trees of Gray's Inn.

'You probably think me a bit young,' he said, then, before Angarad could reply, continued: 'As junior partner, I undertake our legal aid work. Most of what we do is not criminal justice, but, since there is often a grey area between the financial and the criminal, it pays us to keep our nose in the Old Bailey . . .'

'I'm not a criminal!' Angarad blurted.

Shadwell sighed and smiled.

'You are a defendant,' he said. 'I am a defending counsel, whose job is not to ask whether you, ah, *did it*, but to guide you in your best interests. Sometimes, your best interests are to plead guilty, which is what, I am afraid, I must advise in this case. You signed the document, making you solely responsible in the UK for Mr Darren Dodd's offshore dealings, nothing more than an investment, umm, *scam* of several millions. Mr Dodd is untraceable, hence your indictment. You presented a cheque –'

'Which bounced!' Angarad cried.

'– which, in itself, admits complicity in fraud. The fact that Mr Dodd dealt in software, illicitly obtained from your own employer, does not aid your case. A maiden betrayed by her Svengali is a familiar but, at best, mitigating circumstance.'

Angarad put her face in her hands.

'Oh, God,' she sobbed.

Shadwell allowed her to finish her spasm of tears, before clapping his hands and continuing.

'Facts,' he said. 'Twenty-first-century courts view computer fraud very severely. You are looking at a prison sentence of at least three, perhaps five years.'

'*Oh, God! You brute!*'

'Not I,' he said. 'We might get part of the sentence suspended, and remember that tariff is only two-thirds of sentence, so you may be paroled after half your tariff. A sentence of five years may mean only twenty months.'

'Ohh . . .!' Angarad burst into renewed sobbing.

'It is a fiction that so-called plea bargaining is purely an American practice,' he said. 'It exists here, but informally, in a more English manner. Courts do not like time-wasters with frivolous pleas of not guilty; the fact that an unknown benefactor put up your bail money, instead of letting you wait a short while for police bail, is suspicious. Perhaps Mr Dodd has felt remorse for your predicament?'

'That *bastard* . . .!'

'Quite. Do you agree to plead guilty? If so, we may look for light at the end of the tunnel. Don't whine that you have no choice, for we *always* have a choice.'

'I'll plead guilty,' Angarad whispered. 'I *feel* I must atone.'

'Then, Miss Stark, I have an idea of reducing your atonement to the minimum. It involves a deal with both the crown prosecuting counsel and the trial judge. No doubt popular fiction has informed you of different prisons, from the brutal to the sublime, as it were.'

Shadwell laughed; Angarad shrugged.

'There are indeed comfortable prisons, and experimental prisons, just as there are prisons of Victorian vileness. It is my plan to send you for a short time to an . . . *experimental* prison, rather than a longer time in a vile, boring one. You attended Ditton Girls' Grammar School, I believe.'

Angarad nodded.

'Knowing of certain . . . *practices* there, I think you should not have much trouble agreeing to my plan for your immediate future, including this very afternoon.'

Angarad listened to the young lawyer, unspeaking but her face pale, scarlet or aquiver. She crossed her legs several times, as he began to describe HMP Wrigley Scrubs, Yorkshire, but after a while, leaned forward with her nyloned thighs pressed tight, as though they could wet her dry throat, or squeeze the fluttering from her belly . . .

Wrigley Scrubs was an experimental facility only two years old: so far, an unqualified success, and to be joined by others of its model. It developed the open prison of the twentieth century, to restore the moral sense and dignity of its inmates in a uniquely English way. White-collar criminals could only become worse if allowed to mingle with what Shadwell called 'common' ones. A short, sharp shock, as Wrigley Scrubs administered, had proved no use for the hooligan element; yet it worked with decent miscreants who retained some proper morality and understood, instead of resenting, correctional procedures.

'Just *what* correctional procedures?' Angarad asked. 'You mentioned Ditton Girls' Grammar . . .'

Shadwell smiled.

'Imagine that HMP Wrigley Scrubs is just a kind of Ditton Girls' Grammar, only with the rules of a traditional English girls' boarding school,' he said.

'Ditton! *That* beastly place! Nothing could be worse than . . . gym and hikes and games and rotten food and horrible uniforms and . . . oh, *no*!'

Shadwell nodded with a wry smile.

'I'm afraid corporal punishment *is* on the agenda.'

'The *cane*?'

'I do know that unruly girls are sometimes spanked,' he replied. 'I cannot imagine *you* unruly, Miss Stark.'

'You've never been at a school where girls were beaten by other girls,' Angarad hissed. 'It will be more than spanking, with the saintliest girls beaten the most!'

'Then, I suppose, you should try to be unsaintly,' said Shadwell. 'The deal, Miss Stark, is this: six months firm at Wrigley Scrubs, or else taking your chances on a three or five year sentence in a maximum security prison, full of – shall we say, the lower element. At least twelve months in a dismal hole, or six months amongst decent people like yourself, with decorum, fresh air –'

'*And caned on the bare!*' spat Angarad.

Shadwell said nothing but stared at her, a faint, teasing smile playing on his lips. After half a minute, Angarad sighed and nodded.

'I'll take Wrigley Scrubs,' she whispered.

'That is, if Wrigley Scrubs will take *you*,' said Shadwell, rising. 'Miss Horsfall, the governess, is quite particular about her inmates. I can vouch for your decorum but I, and the crown prosecutor, must report to the court on your suitability for the system. If Wrigley Scrubs it is to be, then your immediate future must be a test for that prison.'

Angarad stared at the man, her face pale. Slowly, her lips parted and hung slack.

'Oh, no . . .!' she gasped.

Shadwell nodded and flexed his big, rugby-player's palm, cracking it on the arm of his chair.

'A short spanking, Miss Stark – the minimum, I assure you – for my own peace of mind, so I may assure the court and Miss Horsfall, that you . . .'

'Oh, *damn* it! Damn *me*! Damn, damn, *damn* . . .!'

Angarad sighed, rose and positioned herself to bend over the arm of her chair.

'I've said a bad word, so now I merit punishment,' she said, trembling. 'On the bare?'

'I imagine that would be best.'

'What is your minimum?' she said.

'I'd say that's up to you.'

Angarad removed her suit jacket and folded it on the chair, still warm from her bottom. She unbuckled her shoes and spread her thighs, gripping the floor with her nyloned feet. She reached below the hem of her pleated woollen skirt and raised it over her blouse, so that it lay snug at the small of her back, exposing her crimson lace sussies and garter straps and pink satin knickers, high cut. Slowly, she unfastened each of her garter straps, then rolled the knickers down over her stockings, until they were stretched in a bridge halfway down her thighs. She lowered her head on to her coat, thrusting the naked globes of her bottom upwards for her spanking. Shadwell gasped.

'I say! I had no idea . . .'

'You want to spank me, sir. Go ahead but don't be surprised that you're not the first.'

'That bottom has had more than spanking,' he stammered. 'Those are cane weals. May I . . .?'

His fingers hovered above the dark blue furrows that bruised Angarad's buttocks. She snorted bitterly.

'You're going to *spank* me, remember? Please get on with it. Then you can report I can take it, and my bum can be flogged purple in Wrigley bloody Scrubs, and . . . there, I've said another bad word. *Spank me, please!*'

Crack! Crack! Crack!

'*Mm!*' Angarad whimpered, her eyes shut tight, and her scarlet face screwed in a mask.

Her bare buttocks clenched, squirming, as the male's palm fell in harsh rhythm on the helpless bum-globes. At each spank, Angarad's pubic bush writhed in the pool of come seeping from her slit on to the leather arm-rest.

Crack! Crack! Crack!

'*Oh! Oh!*'

Shadwell sweated, his rolled shirtsleeves damp.

'That's almost a hundred,' he said.

'Surely past your minimum!' she blurted.

'I said it was up to you, didn't I, Miss!'

Crack! Crack! Crack!

'Ouch! *Ahh . . .!*'

'You *want* to be punished,' he exclaimed.

'*No!*'

Crack! Crack! Crack!

'*Ahh . . .!*'

'I'd be a fool not to enjoy spanking such a lovely bottom,' panted the male, 'positively begging for it . . .'

'*No!*'

Crack! Crack! Crack!

Angarad's bare fesses squirmed crimson, her spanker's fingerprints etching deeply over her raw welts.

'Oh! *Oh!* God, that hurts!' she gasped.

There was a knock on the door.

'Are you busy, Shadwell?' said a male voice. 'It's about that Stark girl . . .'

'Come in, Dunton,' said Shadwell. 'I'm working on her now . . .'

'*What?*'

Angie reared but Shadwell pinioned her head.

'Miss Angarad Stark, or rather, Miss Stark's bottom' – Shadwell laughed – 'meet Piers Dunton, the crown prosecutor in your case and, by happy chance, a fellow-member of chambers.'

Crack! Crack! Crack!

'*OOH!*'

Angarad's spanked bare bottom threshed furiously.

'Spirited filly,' drawled Dunton, 'and well used to the cane by the looks of things. Just the job for *la* Horsfall. Mind if I take her for a canter round the track?'

Shadwell delivered a final dozen spanks, in machine-gun rhythm, to Angarad's writhing bare, before yielding place to the slender, mop-haired young prosecutor.

'Oh . . . Oh . . . not more . . .' Angarad sobbed.

Dunton snapped the string of her panties, baring her bottom entirely, then parted her buttocks.

'Her arsehole's well slack,' he drawled.

'Steady on, Dunton!'

'I'd say she's been bummed recently,' Dunton said, 'as well as caned, or flogged. Better tell me how, girly. Are you in the fetish scene?'

'*No! I swear!* Some people I know are . . . I didn't want it to happen! I hate being beaten! You must believe me . . .!'

'Proof is in the pudding,' said Dunton laconically as he unbuckled his belt, a heavy leather strap, three inches thick and half an inch wide, with inset metal studs all along; he folded it in two, with the studs facing outwards. 'How did she take to spanking?'

'Fair to middling.'

'Let's see how she takes the strap.'

Thwap!

The leather jarred Angarad's livid bruised arse and she shrieked.

'*No!* Oh, God!'

Thwap!

'*Oh! Oh! No . . .!*'

Thwap! Thwap! Thwap!

'*AHH!*'

Angarad's naked bum-flesh was a writhing tapestry of bruises and welts, overlaid by the brute leather. The studs left deep indentations at each of the young man's strokes, delivered from above shoulder height.

'Who caned you, girly?' panted Dunton. 'Who buggered you? Truth, now. Don't you want a good report . . .?'

Thwap! Thwap! Thwap!

'*Ah! Ahh . . .!*'

At the thirtieth stroke of the strap, Angarad, choked with tears, broke down and sobbed her whole story. Her strapping did not stop as she spoke and was interrupted by her yelps, and her bottom's continued, frantic twitching.

'. . . I've always tried to do the right thing, and now it seems I'm being punished for it! The ten thousand was going to save my foster-parents – they have a small delicatessen that the Gauntco supermarket is going to destroy and . . . oh, it doesn't seem fair!'

'Gauntco, eh, Rex? Things *aren't* fair, are they, girly?'

Thwap! Thwap! Thwap!

'*OHH!! Stop! Stop!*'

'Funny,' said Shadwell, 'my clients never seem to mind when you fit them up, Piers, for something they didn't do, as part of the game, but they hate being fitted up for something they *did* do.'

'This filly is too good for her own good,' said Piers.

Thwap! Thwap! Thwap!

'*Ahh! Ahh . . . please, please, stop!*'

Angrad's buttocks were puce with welts by the time the belt ceased whopping her naked buttocks. Piers put down the strap but Angarad, sobbing, continued to writhe in her own come, mouthing 'please . . .', and with her fesses still clenching open and shut over her distended anal pucker.

'All right,' said Dunton pleasantly and unzipping his fly. 'You've taken a good hundred, you little slut, so I'll stop.'

Holding her flogged buttocks well parted, Dunton moistened her anus with come from her sodden bush.

'What . . .? *Ahh!*'

Angarad screamed as he plunged his erect cock two inches inside her bumhole.

'Don't you want it, Miss Stark?'

'*No . . .!* I mean, I'm so confused!' she shrieked, as the tool drove into her anus. 'God, haven't I taken enough?'

'Jury's out on that,' said Shadwell, unzipping his own garment. 'Spanking made your quim wet, Miss Stark?'

A further thrust and Dunton's massively stiff cock penetrated her anus right to the hilt. With only his balls visible, Dunton began to bugger Angarad with fierce, pounding strokes. She whinnied and writhed beneath him, her cunt-basin's twitches spraying her thighs with come.

'Not too slack, after all,' panted the bugger. 'Care for some, Shadwell?'

Shadwell's erect cock hovered by Angarad's sweat-soaked tresses. He pulled her head up by the hair and pressed his helmet between her lips. With one thrust, his cock-shaft was at the roof of her mouth and Angarad, eyes closed, began to suck powerfully on the hard flesh. A further thrust drove his cock to the back of her throat, swelling her cheeks and obliging her to bob her head back and forth, while her buttocks squirmed under Dunton's cock poking her anus. Her buttocks clenched, sucking on the bugger's tool, as her throat sucked on Shadwell's.

Freeing one arm, Angarad drove her fist between her soaking cunt lips, opened her fingers and began to masturbate vigorously. Her come dripped down her wrist and glistened on her nylon stockings. She pushed three, then four fingers into her squirming wet slit, pummelling the neck of her womb, as her thumb pressed her swollen clitty.

'Mm . . .' she gasped, sucking one huge cock, with her bum writhing to squeeze the organ impaling her anus.

Dunton began a spanking of her inflamed haunches, bruised purple from his belt.

Slap! Slap! Slap! Slap!

'*Ngg! Mm!*' Angarad gurgled, her head and buttocks bobbing frantically, as both males began to grunt in the onset of spunking.

Slap! Slap! Slap! Slap!

Dunton's thighs slapped her naked bum at each plunge of his cock in her anus; she opened her mouth wider and encompassed Shadwell's tight balls, licking the sac with her tongue.

Slap! Slap! Slap! Slap!

'Mmm . . . *MMM!*'

Angarad wanked herself off to a frenzied, shuddering spasm, come flowing copiously from her wet red slit, and at once the two males bucked harder, filling her holes with sperm. Frothy spunk dribbled from her mouth, down her chin and on to her breasts; from her anus, on to her come-soaked stockings.

'Oh . . . oh . . .' she moaned. 'I *am* guilty . . .'

'Just as well, then, that Shad's on your side,' said Dunton, wiping his arse-slimed cock on her panties. 'In the civvy court, against your wretched parents, he's up for his chums at Gauntco . . .!'

'*Ohh . . .!*'

Angarad's sobs were her deepest yet.

'Enter,' a voice called from within the judge's chamber.

WPC Constance Joule ushered Angarad into the presence of her judge. Faith Dummett was a slim woman in her mid-thirties, seated at her writing desk. She looked over her pince-nez glasses at Angarad, her full breasts rustling the tight cream silk of her blouse. Behind her hung her judicial robes; she was costumed in a sombre business suit of maroon wool. Angarad herself wore the same grey as on her visit to Shadwell the week before.

'The prisoner Stark, as instructed, ma'am,' said WPC Joule, a tall brunette, with her tight black skirt and police blouse encasing big teats, thighs and buttocks that rippled to match Angarad's own; handcuffs, a truncheon and restraining devices of black rubber or gunmetal, jostled at her belt.

Mrs Dummett clicked her tongue.

'Dear me, WPC Joule,' she said. 'Prisoner! Too harsh for such a well-formed young lady. I prefer . . . detainee.'

She instructed Angarad to stand before her desk with her hands behind her back. Angarad did so, biting her lip. Faith Dummett brushed back a strand of her yellow hair and looked her up and down, while WPC Joule took stance at the door.

'It is, of course, quite unusual for a detainee to meet her judge before trial and sentence,' said Miss Dummett. 'However, such is the importance of Wrigley Scrubs to the judicial system that I view your matter with less formality, Miss Stark. How I regret that you stand before me! But – we all make mistakes! – here you do stand. You have agreed to our . . . *proposal*.'

'Yes, ma'am,' Angarad murmured.

'Reports from the prosecutor and your defending counsel are favourable,' said Faith Dummett, wrinkling her nose. 'I shan't ask for details – men can be *beasts* – and I dare say you would prefer not to go into them.'

Angarad nodded, swallowing.

'You are fully aware of the experimental nature of the Wrigley Scrubs regime,' Miss Dummett said, to which Angarad nodded again. 'Good. After my own interview, I shall ask you to sign some papers, and we shall meet again in court, where Mr Shadwell shall suggest you plead guilty; I shall sentence you to a firm period of six months' full rigour at HMP Wrigley Scrubs.'

'Full rigour . . .?'

Angarad paled, while WPC Joule smirked openly.

'A legalism, Miss Stark,' said Miss Dummett quickly, 'to satisfy our *male* lawmakers . . . I and my dear friend Adelaide Horsfall, governess of Wrigley Scrubs, are of one mind: chastisement without reform is no chastisement at all. However, you are aware corporal punishment *is* applied, on occasions.'

'Yes, ma'am,' said Angarad.

'At Shadwell's, you were spanked.'

'Yes, ma'am.'

'Bare bottom?'

Angarad blushed.

'As good as. I was spanked with my knickers on but pulled up very tight, with my string in my cleft and the spanks landing on my skin – that was by Mr Shadwell – then, Mr Dunton ripped my knickers off to strap me on the full bare.'

Miss Dummett sighed.

'You know the term, "full bare", then. I was afraid so. *Men . . .!* It must have hurt.'

'It did, ma'am, awfully!' Angarad blurted. 'It's not so much the pain, or the number of whops that hurt, it's knowing that someone *wants* to hurt me . . .'

'Yes,' said Miss Dummett. 'I know you were at Ditton Grammar and are familiar with corporal punishment. I'm afraid I am now obliged to hurt you just a bit more, as your final test. Or rather, WPC Joule is. Your report says you took spanking, and the strap, well, but were not dusted – caned, that is.'

'Why, no . . .' Angarad gasped.

'Adelaide Horsfall very occasionally approves the use of the cane on thoughtless girls at Wrigley Scrubs,' said the judge, 'and, Angarad – I may call you that? – since you are here because you were thoughtless, it is *possible* you may be thoughtless again. I must sentence you in the knowledge that your bottom *can* take punishment by cane.'

'On . . . on the bare?' Angarad gasped.

'Of course not!' said the judge. 'On your knickers, pulled tight of course, but on the *bare* . . .? My!'

WPC Joule grinned stiffly as she unhooked a short crook-handled sapling cane from her belt's kit.

'I *have* seen a girl caned on the bare,' Miss Dummett said, brushing a speck of dust from her breast. 'It was with Adelaide, actually. We were exploring Morocco in a Land-Rover, and we came to this village in the High Atlas . . . a young man and woman, found – you know, *snogging* – were punished in the public market.'

She brushed her breasts, which quivered as she spoke.

'The young man was stripped to his loincloth and flogged on the bare back – fifty strokes with a bullwhip. Adelaide counted them. He wriggled most horribly! The young lady was caned, bent over a rail with her wrists and ankles held by other women, and her skirts over her head, taking the same number of strokes on the bare, from a male, with a cane over three feet long. I thought it quite awful, although Adelaide didn't agree. She said the girl wept less than the male and could take it. Still, her bare bum was a frightful sight after they'd finished caning her. The women who held her laughed throughout her caning! When she had finished sobbing, they shared a cake with her as they examined her weals: proof, Adelaide insisted, that corporal punishment was healthy. Adelaide can be quite forceful in a good cause . . .'

She sighed.

'Her work at Wrigley Scrubs has convinced me I was right to agree with her,' she said. 'Therefore, Angarad, I should like you to bend over my desk, please, grasping both ends firmly and parting your legs. WPC Joule shall raise your skirt, pull your knickers as tight as they will go and administer four strokes of her cane to your buttocks.'

'Four!' Angarad gasped.

'I know it sounds harsh, but . . .'

'I've no objection, ma'am,' Angarad blurted, taking position as ordered, her face two feet across the desk from the judge's own.

The policewoman lifted her skirt over her back and drew her knickers up tightly till the gusset bit her crotch.

Angarad's buttocks were totally covered by the fabric, apart from a portion of bare haunch, but so tightly were the cotton knickers pulled that the welts, etched on her skin by recent caning, stood up in relief.

WPC Joule smacked her lips.

'Well!' she said, her fingers tracing bruises on Angarad's bare haunches. 'There's been a cane at work here.'

Angarad blushed deeply.

'No, ma'am,' she said. 'I was spanked and strapped! I bruised my thighs falling in the snow.'

'Is that the truth, Angarad?' said Miss Dummett. 'This is technically a court of law.'

Angarad swallowed and nodded. With one hand, WPC Joule rolled a cigarette and lit up. She parked the rollie at the corner of her mouth.

'Very well. Cane the girl, please, WPC Joule. Four brisk ones, not too hard . . .'

She smiled at Angarad.

'. . . but not too soft, either. One!'

Vip!

Angarad winced and her buttocks clenched as the cane lashed her, the tight knickers mere gossamer over full bare.

'Remember, Angarad, Miss Horsfall takes a very dim view of girls who tell fibs . . .'

Miss Dummett's left hand slipped below her desk and began to twitch. She blushed then asked Angarad if her first cut was smarting. Angarad nodded, eyes moistened by tears. Miss Dummett smiled and closed her own eyes for an instant; her shoulder and upper left arm moved rhythmically. She began to stroke Angarad's right-hand knuckles, gripping the desk with her right palm.

'There, there, dear,' she said. 'It'll soon be over. Two!'

Vip!

'*Uhh . . .!*

Angarad gasped as the second canestroke lashed deep in the welt of her first. Her raised bottom squirmed and clenched, with an oily film of moisture trickling into her tightened panties gusset from her quim. Angarad swallowed, closing her eyes in anticipation of the third. Miss

Dummett's voice did not give the command. Instead, she herself panted softly as her nylon stockings hissed, slithering together. WPC Joule sucked contentedly on her cigarette, blowing smoke over Angarad's bare bum.

'Hurt a lot?' Miss Dummett gasped.

'*Awfully*, ma'am. But I know I can take it.'

'Three!'

Vip!

'Ahh . . .' sighed Miss Dummett. 'Just one more, Angarad. Your bottom's wriggling a lot . . . I must warn you against squealing when you take the fourth. Adelaide does not like girls who squeal.'

'I promise, ma'am,' Angarad sobbed. 'But I can't help my bottom wriggling. The officer canes very hard.'

'Yes, I know,' said Miss Dummett. 'Four!'

Vip!

'*Ahh!*'

Angarad screamed. The fourth cut was an upender, taking her right in the bum-cleft and thrashing her anal pucker and the swollen wet lips of her cunt, outlined beneath the tight panties. Miss Dummett's hand gripped Angarad's and she gasped, quickly and harshly, several times, her buttocks squirming in her seat. Miss Dummett gulped and said that Angarad must take the stroke again, but this time without screaming.

'Ma'am,' Angarad sobbed, 'the officer caned me right in the slice! It hurts so! Oh, I don't know if I can take such a stroke without screaming . . .'

'You must. With your permission, WPC Joule will inspect your bottom for welts before proceeding.'

'No!' Angarad cried. But already the policewoman had pulled down her knickers to reveal Angarad's full bare.

'Well . . .!' she hissed. 'I think you might care to inspect the prisoner's buttocks, ma'am.'

Miss Dummett rose, smoothing down her skirt with fingers shiny and moist. She joined the officer behind Angarad's croup. Angarad's eyes closed, her face a blush of crimson, as the judge gasped.

'You have been sparing with the truth, Miss Stark,' she

said drily. 'Your surprise at an award of four strokes was not at my harshness, but at my *leniency*!'

'Y . . . yes,' Angarad sobbed, quivering as the older woman's finger traced the ridges of her caned bottom.

'Why, the little bitch!' spat the policewoman.

'You have been caned for pleasure, Miss Stark.'

'Caned for *pleasure*, ma'am . . .?'

'It is a vile perversion.'

'I *swear* it's not true!'

'Don't make matters worse, you slut! I trusted you . . . The arrangements are made and it is too late to adjust them. Miss Horsfall dislikes untidiness. You are up before me in two hours and I have other, *honest* miscreants to interview beforehand . . .'

'I'm *sorry*, ma'am! I can explain . . . it's just that I've been so unlucky, and – oh! – it's all a misunderstanding!'

'Miss Horsfall *certainly* dislikes misunderstandings!' cried Miss Dummett. 'How can I explain sending her a girl whose bare bottom is already a record of vicious pleasure?'

'If I may suggest, ma'am?' said WPC Joule. 'Miss Horsfall will understand that the condition of the prisoner's buttocks is due to over-zealous caning by the duty officer at this interview.'

'But you've only given her four strokes, Constable!'

'Four so far, ma'am.'

Miss Dummett's fingers probed and caressed the puffy welts from Angarad's past canings, as well as the swellings from her four just taken.

'The report *could* say that but it must be the truth.'

Angarad shuddered as her knickers were ripped away, baring her bottom completely and revealing both her swollen quim lips, the pubic jungle soaked in sweat and come, and the tell-tale slick of moisture at her stocking tops. Miss Dummett gasped sharply. Angarad squealed as her wet knickers were stuffed into her mouth, gagging her, and again as Joule's stubbed cigarette end sizzled on her come-soaked pubic forest.

'You will make it the truth, Constable, for the slut's own good: cane her a full judicial dusting, on the bare.'

'A full dusting, ma'am?' WPC Joule. 'So, a good three dozen – perhaps four.'

Her hand stroked the fresh welts laid by her cane on Angarad's quivering bare bum.

'There is an overlay of weals which I'll have to cover for Miss Horsfall's inspection,' she said. 'Best make it four dozen.'

'Agreed,' said Miss Dummett. 'Perhaps you should strap her down, Constable.'

'*No . . . please!*' Angarad begged. 'I'll take your punishment. You're right, ma'am! I've been caned bare-bum before but I *swear* it was against my will!'

'This kind of pervert takes pleasure from pain,' said Miss Dummett. 'To cure her, the perverse pleasure must be so intense that she comes to detest it. There are sex perverts everywhere, their obscenities mocking justice with rites of corporal punishment, sacred to justice. Cane her.'

Vip! Vip! Vip!

'*Mm! Mm . . .!*'

Angarad's panties gag stifled her scream, as three scalding cuts took her on the tender upper fesses.

Vip! Vip! Vip!

'*Nnhh . . .!*'

Her bare bum clenched and began to wriggle; her knuckles were white, clutching the edges of the desk, and her spread legs and buttocks began to shake like jellies, as the constable delivered the strokes in sets of three.

Vip! Vip! Vip!

'*MMM!*'

Tears ran down Angarad's cheeks, but the tops of her stockings were wet with drip from her cunt, which Miss Dummett touched, squealing: 'The bitch is wet! Cane harder!'

Vip! Vip! Vip!

'*Urr . . . Mm!*'

Angarad's teeth were almost biting through her panties; she turned her tear-blurred eyes, pleading, to the judge standing behind the caner, and saw Miss Dummett's hand beneath her raised maroon skirt, revealing her own lacy stocking tops – sussies but no knickers – a jungle of wet pubic hair garlanded with honeysuckle blossoms and her index finger and thumb firmly masturbating her erect clitoris between the distended red lips of her vulva. Miss Dummett's eyelids were heavy, her eyes fixed on the squirming bare buttocks of the flogged girl.

'Harder . . .' she gasped.

Vip! Vip! Vip!

'*Mmm . . .!*'

Angarad's fesses were crimson with bruises from the policewoman's cane; suddenly she wailed, as a hissing jet of pee sprayed from her cunt, drenching her stockinged thighs. Angarad was dancing on tiptoe, her long coltish legs shuddering at each welt to her helpless bare arse, as the judge masturbated, faster and faster.

'The dirty slut . . .' gasped Miss Dummett, wanking off vigorously. 'Stripe her, Constable! Hurt her mid-arse! I don't want her to sit for a week . . .'

Vip! Vip! Vip!

'*Mm! Mm!*'

Come flowed from Angarad's own swollen cunt, as her slit lips writhed and gaped at each lash of the wood on her naked skin.

'Yes . . . yes . . .' Miss Dummett moaned, as the rod descended. '*Yes . . .!*'

Angarad turned again, to see the policewoman herself masturbating as she caned; her black uniform skirt was pulled up and her hand plunged into her black knickers, which shone moist with her seeping come. Angarad's pubis jolted against the edge of the desk at each stroke; she began to press her clitoris against the wood, her cunt a squelching envelope of swollen wet flesh, using the desk to wank herself off. Angarad's face was deep scarlet, the judge's and constable's growing redder as they masturbated. At the fortieth stroke, Miss Dummett's moans grew to sharp, whinnying gasps; come flowed copiously from her gushing cunt as her belly contracted in her spasm of climax. WPC Joule took Angarad to the full forty-eight, then, still masturbating, with her skirt up to show her own buttocks, turned to the whimpering judge.

'Seems there's more than one slut here,' she snarled. 'Wanking off, ma'am? Scarcely a good example . . .'
'Please, Joule, don't be hard on me,' wailed Faith Dummett. 'Look how tempting that bum of hers is . . .'
The policewoman pushed the quivering woman to the floor to crouch with her buttocks upraised, and her face on Joule's left boot, the right one pinioning her neck.
'No knickers, judge?'
Vip! Vip! Vip!
Angarad's eyes widened, as, still holding her flogging position, she witnessed three stingers stripe the broad firm melons of Miss Dummett's bare arse.
Vip! Vip! Vip!
'You dirty whore . . .!'
'*Oh!* Oh! I can't take it!' whimpered the woman.
'Not like your friend Horsfall,' sneered Joule.
Vip! Vip! Vip!
'*Ahh . . .!*'
Angarad freed a hand which plunged directly between her own throbbing cunt lips. While the poicewoman was distracted by her caning of Miss Dummett and vigorously wanking off, Angarad masturbated the inside of her pouch and her pulsing stiff clitty. Joule caned the woman's bare to scarlet; Angarad's left fingers wanked her cunt while her right hand fingered the deep welts, seared raw on her bare buttocks. Her left palm filled with her come and the liquid flowed down her wrist. At Miss Dummett's fifteenth canestroke, Angarad squealed in climax and Joule turned, as if only just noticing her.
'On your knees, slut!' she cried. 'Lick the monkey!'
Whimpering, Angarad fell to a crouch before the constable's exposed wet cunt, and moaned as her panties were ripped from her mouth while Angarad's face was pressed and held against the policewoman's massive wet cunt bush and the quivering glands of her vulva. As WPC Joule continued to cane Miss Dummett's bare croup, she rubbed Angarad's head up and down between her thighs, where the panties were fully lowered, baring her taut muscled croup and the pubic mound in its damp forest of

curls. Her come deluged Angarad's face and the choking girl drank oily cunt juice. Her tongue found Joule's clitoris, a hard wet button which she took between her teeth, and began to chew and suck. Joule moaned. Angarad's fingers plunged again into her own sopping cunt and as she gamahuched the gushing quim of the policewoman, she thumbed and pinched her her own stiffened nubbin, with her knuckles squelching between her wet gash flaps. She moaned, drinking Joule's come, as the love juice became a torrent of acrid pee; the policewoman pissed long and hard in Angarad's face and, as Angarad swallowed, choking on the hot mixture of pee and come, she masturbated again to a climax that made her shudder, and she bit the policewoman's cunt lips to steady herself. The policewoman howled.

Vip! Vip! Vip! Vip!

A flurry of canestrokes striped Miss Dummett's quivering naked arse-flans.

'*Oh!* I can't take it . . .!' she yelped. 'Oh, God! Joule, you brute! What if Adelaide . . .?'

Her fingers were a blur as she wanked off anew; one by one, the soaked honeysuckle blossoms fell from her writhing pubis. Angarad hung on to the policewoman's cunt lips, clamped between her teeth, as come poured copiously over her nose and lips and Joule grunted louder and louder in her own orgasm. Drinking the cunt juice that dribbled between her fastened teeth, Angarad gurgled, as a new climax flooded her wanked cunt. Miss Dummett's caning was completed, with a thrash right to her slit; she, too, howled in the pain of new orgasm. Angarad sank to the floor, sobbing, hands covering her soaked crotch and piss-drenched face.

'Why . . .?' she moaned. '*Why me . . .?*'

'Why not?' said WPC Joule, rolling another cigarette.

# 7

# A Fair Bum

Angarad stood in the dock amidst the spartan furnishings of the magistrates court. There was only one person in the public gallery, a man. Faith Dummett sat with the other magistrates, ignoring the sobs that came from the defendant and her blush of shame. Shadwell and Dunton made brief statements, a guilty plea having already been entered: Shadwell painting the picture of a thoughtless but innocent slut, and Dunton, in a few cynical and disdainful remarks, contradicting his learned friend, with that of a wicked, deceitful temptress. Angarad silently prayed: *They can't all be against me . . . someone must believe the truth.*

'The prisoner will stand still!' rapped Faith Dummett, as Angarad's skirt rustled over her still-squirming fesses.

*The hypocrite . . .!*

WPC Joule smiled, winking at Angarad, who turned her face away. *No . . . it couldn't have happened!*

Ninety minutes before, in the judge's chambers, she had looked up in shame and the agony of her whipped buttocks, to see Miss Dummett, with judicial robes covering her maroon suiting, and WPC Joule holding a pair of handcuffs.

'This one's a talker,' the policewoman said.

The cuffs snapped on Angarad's wrists and the policewoman frog-marched her to a holding cell. There was no furniture on the board floor; WPC Joule did not remove Angarad's handcuffs, but added to them a rope tied around her ankles and looped into the cuffs, so that

Angarad could choose between standing up, in the bent-over position, or sitting on the floor, with her back and head stretched forward over her knees. Her panties wadded her mouth as a gag after the policewoman had wiped her own vulva dry with the garment and it dripped with fluid. Angarad was left for over an hour before Joule returned to take her to court.

'I'll take the cuffs off,' she said, ungagging the girl, 'as long as you promise that mum's the word.'

'I promise,' said Angarad tonelessly without wiping her own come, drooled on her lips and chin.

'You can say what you like at the Scrubs,' said Joule. 'No one will believe you – or rather, *everybody* will.'

Now, Angarad shut her eyes to stem her tears as the courtroom droned around her. She was jolted from her reverie by Joule's hand clutching her arm.

'. . . to twelve months' firm penal servitude at Wrigley Scrubs special institution for female offenders,' Miss Dummett pronounced, smiling coldly at Angarad.

'*Twelve!* You said *six . . .!*' Angarad cried, to be silenced by WPC Joule's palm pressed over her mouth.

'*Take her down!*' snapped Miss Dummett. '*Vile brat . . .!*'

The man in the public gallery smiled.

'We have one hundred and nine detainees, Isobel,' said Miss Adelaide Horsfall, 'and I expect you to know each one by name. It is our way.'

'Yes, Miss,' said Isobel Coker, staring out at the bleakness of Wrigley Scrubs, around the prison's cluster of low brick cottages; beyond the scrub was the brown valley of Wrigleydale, its worn, denuded hills dusted with snow.

Miss Horsfall smiled.

'You address superiors as "mum",' she said, 'the same way detainees must address you.'

'Oh! I'm sorry . . . yes, mum.'

'Don't apologise, Isobel. Now, I dare say, at first sight Wrigley Scrubs wouldn't strike you as a prison.'

'No, mum. It looks like . . . a medieval manor, really.'

Miss Horsfall clapped.

'How splendid!' she cried. 'I must mention that to Faith – a dear friend of mine on the bench in London. Yes – a feudal manor, of female serfs and wardens, each with her rank, ties, bonds and duties! It was indeed a manor at one time when it was part of the Pollecutt estate. We have no security problems here, I assure you. Our wardens deal summarily with any little . . . *misunderstandings*, and our remoteness makes evasion not only impossible, but undesirable.'

'A place for every girl, and every girl in her place, mum. That's the motto of Wearbridge,' Isobel said.

'*Is* it? I think you will do very well here, Isobel. Mrs Cragg has sent a positively *blush-making* report.'

'Thank you, mum.'

Adelaide Horsfall's eyes sparkled under her flat-combed honey tresses. Pert conic breasts swooped to a pencil waist, which bulged wide at the hips, into long, coltish legs, broad, firm buttocks and generous thighs that quivered like a mare's under her black cashmere suiting and hose. Her age was middle, not more than Mrs Cragg's, with the body hard and lithe under the soft fabric. She looked Isobel up and down, as she stood, holding her raincoat and beret over her arm, and in a dark green pleated skirt with matching polo-neck sweater and stockings.

'Ignoge Brand will be here shortly to get you kitted out and show you the ropes,' Miss Horsfall said. 'She is one of the three senior wardens, to be addressed as "mum", and you are the seventh junior warden, to be addressed by your seniors as "miss". If I may ask you a personal question . . .'

'Please, mum.'

'Are those proper stockings you have on? I mean, with a garter belt and straps? Or . . . *pantyhose*?'

She made a moue of distaste and Isobel laughed.

'They are proper stockings, mum. Force of habit – that was a Wearbridge rule.'

'I am *so* glad. We are rather old-fashioned here, Isobel. Good habits prosper amongst us.'

There was a rap on the door and Miss Horsfall bade entrance. The girl who came in looked at Isobel coolly.

Slightly shorter than the governess, she flaunted a figure of hour-glass beauty, the ripe teats and bottom clinging inside black skirt, with a white tabard halter top, leaving her arms bare, and black epaulettes bearing a gold braid on crossed swords; black leather boots, mirror-shone, with nylon stockings. Her full red lips, framed by a mane of chestnut hair, curled in a half smile, half sneer. Under the armpits sprouted forests of untrimmed hair. Her warden's uniform included a thick leather belt with a heavy buckle and from it dangled a two-foot long cane with its crook handle strapped in a leather holster. Around her belt buckle was coiled a rope, like a cowboy's lariat.

'This the new stroke, mum?' she said.

'Yes,' said Miss Horsfall. 'Isobel Coker – Miss Ignoge Brand, senior warden, or, ah, *colloquially*, stroke. She'll show you the ropes and I'll leave you to her.'

The girl tossed her chestnut tresses, beckoning Isobel into the stone corridor where her boots clacked noisily.

'There are three of us top strokes,' said Ignoge Brand, 'and you're the seventh bottom stroke. You're to be gym stroke, aren't you? The other bottoms will be glad you're here, they've had to take turns moving the equipment and rebricking the labyrinth. I see you're well muscled. Have to be, in this place. There's lots we strokes must do ourselves, 'cos you can't trust stinkers, or slags.'

'There's a lot I don't undersand,' said Isobel nervously.

'*That's* for sure!' said Ignoge. 'It would be pretty weird, otherwise. A stinker is a new slag, see? And a slag is a stinker who's done over three months, or taken a special whopping. There's a new stinker arriving tomorrow and you can help scrub her down. First, we'll go to Chopper's for your medical and your kit.'

'Chopper?'

'The surgical nurse, Miss Maclaren.'

The lithe, petite surgical nurse, in a tight white doctor's robe, invited Isobel to strip for examination. Ignoge made no attempt to leave or hide her curiosity, as Isobel nervously undressed. She looked at Ignoge's cane and saw the surgeon possessed a similar one, hanging from a peg on the wall. She felt her scarred bottom, gulping, as she removed her garter belt, stockings and, finally, her pink cotton panties. Miss Maclaren prodded her with a stethoscope, squeezed her titties between finger and thumb, then made her lie face down on a surgical table, revealing, for the first time, her bare buttocks.

'Spread your cheeks,' said Miss Maclaren. '*Well!*'

She donned rubber gloves, while Ignoge casually kneaded the bare, wealed melons of Angarad's bottom.

'Please, Ignoge,' said Miss Maclaren mildly. 'I must examine the anus and vulva.'

'Of course, mum – it's not often you see such a ripe arse, though. That would be a fine crop of welts, even on a slag.'

The nurse took her speculum, a metal device like a pair of compasses, and prised open the pucker of Isobel's anus, leaving the speculum to hold it stretched wide open. Isobel groaned as her index finger penetrated the anal shaft, extending to its full length, and probing.

'Well,' said Miss Maclaren, 'Isobel may or may not choose to tell us how she came by them. We may surmise that her job interview was more . . . *testing* than usual.'

'Ouch!' squealed Angarad, as Miss Maclaren pulled open the flaps of her vulva and inserted a second, larger, vaginal speculum, to hold open her pouch, then inserted three rubbered fingers.

Isobel began to squirm slightly.

'You have a very large, or else swollen, clitoris,' said Officer Maclaren. 'Most interesting – do you feel excited in a situation like this? Nude and helpless?'

'*No!*' yelped Isobel. 'I mean, no, mum.'

'Good,' said Miss Maclaren. 'A slag – *detainee* – is quick to sense weakness, or the enjoyment of weakness . . .'

Isobel twisted to look at Ignoge's face: the lips were slack and filmed with drool, the eyes heavy slits, fixed on Isobel's bare.

'The vagina is also abnormally large,' said Miss Maclaren.

'I am a big girl, mum,' said Isobel. 'And as for my welts, mum' – directed at Ignoge – 'I'm a Durham lass, and I dare say a mite tougher than you *southern* folk. We played tough games at Wearbridge Girls' Grammar.'

Ignoge's nostrils flared and Miss Maclaren chuckled.

'You English are *all* southerners to *us*,' she said. 'Perhaps Durham lasses all have large pouches, and the men tarses to fit! You were a staff member at Wearbridge?'

Her finger poked at the neck of Isobel's womb and the nude girl shuddered; moisture seeped from her slit. Isobel took a deep breath and swallowed.

'Yes, mum,' she said, 'and Mrs Cragg told me, a staff member *here* must be able to take whatever she dishes out, and, yes, she tested me. I didn't know it would be *that* hard, but I promise I took it without a squeal. '

'Are you looking forward to *dishing it out*, then, Isobel?' murmured Miss Maclaren, as she removed her fingers and speculums from Isobel's holes and wiped her rubber glove clean of Isobel's cunt fluid.

'If it's needed, yes, I am,' said Isobel, sitting up.

Both Miss Maclaren and Ignoge Brand smiled.

'Judging by the bare bottoms it is my duty to tend,' Miss Maclaren said, 'I would imagine it is often needed.'

Isobel wriggled uncomfortably in her new warden's uniform; despite her suggestion that the clothes, especially the regulation black bra and panties, were a size too small, Miss Maclaren said they were a perfect fit and any initial discomfort would vanish when she had got used to her thermal corselet, worn over her bra. Junior wardens wore standard white shirts, short-sleeved; the display of underarm hair, like the antique tabard, was a privilege of top strokes, though even they were forbidden to shave or trim their cunt bushes. The stockings were of extra-thick, sheened nylon, and the only area visited by air gusts was the sliver of thigh, uncovered by the heavy rubber garter straps, between Isobel's panties, high in cut, and her stocking-tops. The garter belt, like the straps, was of black latex and bit into Isobel's haunches. Her fingers brushed the gleaming new cane dangling from the wide leather belt at her waist and her coiled rope, with its sliding noose, on her belt buckle: it *was* a lariat.

Ignoge showed her the room in the wardens' block that was to be her home: a tidy bedsit, furnished with table, chair, sofa and bed, and the board floor brightly polished.

'Bathroom is down at the end of the corridor,' she said. 'When you're on night duty, you share the spare bedroom in the cell block with another bottom stroke, so you have to cross the courtyard to come back here if you need the bathroom. Unless you're brave enough to pee with the stinkers and slags, which I don't advise. By the way, you *must* shave your legs and armpits but *never* your mound. Public shaving is a slag's punishment, usually before she's flogged.'

'*Flogged?*' Isobel blurted.

'As in "beaten",' said Ignoge, 'with a cane, quirt or whip, on the naked back or arse. Clear enough, *miss*?'

They proceeded to a rapid tour of the prison's inner corridors and outer courts. The cell block was in the shape of a cross, with the wardens' office and bedroom at its centre, so that two wardens could observe all four cell corridors at once. The wardens' area was sealed off from the cells by steel doors and accessed directly from the courtyard. The inner courtyard circled the cell block and contained refectory-cum-assembly hall, gymnasium, cells for solitary confinement and classrooms, occupied by girls at woodwork or other crafts, sewing or book instruction. There were bathrooms throughout the prison for detainees and wardens but the crux of the cell block was too small to contain one. Both wardens' and detainees' bathrooms had long troughs for squatting and indented with bum-rests, through which running water gurgled constantly; the wardens also enjoyed separate lavatory cubicles. The outer courtyard led to workshops and stables, beyond that were the swimming pool and sports fields, and then the scrubs stretched to the River Wrigley and its flanking hillocks of moorland.

'I'm not sure I've taken everything in, mum,' Isobel said.

'You will,' replied Ignoge. 'First thing is to learn the names of your sister strokes.'

The three top strokes were Ignoge herself, Althea Tite and Goiswinth Moss; Isobel's colleagues as bottom strokes were Belinda Garce, Judon Oates, Sarah Bunn, Amy Patel, Imogen Tandy and Edra Forge. Ignoge explained that every detainee had her own private cell, a luxury in regular prisons, where the indignities of the day could heal.

'Or where we can inflict new ones,' she sneered.

'I've . . . I've never carried a cane before,' Isobel said, as they paused to visit the wardens' bathroom at the gate lodge of the inner courtyard. 'I knew corporal punishment was part of discipline here, but not to what extent.'

Ignoge squatted in a cubicle, after unfastening her garter straps and lowering her stockings and knickers in a swift, practised thrust. Isobel took the stall beside her, after a brief glimpse of Ignoge's luxuriant pubic mane, dangling between her large ruby cunt lips. She removed her new underclothing carefully and her hiss of pee joined her superior's beside her. As the steam rose above the low cubicle partitions, Ignoge said it was at the warden's discretion.

'That cane is not for show,' she said curtly. 'If you don't use it, the slags won't respect you – and I mean use it at will, outside of formal canings and whippings. The belt comes in handy, too, buckle out.'

'*Formal* whippings?' Isobel said.

There was a rapid plop-plop as a jet of stools filled the pan beneath her thighs. Ignoge laughed.

'Frightened of whipping a girl on the bare?' she said. 'After seeing that scorched bum of yours, I'd think not.'

'No . . . no, of course not,' said Isobel.

'As gym mistress, you're i/c equipment, understand? We whip the slags on vaulting horses, wall bars, that sort of thing . . .'

In the near distance came a faint rhythmic sound: tap-tap-tap, like a blacksmith's hammer.

'What's that, mum?' Isobel asked.

'Some girl taking bare-bum caning, of course. I'd say it was Miss Oates, she should be on patrol, and that sounds like her style. She likes to lay it on hard.'

Tap . . . tap . . . tap . . .

*Some girl taking bare-bum caning . . .*

'It doesn't sound very hard,' Isobel murmured. 'It's funny, from a distance, you miss the terrible whistle of the cane, and the whop on the bare. It's a drier sound.'

*Some girl taking bare-bum caning . . .*

Isobel's fingers slid down her woollen corselet, raised above her belly-button; over her tingling bare belly, to plunge within her forest of pubic curls and delve between her slit lips. She sighed as her thumb found her clitoris.

'You all right? Nearly finished?' said Ignoge. 'I have other things to do, Miss Coker – one of the bottoms, Miss Garce or Miss Oates, perhaps, will brief you more thoroughly.'

'I . . . I think I'm a bit bunged up, mum. The coach trip . . .'

Isobel gulped as her fingers began to dance in the rhythm of the tapping between her juicing cunt flaps, and her thumb rubbed her swelling clitty round and round. She shut her eyes, shaking her head, but her breath came as a hoarse rattle as she masturbated more and more vigorously. Four fingers inside her pouch, not filling her big wet cavern but scratching the walls – *yes! the g-spot!* – and the thumb wanking the clit . . .

Tap . . . tap . . . tap . . .

Twelve . . . thirteen . . . fourteen . . .

'How many strokes are there in a caning, mum?' she blurted.

'Why, as many as it takes,' snapped Ignoge.

'Isn't there a tariff of offences?'

'There are only two offences at Wrigley Scrubs, Miss Coker: *dumb insolence* and *insolence.* When a slag or stinker reaches a certain number of points in her tariff book, she is formally beaten in public, a stroke for each point, which cleans her slate: say, a caning of fifteen for fifteen offences, or a whipping if it's over twenty-one. Or she can accept an informal swishing on the bare, for each separate offence, and get it over with leaving her tariff book clean.'

*Formally beaten in public, a stroke for each point . . .*

Isobel's fingers wanked her clitty harder.

'But why not let her points mount up, mum, and have all the offences punished at once? Taken into consideration, they call it. Then she'd take fifteen in one go, instead of a separate caning for *each* of fifteen offences.'

'If her tariff book's full, she risks being transferred to another jail! Aren't you finished?'

Tap . . . tap . . . tap . . .

Fifteen . . . sixteen . . . seventeen . . .

'*Ahhh . . .!*'

A girl's choking sob.

*Her bare buttocks quivering, bruised, helpless under cane . . .*

'Nearly, mum,' gasped Isobel, masturbating her swollen clit and trying to stop her gushing come from soiling her stockings, stretched between her thighs. 'I've never seen a girl whipped bare, in public . . . do they wriggle awfully?'

There was another plopping, as a further jet of stools left her anus.

'Listen, mum,' she said, 'I'm loosening . . .'

Tap . . . tap . . .

Eighteen . . . nineteen . . .

Tap . . . tap!

Twenty . . . twenty-one!

'*Oh! Ahh . . .!*' screamed the distant girl, her voice just loud enough to drown Isobel's own panting as her belly convulsed in climax, and her come-soaked fingers pummelled her stiff, swollen clit.

Isobel rapidly wiped herself, pulled the chain and joined Ignoge outside the cubicle, where Ignoge was smoking a hand-rolled cigarette.

'By the way, Miss Coker, I watched you through a knothole. You were too busy wanking yourself off to notice. You *do* have a big pouch!'

'*Oh . . .!*' Isobel blushed fiery red.

Ignoge smiled, blowing a plume of smoke in Isobel's face.

'I'm sure you wank off as much as the rest of us, but wardens must be *discreet*,' she said. 'As for any slag caught wanking, singly or together, well, it's a caning, just for starters. Just remember that the code of discipline covers *every* girl at Wrigley Scrubs . . . You'll have to make your own arrangements for snout, unless you want to cycle to the village ten miles away.'

'Oh . . . I don't smoke,' said Isobel.

'You will,' said Ignoge.

It was lunchtime. Wardens lined the half-timbered brick walls of the refectory, supervising the detainees, who ate, seated on benches at oak tables under a low, beamed ceiling. Isobel stood to attention beside Belinda Garce. The girls, uniformed in short grey skirts, white cotton stockings and white blouses, received their food on trays from a counter, where other detainees served. Some girls wore only bra and panties, the panties no more than a g-string that left the buttocks bared, and in most cases marked by recent chastisement. Those girls were barefoot and had their wrists strapped behind their backs. They were obliged to pick up their trays by clamping the rope handles with their teeth; they ate by plunging their faces into their food, being unable to use wooden spoons like the others. Belinda explained that they were stinkers who had committed an offence and been caned for it, then 'stripped to smalls'. All detainees wore a skimpy thong as standard issue so that, if awarded a bare-bottom caning, they had only to lift their skirts. It was cold in the refectory and the girls ate fast, shivering; beneath their thin blouses, only a white bra was visible, with no thermal bodice.

Belinda said that on Miss Brand's order, Isobel was to accompany her on patrol that afternoon. Belinda was a muscular Welsh girl of Isobel's age, with ash-blond tresses in a pony-tail. Like Isobel, and every warden's, her spic-and-span uniform, designed to cling, hugged a ripe figure, accentuating the breasts, thighs and buttocks. The slags, too, had clothing apparently a size too small, causing bare flesh to bulge at midriff, breast or thigh top, where seemlier kit might have hidden it. The discrepancy between body and kit size was most noticeable in the bra, from which breasts thrust, jutting and swelling.

Isobel commented on this in a whisper and Belinda told her that Miss Maclaren, i/c uniforms, thought all girls should be wiry and petite, like herself.

'Also, it looks good when the Home Office inspectors or the TV news people come round,' she said, grinning slyly. 'Maclaren's a tough nut – if you really want to terrify a slag, threaten her with a visit to surgery for her beating. I hear you've been pretty well tested yourself,' she added, licking her wide pink lips.

'What . . .?'

'I mean, your bum's been well dusted. No need to tell me why . . . but word gets around fast in here. It's good for a stroke to know that what she dishes, she can take – and *enjoy* how much a slag's arse is hurting under her cane.'

'*Fucking bum bitch!*'

'*Fucking gob whore!*'

Isobel looked up to see a tussle between two slags, each tugging at a sliver of meat and accusing the other of stealing it. Suddenly, there was a whistle, then a crack, as two lariats snaked through the air, each one looping a girl under the breasts, pinioning her and dragging her from the bench on to the floor. Ignoge Brand and Goiswinth Moss approached the girls and pressed their heads to the floor with their boots, whilst a table was cleared by other slags, protective of their own food. The strokes hauled the roped girls on to the table, with their bottoms in the air, and gave their lariats to two of the bottom strokes to hold the girls helpless. Their skirts went up, revealing the bare orbs of their g-stringed bottoms. Ignoge and Goiswinth raised their canes.

Vip! Vip! Vip! Vip! Vip! Vip! – six strokes cut smartly on each wriggling girl's bare arse, their beatings delivered in exactly six seconds. Both howled at the first and second strokes, but were told by the other girls to 'shut it, bitch'. The two slags, sobbing, were not permitted to rub their wealed bare bums as their wrists were strapped behind their backs with rubber thongs, and their shirts, skirts, stockings and footwear were removed. Nude but for bra and panties, they were obliged to resume their places at table, clad as stinkers and delving with their faces into the remains on their food trays. The two wardens holding the girls released them from their nooses and threw the lariats back to the caners, who caught the ropes with their teeth.

'They don't get much food,' said Belinda, 'so that tends to happen quite a lot. Many of the stinkers are in fact slags, who've suffered a month's loss of privilege after being caned bare for wanking off or other insolence.'

'Will I have to learn how to use a lariat?' Isobel said.

'Of course,' said Belinda.

At the wardens' luncheon, where food was plentiful, Isobel met all of her new colleagues. She sat between Belinda and the top stroke Althea Tite, a tall girl, with a rich russet mane and figure like Miss Horsfall's: slim frame ripening into ripe thighs and croup, and pert, jutting breasts straining under her shirt. Her long colt's legs slithered as she crossed and uncrossed her nylon-sheen thighs, brushing against Isobel's. Suddenly, over pudding, she felt Isobel's biceps.

'Gym mistress, eh?' she said, her voice a silky Home Counties drawl. 'Good caning muscle, there.'

Her hand strayed to Isobel's thigh.

'Well-built all round, I'd say, with a fair bum.'

Althea's fingers strayed to Isobel's arse-cleft and pressed briefly on her buttocks.

'*Althea*,' said Ignoge, mildly.

'Just testing the beef,' said Althea, which raised a laugh.

'I can assure you, the girl has more than a fair bum,' said Miss Maclaren. 'Pure Aberdeen Angus! She's lucky not to be a slag, or I'd swish that juicy rump . . . *my* way.'

Isobel blushed but returned Miss Maclaren's gaze with a stare of her own, at the two top buttons of Miss Maclaren's blouse unfastened, showing bra and tight, jutting teat-flesh; the trim surgical officer grinned and allowed her eyes to fall. After pudding, most of the girls rolled and lit cigarettes. Then, after coffee, it was time for afternoon patrol. Isobel accompanied Belinda, who explained that the inmates were occupied as fully as possible during waking hours at class or in physical pursuits. 'Frisky' girls had to break rocks in the quarry, half a mile distant. Classwork consisted of calligraphy, sewing, arts and crafts.

'I suppose there are computer studies?' Isobel said.

'Heavens, no,' said Belinda. 'Miss Horsfall doesn't approve of things like that.'

'Is there a chapel with religious services?'

Belinda laughed.

'You could call it that. Let's go straight to the gym – you'll probably need a squad of stinkers to help you move things around when there's a public punishment. Miss Horsfall likes things . . . theatrical.'

The gymnasium was a low, vaulted chamber, like the refectory, with mullioned windows, and Isobel remarked that it looked more like a chapel than a gym. Solid fixtures like wall bars looked incongruous against the oak-panelled or white plaster walls. A doorway led to a chamber almost as large, which was the store. Here, Isobel saw ranks of vaulting-horses, jumping bars, skipping-ropes, dumb-bells, and exercise machines; also, devices punitive.

'There's the rack,' said Belinda quite casually, 'and the stocks and the whipping-frames and the caning-horses – see the rubber cufflets for the wrists and ankles and the waistband. A girl caned on the horse is absolutely helpless.'

She licked her teeth.

Isobel swallowed nervously.

'So many! It's hard to imagine decent girls needing such . . . *draconian* treatment,' she said. 'I thought corporal punishment was an occasional usage.'

Belinda shrugged.

'Corporal punishment makes decent girls less brutish because they understand it.'

'It all looks nicely polished and dusted.'

'From use,' said Belinda, opening a cupboard, at which Isobel gasped: the space was neatly packed with canes and whips, as well as restraining harnesses, rubber corsets and cuffs, and metal branks and gagging devices.

'Will I have to use all those?' Isobel gasped.

'Not all on your first day,' smirked Belinda. 'There's an inventory book and list of punishments, here' – she indicated a thick leather folio. 'Ghislaine Bassin, the trusty, will show you how to decode it. Sound slag, Ghislaine – been here the longest and never accepts promotion.'

Beside the door was a row of four structures with pointed tops, each mounted on wheels and covered by a dust sheet. Belinda pulled off one sheet.

'That is the cage,' she said. 'It is for really naughty slags and is designed to be too narrow to sit down, so that a miscreant caged must stand up. It is an antique, actually: look how carefully the rods and eyelets are pierced in the bars, so that a victim may be trussed, or skewered, by any combination of restraint. The bars are hinged and can be lowered separately to show her bare for whipping.'

The cage bars were painted ochre and red, and atop the spire was coiled a chain with a hook. The four-sided ceiling of the cage was painted in swirling, abstract symbols; Belinda said they were supposed to be from North Africa, representing the four forces of earth, air, fire and water.

'Sometimes, the cage is hung from the refectory ceiling,' said Belinda, 'or outside, from one of the turrets. Especially when it's snowing. Miss Horsfall says that corporal punishment is a movable feast, so that almost any chamber can be used for an informal caning, while formal floggings tend to be in the gym or the refectory. You'll see the whipping posts outside and the ducking gibbet by the river. That's an antique too, from when the place was Pollecutt Manor.'

Isobel and Belinda visited the main bathroom where a group of stinkers, all nude, were at latrine duty. Under the canes of Sarah Bunn and Edra Forge, the bottom strokes, the girls crouched, contorted, to clean the floor with their pubic bushes as mops. One girl was held by wrists and ankles bent back over her head by two muscular inmates, who swung her pubis along the latrine channel, wiping it dry after two nude stinkers had licked it clean.

'Want to pee?' said Belinda. 'I do.'

Without ceremony, she nodded at Sarah and Edra and squatted on the toilet runnel, just before the girl's swabbing tongue. The aluminium was already bright but

Belinda stained it with her copious jet of steaming piss. The girl did not pause in her cleaning duty and any droplets of pee left unlicked were wiped off by the suspended girl's pubic mop. From time to time, her piss-soaked curls were sucked dry like a sponge by one of the other latrine girls.

'Yes,' said Isobel, as she watched Belinda's bush of ash-blond curls disappear back into her black panties, 'I feel like a pee, too.'

Trembling, she squatted and let flood a torrent of yellow fluid, some of it splashing the duty stinker's face and lips. The girl looked up sullenly at Isobel's buttocks as she licked her pond of golden piss. Isobel pulled up her panties and followed Belinda in rinsing her hands, then wiping them dry on the cunt bush of the nearest nude girl.

'Slags are muck,' she said loudly, 'so don't treat them as anything less.'

In the courtyard again, Belinda asked Isobel if she would mind exploring on her own. 'I've some things to do,' she said. 'Actually, I'm out of snout and that bitch Ignoge won't lend me any more.'

'Of course,' Isobel replied, 'but let me ask – Ignoge mentioned a thing called the labyrinth which had to be rebricked . . .'

Belinda pointed beneath.

'Down there,' she said. 'That's where slags have to go when a spell in solitary, and twice-daily canings, aren't enough to correct them. They must find their way out, which is why we keep changing the configuration. Anything may happen down there – you *don't* want to be in the labyrinth, Isobel. It is accessed by a tunnel beside the Pollecutt Room, which, by the way, is always kept locked – it's the only room that neither slags nor wardens are allowed to enter.'

'And you mentioned slags being promoted – if Ghislaine Bassin is already a trusty, surely that is a promotion?'

Belinda's response was to look cautiously round, then raise her skirts and lower her panties, to give Isobel a glimpse of her bare arse, ridged with crusted cane welts.

'I was a slag for six months, then trusty for nine, before *I* was promoted to warden,' Belinda said.

# 8

# Scared of Strokes

The scrubland darkened quickly and a fine dust of snow began to fall, so that Isobel curtailed her walk down to the River Wrigley and headed back towards her room. The prison buildings, cosy even in the bleak midwinter daylight, were now shadowy and menacing. There were solitary cries, rhythmic tapping noises, muffled groans. Isobel shivered as she entered a corridor unfamiliar to her but with a bathroom visible at one end. She hurried towards its sign, announcing 'Senior Wardens Only'; she peeked inside to find the place empty. Bladder bursting, she locked herself in a cubicle, unfastened her garter straps, fumbling in haste, then, lowering her panties, peed copiously and sighed. The bathroom for top strokes was painted in lemon yellow, with padded satin toilet seats, bidets, scent, tissue, nail files and cotton buds, and other tools of the boudoir. There was a commotion in the chamber; Isobel bit her lip, left her panties at her ankles, but pulled her feet up, to squat, invisible to the outside.

'Well, Ghislaine,' said a girl's voice – that of top stroke Althea Tite – 'I'm not at all pleased with you. You were supposed to deliver me my aubergine bra and panties today . . . I don't know what you *do* in the sewing room!'

'Please, mum,' whined a girl, 'it's not my fault. Miss Horsfall had me down for a waspie corset, in mauve silk, which takes a long time, and then Miss Brand wanted one the same, only in peach . . .'

Slap!

'Ouch, mum! That hurt!'
'Are you saying that Miss Brand takes precedence over me, bitch? After all I've done for you?'
'No, mum . . .'
Slap!
'Oh!'
Slap!'
'Please, mum! I promise . . . please, don't be cruel!'
'Cruel? Wait till you meet the new stroke, Miss Coker. She's gym mistress, and she told me at lunch she would test every single appliance on her trusty . . .'
Slap!
'*Ohh!*'
'Strip down, slut, for full inspection.'
'Y – yes, mum. Of course.'
There was a rustling and snapping, and the sound of dress and underthings slithering on skin. Boots clattered to the floor.
'I don't believe it! You're wearing my panties!'
'No! honestly, mum, I made these long ago.'
'Still a crime, *bitch!*'
'But Miss Horsfall has never said anything –'
Slap! Slap!
'Take them off, then lift your arms for pit inspection.'
The panties slithered off the girl.
'You haven't shaved your armpits!' hissed Althea Tite.
'I ran out of razors, mum. You see, I owed Emma Shadwell a quarter ounce of snout and I didn't have any, and she said she'd take a razor instead because Oswald wouldn't give her any more credit at the shop, and she owed June Dunton half a quarter ounce, and . . .'
Slap!
'*Ohh* . . .'
'You slags are all the same with your pathetic excuses. Get into that toilet. *Now!*'
Slap!
'Y – yes, mum,' Ghislaine stammered.
The two girls entered the cubicle at the end of the row, next to Isobel's, and Isobel was able to survey the scene

through a knothole in the wooden partition. The victim of Althea Tite's displeasure was a lithe girl, an inch shorter than Isobel, with big, pendulous bubbies and a firm, jutting arse over powerfully muscled thighs. Her skin was a delicate uniform olive. Though long, the breasts were nevertheless firm, jutting up pertly and outwards. Muscle bunched her spinal cleft, giving her back the aspect of two stretched peach-halves. The tight buttocks dimpled at the top, forming a cup, or pouch, and curved abruptly over the thigh-tops to make separate clefts where thigh joined fesse. The waist was narrow, which exaggerated the swellings of teat and arse; her breasts bobbed, quivering, as Althea Tite pushed her into the cubicle. Her raven hair was flat around her skull but gathered in a slide, with braided ringlets cascading over her shoulders and caressing dark nipples like fat, glossy dates. Althea held her by an earlobe. Kneeing her between her buttocks on the anus bud, Althea forced her head down to the toilet seat, and ripped the slide from her tresses so that the girl's hair fanned across the toilet bowl.

'Clean it, slag,' Althea hissed.

'No, please . . .' wailed Ghislaine.

'What gang are you with, slut?'

'Gang, mum? Gangs are illicit . . .'

Slap!

The palm of Althea's hand cracked acros the girl's bare buttocks.

'*Oh!*'

'Illicit, like smoking and coloured panties. Which gang is it, bitch? Franks, Goths, Vandals, Saracens?'

'Saracens, mum – remember?'

'You *are* a dirty bitch.'

'You should know, mum.'

Slap! Slap! Ghislaine's bare bum jerked.

'Fucking whore!'

Isobel held her breath, craning to watch, as the top stroke pushed the squirming slag further into the toilet bowl.

'No . . . please, mum,' came her muffled moans, but her head began to revolve, scrubbing the bowl with her hair.

'Tongue and lips, too, bitch,' Althea snapped.
Ghislaine made licking sounds.
'That's better. Keep at it, bitch,' Althea said, unfastening her cane and rope from her waistband.
She grasped Ghislaine's hands, removing them as props from the toilet seat so that her head sank deeper. She roped the girl's wrists at the small of her back, perched at the top of her buttocks, but leaving the fesses clear. Lifting her cane, Althea patted each buttock, then brushed her fingers down the crack of Ghislaine's arse. Her fingers poked the cleft wider and Ghislaine obeyed the mute command; she spread her legs, clinging to the toilet bowl with her calves, and parted her fesses.
'Oh . . . how many, please, mum?'
'Just fifteen.'
Vip!
The cane whistled and sliced Ghislaine's bare bum. The girl shuddered and her buttocks clenched before the next stroke took her on top croup, making her cry out.
'*Mmm!*'
'The second doesn't count, for blubbing. I should stick a fistful of goosefeathers in your cunt, you brat.'
Vip!
Ghislaine's head banged the inside of the toilet bowl; her bare bottom, striped by three livid pink weals, began to squirm, opening and closing rapidly. Althea waited for a relaxation of the bum muscles to allow the cleft, and the raven forest surrounding the red gash, to appear beneath the anus bud, before lashing Ghislaine an upender, hard in the perineum, and slicing both cunt and anus.
'*AHH! Mum! Oh, please!*'
'That doesn't count, either, Ghislaine. This may be a long set . . .'
Isobel's gaze was fixed on the trembling bare bottom of the beaten girl, the top pouch of her bum-cleft opening and closing like a mouth, and her spine writhing, with bone and muscle rippling beneath the skin. Her fingers crept between her thighs, to her own gash, swollen and seeping come. Isobel grimaced and shut her eyes, but only for an instant:

returning to the scene, she fastened two fingers on her stiffening clitty and began to masturbate as she watched Ghislaine's bare-bum caning.

The vip! vip! of the cane echoed over the flushing sounds of water in the bathroom, with Ghislaine's head churning the toilet bowl, sometimes rising for air, only to have the soaked tresses pushed down again by her caner. The soft olive skin of her bottom, though scarred with old weals, had seemed creamy and whole. Now, it was bruised by stripes of pink, darkening to crimson, then to purple, laid in delicate pattern over haunches – which bruised the darkest – to top buttock, to the shuddering compact flesh of the mid-croup and the clefts between thigh and under-fesse. Ghislaine had taken nineteen strokes of Althea's cane on the bare, including repeaters, when Althea stopped the beating. Isobel wanked herself as slowly as she could, yet unable to stop her fingers quickening as she peered back at the caner and saw her with skirt lifted and fingers under her knickers, glistening with seeped come. Althea Tite was wanking off as she caned her slag.

Althea poked between Ghislaine's thighs and her fingers came up dripping with oily come from Ghislaine's pouch. Ghislaine remained in position, not shifting her roped wrists, while Althea departed, to return, moments later, with a cluster of rubber thongs at her pubis enclosing a strap-on dildo. Unwrapped, this was a double prong, with one giant rubber phallus, in pink, already impaling Althea's cunt; the other shaft quickly nuzzled the lips of Ghislaine's anus bud. Both prongs were over a foot in length and the girth of a girl's wrist. Beneath them hung two rubber balls.

Althea prodded Ghislaine's bumhole, the caned girl jerking with sobs, until she penetrated her to about an inch. Ghislaine squealed. An inch more and her squeal became an unbroken wail; as Althea thrust her buttocks to plunge the dildo as far as the balls in Ghislaine's anal elastic, the girl screamed, once. Thereafter, she took Althea's buggery in squirming silence. Althea fucked her in the bum vigorously, while masturbating her own distended clitty, below which the cunt-slimed pink rubber slid in and out of her own soaking gash. Ghislaine began to rub her cunt and clitty on the toilet seat, and rivulets of come trickled down the cane-wealed olive skin of her inner thighs. Both girls groaned, mewling in unison.

'Going to come, slut?' panted Althea.

Isobel wanked faster, come gushing on her wrist and soiling her panties at her ankles.

'You *know*, mum . . .' gasped Ghislaine. 'God, yes, fuck my hole harder, mum . . . yes, bugger me. You *know* me so! God! Ah! I'm coming! Oh! *Ohh* . . .'

Althea's belly heaved; her fingers were a blur as they wanked her clitty and, as her own moans grew to gasping squeals, she squeezed hard on the rubber ball-sac hanging between the two dildos.

'*Yes!*'

'*Ahh* . . .'

Isobel's own gasps as she wanked off to spasm, with come wetting her thighs, stockings, boots and panties, were drowned by the tribadists' squeals, as white cream from the rubber ball-sac frothed at Althea's cunt and Ghislaine's anus, splattering their pube-jungles, thighs and lower buttocks. Isobel's crouching thighs trembled so that she almost toppled, grasping the cistern top for support, and making a dull clank, as her weight shifted its lid. She sat, shivering and trying to mop her flood of cunt-juice from her skin and clothing with a toilet tissue. Suddenly, an eye appeared at the knothole she had just peered through. The eye winked. There was a rapping on the cubicle door.

'Come out, come out, whoever you are . . . *Miss Coker*!' Althea sang.

Numbly, Isobel corrected her stockings and panties without taking time to fasten her garter straps, smoothed down her skirt and opened the cubicle door, to be greeted by the sight of three of the bottom strokes: Imogen Tandy, Amy Patel and Belinda Garce. All had rolled cigarettes in the corners of their mouths. They jeered; Belinda was the first to seize her. Althea lit up a half-smoked rollie while untying the ropes from Ghislaine's wrists. Ghislaine emerged, head and face dripping from the toilet bowl, and rubbed her bare bum before going in search of her discarded knickers.

'That really hurt, mum,' she said.

'Thought Saracen bitches could take it,' snapped Althea.

'Well, I *did*, mum, didn't I?'

'Let me go!' Isobel cried.

'She was wanking!' said Amy Patel brightly, with a flick of her shiny black mane and a trembling of her conic breasts under her clinging white uniform shirt.

Her stockings slithered as she rubbed her thighs together and grinned, at Isobel, then the others.

'Wanking off, and in the top stroke bog!' said Althea. 'That's *very* serious, miss. Lucky these ladies happened to be passing. You're a stroppy one and I'll need help holding you down.'

'What for?' wailed Isobel. 'Surely, you don't mean –'

'A caning,' drawled Althea, with a puff of smoke in Isobel's face. 'Yes, that's exactly what I mean.'

'Belinda!' cried Isobel, as the girls pinioned her wrists and head, holding her bent over a washbasin with her face pressed against the mirror.

Belinda shrugged as Althea lifted Isobel's skirt and pulled down her sopping knickers. She knelt and clung to Isobel's left foot, immobilising her. Another girl held her by the right foot; it was Ghislaine, her trusty, grinning impishly.

'You were witnessed wanking off, *in flagrante*,' said Althea. 'I wouldn't advise an appeal to higher authority.'

'You forget what *I* witnessed!' Isobel blurted.

'An unruly detainee, whom I corrected with reasonable force. Isn't that what happened, Ghislaine?'

'Yes, mum,' said Ghislaine, 'no more and no less.'

Althea lifted her cane over Isobel's quivering bare bottom.

'Better get it over with, Miss Coker, with a swift fifteen to the bare.'

'We all have to bare up below sometimes,' said Imogen Tandy, licking her lips.

'If we can dish it out, we must be able to take it,' said Amy Patel. 'That's reasonable, isn't it . . . *Isobel*?'

Her hand stroked Isobel's bare bottom.

'It's not as if you haven't been caned before.'

'But proper stingers, this time,' added Belinda.

'Only fifteen!' said Imogen. 'Come on, agree.'

Althea swished her cane, inches from the trembling bare flans of Isobel's bum; Isobel's buttocks clenched. Althea swished again, closer, but Isobel's cleft remained open, showing her anus bud shut tight, but her gash swollen, open and dripping come from her tangled fronds of wet, underhanging pubic forest.

'She's juicing,' murmured Belinda Garce. 'There's a seep from her cooze. She's not scared of strokes.'

'Perhaps fifteen isn't enough, mum,' said Amy.

'No!' said Isobel hoarsely. 'I agree, damn you. *I agree.*'

Vip!

At once, Althea lashed her full across middle fesse, and the buttocks jerked as a pink stripe flamed the naked skin.

'*Uh!*' Isobel gasped, as her bottom squirmed.

Vip!

'*Uh!*'

Vip!

'*Uhh . . .!*'

'The first five are the worst,' said Belinda. 'After those, it's plain sailing.'

Isobel's buttocks writhed, awaiting the next of the set, the weals now darkening, lying in a patchwork of stripes on the bare flesh.

Vip! Vip!

'*UHH . . .!*'

The bare bum squirmed, clenching furiously at two strokes, laid backhand and forehand.

'She *is* juicing,' said Imogen Tandy, her fingers dabbling Isobel's pendant cunt flaps.

Amy reached down Isobel's pubic mound and her hand slid into Isobel's cunt, right to her wrist.

'What a monstrous box!' she cried.

'Let me have a grope!' said Belinda, Amy withdrawing to permit her entrance to the slit.

Vip! Vip!

'*Uh!*'

'You're right! What a cavern! And well juicy!'

Imogen took her turn; her fist penetrated Isobel's gash and pressed her clitoris.

'Big nubbin, too,' she said. 'She must wank off a lot.'

'Quite a challenge for Oswald at the shop.'

'Give *our* holes a rest.'

'She'll get all the snout she wants on credit, jammy bitch.'

'But she doesn't smoke.'

Vip!

'*Uhh . . .*'

Buttocks writhing, Isobel moaned as her flow of come grew stronger, sliming her thighs. Each stroke of the whippy little cane slammed her breasts against the mirror, squashing her stiff nipples. Each girl in turn rubbed her distended clitty. Ghislaine's face glistened with droplets of come, sprayed from Isobel's quivering cunt.

'All right, Miss Coker?' said Althea pleasantly. 'Nearly over.'

The tufts of russet hair, billowing at her armpits, dripped sweat down her tabard top.

'Oh, mum,' gasped Isobel. '*It hurts so* . . . you cane hard.'

Vip!

'*Ahh! Oh!*'

'I know. Next time, try making a little less noise.'

'*Next* time, mum? I don't understand.'

Vip!

'*Ah! Ah!*' Isobel sobbed. 'Please, mum – may I know? – *how many* of you, how many wardens, were promoted from slags? Am I the only one –'

Vip!

'*OHH!*'

'That's for us to know and you to find out, bitch,' said Althea Tite coolly.

The girls giggled; they took turns frotting Isobel's stiff clitty, while her bare bum writhed under the cane and the skin darkened to a crisscross of purpling weals. The mirror steamed with Isobel's panting breath and in it were the blurred reflections of the three bottom strokes, each with a hand beneath her skirt and rubbing herself. Ghislaine, crouching, held Isobel's shuddering legs; her head was beneath Althea's skirt, bobbing at her crotch.

Vip! Vip!

'Please . . .' Isobel moaned, her lips pressing the glass. 'Please . . .'

Fists punched her gash and thumbs flicked her stiff nubbin, while come gushed from her twitching cunt flaps.

Vip!

'*Uhh* . . . yes . . . Oh! *Oh! I'm coming!*' Isobel cried, her belly knotting in her spasm of climax, her come-gush a torrent of oily juice.

Althea delivered the final strokes with her eyes screwed shut, her face scarlet and her own loins writhing as Ghislaine tongued her.

'Yes!' moaned Belinda.

'Mmm . . .' cried Amy.

'A fair bum!' gasped Imogen, licking Isobel's cunt juice from her slimy fingers as she wanked her own cunt.

Isobel's flogged buttocks continued to writhe, long after her beating was complete. She arose, shaking, her face red and her voice a choking sob. The other wardens and the detainee Ghislaine faced her, standing to attention, drawing on lit rollies. When Isobel struggled back into her underthings, stained with come, and smoothed down her uniform, they patted her on the shoulders.

'Good girl,' said Belinda Garce.

She proffered her half-smoked rollie.

'Want a smoke? You can pay me back when you get yourself sorted for snout.'

Isobel Coker took the cigarette with trembling fingers, put it between her lips, inhaled, then exhaled a strong plume of blue smoke. She repeated the operation at once, taking her time exhaling, this time with a sigh of relief.

'Thanks, Belinda,' she said.

From the outside, the white prison van was no more than a tradesman's vehicle, except that the narrow portholes were covered in fine wire mesh. Inside were seating cubicles for a dozen prisoners, each one a toilet: journeys in HMP vans could last a long time. Angarad's trip from London had taken several hours of darkness, during which she was obliged to sleep, leaning on the wall of her cubicle. Food and drink were passed through a slot by Officer Joule, without facial contact. Her feet were enclosed in a wooden hobble bar but her hands were free. After a while, Angarad did not bother with lowering and raising her underthings to pee, but sat slumped, with her knickers at her ankles, peeing and stooling in dribbles, although at times she rose to rub her itchy bottom. Dawn broke and a chill Yorkshire air blew. She woke with a shiver; sensing commotion, and an imminent arrival, she peed, fastened her underthings and smoothed down her skirt.

The van stopped. Doors slanged and WPC Joule unlocked the door of her cubicle. She freed Angarad from her hobble bar, then handcuffed her wrists behind her back before leading her to the door at the van's rear. Angarad stumbled going down the step and a buxom girl in prison officer's uniform caught her, preventing her from falling. WPC Joule descended and saluted the prison officer.

'WPC Joule, delivering prisoner Stark, Angarad,' she snapped.

'Junior Warden Coker, accepting delivery,' said the officer, returning the salute. 'You may remove her handcuffs, officer. No need for them here.'

Her voice had a soft northern lilt and her eyes smiled at Angarad. WPC Joule shivered and looked round at the snow-covered scrubland. She accepted the delivery note which Isobel had signed and returned in a hurry to the thrumming warmth of the vehicle. Angarad watched her home for the past ten hours retreating into the light dawn snowfall. It was scarcely past dawn and already the prison was busy. In the distance trudged a work party, carrying pickaxes and, obscured by snowflakes, clad in bras and panties. Other detainees wore uniform prison garb, while some were barefoot and wrapped in grey blankets. She rubbed her eyes.

'Don't be frightened, love,' said the prison officer. 'You'll adapt soon enough. I'm a warden and you are a detainee, and you call wardens "mum". Just remember that, and you'll be OK. We'll get you fed, scrubbed up, medically examined and kitted out, then you can met Miss Horsfall, our governess. I'm a bit of a new girl myself. I was posted here last week.'

'I'm going to be here for a *year*,' said Angarad bitterly, as Isobel steered her towards the central block with her cane swinging from her black belt as naturally as a purse.

Isobel saluted a senior officer, tall, coltish and blond of tress, who grinned and saluted back; unlike Isobel, her uniform shirt was merely a tabard top, which left her arms wholly bare, with huge bushes of hair under the armpits.

'May I ask a question?' Angarad said.

'Of course.'

'Why are some of the girls wearing blankets?'

'Stinkers – new detainees are issued only with bra and panties,' said Isobel, 'and, of course, a blanket. You have to *earn* your uniform here at the Scrubs, and that includes stockings and suspenders. If you play up well, then you'll be proud of your Scrubs uniform.'

'And if I don't?' murmured Angarad.

'Don't be a smart arse, miss,' Isobel retorted, her Durham accent making the words 'smott oss'. 'You know full well that our regime allows strict corporal punishment. You aren't scared of strokes or you wouldn't be here. Try to enjoy it.'

Her voice sank to a whisper.

'*I have to . . .*'

After breakfast of tea and porridge, Angarad was escorted to the cleansing room, a normal bathroom but equipped with a set of brushes like a carwash, and amid them a cage of steel hoops, open on its hinges, and with an eyeless, mouthless metal face-plate. The cage was in the form of a human body, with the arms and legs parted like a gingerbread man. Two girls in prison issue bra and g-string panties stood by the device. Isobel ordered Angarad to strip naked and enter the cleaning hoop, which would then be buckled around her nude body. Angarad flinched.

'Don't worry,' said Isobel. 'You must be fully scrubbed and deloused before the surgical nurse, Miss Maclaren, gives you your medical. Clare and Ingrid are trusties.'

Sighing, Angarad stripped and watched the warden place her clothes in a laundry bag, tagged with her name. Everything, including her watch, went into the bag. Nude and shivering, she stepped into the cage of steel hoops. The door clanged shut and was locked, its hoops constricting her breasts, belly, thighs and ankles, with a vertical hoop biting into her vulva, and fastened to the metal plate snapped around her head, covering the face but leaving her mane free. The wire cleansing brushes began to whir and Angarad shrieked as jets of ice-cold water sprayed her.

The hoop cage held Angarad's legs parted, her vulva defenceless against the powerful sluice of disinfectant fluid and the wire cleansing brushes that followed. The fluid penetrated her cunt and bum-cleft, with vertical rotor-brushes whirring between her parted thighs, while side brushes scraped her flanks, belly, breasts and armpits. The brushes sliced her scalp and penetrated the exposed folds of her vulva, and the wrenched pucker of the anus bud. She shuddered, sobbing, as the rotors attacked those parts again and again, roaring as they scraped her protective face-mask.

The machine stopped; Angarad was released, gasping and shivering, and made to lie belly up on a metal frame table, with cuffs and straps at each corner and a buckled rubber corset at its waist. The girls began to examine Angarad's soaked hair with tweezers, one at her head and the other at her pubis. Eventually, after extracting several pube-hairs by the roots, they pronounced her clean. Isobel held a hosepipe and rinsed Angarad's upper body of the cleansing fluid, directing the jet generously between her legs and to the stiffening nipples; her titties trembled under the spray, which lashed her like a whip.

'You're hairy, miss,' said Isobel. 'Rules are that detainees must shave the body completely every day, except for the pubic bush, which you must leave completely untouched.'

Angarad began to cry as her naked body was attacked by the two girls with wire pads and razors probing every crevice of her body – arse-cleft, armpits and navel – while leaving the pubic bush standing, a blond curly forest amid an expanse of belly and thigh-skin, bared of golden down.

'If you like, I can strap you,' said Isobel gently. 'But I dare say you'd prefer not, so early on.'

Angarad sobbed that she could take it. At last, she was ordered to turn over and lie on her belly for the cleansing and shaving to be repeated on her hindquarters. As she shifted, to expose her bare bum, all three females gasped.

'You *have* taken it,' said Isobel, 'haven't you?'

Her palm stroked Angarad's wet buttocks.

'Yes, I've been caned – and worse! Laugh all you want,' sobbed Angarad.

'When was the last time?'

'My . . . my judicial interview, before my court appearance.'

Vip!

'*Oh!*'

Isobel's cane sliced Angarad a cut on her wet buttocks.

'My court appearance, *mum*,' said Isobel, sighing. 'You'll have to learn decorum, girl, the hard way, or . . .'

'*Or*, mum?' Angarad sobbed. 'Is there another?'

'Not really,' said Isobel. 'But . . . you've been caned frequently, miss – I'd say, on the bare.'

'Yes.'

Vip!

'*Ouch!* Yes, *mum*!'

'That's better.'

The soapy wire wool penetrated Angarad's vulva, making her wince. The girl scrubbed vigorously, covering Angarad's inner and outer cunt lips, her clit, perineum and her whole cleft, including the anus pucker.

'God! – I mean, mum, that hurts,' Angarad sobbed.

'Your arse is used to pain,' said Isobel drily. 'Your file has a pink sticker, meaning that you are a pervert.'

'*What?*'

Vip!

'What, *mum*!'

'What . . . mum?' Angared sobbed, her teeth a rictus, as a fresh pink weal glowed on her bare bum.

'One who takes pleasure in corporal punishment,' said Isobel, with the slightest of tremors in her voice. 'Who *likes* being caned on . . . *on her bare bottom.*'

'Oh, mum, it's not true!' Angarad cried. 'I can explain! If only someone would listen . . .!'

'No names, no packdrill, miss,' snapped Isobel. 'You are here for correction, not gloating on past misdeeds.'

'But . . . but I was wrongly –'

Vip!

'*Ahh!*'

'Enough!' said Isobel, her face red. 'I'll be back in twenty minutes, and I expect you slags to have her presentable.'

'Yes, mum,' said the two girls in bras and panties.

When Isobel departed, they sniggered, the larger of the two twisting Angarad's arms up her back in a half-nelson.

'Twenty minutes! Plenty of time for the slut to wank off,' she said. 'Didn't you see her quim damp? She's as new as this stinker – not here a week and a slag already!'

'And plenty of time for us,' said the other.

'Wait a minute –' Angarad began, but was silenced: the smaller girl pulled aside the gusset of her panties and pushed her huge quim-bush into Angarad's face.

'Lick me, slut,' she said.

'*Mm!*' squealed Angarad, as wet cunt lips squelched her mouth and her nose pressed a clitoris already throbbing. The girl's hips swayed, grinding her pubis into Angarad's face and sliming her with come.

'*Mm!*' she moaned, as her wrists and upper arms were swiftly roped together, the rope encircling her nipples and fixing her armlock, with her fingers pressed between her shoulder-blades.

The rubber corset was buckled over her back to its tightest notch, pinioning her to the table frame.

Smack! Smack! Smack!

The larger girl began to spank Angarad's bared fesses, while her cunt flaps were prised open and two, then three, fingers thrust into her pouch, with a thumb pressing her clitty. The girl penetrated her cunt to the wrist and began to fist her, with jabs to her wombneck. Angarad squealed and threshed but, as her mouth opened, the small girl's swollen cunt-flaps pressed on her tongue, obliging her to lick them. The girl sighed and shifted, so that Angarad's tongue was pushed against her stiff nubbin.

'Nothing personal,' she said. '*Ohh* . . . that's nice. I'm Ingrid Fage, by the way, and she's Clare Cubitt. All stinkers must be broken in.'

'*We* were,' said Clare.

Clare was tall, big-breasted and massively crouped, with auburn hair, thick at head and pubis; Ingrid, blonde and wiry, her breasts conic and her frame lean as a whippet's, the narrow waist and ribcage billowing to a broad, taut croup and the crotch adorned with a jungle of cunt hairs that stretched almost from hip to hip, creeping up her flat, muscled belly to her navel, while its unkempt lower fronds wreathed long, swollen gash flaps of livid crimson.

Smack! Smack! Smack!

'*Mm! Mm!*'

Angarad's spanked bare buttocks writhed as her mouth and tongue were slammed against Ingrid's dripping cunt. Her lips closed on the clitoris of the tribadist and her throat bobbed as she swallowed the girl's come.

'She's not bad, for a stinker,' gasped Ingrid. 'I'm nearly off . . .'

'You Goths wank off too much,' grunted Clare.

'Fucking Franks,' responded Ingrid. 'Pack of rug-munchers . . .'

'You'll have to join one tribe or the other to survive, stinker,' Clare said, as she spanked Angarad's bare. 'Jails are run by inmates and this cage is no exception. There are four gangs, the Franks, Goths, Vandals and Saracens, and we all claim territories, like squares on a chessboard, and if a slag is caught in enemy territory, then she can be thrashed, or wanked, till she can't take it. Problem is, the territories are always changing, and no one is ever quite sure who's occupied what. It's a good game.'

'From your perve's welts, I'd put you down as a Saracen or Vandal,' said Ingrid. 'We all wank off and cane bare, but Saracen canings are the juiciest. Vandals cane hard, too, but they have big bumholes because they like it best up the rear. Isn't that *soo* filthy?'

Both slags laughed.

Smack! Smack! Smack!

'*Oh!*'

Angarad's bum quivered; Clare vigorously fisted Angarad's gash, thumbing her clitty until the new girl's slit lips dripped oil. Angarad's cunt basin began to writhe in time with her fisting, her pouch drawing Clare's knuckles into her wetness. Clare squatted at the small of Angarad's back, her panties lowered to her thighs and her naked quim, with its wet tangle of cunt hair, rubbing against the spinal nubbin. Clare's come tricked down Angarad's bum-cleft, spilling on to her spanked buttocks, now mottled red. Each clenching of her fesses revealed Angarad's anal pucker squirming and open.

'She *has* got a fair bumhole,' said Clare. '*Well!*'

'I'm going to come,' gasped Ingrid.

'Me, too,' said Clare, squirming on Angarad's pinioned back. 'How's her tongue?'

'Agile,' was Ingrid's panted reply.

'She's a perve, a real Vandal,' said Clare. 'Needs it up the bum for her to come. Caning would get her off, but not just spanks.'

Smack! Smack! Smack!

'Mmm . . .!'

Angarad's scarlet bare bum had taken over seventy spanks when Clare withdrew her fist from the dripping pouch and plugged Angarad's anus with her forefinger, poking and widening the aperture until she had two, three and then four fingers plunged into the anal elastic. Angarad's moans grew to shrieks, muffled by Ingrid's dank wet cunt hairs, as Clare began to finger-fuck Angarad's squirming anal hole while maintaining the vigour of her spanks. After each set of three spanks, she paused to wank her own distended clitty, pressing the nubbin between fingernail and Angarad's shuddering spine.

'I think her bumhole would take fist,' said Clare. 'It's well slack.'

'Do it!' cried Ingrid. '*Dirty little perve.*'

'*Fucking Vandal.*'

'*Mm! Mm! Mm!*' squealed Angarad, furiously shaking her head against Ingrid's pubis.

'*Yes . . .*' hissed Ingrid, her belly beginning to heave in spasm. 'Oh! Oh! *Ohh . . .!*'

'Cunt's tight, though,' said Clare, climbing down from her saddled position. 'She's in for a rough ride with Oswald . . . *there*!'

Angarad howled, her tears mingling with Ingrid's gushing come; Clare's fist was fully plunged in her anus. Clare began to fist the bumhole, buggering the squirming, squealing girl with rapid jabs to her anal root and continuing to spank her blotched bare bottom.

Smack! Smack! Smack!

'*Ahh . . .!*' screamed Angarad. 'Ah! Ah! *Ahh . . .*'

Her belly began to writhe against the table.

'The slut's coming!' panted Clare, as she fisted Angarad's gaping bumhole, stretched several times the normal pucker. 'She *will* make a good Vandal.'

'And Oswald should be pleased . . . especially if she's cycled to the village on a Vandal bike.'

Both girls giggled.

'That's one without a saddle, see,' said Ingrid. 'Oswald likes his arseholes good and raw.'

'Oh . . .' Angarad sobbed, slumping, as her belly ceased to flutter in spasm. 'God! I'm so ashamed!'

'The A word!' said Clare. 'We don't use that much at the Scrubs. Oswald does, though. He loves it when you're ashamed, riding his . . . *cock* doesn't do the monster justice.'

'Despite our absolute *longing* for justice,' said Ingrid.

Clare withdrew her fist, took Angarad's bare foot and applied it to her own cunt, wanking herself to a swift orgasm with the girl's big toe, as Isobel Coker's steps were heard returning to the cleansing room. When the bottom stroke arrived, she found the nude Angarad wrapped in a grey blanket.

'All done and dusted, mum,' said Clare, 'and ready for Miss Maclaren.'

'Good,' said Isobel Coker, shifting her thighs under a skirt gleaming with fluid at her crotch. 'Let me just have a last look at . . .'

She lifted Angarad's blanket and gazed at her croup.

'Clean enough. She had a hard judicial interview in London, I believe,' she said, stroking Angarad's freshly spanked bottom. 'I only tickled her – you saw, ladies! – but those pervert's welts will take a long time to . . . to . . .'

'Fade, mum?' said Ingrid.

Isobel blushed.

'Yes,' she snapped.

'If they ever do, mum,' said Clare.

'Men are such beasts,' said Isobel Coker.

# 9

# Womancart

Filming had ceased for the day and Habren was bathing. Pink light slanted through the open window-turrets, as two of her cast, wearing crotchless harem pantaloons, sponged her, and poured pails of hot water and scented unguents. She lay in the hot tub, gazing upwards at her nude reflection in her ceiling mirror. She parted her thighs and watched her hand squeeze first one engorged nipple, then the other; slide across her belly in a caress, to the jungle of pubic hair, within which gleamed the ruby wet lips of her open cunt. She placed finger and thumb between the pouch flaps and parted them, to reveal the gleaming red cavern of her cunt. Two, then three fingers penetrated her gash and her thumb rubbed her swollen clitoris, while her free hand crept into her bum-cleft and with two fingers she penetrated her anus, right to the knuckle. Slowly, with a smile of pleasure at her reflected self, Habren masturbated to a climax, her moans soft and mewling, and the gush of come from her wanked cunt spiralling in the water like fronds of anemones. The two girls silently aided her masturbation with a rolling pressure on her nipples, while wanking their own cunts through the open pantaloons and pressing come-slimed finger-kisses to Habren's lips. As Habren's breath of orgasm ebbed, Aggar knocked on the stone wall and brushed aside the door hangings. He apologised gravely for interrupting his mistress's most sacred daily ritual, at which Habren smiled and replied that her rite of masturbating to her own image was complete.

He had come to advise her a vehicle was approaching the fort. Habren dismissed her girls, now mutually masturbating and, still frotting, they retreated, heads bowed, and backwards from her presence. Habren rose from her bath without bothering to cover her nudity and padded, dripping, to the slit window. Wreathed in dust, a vehicle was slowly descending the mountainside. Habren donned a cotton robe, fastening it loosely at the waist, and descended barefoot to meet the newcomers. The cast and crew were busy at their evening meal or else lounging by the oasis pool, where Joss squatted, wearing his white suit and observing the naked girls comparing the day's whipmarks, highlighted by the crimson rays of the sunset.

The vehicle loosed its brakes and speeded as it reached flatland; wreathed in dust, it was a primitive cart, with wooden unspoked wheels and a creature between the shafts drawing it, while the driver stood in the cart itself holding a map. Habren licked her lips and whistled: the yoked draught animal was a human female. The cart drew to a halt; from the swirl of dust emerged a young man and woman, both tall, blond and alike. They wore desert boots and socks, khaki shorts and check headcloths; beneath the girl's, lush blond tresses strayed. The male was shirtless, the female had her khaki shirt knotted under her huge breasts, with only a single button of the garment fastened. She was drenched in sweat. Habren eyed both before addressing the young man with her eyes and her lips.

'This is private property,' she said.

'Of course – we beg merely some shelter for the night, and will pay, of course,' said the male, with a slight accent.

'There is no question of payment,' said Habren. 'Please refresh yourselves, then go. This is a film set, you see, and our proceedings are . . . discreet.'

The girl's eye had fastened on the nude girls bathing in the oasis and their mottled skins. She smiled at Habren, first shyly, then with a wide, sunny beam, exposing bright white teeth against her thick red lips and tan face. She shifted in her sweat-drenched shirt, so that her full, heavy breasts were squeezed together, and the hard damsons of her nipples pressed, braless, against the cloth. The full pears of her croup clung to the wet, tiny shorts, revealing no panty line, above long, coltish, thigh and calf muscles that glistened, rippling and tense, in the red sunlight.

'I am Truud Wegener,' she said, 'and this is my twin brother, Jan. Our vehicle's axles require adjustment – simple maintenance, but will need perhaps a night. Thus, we should not disturb your film-making. I assume you do not film at night. By the way, we are very . . . wide-minded. We, too, are making a film, of our journey and its strange phenomena.'

Habren pursed her lips, glancing behind her at her girls, who made no attempt to conceal their whipmarked nudity. She placed her hand on Truud's shoulder, let it slide down her spine, with her fingernails grating, and rested her palm on the girl's buttocks. Truud shivered and her bottom trembled, as Habren's fingers brushed her cleft.

'My, you do need a bath,' she said, 'but uninvited guests should make no assumptions, especially when interrupting a lady's toilette. It's *broad*-minded, by the way.'

'Oh! I'm sorry,' cried Truud, seeming genuinely alarmed. 'I have made an error.'

Jan smiled.

'I prefer *open*-minded, but the point is moot,' he said. 'Truud is very Frisian. She does not like to make mistakes.'

'What about you?' asked Habren.

'I do not make mistakes,' said Jan, staring blatantly at Habren's half-fastened robe, which showed most of her belly, and the first thick sprays of her pubic bush.

'There is the tradition of desert hospitality,' said Habren, her eyes on Truud's full, ripe arse-melons. 'Since you're here, we'll put you up.'

Truud's smile was radiant as Habren's arm circled her waist, allowing the inside of her wrist to brush the young woman's full pubic mound. Habren's nostrils flared; she breathed hard, scanning the girl's tan breasts and taut, slightly trembling, buttocks, which she impishly patted, while stroking her own bum, as though in comparison. The male's crotch stirred.

'I am sure you are curious *what* you interrupted,' she said coolly. 'I have desert habits, and was masturbating in the bath, as I do every afternoon, looking at my reflection in the mirror. I dare say, Truud, you are familiar with the practice, especially on such a lonely trek.'

'Oh!' said Truud, blushing, 'I admit that, once or twice, I may have . . . looked at my body.'

'And masturbated in this sensuous heat. We all do.'

'That is a very personal question! But yes, I masturbate, whenever I have privacy. Do not all girls? Once, when I was alone in the labyrinth of Oum El Hanch, I found a secret chamber, carved in erotic scuplture. No, not erotic – flagellant. Women in cages, or roped and bound, were whipped by males with . . . with erect appendages. Their bodies were depicted in a very lifelike manner and I could almost hear their screams and feel their pain as they were flogged, and squirm with them. The chamber filled me with strange joy, despite the sufferings of the whipped girls! Some of them bore the marks of whipping but had their bodies beneath the neck entirely cased in wax. The cage, and the dripping of hot beeswax or molten Baltic amber, were Vandal tortures so refined as to be cult rituals. I could not resist my urge – I stripped and masturbated, rubbing my clitoris on a stone dildo, carved on a male who appeared European. I admit, too, that . . . that I spanked myself on my bare buttocks as I masturbated. It was not painful compared to the agonies of the girls in the carvings, yet I wanted to share their joy, for . . . *they were smiling*. I took many photographs and think I may have found a sacred maze of Vandal flagellant worship, where the whipped girls were priestesses of the rod.'

'Please use my bathtub, Truud, and relax,' said Habren, 'though there is not much room for self-flagellance, and it might be fun for us, if you are not *too* wide-minded.'

Over supper, Jan and Truud explained their journey. They squatted on cushions on the stone floor, eating with their fingers, with Joss having abandoned his daytime suit for a silk dressing-gown, while Habren wore a tabard halter top, cut off just below her breasts, and billowing harem pants. The Dutch, or Frisians, as they insisted, had fresh kit, the same as they had worn on arrival.

'We are on the trail of the Vandals, who we believe to be our ancestors,' said Jan, 'using their traditional method of transportation, across Europe and then across Africa, namely, the womancart. We are writing our joint doctoral thesis on the subject at the University of Leeuwaarden.'

Vandals, from Germany, had migrated north, to Frisia, Denmark and northern England, or south, through Gaul and Spain, until, in the year 429, King Gaiseric took his entire nation of eighty thousand people across the Straits of Gibraltar to Africa. They established an African kingdom, which lasted a century, until their defeat by the Byzantine Empire. During that time, they occupied Sicily, Corsica and Sardinia, and even pillaged Rome.

'Yet, after a lightning Byzantine conquest,' said Jan, 'the south Vandals disappeared. How? To where? Eighty thousand people, or more, do not disappear. We believe many migrated south and west, to the remote areas of Morocco and perhaps as far as the Gold Coast. Our purpose is to find settlements where Vandal artefacts, customs, perhaps the Vandal gene pool, survive, as in Friesland or Northumberland and Durham – even Yorkshire. Research was undertaken by Sir George Pollecutt, deputy governor of Tangier, when it belonged to the English crown in the reign of King Charles II. He wrote of blue-eyed Berbers and the legend of the sacred maze of Oum El Hanch, and added his own legend, that of Pollecutt's box, containing the treasure of the Vandals. But it was not in the maze. I found *this*' – she showed a square of pink brocade, foxed with age.

'What and where is this box?' Habren asked.

'We shall not know until we find it,' said Truud. 'The Englishman was eccentric, in the English tradition we Dutch so admire. He was a . . . a lecher, of bizarre tendency. He established a series of whipping forts for his pleasure, where the tribal girls would be brought for chastisement if they erred. Many tribes adhere to his custom, after centuries, and permitted us to film their rites, in which girls are whipped naked, then hung in cages overnight. I was appalled, but fascinated, that the girls *welcomed* their chastisements, as the flogged female buttocks become enhanced, or sacred, when the entire croup and loins are enshrined in hot dripped wax, cooling to a solid case, and worn for a period of days after a whipping. The maze of Oum El Hanch is a clue to an ancient cult, either discovered, or *imported*, by Vandal migrants – then rediscovered by the, ah, lustful Englishman. In England, Pollecutt founded a club called . . . *Pinkarse.*'

Truud blushed.

'When I bathed in your tub, I did look at myself and masturbated,' she whispered. 'It was like having a twin.'

'You mean you are *not* identical twins?' Habren asked. 'I overheard my foster-parents in Knutsford once, not clearly, but . . . I think *I* may have one, somewhere. It makes me dream . . . They were appallingly *nouveau* and quite amoral, but couldn't tell me for sure.'

'For practical purposes, we are twins,' said Jan, 'but being differently sexed, cannot be identical twins. Monozygotic twins, from a single egg, are identical in every detail of their genome, hence of the same sex. Only their fingerprints differ! Dizygotic twins like us are merely members of the same litter. However, we are very close . . . we have shared our lives, in *and* outside the womb.'

Truud's face reddened further.

'What will you do with your discoveries?' asked Joss.

'The thrill of discovery is enough,' said Truud.

Joss blurted that if they needed money, his company logo would look nice on the sides of their cart.

'Don't be an ass, Joss,' said Habren, without looking at him. 'So – just the thrill of discovery?'

'Perhaps discreet publication, for the discerning public,' said Jan. Habren laughed.

'Healthy exhibitionism,' she said. 'Not unlike my films. My girls are on a voyage of *self*-discovery and self-exposure, for a discerning public . . .'

She explained crisply.

'They are porno films?' said Truud.

'There *is* a sexual dimension, as in all things,' said Habren. 'The nerves of a girl's arse are her most sensitive, apart from nipples or clitoris – so, a bare-bum spanking is both discipline and stimulus. More important are the roles of dominant and submissive, expressed through the lash. It is the pride that you *can take it* – and learn your true nature in doing so. The *scene* is world-wide and ageless, a cult of flagellance, teaching that the highest wisdom and pleasure are in the pain of whip on bare skin. My cast are girl submissives, who gain pleasure from their whippings and their exposing. I accept no one unless her dedication is real – that she is a real sub.'

'Proved by practical test?' said Truud.

'Exactly. I see my work as part of a flagellant tradition as old as humanity. Thus, we make our film *Whipping Fort* in a place which actually *was* a whipping fort.'

'Sir George Pollecutt writes of such a cult,' said Jan. 'The goddess Flagella, or, in Old Vandalic, Rodd or Roden, and in Africa, Ishtar, harlot goddess of the date clusters . . . yet, it was the *goddess* who was whipped, by *males.* I believe Sir George added to the cult practice. He dealt in American sotweed, or tobacco, and Berbers still place rolled tobacco in the anal and vulval holes of caned women, to inhale the fumes of the burning leaves moistened by her fluids.'

Truud swallowed nervously.

'A woman has an instinct to submit to a male, but it must be dreadful to be *whipped*,' she murmured, 'though I did spank myself at Oum El Hanch, on the bare bottom, and also when I was masturbating in your bathtub. I pull our womancart – my duty, as the Vandal woman I believe myself to be – but I don't need whipping, even though, in more unruly times, the males certainly whipped their women along and often caged them. Quite awful!'

Truud shuddered, her breasts quivering like jellies.

'No more awful than eating chilli peppers!' Jan laughed. 'And what about the flagellant sect of the Middle Ages? How can you, as a historian, be unaware?'

'Jan,' she said in English, 'stop putting me down!'

'Ignorance deserves to be put down!' he snapped.

'*Ach! Varken!*'

'You sound more like man and wife than brother and sister,' Habren murmured.

Balling her fists in a gesture of rage, Truud spilled a flagon of wine over Habren's silk pantaloons.

'Oh! I'm sorry!' she cried.

'It's no problem at all,' said Habren, smiling at Jan.

'On the contrary,' he said, 'it is just this thoughtless petulance that so often spoils things!'

'What about your *male* arrogance?' responded Truud. 'I said sorry and Habren said she wasn't upset!'

'No, Truud,' Habren replied. 'I said it was *no problem.* Those were my favourite pantaloons, worn specially for you and now ruined. The question is, Jan, how should your twin make amends, so that we can be friends again?'

Jan watched Habren strip off her pantaloons, down to the pubic string that was her only adornment and scarcely hid her luxuriant cunt-bush. She cast the soaked garment in Truud's lap.

'I know exactly how,' Jan said. 'First, Truud should be made to wear your soaked pantaloons, for shame.'

'And then?'

'Then, I shall spank her bottom.'

'That's ridiculous!' Truud cried.

'Please put on the wet pants,' said Habren.

'No!'

'Obey!' said Jan. 'You are a Vandal woman!'

Truud glanced from Habren to Jan, then to Joss, and at the impassive Aggar. Her lip trembled.

'I've never been spanked before,' she said. 'Perhaps I do deserve it. My loss of self-control was unacceptable . . .'

She rose, turned her back on the others and slid down her khaki shorts, beneath which she had no knickers. The golden melons of her croup gleamed in the candlelight, their tan unbroken by strapmarks. She stepped into the wet pantaloons and pulled them up tight, so that the stained red fabric clung to her vulval folds, arse-cleft and fesses.

'My chamber is at your disposal, if you'd prefer Jan spanked you in private,' Habren said.

Truud glanced from one face to the other, at the crotches of the three males, all astir. She licked her teeth and rubbed her wet buttocks, pulling the pantaloons as tight as she could, with her finger lodged in her crack. Slowly, she unfastened the buttons of her shirt, opening it to her midriff and, finally, letting it slide to the floor, to bare her golden breasts, topped with dark red nipples already stiff.

'No,' she whispered, 'I'd like you all to watch.'

Truud bent over, supporting herself on tiptoes and fingertips, with her legs apart, her bottom thrust high and her firm, massive teats hanging like golden marrows below her ribs; she rolled the wet pantaloons to her ankles, leaving the bare melons of her bum taut and trembling in the firelight, with droplets of wine dribbling into her jungle of blond pubic curls.

'To avoid further mess,' she said, 'it is better I should be spanked on my bare arse.'

Jan took position behind his twin's bare bum and raised his arm.

'I have never spanked her before,' he said.

'Have you spanked any girl before?' said Habren.

'I . . . yes, I have.'

'*Jan!*' cried Truud, though without shifting from her submissive posture.

'Then you know about relaxing the buttocks with a warming-up, the building of pain until the subject crosses her threshold, after which a beating may continue indefinitely . . .'

Smack!

'*Oh!*'

Truud's fesses trembled at Jan's first spank.

'Be quiet!' hissed Jan.

Smack! Smack! Smack!

'*Ohh . . .! It hurts!*'

The golden bum-flans began to clench and quiver.

Smack! Smack! Smack! Smack!

'*Ahhh . . .!*'

Truud's naked arse jerked as each spank bruised her smooth flesh, leaving spanker's red marks on her bum-skin. Her long legs shuddered and her arms trembled; at each spank, her titties wobbled violently. Jan frowned, his eyes fixed on his twin's bare bum; his cock bulged proud. He continued the spanking to a hundred slaps, Truud's wails growing more subdued, until his blows drew only a grunt from her. The posture had steadied, the legs and arms holding firm, although the fesses clenched tight before and after each flurry of four or five spanks. Jan dripped with sweat, his penis now rock-hard under his garment.

'Perhaps you would like to make yourself more comfortable, Jan,' said Habren.

Jan looked round, seeing her eyes on his erect cock, and her fingers slipping in and out of her loinstring as she rubbed herself between the thighs. Unsmiling, he shed his shirt and unzipped his shorts, letting them fall, to reveal his stiff cock. Truud looked round and whimpered, as Habren handed Jan a short, whippy cane. The girl's bottom was a smooth blossom of scarlet, dappled by the imprints of her spanker's fingertips. Habren raised her tabard over her breasts and stroked her own stiff nipples, kneading the plums between finger and thumb; her cunt-bush gleamed with come seeping from her wanked pouch.

'You said nothing about *caning*!' blurted Truud, bitterly. 'I suppose you caned those . . . those *sluts*!'

Habren's hand clamped the girl's cunt, rubbing her hard on the swollen gash flaps, and emerged dripping with Truud's own come.

'You are sopping! If spanking turns you on, then think what a caning must do,' Habren said. 'Twenty-one brisk stingers should teach her pleasure . . . Joss! Keep your hands behind your back, you whelp!'

'*No . . .!*' Truud moaned, but braced herself, thighs and bum taut, at the whistle of the cane.

Vip!

'*Oh!*'

Vip!

'*Ah!*'

Vip! Vip! Vip!

'*Ahh . . . Mm!*'

Her bare buttocks squirmed as the cane laid fine pink stripes on the golden skin, and her legs trembled like reeds.

Vip! Vip! Vip!

'*Oh . . . oh . . . ach, nee . . .*'

Eyes tight shut, Truud's head jerked from side to side, her teeth alternately gritting in a wall of white, or slackening to let her tongue loll from her lips, slimed with drool, as her cunt oozed come over her inner thighs. The force of the strokes banged her quivering titties together like bells of flesh, her nipples too stiff to avoid jarring.

Jan slackened the pace of his caning, taking careful aim and placing his strokes so as to cover the whole bottom. The legs quivered at each cut of the rod; Truud's ankles pushed the elastic of the wine-dark pantaloons to bursting. Her face was crimson, her eyes flodded with tears, yet, between canestrokes, there was a plopping sound as come dripped from her writhing cunt on to the puddled gusset of Habren's harem pants.

Still masturbating, Habren knelt and, with a swift, birdlike swoop of her head, took the glans of Jan's erect cock between her lips. She sucked his glans while he dealt three more strokes to the crimson bare of his sister, then, at the next, plunged her head to engorge his cock, right to his balls. Habren wanked herself vigorously, come streaming from her tangled pube-hairs as she sucked the Vandal's cock. Her husband watched, his own cock throbbing against his silk robe. Jan dealt the twenty-first stroke and flung aside the cane, using both hands to press Habren's blond tresses to his loins. She shook her head, opened her mouth and withdrew.

'I've better use for you,' she panted, licking drool from her chin, 'and for your twin sister. She is more than your sister, though – *isn't she*?'

She accompanied her question with a nip to the skin of his ball-sac, beneath his orbs, after which her palm cupped his balls entire.

'*Ah!* I admit it,' he gasped. 'We share and *pleasure* each other . . . *but my sister's cunt is virgin*!'

Habren snapped her fingers and Joss stepped forward.

'Husband,' she snapped, 'do the bitch in her bumhole.'

Still holding Jan's cock, she pushed Truud's body prone on to the stone floor, where the girl wriggled in a pool of her own come, her legs still locked by the waistband of the silk pantaloons. Habren prised apart her wealed, crimson buttocks and stuck her index in the girl's anus. Truud screamed. Aggar moved from the room and the faint whir of a film camera started as Joss doffed his robe and stood erect before Truud's squirming buttocks.

'Please, no . . .' groaned Jan, as Habren rolled his balls in her palm like dice.

Joss dropped on top of Truud and his swollen helmet poked her anus pucker. He thrust three or four times before penetrating her a few inches. Sweat poured from his muscular body as he thrust at the arse-shaft, until Truud moaned, her body sagged, and Joss cried in triumph as his cock sank into her anal elastic, right to his balls. His arse began to pump vigorously as he buggered the girl.

'*Nnngh! Urrgh!*'

Truud moaned, drooling and slapping her chin against the flagstones. Yet her buttocks parted and began to thrust in time with her buggery, as the fesses squeezed suck Joss's cock, holding it at the root of her anus; her sobs grew to squeals of pleasure.

'Yes . . . *yes* . . . fuck me harder . . . *ahh* . . .!'

Come gushed from her cunt, squelching and slapping the floor. Jan grimaced and sighed, his cock rigid.

'The first time you've seen her fucked by another man?'

'*Yes* . . . oh, damn you!'

Habren, smiling, squeezed Jan's balls. Joss grunted as he spurted his spunk into Truud's bumhole.

'*Ach . . . Jazeker! Ja . . .!*'

Her belly clapped the floor as she writhed in her own orgasm. Habren drew Joss from the girl's writhing bum and herself squatted over it. Tickling Jan's balls and flicking his peehole with a thumbnail, she pissed heavily, splattering the girl's raw cane weals with golden fluid, then ordered Joss to kneel and lick her cunt clean. As her husband's lips and tongue slobbered in her swollen pouch, Habren flopped Truud on to her back and ripped the pantaloons from her. She delivered the last of her pee directly into the garment's gusset, stained with wine and slimed with her come. Aggar approached and knelt by his mistress, buckling a strap-on dildo around her waist. Habren released Jan's balls and forced Truud's come-soaked thighs apart, squatting over her, ready to fuck. The tip of her pink, knobbled dildo touched Truud's clitoris and the girl shuddered, moaning. Drool flecked her lips.

'*No . . . please . . . enough . . .!*'

Habren ordered Jan to bugger her own arse from the rear, while she fucked his twin's virgin cunt with the strap-on. She bound the piss-soaked pantaloons tightly around Truud's trembling titties, so that the breast-flesh was pinioned and swelled, puffy and wrinkled, from its bonds. Truud squealed and was silenced as Habren stuffed the dripping gusset of the pantaloons into her mouth, gagging her. Truud's eyes were wide as Habren parted her bum-cheeks and Jan mounted her. Habren's dildo pierced Truud's wet cunt, just before her own anus yielded to Jan's cock-thrusts and she groaned 'Yes . . .!' as his tool pounded her arse-root.

Habren fucked the squirming, sobbing Truud with her dildo, its gnarled extrusions catching her swollen clitty at each stroke, in the same rhythm that Jan buggered her, their strokes becoming faster. Truud gasped, crushed under the weight of two bodies and, if she closed her eyes, Habren slapped her.

'Look at the brute!' she hissed. 'Your twin, your lover . . . bum-fucking another woman! See, he loves it! Jan, fuck me harder! Bugger me deep . . .!'

Habren's buttocks clutched the penis that impaled her, her fesses clenched and wriggling fiercely, as if to suck in his ball-sac. Her husband knelt before her, erect again, and presented his cock to her lips. Habren snarled that Joss had earned a flogging, not a spurt.

'Bring me a real man,' she hissed, 'and watch us – hands behind your back, worm.'

Her husband summoned Aggar and watched as the black man's cock plunged to the back of his wife's throat; buggered, fucking the squealing girl and her mouth impaled on the giant black cock, Habren sucked Aggar, until creamy spunk burst from her lips. Jan cried out as his own spunk flooded Habren's anus and frothed at her pucker; Truud sobbed, pissing copiously, as the dildo rammed her cunt, tickling her clit to orgasm.

Gasping, they rose. Habren picked up the cane and threw it between Truud's legs. She pulled the gag from her mouth and untied her bound breasts, which sprang back to fullness, their golden skin turned white in bondage.

'You may cane my worm of a husband,' she said. 'A good fifteen on the bare, while he licks your piss from my floor.'

Truud shivered and said shyly, 'I'd rather lick up my own mess, if you don't mind, even if it's my bare that takes the cane. I cannot hurt anyone.'

'*Do it*, then, Truud . . . as you *intended.*'

'I don't understand.'

'The road map was in *your* purse and in *your* handwriting?'

'Why, yes, but –'

'You have the route sketched in turquoise ink and the places you've stopped marked in black. Yet the turquoise route doesn't go to the Gold Coast. *It stops here.* The halt wasn't to fix your vehicle, it was to fix *you.* My film sets are no secret. You *knew* you would find Vandals . . .'

Truud smiled as she began to lick the floor clean of her pee and come. She wiggled her bare arse and slapped her buttocks with wide, appealing eyes.

'I wanted to surprise Jan,' she said. 'He is addicted to your films and the practices in them. If he can cane *sluts*' – Jan growled – 'it's only fair he should serve *me* . . .'

Vip!

'*Ahh!*'

Jan lashed his twin sister's bare bum.

'My arse has waited so long,' panted Truud, as her buttocks clenched for caning, the square of pink brocade, a fluttering pennant, in her anus.

# 10

# Snout Run

Angarad's cell door slid open and Isobel Coker entered, closing the door quickly behind her. Angarad, sitting on her bunk, wearing only her plain white cotton nightie, cringed a moment, then gave a guarded smile and sprang to attention. Her stinker's uniform bra and string knickers lay, folded neatly, on her grey blanket.

'It's only me,' Isobel said. 'Smoke? I've half a rollie left.'

She lit up and the two girls sucked hungrily on the scragend of tobacco.

'I thought strokes always had full pouches,' said Angarad.

'We strokes are more like slags than you imagine,' Isobel replied. 'Most of us *are* former slags.'

'I know, mum. But not you.'

'Would you be afraid if another warden visited you?'

'It's not my place to say, mum,' said Angarad, averting her gaze.

'But some of them like to make a surprise inspection after lights out? And whop you, bare bum?'

'I'm only a stinker, mum,' Angarad sighed, 'with a pink sticker for *pervert.* A warden may do as she pleases.'

'I suppose I'm something of a stinker, myself,' Isobel said, 'as a newcomer. You *are* a pervert, aren't you?'

'Mum, in a week here,' Angarad replied, 'I've given up trying to persuade people otherwise. I've given up trying to persuade myself! I'm a pervert. The system says so. If I'm whopped, it's because I deserve it.'

'But do you *like* whopping? Remember, you came here with a well-striped arse.'

'Not my choice, mum.'

'You haven't answered my question. Raise your nightie, stinker, and show me your bum!'

At once, Angarad obeyed, taking the hem of her nightie between her teeth and bending over her bunk, her arms and thighs stretched wide, with her hands clutching the ends of the bunk, as though to take a beating. Isobel ran her fingers down fresh dark welts on Angarad's bare arse.

'Who did *that*?' she whispered.

'Perhaps Miss Brand, mum. She roped and flogged me last night with her belt, fifty lashes. Or, perhaps Miss Maclaren. She gave me an enema yesterday and caned me fifteen, while my arse filled. I've taken a dozen from Miss Garce and Miss Forge and Miss Oates and . . . well, from almost all the strokes. They all seem to have their own . . . preferences, with a new stinker's bum – with *my* bum! – as a testing ground. Miss Oates likes her cane, Miss Brand ropes my wrists and ankles like a pony, Miss Garce makes me swallow my own panties as a gag while she canes my bare! I've never been flogged in public, so my book is clean! I watched Ghislaine Bassin take two dozen, with the rubber ten-thong whip, on her back from Miss Tite, then two dozen with the cane on the bare bum from Miss Brand, and we had to eat while we watched. It was horrible! Afterwards, Ghislaine showed us her bruises, as though she was proud of them and . . . and wanked off as we touched her. Ghislaine said she'd been sentenced to the labyrinth, twice . . . but she wouldn't tell, even when two Saracens slippered her bare bum with a gym shoe – and I held her down! She *made* me! The bitch!'

Angarad's breasts and buttocks quivered as her spine shook. She grimaced, sobbing.

'Ghislaine is my trusty, as gym mistress,' said Isobel. 'But she seems to court trouble, almost on purpose. She takes an owner's delight in the punishment apparatus you stinkers must polish with your quim-bushes every day. Has Miss Tite taken an interest in you?'

'Miss Tite caned me two dozen on bare, mum, as I'm sure you know,' said Angarad bitterly. 'She caught Ghislaine and me wanking off, as Ghislaine was showing me her scars. Ghislaine got another two dozen with the cane, on top of her public thrashing. This prison is not . . . what I was led to expect, mum.'

'Did Miss Tite do anything else?'

Angarad was silent; Isobel slapped her bare left fesse, hard, and Angarad winced, briefly closing her eyes.

'Did she tool your bumhole with a strap-on?'

'I'd prefer not to say, mum.'

'I'll take that as a yes. I could cane you for insolence, bare as you stand,' said Isobel.

'Yes, mum.'

'Would you enjoy it, Angarad? The same as you *enjoyed* Miss Tite's bumming?'

Angarad paused. Isobel took her warden's cane from her belt, raised it over Angarad's quivering bare arse-flans and struck them.

Vip!

The cane left a faint pink weal, overlaying her darker, older bruises. Angarad shivered and gasped.

'*Would you enjoy it, Angarad?*'

Angarad stretched her legs and curled a foot around the legs of her bunk, so that her buttocks were fully parted, showing the arse-cleft, the cunt and the thick pubic bush dangling shiny and moist beneath the gash flaps. Her eyes were fixed ahead on the wall and she swallowed.

Vip!

Angarad's buttocks clenched but her spread was too wide to shield her cleft; the cane drew a raw stripe right across the fesses, just above the exposed anal pucker.

'*Would you, miss?*'

Angarad was silent, her face red and her lips pressed shut.

Vip! Vip! Vip!

Three strokes took her on top buttock, just below the spinal nubbin where her skin was thinnest.

'*Uhh . . .!*'

Angarad's bare fesses began to squirm, writhing in slow undulation, yet unable to meet in defence of her exposed holes, as her toes kept their lock on the iron bedpost.

Vip!

'*Ah!*'

Isobel thrashed her anus bud.

Vip! Vip! Vip! Vip!

Four slices followed, two on each haunch, and pinking at once.

'*Oh! Oh; God, mum!*'

'You haven't . . .'

Vip! Vip! Vip!

'*Ahh . . .!*'

The bare arse squirmed frantically, as the pink welts deepened to crimson, new slices landing in first weal.

'. . . answered . . .'

Vip! Vip! Vip!

'*God, it hurts! Please, no . . .*'

Vip! Vip! Vip! Vip!

'*Ahh . . . ahh . . .!*'

Four more haunch-cuts made Angarad's whole body jerk and shudder as though in spasm; her spine and legs writhed in unison; droplets of fluid welled at the tips of her pubic bush: lengthening, stretching into pearls of come, preparing to splatter the stone floor between her quivering thighs. Isobel's face was as red as her victim's; she, too, swallowed and her hand crept under her skirt, already moist at the crotch, to her panties' gusset, where she began a slow frotting as she raised her cane.

Vip! Vip! Vip! Vip!

'*AHH . . .!*'

'. . . *my question!*'

Angarad's entire body trembled; tears coursed down her cheeks, dropping to the tips of her erect nipples, as drips of come splashed beneath her juicing cunt, sliming the floor.

Vip!

'*Would* you . . .'

Vip!

'... enjoy it ...'
Vip!
'... if I caned you ...'
Vip!
'... *on the bare?*'
At every stroke of her cane on Angarad's threshing bare bum-flans, Isobel's fingers pressed her clitoris, the panties thrust aside to bare her own bush and cunt lips to her masturbating fingers. Her stocking tops, garter straps and naked inner thighs were wet with her own come. Isobel gasped out loud and Angarad's head twisted to look.
Vip! Vip! Vip!
Isobel's response was furious, with three cuts across top buttock, the delicate skin already puffy and crimsoned.
'*Ahh ...!*' Angarad screamed, sobbing bitterly. 'It's OK, mum. All the strokes wank off when they cane me ...'
'*Cheeky bitch!* Still not answering ...'
Vip!
'... a simple ...'
Vip!
'... *question!*'
Come dripped copiously from Angarad's cunt; her face, glowing as red as her caned arse, wrinkled tightly in a grimace, but her only sound was a soft, choking hiccup. Her body quivered, titties and arse-flans clenching like pairs of leather bellows. Hanging beneath her the nipples were so stiff and swollen; they seemed like big new dugs grown from her breasts.
'Beating excites you, miss.'
Vip! Vip!
A pair of strokes on the haunches.
'Ah ... ah ...'
'Admit it!'
Vip! Vip!
Two, slanting on inner thighs, beneath the cunt lips.
'*OWW! Oh, mum ...!*'
Vip! Isobel dealt an upender, right between the wet flaps of Angarad's gash.
'*AHH!*'

Angarad's scream filled her cell, yet the come trickled from between the lashed flaps in a steady flow of clear oily juice.

'Your pouch speaks for you, miss,' Isobel panted, her knuckles pummelling the wet walls of her own cunt. 'You'd like me to wank you off, miss? Perhaps you'll answer *that* question. Damn you, damn all *submissives* . . .!'

Vip!

Another upender took Angarad squarely on her distended bum pucker; she squealed and nodded, gasping harshly.

'*Ah!* I need it for my shame. I need to be beaten, for the badness in me . . .'

Isobel completed Angarad's caning with a crisp three that had the girl gasping and her bum wincing, but now Isobel's fingers were on Angarad's cunt, wrenching at the swollen gash flaps and distended clitoris. Angarad's come slopped on Isobel's wrist as her fist penetrated the girl's cunt, and Isobel laid down her cane on the bunk.

'We are so alike,' she gasped. 'We could be twins. You could fit into my uniform and I . . . I could so well fit your submission . . .'

Her thumb frotted Angarad's swollen clitty, while her fingers clenched, spreading inside the girl's gash. Isobel wanked off her own cunt, her panties, garter straps and stockings now a mess of oily come.

'Make yourself comfortable on your bunk, miss,' gasped Isobel. 'I ask permission to join you.'

Angarad slumped, stretching her nude body belly down, with her glowing arse raised, her head at the foot of her bunk and her bare feet on the pillow. Isobel lowered her own head within inches of Angarad's feet, while her cunt danced before the girl's face.

'*Yes, mum*,' sobbed Angarad. 'To *all* your questions.'

Shafts of moonlight streaked the darkness of the cell, where two female bodies, one in prison officer's uniform, the other gooseflesh-naked, writhed in tribadic embrace. The uniformed girl's head was plunged between the open naked thighs, her nose and mouth frotting wet cunt, while the naked girl moaned, her head beneath black skirt, and tongue flickering on a fleshy red nubbin, standing stiff amid swollen cunt folds and damp forest of pubic curls.

'I have this . . .' one whispered and the other giggled, her giggle freezing to a gasp, as a dry corn cob easily penetrated her gushing wet cunt.

'Oh, yes . . .' she moaned. 'Oh, fuck me there . . . you use it to wank?'

'I must,' whispered the second tribadist, nude, her fingers expertly manoeuvring the makeshift dildo under the uniform skirt panties, rhythmically, in and out of the wriggling girl's pouch. 'I'm . . . I'm *too big*. Feel for yourself.'

Isobel, nude, manipulated Angarad's fingers into her own gushing slit, then the cavern of her vulva.

'Wank me,' she pleaded. 'Fist-fuck me.'

Angarad lifted her head and licked her lips, drooled with Isobel's cunt-slime. She replaced her tongue with her balled fist, sliding it easily into the naked warden's cunt.

'It is nice to be warm at night,' she whispered, as she masturbated nude, writhing Isobel, whose own mouth, clamped on the wet blond pubic jungle, continued to lap the flow of Angarad's come. 'They give you a nightie and a blanket, just enough to stop you freezing but not enough to be cosy.'

'It's part of your discipline,' gasped Isobel, as Angarad's fist slammed the neck of her womb and the girl's forearm plunged two inches into her cunt. 'God, a hot fist is better than a cob.'

'Ohh . . .' Angarad moaned, as the corn cob fucked her own flowing cunt. 'That's good . . . it is funny, but nice, to be wearing your clothes. But why, mum?'

'Call me Isobel!'

'You can't make me, mum!' said Angarad, pausing in her gamahuche of her squirming partner. 'I don't trust you, or anybody.'

'I can make you,' Isobel hissed. 'I've read your file.'

Isobel suddenly plucked the cob from Angarad's cunt, straddled her and forced her buttocks apart. The cob, oiled from Angarad's gash, slid into her anus smoothly to a depth of three inches, with Angarad squirming violently; then conquered as the anal elastic gave way.

'*Ohh . . .*' Angarad squealed, her anus gripping the dildo, '*yes . . .!*'

'You *are* a pervert,' Isobel continued.

'And *you* aren't?'

'*OOH!*'

Angarad shrieked as Isobel slammed the dildo hard on her anal root. Her fingers rubbed her nubbin, masturbating vigorously, as she writhed under the corn cob's buggery.

'*Oh! I'm coming*,' Angarad blurted.

'Yes, yes, *yes . . .*' gasped Isobel.

There was silence as two faces sank back on to open cunts, teeth and lips kissing swollen nubbins, as come slopped from their writhing cunt flaps and they panted together in orgasm.

'I have seduced you,' whispered Isobel, as a chilly grey dawn broke through the cell window. 'You took forty strokes from my cane, on the bare, without cause. Now you must punish me.'

'Since when does a stroke need cause –' Angarad began.

'*You must punish me!* Take my cane and give me forty strokes on the bare, *stinker*!'

Angarad rose from the bunk, smoothed down her stroke's uniform and lifted the cane. She laid it in Isobel's bum-cleft, across the cunt and anus bud; Isobel shivered, then brushed back her blond mane before spreading her thighs and gripping the bunk ends with her hands.

'I've never – I've never caned a girl's bare before,' said Angarad, then blurted: 'What's in it for me, *mum*?'

'You've heard of the snout run,' said Isobel hoarsely. 'I want you to go, dressed in my uniform.'

'Cycling to Oswald's shop in the village, for tobacco?' said Angarad drily. 'I hear he's well built . . . fit to service a box like yours, mum.'

'It's my turn but I'm scared,' Isobel whimpered. 'He won't fuck me where I want – *need* it – in my pouch. He likes it only in a girl's bumhole – his tastes are yours, Angarad – he is a confirmed pervert, a . . . a *bugger*.'

'You cheeky *fucking bitch*!' Angarad blurted. 'Right! I'll do the snout run, for a half ounce for me . . .'

'Yes! Agreed!'

'And I'll cane you till you beg for mercy, bitch!'

'Oh! Yes . . .!'

'Forty on the bare, *Isobel*,' Angarad hissed, her hand trembling as much as the bare girl's buttocks that lay under her whistling cane.

Sunrise was only a faint gleam in the cloud mass, as Angarad pedalled, standing up, along the bank of the River Wrigley: five miles to the bridge, another five across the moors to the village. It was an air chill enough to bite the bones. Her bicycle skidded in the slush but only with reluctance did she permit herself the comfort of sitting: the bike, all that she could borrow – *steal!* – from the wardens' shed, had a saddle that was almost no saddle at all, but a simple steel tube tilting upwards, in the dimension of an outsize phallus. To sit meant a constant shifting of the buttocks to avoid the prong from penetrating either of her nether holes; at best, it stuck awkwardly against her spinal nubbin, leaving her perched, with her long legs stretched to the full to reach the pedals.

A moss-covered stone bridge, steeply arched, led over the Wrigley's pebbly stream and Angarad dismounted to cross it. On the other bank, a wall of scrub obscured the road, with broad undulating dale stretching to the prison, now a specked cluster, and the village, faintly visible through the misty air. She remounted the cycle, forgetting the oddly formed saddle and gasped as the tube penetrated her cleft and pushed her loinstring into her vulva to a depth of three inches. Angarad began to rise, got the hem of her warden's raincoat caught in the chain and, with a curse, sank back on to the saddle to free herself. There was a snap of knicker-cloth; this time, the prong penetrated her cunt, right to Angarad's wombneck.

Swallowing hard, Angarad adjusted her raincoat and sat astride the cycle, with her feet on the roadway, before hoisting them once more to the pedals and pushing on, a faint grin playing on her lips, as her thighs pumped and the prong slid rhythmically in and out of her gash. A seep of vulval fluid moistened the tops of her stockings and she leaned, so that the prong thrust against her naked clitoris. Her face reddened as she progressed beside open, rolling dales, and her grin turned to a frown. She stopped, shook her head, gulped and raised her buttocks a few inches, replacing them at once on the saddle – but now so that the come-slimed prong plunged into her anal cavity. She wriggled, getting the tool well inside her anus, gasped, then pedalled on. As her buttocks worked the cylinder further and further to her anal root, her cunt continued to seep heavy come, over her thighs and wet stockings.

After a mile, the mist became a fog and the village, nestling in its valley, disappeared. A tinkling of cowbells filled the air; Angarad pedalled further, gasping as the saddle anally tooled her and her vehicle veering as the pumping of her thighs drove the tube hard against her arse-root. Above the cowbells, whips cracked and female voices yelped. Rounding a bend in the road, Angarad faced a flat heath, bordered by scrubs that concealed her from view. She did not dismount but propped the cycle with her feet and crouched low over the handlebars, keeping her arse-slit on the saddle and her bare buttocks, shrouded by her raincoat, moving gently up and down on the oily dildo. She fished in Isobel's raincoat pocket, found a plastic tobacco pouch with two half-rollies and a matchbox and, with trembling hands, lit a cigarette, careful to blow smoke away from the spectacle on the snow-drifted heath. It was a chariot race.

The chariots were crudely crafted boxes of wood, on spokeless wheels, made of planks nailed crosswise, bound in metal strips, and rounded. Each of the two chariots was drawn by girls in harness, whipped on by its driver, a girl in fur, that parted at each whipstroke to reveal bare legs and breasts. The drivers were Ignoge Brand and Althea Tite: the steeds were pairs of nude girls, in bits, hobbled in horse-shoes and strapped tightly in rubber harnesses. Under Ignoge, Clare Cubitt was teamed with Emma Beare and under Althea, Ingrid Fage with June Thorbeck. Each chariot flew a pennant: Goths versus Franks.

Each nude girl had cowbells pinned through her nipples and cunt flaps and, at each thrash to their pumping bare buttocks, the bells jangled. Their harnesses clutched the ribcages, forcing the titties up, and circled the crotch, waist and buttocks. Each girl's vulva was filled with a leather pizzle attached to her harness, that pumped in and out of her slimed cunt as she raced. The chariots were cumbersome and moved at a creaking pace, scarcely faster than a bicycle's; yet both Ignoge and Althea, glaring furiously at each other and at their animals, whooped and threatened as though at a horserace.

Vap! Vap! Vap!

'Giddy-up, you bitches!'

Vap! Vap! Vap!

'Faster, sluts!'

The wheels hissed in the slushy snow, as the long hide whips cracked on the striped backs and buttocks of the draft animals. Each whiplash across their naked flesh drew mewling cries from the pony-girls. All four were scarlet and panting, their faces streaked with tears, yet with copious cunt-slime oozing from their shafted pouches, trickling over their thighs and leaving hot droplets in the snow. Tracks circled the arena over a number of laps; the cries of both drivers suggested the finish was near. Both Althea and Ignoge were wild, with all modesty forgotten as they lashed their animals: their fur coats flew, revealing both girls nude beneath, with their discarded warden's uniforms strapped to the backs of their carts. Unlike the hobbled pony-girls, they were barefoot, clinging with their toes to the sides of their vehicles.

A knot of bottom strokes, in uniform, stood in the distance, holding flags to mark the finishing line. The chariots were neck and neck, their drivers' whips a blur as they thrashed the livid, bruised bums and shoulders of the naked pony-girls. As their arms rose and fell, slabs of hair gleamed at their armpits. Seconds before the finishing line, Ignoge Brand turned and lashed Althea hard across her exposed bare breasts. Althea screamed, dropped her whip and almost toppled from her chariot.

Unwhipped, Ingrid and June slackened their pace to a stumble and the Goth chariot cruised past them across the finishing line, to applause from the spectators. No sooner was Ignoge Brand surrounded by the cheering bottom strokes, than Althea leapt from her chariot and threw aside her fur coat. Her lariat flew, trapping Ignoge around her breasts and dragging her to the slushy ground. Althea forced her way through the throng, lifted Ignoge's soaked fur over her head and sat on her face. She folded her whip in two and began to flog Ignoge on the bare bottom. Ignoge howled, writhing, as her arse-globes turned scarlet with the cuts from the double whip-thong, and the bottom strokes cheered her humiliance as they had her victory. Althea whipped Ignoge's bare for twenty strokes, until the reddened arse-pears squirmed in the helpless rhythm of the flogged girl's shrieks. Althea paused to acknowledge the cheers, permitting Ignoge to twist in the slush and topple her chastiser. In the tussle, Ignoge slipped from her fur and both girls grappled nude, clawing at hair, quim and breasts: until Ignoge drew back, feinted and landed a barefoot kick between the folds of Althea's cunt.

Althea screamed and doubled up, clutching her crotch; Ignoge followed with a kick to Althea's pendant bare teats, toppling the taller girl. Ignoge pressed Althea's face into the snow and picked up the whip. She began to flog her aggressor as hard as she herself had been flogged, to the same cheers. Several of the wardens rubbed their crotches under their raincoats or, blatantly, had the coats open and wanked off, with knuckles grinding beneath exposed knickers. The four steeds pawed the ground and snorted, like real ponies, but with smiles and gasps, as each pony-girl rubbed the buttocks and wanked the naked cunt of her partner. Belinda Garce and Amy Patel smiled, hands busy frotting beneath their panties, as each masturbated the other. Angarad moved her own buttocks in stealthy rhythm on the tubular saddle impaling her anus and her fingers fumbled beneath Isobel's raincoat and skirt, meeting no resistance from the panties, already split by the saddle tube. She moaned softly, wanking off faster and faster, as she watched the helpless, wriggling buttocks of Althea turn red, then crimson, under the stronger girl's whipstrokes.

Ignoge flipped the screaming Althea over on to her back and began whipping her bare breasts, lashing hard on the nipples; then flogging the raw red gash between the cunt flaps, swollen and shiny with slime. Angarad fingered her swollen clitty, ramming the tube all the way to her anal root, again and again, with her legs stiff and shuddering, threatening to buckle, as waves of pleasure coursed through her belly and spine. Althea's resistance ebbed and she opened her thighs wide to the whip, her own fingers masturbating her cunt. Watching her, Angarad let her belly heave; a gush of cunt oil signalled her onrush of climax and, fingers working her stiff nubbin as the metal tube buggered her, she began to gasp in orgasm. Droplets of her cunt slime, like flower petals, patterned the snow beneath her quivering thighs.

'Well, Miss Coker,' said Miss Horsfall, several feet behind Angarad, who jumped in shock and looked round, drawing her woolly scarf over her mouth and nose.

Miss Horsfall sat at the wheel of her dark green Bentley motorcar. She wore a fur coat, like the two racers.

'Going to the village, so early, Isobel?' she drawled.

Angarad nodded, drawing her scarf up, so that only her eyes were visible.

'I like to watch the semi-finals and, of course, the final,' said Miss Horsfall, 'although the dear girls think I don't know. That's why they race so far from prison . . . I dare say Ignoge has won this for the Goths, despite her little naughtiness at the finish – but who said life was fair? Of course, it scarcely matters, as the Vandals always seem to win anyway. Speaking of fair, I do hope that new girl, Angarad Stark, isn't in thrall of some gang. She seems such a delight – almost your twin.'

'I certainly wouldn't know, mum,' said Angarad, imitating Isobel's Durham accent.

'Such an unfortunate word, "gang",' sighed Miss Horsfall. 'It reeks of the lower classes. Yet prisoners must have some outlet for their . . . girlish enthusiasms, and it helps if they think we ignore or even condone it. That is the beauty of our British system: the only crime is getting caught or, worse, swanking in victory. Now, I would place Angarad as a decent bare-breast boxer. She has the agility, although it would be a shame to see those pretty teats take the drubbing in store for them. Come to think of it, Isobel, you might consider taking up boxing yourself, if only as a referee. The girls fight in loinstrings, bare-breasted and bare-knuckled, but with the ladylike refinement that victory is decided by securing possession of the opponent's undergarment rather than by knocking her down.'

'I'll consider it, mum,' mumbled Angarad.

'Well, I mustn't detain you, Miss Coker. If you call at the village shop, you might ask Oswald if that shipment of claret has arrived for me. I do like to patronise the traditional English shop, not these ghastly supermarkets, and of course Oswald Pollecutt is the bearer of a fine name in these parts.'

'Oswald *Pollecutt*, mum?'

'Why, yes. Wrigley Scrubs itself was bequeathed to the nation by his forebear, Sir George. Our labyrinth – to whose oppressions it is sometimes my duty to sentence an unruly girl – is said to be modelled on the great labyrinth of Oum El Hanch, discovered by Sir George in the Moroccan desert, when he was deputy governor of Tangier.'

The glove-box of Miss Horsfall's car was not fully closed and from it jutted a leather pizzle, like the dildos attached to the racing girls' harnesses: like them, it was shiny with oil. Miss Horsfall shifted in her seat, permitting her fur coat to fall open for an instant, before she gathered it in. She wore silk stockings, suspenders and garter straps but no knickers, and her luxuriant cunt bush glistened with come.

'You appear to be riding what, I believe, is called a "Vandal" bicycle, Miss Coker.'

'I wasn't aware, mum,' Angarad stammered.

'It must be rather uncomfortable.'

'No . . . not really, mum.'

'Of course, a ticketed pervert, like Miss Angarad Stark, would find such a vehicle entirely to her satisfaction. I recall apprehending the detainee Susan Race – now released – on what is called a "snout run", riding such a contraption. I let her complete her errand, but running in her stockings, holding her shoes in her teeth, with her skirts pinned up, while *I* rode her cycle, caning her on the bare, all the way into the village. Forty-three strokes in all, and quite as painful for me as it was for her . . .'

'I am sure she merited them, mum.'

'What were you looking at, just now, Miss Stark? When my coat fell from my thighs?'

'Why, nothing, mum! *Wait a minute – what –?*'

'You are Angarad Stark, miss,' said Miss Horsfall. 'You may have seduced, or overpowered, your lookalike, Miss Coker, but you cannot hide your pervert's eyes. So innocent and beguiling, yet begging for chastisement.'

'Oh, please, mum!' Angarad wailed, throwing aside her scarf. '*I can explain –*'

'Of course you can, but think – do you *wish* to?'

Angarad bit her lip and swallowed. Tears formed at her eyes.

'No, mum.'

Miss Horsfall clapped and once more her fur fell away, revealing her unpantied pubic bush and the leather car seat slimed beneath her bare bum. She did not recover herself.

'The correct answer, Angarad! Whatever you say, you are in trouble, and implicating Miss Coker would make things worse – possibly for her as well. Such a delicious dilemma! Were you masturbating as you watched the chariot race?'

'Yes, mum,' blurted Angarad, her face scarlet and moist with tears.

'*With the prong pleasuring your pervert's anus.*'

There was silence, for a moment.

'Yes, mum,' Angarad whispered, sobbing. '*Yes . . .*'

'You shall continue about your business and take your tea early this afternoon. Then you shall be caned publicly, while the other girls take theirs. I expect you to be in your own uniform and Miss Coker in hers.'

'Yes, mum. Thank you, mum. I'm so sorry, mum.'

'Please give my fond regards to Oswald.'

'Yes, mum.'

Miss Horsfall slipped her car into first gear. Her fur coat shifted, revealing a square of brocade clinging to her bare right buttock.

'Oh, and a week or so after your public flogging, miss, you shall spend a night in the labyrinth.'

# 11

# Twin Prongs

The village of Wrigley Scrubs sat grey and gloomy, like an extrusion of the bleak scrubland around it. There was an inn and a street of huddled dwellings, but no church and a single shop bearing the legend 'Jos. Pollecutt, Esq., Haberdasher and Licensed Victualler' in gothic script. The River Wrigley looped sluggishly behind the terrace where the shop squatted. The shop door tinkled, with the same cowbell as was fastened to the nipple or quim of a chariot girl. Inside, the air was foggy with warmth from a blazing log fire in a cast-iron fireplace, the metal design showing interlaced female bodies, nude and thrashed by impish cupids with erect penises for wings. Tongs, pokers, and leather bellows hung on either side of the fireplace, above a pair of brass fire dogs, their metal bodies dancing with light. Above the fireplace, an antique enamel sign proclaimed that 'Pinkar's Brandy Will Bring A Glow To Your Cheeks'. Goods were piled at random: unopened cases of wines and spirits; corsets and corselets of leather, nylon, rubber and pink brocade; shears, ploughshares, bullwhips, riding crops, harnesses, bits and buckles; cheeses, hams and haunches of meat, hanging on ceiling hooks; blocks of compacted rolling tobacco and boxes of cigars. Perfumed smoke trickled from a censer, hanging above the glowing logs in the fireplace. The shop was unattended; Angarad wiped sweat from her brow and removed her raincoat, folding it over her arm. She passed some minutes touching the items displayed, ending at a riding crop, of whalebone or fibreglass, braided in leather with a metal thorn at the tip. Shivering, she stroked the shining fabric of the crop and started when a man's voice interrupted her.

'Penny for your thoughts, miss.'

It was a command, rather than a question. A young, tow-haired male, red-faced and swarthy over a muscled frame, stood with his thumbs in the waistband of leather breeches, staring at Angarad up and down. He leered.

'An't seen ye before. Come for snout, I suppose. Unless haberdashery's more your line ... I've a corset or two could squeeze that pretty frame and tighten those bubbies.'

'Miss Horsfall asked if her case of claret had arrived,' Angarad blurted, blushing.

The male nodded towards the pile of bottles.

'Could have asked an hour ago,' he sneered. 'Likes her breakfast, that one.'

'Wine ... for breakfast?' Angarad said.

'Not wine, no. The *colour* of wine, maybe ...'

His leer deepened.

'I'm here for Miss Isobel Coker,' Angarad said. 'She hasn't had the pleasure of meeting you yet, but said you would know what I wanted ... Mr Oswald?'

'What *do* you want?' he said.

'Isobel said ... you'd know ...' Angarad gasped lamely, for her eyes were at the crotch of the man's breeches, now swelling blatantly in erection.

'Like it, do you?' said Oswald.

'*What?*'

Angarad jumped, taking her fingers from the riding crop.

'The riding crop.'

'It's very nice.'

'Is that all?'

He looked at her with glittering, amused eyes.

'I mean ... it's strange that a thing of such beauty should be used to inflict pain,' Angarad blurted.

'Instruments of supplice are often the most beautiful works of art. Ever seen the jewelled iron maiden in the dungeons under Rouen cathedral? Or the silver rack of the Visigoths at Salamanca? This one's my own work, like the rest. Family firm, and I'm the family. Do everything myself.'

He approached the trembling Angarad and brushed her skirted haunches with his fingers.

'*Everything* . . .'

His penis was uncoiled like a snake, straining at the leather. Angarad stared, not resisting, as his fingers crept beneath her skirt and touched her stocking tops. She swallowed, gasping, and her eyelids flickered shut for an instant.

'Who was Jos Pollecutt?' she asked, as the male's fingertips squelched her come-damp nylons.

'Oh, great-something-great grandpa. And his great-something-great grandpa was Sir George, who started the whole pretty show. Deputy governor of Tangier, had a chain of whipping forts in the Atlas mountains where he kept pleasure girls, some notion they descended from the Vandal tribe, whose treasure he hid in a box. Got a bit carried away, like all enthusiasts, thought everybody was a Vandal – or, at any rate, a flagellant, which ain't wrong at all. He gave Wrigley Scrubs manor to the nation! Rather, the *discerning* nation . . .'

'What was it, before it was a prison?'

'The same. Dare say you've heard of Pinkarse Club, in the reign of King Charles the Second.'

'The Pinkarse Club? I *have* heard of it . . . I thought . . .'

'What a slut thinks don't matter. Pinkarse never really went away, d'you see. Wrigley Scrubs – secluded, far from town and the unthinking masses, fit for pleasures of gentlemen and gentlewomen, even in this woeful modern age. Four ounce block of snout, was it?'

'I think . . . yes. No, six ounces.'

'I sell blocks of four ounces. Six strokes per ounce, it costs. If you want me to cut one in half, there'll be extra – more than strokes.'

'I don't understand . . .'

'Yes, you do. Got any cash?'

'Why, no . . .'

'On the slate, then. Got some famous hussies on the family slate.'

'*Ouch! How dare you!*'

Oswald's fingers suddenly clamped her wet bare cunt, unprotected by her broken panty string. He slid his thumb into her slit.

'You must have enjoyed your cycle ride, Miss Angarad Stark,' he hissed. 'Nice and wet. Whipping wet filly is all the easier, for both parties. Six strokes an ounce, on the bare, miss, with that very crop. Followed by my *extra*.'

He nodded at the the bulge in his leather breeches.

Angarad's buttocks shifted, clenching, as her eyes fixed on the male's monstrous penis.

'How did you know my name?'

'More important is how I know your *tastes*, miss. In fact, I'm surprised your name isn't Dodd.'

'*Dodd?*'

'You look just like Habren Dodd, the film star: a voluptuous *sadique*, the queen of flagellance. She married a Gaunt, of the beastly supermarkets . . . a *Lancashire* family, I believe, who have had the impudence to bid for the Wrigley Scrubs franchise. So, you may make Mrs Gaunt's, or Miss Dodd's, acquaintance sooner than you'd like . . .'

His thumb reamed her sopping cunt and Angarad, wincing, clenched her thighs, trapping it inside her, and rubbing her throbbing clitty against its calloused roughness.

'*Ohh . . . don't make me* . . .' she gasped.

Two fingers, slimed with Angarad's copious come, artfully straddled her perineum to penetrate her anus, sliding into the elastic shaft which yielded, allowing him to poke her bumhole right to the knuckle. She squealed as his sharp nails pinched the elastic of her arse-root. The two fingers parted, stretching her anal shaft, and began to slide slowly in and out. Angarad moaned, her eyes closed and face scarlet.

'Ohh . . . please, don't . . . *Ouch!*'

She screamed as his fingers jabbed hard at her arse-root, remaining embedded in the anus, and pulling her towards him.

'My . . . my *tastes*?' she sobbed.

'You have a pervert's arsehole, miss, and a pervert's eyes, but differ in – shall we say, *posture* – from *la* Dodd. Take the crop from the wall with your teeth.'

'Oh! Please, no! Don't make me submit to this!'

'You may leave snoutless, if you wish, and disappoint a jail full of tobacco-starved sluts. Or you may be a good girl and obey. Kneel, first.'

Oswald shuttered his shop. Sobbing, Angarad opened her mouth and fastened her teeth on to the cool leather braids of the riding crop. She crouched, the man flicking up the back of her skirt as he bent over her, to secure his fingers in her anus. On all fours, clutching the riding crop in her teeth, Angarad was pushed by the man's fingers in her bumhole to the back of the shop where the fire blazed. Sweat glazed her eyes as she approached the flames.

'No, wait!' she whimpered. '*Please!* What are you doing?'

'As you desire, my lady,' he hissed. 'I shall warm you, this cold winter's morn . . .'

With a plop, his fingers left her bumhole. Oswald took the crop from her mouth and hung it over her head above the flames. His fingers wrenched her blouse buttons and the garment came off; Angarad's face was inches from the fire and her sweat poured. There was a snap! as her bra came loose and her bare breasts spilled out, slapping the brass fire dogs. Another snap! and her suspender belt was undone, the garters flapping and her stocking tops sagging, as steam hissed from her drying come that soaked them.

'*Ahh! It's hot!*' she squealed, but Oswald held her down, squashing her nipples on to the metal.

He seized each arm and plunged her hands into coal-scuttles on either side of the fireplace, locking her wrists with hinged brass handles snapped shut. He placed his boot on her nape, pinning her teats to the hot brass, with her face twisting away from the flames. He lifted a leather bellows, slid his fingers between her legs and penetrated her wet slit, where they dabbled several seconds before emerging, slopped with her come, to oil the brass nozzle of the bellows.

'*No! Don't . . .!*' Angarad screamed.

The hot, oiled metal slid into her anus and sank to its full depth. As Oswald began to pump, Angarad's screams turned to a sobbing, continuous whimper.

'*Oh! Oh! You'll burst me!*'

The bellows wheezed and Angarad's belly swelled as her bottom wriggled; helpless, she was pinned by the man's foot on her nape and by the pinioning force of the leather bladder, forcing air into her rectum. Her bare titties, squashed on the searing fire dogs, squirmed as frantically as her bum-flans. Oswald pumped her arsehole for several minutes, before laying aside the bellows and taking down the riding crop, its leather seared hot from the fireplace. Scarcely had Angarad's anus expelled the last gasp of wind, than her groans turned to new screaming as Oswald began to beat her on the bare.

Vip! Vip!

'*Ahh! God! Why me?*'

The crop lashed twice, hard, across her bare buttocks, making them clench and wriggle and slamming her teats against the hot metal. A thick red stripe rose on each white arse-globe.

'The Pinkarse discouraged usage of such names,' said Oswald. 'Unless, of course, you have some personal, pagan deity in mind, whose answer would undoubtedly be, *because you want it, slut!*'

Vip! Vip!

'*Ah . . . oh!*'

Vip! Vip!

Her bruised bare croup squirmed, the fesses clenching.

'*AHH! Please, stop!*'

'While your arse is blushing so pretty, my dear? I am most fond of a warm entrance . . .'

Vip! Vip!

'*Oh . . . oh . . . oh . . .!*'

Angarad's naked arse glowed scarlet, the jagged edges of her new welts thrown into relief by the flames. Her bare fesses danced like the flames before her, as the logs spat and crackled. Her titties and belly writhed, helpless, as her bare bum quivered; Oswald delivered his strokes in sets of two, with one clean cut across each fesse or haunch so that, in her first minute, Angarad took ten lashes on the bare; in her second minute's thrashing, she took six; a third minute brought her to twenty-four, which, Oswald declared, completed her tariff. He unrolled his leather breeches to mid-thigh, revealing his cock monstrously erect. Without warning, he grasped her belly and pulled her loins upwards towards his. The coal-scuttles rattled as Angarad's arms were stretched by her clamped wrists; her titties sprang free of the fire dogs and glowed blushing hot, with the nipples dark crimson. He grasped her cunt flaps and squeezed, milking her pouch of its copious come.

'Please, no. Don't fuck me, sir . . .'

'You common bawd! You whore! Like the rest, you beg for it . . .'

'No! My pouch won't take one that big!'

'We can accommodate . . .' he hissed.

'*Ahh!*'

Slopping the come on the shaft of his cock, Oswald drove hard into her anus pucker, penetrating her to three inches; a second thrust plunged his cock all the way to her anal root, with his balls almost sucked in by Angarad's bum elastic, writhing to accept the invading cock.

'*Ah! Ah! Please! Not there!*'

'You want it, whore!'

He began to bugger her, holding her by her hair, which he pulled savagely at each slam of his cock into her squirming arse-shaft.

'*No!*'

'Liar.'

'*Oh! Oh! Please . . . please . . .*'

Angarad's cunt basin jerked at the force of her buggery, spewing droplets of come on to the fire, until her squeals were drowned by the hissing of steam. Her thighs glistened with the juices pouring from her swollen cunt, jerking and jolting as the giant tool impaled her anus, squeezing the cock and bucking to his every thrust.

Thwap! Thwap! Thwap! Thwap! Oswald's hips smacked against the reddened bare flans of her quivering buttocks as he buggered the girl. Her bum leapt to meet his tool's onlslaught, her twitching buttock-meat clutching the ball-sac as the shaft plunged inside her. His grasp on her cunt basin slackened an instant, as his hands left her hips to clamp her soaked pubic bush and the trembling bone beneath, then penetrate her oily wet slit with his fingers. Oswald vigorously masturbated Angarad's swollen, stiff clitoris as he fucked her anus, getting his whole fist inside the pouring slit, and the girl thrust her cunt up, to squash her nubbin and gash flaps on his knuckles.

'*Oh . . . yes . . .*' she moaned.

'*Yes, what*, bitch?'

'Yes! Do me . . . *do me . . .*' panted Angarad.

'That's better.'

'I'm going to come . . . please fuck my arse harder . . . yes! *Oh, God! Yes! Do me!*'

Angarad pissed and the splatter of hissing come-drops on the embers grew to a roar, as a jet of powerful golden pee sprang from her pouch-hole on to the flames, dousing them for a moment. Her belly flattened and heaved; her squeals grew to a sobbing, staccato scream; Oswald grunted and creamy spunk frothed at her anal pucker just as she cried out in her peak of orgasm. Angarad slumped, sobbing, as Oswald buckled his slimed cock back into his breeches.

'I'll never forgive you . . .' she whimpered. 'Never!'

'Splendid, bitch!' Oswald cried, slapping her bottom. 'That means you'll come back for more. I believe that a certain Miss Isobel Coker, whose uniform you have, would herself benefit from a snout run: be so kind as to inform her of the size of a Pollecutt tarse, fit to accommodate ladies with even the largest boxes.'

'Never!' cried Angarad.

'Good,' said Oswald. 'When a slut says no, she means perhaps, and when she says never, she means most certainly. *Why*, you'll be thinking on the painful ride home, should *my* arse suffer, and not *hers* . . .?'

Angarad sobbed.

'You bastard,' she whimpered, as Oswald grasped her between the thighs and jerked her to her feet.

'Quite so! A proud tradition of the Pollecutts, like our care for our common folk. I myself see to the swiving and spanking of every single beldam in the village . . . young Misses Race, Shadwell and Cardus, for example, respectable spinsters all, being some of the juicier rumps that squirm under me. Now, miss, to conclude our business . . . I believe it was six ounces of snout?'

'Yes,' Angarad said. 'Yes, please.'

'Try and eat something, Miss Stark,' said Miss Horsfall. 'It doesn't do to be whipped on an empty stomach.'

'I . . . I can't find the appetite, mum,' said Angarad, toying with her supper.

'And stop shifting like that. It is unladylike. Your derriere will have ample time to move, I can promise, when you are chastised in the cage.'

Angarad shuddered.

'Miss Maclaren gave me an enema, mum,' she murmured, 'after examining me, to certify me fit for punishment. She said it was so I shouldn't foul myself when whipped, though she couldn't guarantee I mightn't . . . you know, make water. She pushed the tube right up my rectum and it hurt terribly.'

'*Please!*' snapped Miss Horsfall, and beckoned to Ghislaine Bassin at the doorway of the deserted refectory pushing a wheeled cage, supervised by Isobel Coker.

Isobel blushed and lowered her gaze, seeing the slumped figure of Angarad in her nightshift and barefoot. She carried a leather quirt of nine thongs, folded in two, and a long whip of a single thong, coiled at her waist. The cage trundled to the centre of the hall, where a hook hung from a chain embedded between the rafters.

'It is time,' said Miss Horsfall.

Angarad took a last sip of tea before standing and meekly raising her arms with lowered head. Isobel grasped the bottom of her nightie and pulled it up, making her breasts quiver as she drew it off the girl's body. Nude, Angarad stepped into the cage, with her back and buttocks facing out through the opened door. She made a cross of her body, gripping the holds at top and bottom of the cage corners with her toes and fingers, and the centre bar with her teeth. Her nightie was folded and placed on the cage floor, beneath her pubis, for modesty Miss Horsfall explained, and in case she wetted herself. She was hoisted thus, to hover over the dining tables. Ghislaine fetched a ladder, which she raised beside the cage at a three-foot distance, propping its head on the rafters and securing its foot beneath a table. Angarad's naked body tensed, as she clung, unstrapped, to her prison bars.

'You have chosen the cage, miss, and a public whipping on back and buttocks, rather than a simpler, but longer, bare-bottom caning,' said Miss Horsfall. 'Do you stand by your choice?'

'Yes, mum,' said Angarad, from her perch.

'I have warned that you risk pain just as severe from Miss Coker's bullwhip as from the stoutest cane,' Miss Horsfall added.

'I'll take the whipping, mum, if you please,' Angarad replied.

'You understand the purpose of the cage. Without the aid of restraints, normal in a public caning, taken bent over a flogging-horse, the *caged* miscreant must hold herself in position, by exercising her will.'

'I understand, mum,' said Angarad.

'Then let the tea bell be rung,' commanded Miss Horsfall, as Isobel ascended the whipper's ladder.

The slags, in their uniforms, and stinkers, in blankets or bra and panties, rushed into the hall, urged on by the warden's drawn canes. There was a breathless hush as Miss Horsfall announced teatime would be accompanied by a public whipping of the detainee Angarad Stark, for gross insolence. Her tariff was twenty-one strokes of the quirt, on the back, and twenty-one with the bullwhip, on the buttocks; punishments to be taken consecutively and both on the bare. Slags and strokes alike craned to see the figures of Isobel and Angarad aloft.

'Remember, Angarad, it's not me who's whipping you,' Isobel whispered. 'Just . . . some warden.'

'I'd *rather* it was you, Isobel,' said Angarad, glancing down through the bars of her cage.

'I'll have to go hard on you,' said Isobel.

'I know.'

'Miss Horsfall . . . well, she said she'd judge me by my standard of punishment today. I'm not out of the woods in this affair.'

'Whip me as hard as you can,' said Angarad tonelessly. 'See the welts on my bum? Those were with a riding crop, from Oswald, at the shop, before he practically split my arse in two with a terribly hard bumming. Next time, do the snout run *yourself*, Isobel, because if you can persuade the brute to do you in the cunt, you'll be well pleased. He's *your size and more.*'

'Oh . . .' said Isobel, with a blush, clutching the ladder's side and smoothing down her skirt. 'Well, try to crouch with your bum cheeks as far as possible apart. It sounds nasty, but it'll help you squirm and clench more freely, to dissipate the pain. For your back, I'm afraid nothing much will help. I'll do your back first, close up, then take you on the bum from a couple of rungs further down to accommodate the longer whip. I'm afraid both sets will smart horribly.'

Angarad looked down at the murmuring ranks of girls, eyes sparkling as they gazed, and their teas untouched.

'Give them a good show, Isobel,' said Angarad, her lips twisted in a smile on the left side only. 'Remember, I'm a ticketed pervert . . . I *want* to smart.'

Isobel bit her lip.

'Don't make it hard for me,' she whispered.

'*Do your duty, you fucking whore!*' Angarad spat.

Her face crimson, Isobel lifted the quirt over Angarad's back.

'You cheeky bitch,' she hissed.

Thwap!

The thongs bit the girl's bare shoulders, jolting her against the cage bars, and the crowd below cheered, while Miss Horsfall, standing with arms folded, smiled thinly.

'One,' she said.

The quirt left an angry row of weals, sliced on Angarad's bare back-flesh. Isobel paused for ten seconds, until Angarad's quivering had subsided.

Thwap!

Ten seconds' pause, and Angarad was still shaking.

'Two . . .'

Thwap!

'Three . . .'

Tears streamed from the flogged girl's eyes and her teeth bit hard on the restraining bar; her limbs strained, shivering violently as her back was striped, but she made no sound.

Thwap!

'Four . . .'

The heavy quirt was as much a bludgeon as a flogging device, sending Angarad's bare breasts cannoning against the bars of her cage at each stroke, delivered on the ten seconds. By the fifteenth stroke, her mottled shoulder welts were a deep, puffy crimson and her breath came in harsh gasps. Yet her nightie beneath her moistened steadily, as drops of come seeped from her gash.

Thwap!

'Sixteen . . .'

Angarad moaned, her wail wracking her whole body, as a jet of piss erupted from her cunt, splattering her nightie, but the stream so strong that drops fell on the tea-tables; her piss, mingled with her oozed cunt slime, was so copious that the garment was soaked through and the fluid continued to drip steadily. Stealthy winks and murmurs of approval were exchanged, as the girls saw Angarad pressing her clearly enlarged clitoris against the bars of the cage, and rubbing her slit on the come-slimed metal, as her body thrust forward at each lash.

'Wanking off!' said Amy Patel, her own fingers busy at her soaked panties' gusset.

'A real pervert,' said Belinda Garce, as she, too, masturbated under the table, skirt up and fingers wanking her naked cunt.

After the twenty-first and final stroke of her first set, Angarad, eyes closed tight, continued to rub her gushing slit up and down against the cage bars, as though still being whipped. Isobel paused for five minutes, allowing the sobbing victim to calm herself, before descending to a lower rung of the whipping ladder and uncoiling her bullwhip. Isobel's skirt was only a few feet above the tea tables and, since her knee was bent with her feet two rungs apart, her knickers, sussies and stockings were clearly visible. The girls giggled; Isobel's panties were wet with come. After the pause, Miss Horsfall signalled the start of the bum-flogging and Isobel's whip snaked upwards, aslant, to take Angarad hard across the bare buttocks.

Vap!

Angarad shook, but the whip did not carry the same slamming force of the heavy rubber thongs. Nevertheless, her fesses at once clenched and began to squirm, as a thick red weal darkened the naked arse-globes.

'One . . .' Miss Horsfall intoned, her eyes fixed on Angarad's quivering bare buttocks and oblivious of the teacup Amy Patel held, slyly placed below Isobel's own crotch and knickers.

Vap!

Angarad's toes clutched her cage bars, as her long legs shuddered, kicking, under the leather's sting on her bare.

Vap!

'Three . . .'

By the time the twenty-first stroke was laid, Angarad's back and buttocks were a mass of welts, and the girls had managed to consume their tea in its entirety, with not a teacup full, nor crumb of bread or spoonful of jam left. Amy Patel, though, held on to her teacup as the tea things were cleared and Ghislaine Bassin winched the cage down. Isobel, panting hard, descended from her whipper's ladder.

'Not bad, miss,' said Miss Horsfall.
'Thank you, mum,' said Isobel.
As Angarad stumbled, panting, from her cage, Miss Horsfall brushed a square of pink brocade across her come-soaked pubic bush and stuck the cloth to her arse-cleft, poking it as a pennant into her anus. Amy advanced.
'I've saved you a cupful, Miss Coker,' she said.
'Why, thanks,' said Isobel, smiling and sipping from the cup, only to spit out the oily fluid at once. '*What . . .*'
'It's your come, miss,' said Amy. 'I thought you'd like to have it back.'
'Amy!' cried Miss Horsfall. 'This is carrying drollery a little far!'
She took the cup, brimful of Isobel's come, then stared balefully at the red-faced whipper.
'If this is really your . . . *exudation*, Miss Coker,' she said icily, 'then it appears that Angarad Stark is not the only newcomer who merits a pervert's ticket. Report to my office, if you please, after your tea.'
The bottom strokes tittered and made victory signs.
'And, Miss Coker –'
'Yes, mum?'
'Don't bother to wear your knickers.'

'Mistress?' said Joss Gaunt.
'What is it, worm?' snapped Habren.
She lay nude, on her belly, her divan shaded by silk from the afternoon glare of the sun. Sipping clear liquid from a wine glass, she smacked her lips. Truud, her silken harem pants at her ankles and her naked breasts bobbing with nipples erect, had her face between Habren's parted thighs and was tonguing her, at the same time masturbating to fill a new wine glass with her come. Her twin Jan buggered the reclining mistress, his rigid cock glistening with arse-grease, as it slid, slowly, dreamily, in and out of her rectum. The perfume of incense filled the air; Aggar stood, fanning the trio with ostrich plumes.
'The bid for the franchise of Wrigley Scrubs prison has been accepted.'

'What of it?'

'One of us shall have to go to England to complete the paperwork, my darling.'

'Mm! Yes, Truud, that's so *good.* Jan – when you've spunked in me, you may remove her pantaloons and cane her fifteen on the bare.'

'Shall I go, darling?' Joss quavered.

'Certainly not.'

'It's just that, since your new friends' arrival, the film is, ah, rather behind schedule.'

'*You dare . . .!* Truud, after your caning, you shall give my husband fifteen strokes on the bare. Joss, assume position.'

Joss obeyed, baring his arse and bending over.

'Must I, Mistress?' said Truud.

'Of course. Jan, are you going to spunk?'

'Not yet.'

'Aggar can take over when you've done me. Mmm . . . Lick harder, Truud, and make sure you swallow every drop. After you've beaten my husband, I want you to continue wanking yourself off and clean the floor in come with your titties.'

'Thank you, Mistress,' said the Frisian girl, her voice muffled as she gulped Habren's come.

'The girls *are* beginning to murmur,' said Jan, quickening his buggery, until his back arched and his loins slammed Habren's gently writhing bare arse-globes.

'Let them,' gasped Habren. 'Dirty little subs, all.'

'Idleness is not good for them,' Jan panted. 'They loll at the pool, masturbating each other and intriguing. I have seen Edwige and Susan caning other girls.'

'Impossible!' Habren snorted. 'If you won't spunk in me, take your twin's pants off and cane her while Aggar attends my hole. I'll have to bring myself off with my fingers.'

'Mistress,' said Truud, as Jan ripped off her pantaloons, exposing her scarred bare moons, 'may I polish the floor *before* my caning? My bum still smarts from my lunchtime dozen.'

'You disobedient slut!' Habren said, then, '*Ahh* . . .' as Aggar's stiff black cock penetrated her slime-greased anus. 'You'll take a double caning for that . . .! Yes, Aggar . . . *ohh* . . . *fuck me* . . . *deep*!'

Habren began to writhe, as she wanked her clitoris under the giant cock's buggery.

'Perhaps you are too harsh on my twin,' said Jan stiffly. 'It is, after all, not a month since you – *we* – initiated her into the joys of submission. Don't you remember your own initiation, Habren? Your arse must have taken ample weals, to learn to inflict them so well.'

'I, bare my bum as a filthy *sub*? Certainly not! You *insolent*! Now, cane your sister, as I commanded! Ah . . . yes, Aggar, don't stop . . . bugger me harder . . .'

'Perhaps Edwige and the others are right,' murmured Jan. 'It is *you* whom the desert sun has made insolent.'

He opened the door and Edwige entered, followed by Susan Race. Both wore only white loinstrings and carried canes. They grinned, teeth sparkling in tan faces and bare breasts bobbing with nipples erect. Edwige barked a command in Berber dialect. Aggar placed his forearms around Habren's breasts and pressed her to his chest, then lifted her, helplessly impaled and writhing on his cock, with her legs jerking furiously.

'*Stop, you sluts!*' Habren screamed.

'I say,' bleated Joss, 'you can't just –'

Vip!

'*Oh!*'

Susan's cane cracked across his own bare bum.

'This is outrageous!' Habren screamed.

'We thought it would be good cinema,' said Jan.

Followed by the girl invaders and the twins, with Joss protesting feebly, Aggar carried the kicking, squealing Habren outside to Truud's womancart, with her body helplessly impaled on his tool; he lifted her from his cock with a plopping sound and threw her sprawling in the dirt. A knot of giggling girls lifted her, squealing and sobbing, and helped truss her in harness, with her feet hobbled. Aggar thrust his cock between her lips and a flurry of canestrokes on her bare bum made her jump, as Edwige told her to suck his arse-greased tool to orgasm; gasping, Habren tongued the glans and shaft of the giant black cock, as it slid in and out of her mouth, powerfully fucking the back of her throat and, as she sobbed, spunk spurted from her lips, dribbling down her chin on to her quivering titties.

Vip! Vip!

'*Oh!*'

Edwige and Susan each lashed Habren on the naked flank. Her mouth gaped in a scream, drooling Aggar's spunk.

'*You fucking sluts! You're all sacked!*'

'You may reconsider that threat in the cage, Mistress, after your whipping,' said Edwige. 'In the absence of your cooperation, Miss Truud is a talented film-maker.'

From a sack, she took a huge double phallus of sculpted white limestone, put her fingers between Habren's thighs, and masturbated the squealing woman for two minutes, pausing frequently to oil the dildos. When they were dripping with Habren's come, she inserted the twin prongs into her anus and cunt, pushed smartly and thrust, until both shafts had disappeared to their sculpted ball-sac. Edwige strapped the device around Habren's cunt basin with three zipped flanges of rubber. Habren wailed and whimpered, her loins shifting to ease the pain of the massive penetrators, as tears coursed on her cheeks.

'We are going to have a race,' Edwige said, 'with only one contestant. Miss Habren is going to pull the cart to the cage, in which she is going to dine this evening. Mr Gaunt, you shall be the driver, with myself and Susan as outriders.'

She uncoiled a heavy bullwhip and handed it to him.

'I? I can't – it's outrageous – I won't –'

'You shall strip, naked as your wife, and Truud shall stand behind you to urge you on with the cane, while Susan and I run beside Miss Habren with our own canes. You shall whip her back and we her bum and haunches.'

'Truud is going to cane me on the bare?'

Joss's eyes sparkled.

'Assuredly. Unless you wish to be whipped in the cage along with your bitch. You have been fucking Truud in the cunt with some frequency, have you not, Mr Gaunt?'

'Why, yes, but –'

'*What?*' cried Habren. 'You disobedient *wretch*!'

The cage shimmered, half a mile distant, with its door open and the pulley rope slack, ready to hoist it.

'I see,' said Joss. 'Well, then – in that case – it seems –'

In an instant, Joss was stripped and, towering over the nude, harnessed body of his wife, flourished his whip. Truud, still in her harem pantaloons, climbed behind him and striped his bare arse with a vicious cut.

Vip!

'Ouch! That hurt!'

Vip! Vip! Vip! Vip!

The girls' canes landed smartly on Habren's bare arse-central globes.

'*AHH . . .!*'

Thwap!

Joss laid a broad pink weal across his wife's bare shoulders.

'*Mmm! No, please!*'

Thwap!

'*Oh . . .!* Oh . . . *please*, darling, *no* . . .!'

Habren's naked flesh wriggled, her back shuddering, as the hide whip stroked her shoulder-blades. Joss smiled as Truud began to flick her whippy little cane across his own bare arse; his cock swelled. Jan lowered his garment and thrust his stiff cock into Habren's mouth. Gagging, she began to suck the erect flesh, her tears dripping on the massive stiff stool as it fucked her mouth.

Thwap!

'Mmm . . .!'

'You must be whipped at womancart,' said Jan, 'but may spare yourself the agony of the cage if you tell us *where to find Pollecutt's box.*'

Habren raised her lips from his cock.

'I swear,' she wailed, 'I have no idea, neither where it is nor what it contains!'

The girls raised their canes and Joss his whip. Jan plunged his cock back into her throat.

Vip! Vip!

Thwap!

'*Mmm!*'

'Then,' groaned Jan, as his cock began to buck in spurt, 'it is the cage, you *fucking whore*!'

'Ohh . . .'

Habren whimpered as Jan's spunk spurted, dribbling from her teeth, and her throat bobbed as she swallowed cream. Jan grinned fiercely, slapping her cheeks hard and his pubic bone slamming her lips, as he spermed into her mouth. He withdrew; Aggar, too, slapped Habren's spunk-slimed face, before placing a bit in her mouth to gag her.

Thwap!

'Giddy-up, nag!' her husband cried.

'*MMM . . .!*' Habren wailed.

Her bare back and buttocks shivering under a rain of strokes, she strained, with belly knotted and thighs and titties quivering. The womancart began to trundle.

# 12

# Vice Versa

'Did you enjoy your tea, Miss Coker?' said Miss Horsfall, closing her heavy curtains against the snowflakes falling softly against her mullioned windowpane.

'I hadn't much appetite, mum,' said Isobel.

'Not after your exertion in whipping the slut Stark? You whipped her rather well, by the way.'

'Please, mum, you told me to come without wearing knickers.'

'And are you?'

'Of course not, mum.'

'That doesn't explain your loss of appetite.'

'Please don't toy with me, mum,' said Isobel. 'I've been a stroke here long enough to know the slags aren't the only ones who . . . who have to bare their bottoms. I'm the only stroke who hasn't herself been a slag. If you intend to thrash me, please get it over with.'

Miss Horsfall sat at her desk, leather-topped, in her large, thickly carpeted apartment, whose several easy chairs and sofa also shone with leather. Its smell was musty, with a rack of belts, whips and canes hanging in a bookcase beside leather-bound volumes. Isobel glanced at the instruments of discipline, and trembled, fingering the cane and rope at her own belt.

'Did you enjoy whipping Miss Stark?' said Miss Horsfall suddenly. 'Amy Patel played a cruel jape on you, but . . . it *was* your fluid in the cup, wasn't it?'

'I . . . I did my duty, mum.'

'Answer the question.'

'Yes, mum. I . . . I juiced, seeing her naked body squirm. The girl cheeked me. Called me . . . a rude word.'

'Specifically?'

'A whore, mum.'

'Which you aren't . . .'

'*Mum!* It was an insult! I got angry. I know I shouldn't have . . . and I deserve punishment for losing my temper.'

Miss Horsfall wrinkled her nose.

'I haven't asked you how Angarad came to be wearing your uniform on the way to the village. Perhaps you enjoyed beating a girl you felt had betrayed you. Never mind . . . you hum, rather. A bit sweaty. Take a shower.'

She gestured to her bathroom.

'You'll find everything you need.'

Isobel hesitated, then entered the bathroom, closed the door and stripped, carefully folding her clothes. The bathroom was all in pink: bathtub, shower curtains and fluffy towels, and luxurious with lotions, cream and scent, including several tubes of lubricating jelly. She climbed into the bathtub, closed the curtains and turned on a scalding shower, sighing as the hot water caressed her skin. Miss Horsfall's voice came from the sitting-room.

'As you know, this is a privatised prison,' she said, 'and there has been a change of ownership. There may be some changes here at Wrigley Scrubs soon. I must know which wardens I can trust to remain loyal and obey my orders. I sense you are one of them.'

'Thank you, mum,' Isobel replied, lathering her belly and breasts with soapsuds. 'You *are* going to beat me, I think.'

'A camera crew from the BBC is to visit tomorrow, for the purpose of showing Wrigley Scrubs as the model prison of the future. Of course, we wish to show our best side. The mild deception I plan, of showing trustworthy wardens lightly spanked as slags, is, I think, in the public interest.'

'I hope to be trustworthy, mum,' said Isobel, with a gulp.

'I'm going to test your obedience, Miss Coker,' said Miss Horsfall, her voice distant and muffled. 'When you emerge from the bathroom, you will show your ability to obey my orders to the full, and *without question.*'

'Yes, mum,' said Isobel, and continued to sluice herself for minutes, until the lights suddenly went out.

She groped for a towel and wrapped herself, before searching for her uniform. It was gone. She crept from the bathroom to find the sitting-room in darkness, save for a tiny spotlight played on the back of the sofa: on the broad, pear-shaped naked buttocks of a female, squatting on the sofa seat, with her head over its back. The cheeks were fully parted, to show a tangle of cunt-hairs and dripping red labia, with the anal pucker well distended. The arse-globes were already mottled and puffy, as though from a distant beating.

'You will show your ability to obey my orders to the full, and *without question*,' said Miss Horsfall, her voice muffled, from the direction of the closed curtains. 'You see the exposed croup of a slag, who has been exceptionally insolent and requires chastisement more severe than can be publicly administered. I wish to see if you have the will, Isobel, to administer that chastisement.'

'I'll do my best, mum,' gulped Isobel.

'From the bookshelf, you will take a rope and bind the miscreant's ankles securely together, with ropes extending to the sofa legs. You will find two straps hanging from the top of the sofa. Those, you shall buckle over the small of the girl's back, rendering her helpless.'

Trembling, Isobel obeyed, roping and buckling the immobile naked girl, until she was helpless. Still, she did not look at the inky depths beneath the sofa, where the girl's hair fanned out, covering her head pressed to the floor, and her supporting fists.

'Done and dusted, mum,' she said, after her work.

'From the bookshelf, take the rattan cane, furthest to the left. You will administer one hundred strokes, in sets of four, over a period not to exceed one hour, on the full bare. You will attend to every portion of her croup, extending from top buttock to underfesses, and including a sound marking of the haunches halfway around to the thighs. At no time will you heed any expressions of distress, either verbal or physical. If you observe the girl rubbing her pubis on the sofa in an attempt to masturbate, you will ignore it. If she loses control of her bowels, or makes water, you will ignore it. Replace your towel in the bathroom and return to do your duty in the nude. You will obey.'

Isobel returned her towel as ordered and, naked, took down the heavy tool of chastisement, a long rattan, half an inch thick. She shuddered.

'A full hundred, mum?' she gasped.

'You will obey.'

'What if she faints?'

'You will obey.'

Placing her bare feet firmly apart, in caning stance, Isobel lifted the rattan, then lashed down. It made a cool, swishing sound, as it sliced the air.

Vap! Vap! Vap! Vap!

Isobel delivered the first four strokes full on the girl's centre bare. The girl's belly jolted against the sofa and her fesses trembled, clenching, but she made no sound other than a soft, purring sigh.

Vap! Vap! Vap! Vap!

The rattan raised rapid, cruel weals, already crimson, and instantly puffing the bare arse-globes. The buttocks began to clench rhythmically.

Vap! Vap! Vap! Vap!

Isobel dripped with sweat in the room's closeness.

Vap! Vap! Vap! Vap!

After the first dozen, Isobel paused to wipe her brow. The bare bum she had flogged was a patchwork of crimson welts, darkening and puffing to ridges. The girl's buttocks continued to clench and unclench during the pause and her hips undulated gently, grinding the sofa back with her pubis. Isobel glanced at the curtains, but they were shrouded in the darkness, the pencil light illumining only the whipped bare bum beneath her. She gasped, swallowed and shut her eyes, then, slowly, her fingers crept across her belly, to her jungle of moist pube-hair; into her soft wet slit to brush her swollen clitoris. Isobel stroked herself in the slit for several seconds, masturbating in the trickle of come that seeped faster and faster from her cunt and gazing at the rippling whorled welts she had raised on the ripe naked fesses, helpless before her.

'You will show your ability to obey my orders to the full, and *without question*,' came Miss Horsfall's instruction.

Vap! Vap! Vap! Vap !

Isobel delivered four lashes straight to the left haunch, following them at once with a set to the right. The tender haunch skin leapt to bruised darkness and the flogged girl squirmed against her restraining girdle, while her legs threshed in her ropes. There was a thump, as her head banged the padded sofa back.

'Are you masturbating, Miss Coker?' rasped Miss Horsfall's voice.

'I . . . *Oh*! Mum, I . . . oh . . .!'

'*Are you masturbating, Miss Coker?*'

'Y-yes, mum. '

'It is in order. You will show your ability to obey my orders to the full, and *without question.*'

'I can't help . . . a flogged girl's bare . . . oh, my God!'

'It is in order.'

Vap! Vap! Vap! Vap!

Isobel masturbated rhythmically as she caned, and the girl's whinnies turned to a muffled slurp: she was chewing the carpet. Her bare arse jerked and squirmed wildly, yet there was no sound from her, even when Isobel sliced the same welt twice, other than the chewing noise and little gasps and swallows. Suddenly, the whipped girl moaned, pissed all over the sofa, a lake of golden fluid puddling the seat and cascading to the carpet. Isobel paused, at the forty-first stroke, watching the girl's bum squirming, as the yellow torrent erupted from her swollen gash flaps.

'My God . . .' Isobel murmured, yet continued to masturbate, while the puffy welts of the bare flogged bum writhed, as though wringing the pee from the girl's bowels.

'You will show your ability to obey my orders to the full, and *without question*,' Miss Horsfall's voice intoned.

Gulping, Isobel raised an unsteady cane, using both her hands, and brought it down on the clenched bum. The last droplets of pee squirted from the squashed cunt and glistening with copious come oil. The girl made slurping noises as she chewed the carpet and rubbed her loins harder against the sofa back. She, too, masturbated, along with her caner. Isobel went back to one-handed caning; her belly rose and fell, as her fingers pounded her swollen clitoris, bringing her closer and closer to climax.

'You will show your ability to obey my orders to the full, and *without question.*'

Vap! Vap! Vap! Vap!

The rattan flew like a feather, in Isobel's grasp, slapping the naked buttocks with as much force as a quirt, with all its rubber thongs concentrated in the single springy shaft of wood. The weals on the squirming girl's flogged buttocks were crimson trenches, puffy at the edges, and formed a crisscross pattern, already blurring, with Isobel's strokes now lashing already open welts.

Vap! Vap! Vap! Vap!

'*Mm . . .!*' panted Isobel, wanking herself off to climax; pools of girl-pee moistened her bare feet.

At the eighty-eighth stroke, the flogged girl began to lift her cunt basin from the chair, a few inches, then slam her engorged clitoris and cunt lips on to the leather, sopping wet and streaming with her come. Isobel delivered the final dozen with scarcely a pause between sets of four and, at the ninety-sixth, the girl peed once more, but now with sharp shrill cries of orgasm, subsiding to a whimper, long after Isobel had delivered the hundredth canestroke. Isobel lowered her hot cane, wiping the sweat from her face and the dripping come from her cunt and thighs, smearing the fluid awkwardly on her hair. The beaten girl crooned to herself, as Miss Horsfall's voice snapped: 'You may collect your uniform from the armoire, in darkness, Miss Coker, and depart. You have passed your test. Do not attempt to examine your subject's face. She has received just chastisement but will never thank you for it, as you may not know her name. Her offence was vile: she sought punishment *for her pleasure*, outside the confines of HMP Wrigley Scrubs, and delivered her back orifice to a brute male, for *his* pleasure – *and hers, too.* Your thrashing will teach her a lesson not to seek pleasure in pain – that most obscene perversion! She is already ashamed of her perverted lust, and the fact that you masturbated, gloating over her flogged buttocks, shall add to her shame. I ordered you to report without knickers, knowing you would only wet them. She shall work free from your bonds in appropriate time, knowing that if she is late for lights-out, she shall merit further chastisement.'

Isobel scrabbled in the darkness, found her uniform and dressed hurriedly.

'Please, mum, I'll find it hard not to look at the slags and guess which one I've beaten,' she said, politely. 'But I suppose it is for her to know and me to find out.'

'You will show your ability to obey my orders to the full, and *without question.*'

'Very well, mum. I'm glad I've given satisfaction.'

'You will show your ability to obey my orders to the full, and *without question.*'

Isobel slipped out of the door, with a last glance at the bare bum she had just caned purple. Miss Horsfall's voice echoed tinnily after her, as she passed along the corridor.

'You will show your ability to obey my orders to the full, and *without question.*'

Click.

'You will show your ability to obey my orders to the full, and *without question.*'

Click.

'You will show your ability to obey my orders to the full, and *without question* . . .'

The face a golden tan, and her breasts and croup clinging in a business suit of shimmering grey shantung silk, over which her blond mane artlessly cascaded, the tall young woman stepped from the London train. She carried a pigskin briefcase and strode to the car rental office, her gait awkward, and keeping well apart her white-stockinged legs, and feet encased in red patent stilettos. She shifted her croup restlessly as she did the paperwork and took the keys to her vehicle. The clerk accompanied her to the car and opened the door; she grimaced as her buttocks touched the seat.

'Are you all right, Mrs Gaunt?' he asked. 'You seem to be in a little discomfort, if you don't mind my saying so.'

The woman snapped opened her mouth but twisted her lips in a radiant smile, showing snow-white teeth.

'Why, so would you be, if you had just been driven as a carthorse in the Moroccan desert, whipped in a cage and left caged and shackled through the night, with a bare-bottom caning before breakfast,' she said.

'I don't understand, ma'am,' he stammered.

'Intriguing, though, isn't it? Especially as it's true. There are people – *perverts* – who like that sort of thing, you see, and I happen to be one of them. I require from you only directions to the prison at Wrigley Scrubs.'

He blushed and nodded.

'Easy, ma'am,' he said. 'I think I *do* understand.'

Ignoge Brand was on duty at the gate when Habren's car pulled up at Wrigley Scrubs.

'Stark! Since when did you have a car pass, or an exeat? Anyway, you're supposed to be in the infirmary with flu.'

'You are mistaken,' said Habren. 'I am Mrs Habren Gaunt, a director of Gauntco, responsible for the prison franchise, as of tomorrow.'

'Don't come it, you fucking scrubber. I don't believe you,' sneered Ignoge. 'You faked the flu and sneaked out, you dirty little sub, and Oswald's buggered you so much, he's got soppy and lent you his motor.'

Habren showed her identification and Ignoge blushed, stammering apology.

'You could be twins . . .' she blurted. 'You and Angarad Stark! I'm sorry, mum . . . she's a *real* perve, that one!'

'Which, I take it, you're not. Would you please identify yourself?' said Habren mildly.

As she spoke, she turned to look at a gang of slags trudging through the morning fog; barefoot, they wore only bras and panties and shouldered shovels. The girls were roped together at the waist and at the wooden hobble bars enclosing their ankles. Their shuffling gait was accompanied by a tinkling of cowbells pierced, through the fabric of each girl's bra, at her nipples. Some wore crotchless panties, with bouquets of goose feathers rammed inside their quims.

'Top stroke – senior warden Ignoge Brand, mum,' said Ignoge. 'Those slags, I mean detainees, are a morning work party, going to dredge silt from the river.'

'Tethered like animals? How shameful for them. And why the goose feathers?'

'For blubbing, during a whopping. It's penal policy, mum. We like to get them off early, before too many people see and get the wrong impression – well, I'm really sorry for any misunderstanding, and welcome to HMP Wrigley Scrubs, mum.'

'And what would be the right impression, I wonder. Thank you,' said Habren, accelerating her car so that slush drenched Ignoge's stockings. 'You may expect to see a lot more of me.'

She drove to the governess's lodging, stopped the car and got out, moving stiffly. Before she could ring the doorbell, the door opened and Miss Horsfall herself greeted Habren.

'Mrs Gaunt! I . . . we weren't expecting you so soon.'

'I took the earlier train. May I come in?' Habren said.

'Yes, of course . . . please excuse the mess, we're in quite a tizzy, preparing for a BBC camera crew to film this afternoon, and my cleaning slag hasn't reported yet . . . I had to cane the last one for sloppiness . . . but I'm sure you don't want to hear all the gory details just yet. Do call me Adelaide. I just adore your outfit, Mrs Gaunt. Only true beauty can carry grey.'

With a slither of her seamed nylon stockings, Miss Horsfall, buttocks wiggling, led Habren into her living-room, with its leather furniture and bookshelf full of canes. Miss Horsfall said shyly that her guest must excuse her fidgeting in her seat as she had piles. Habren sat beside the governess on the sofa, after glancing at the well-chewed carpet behind it and the damp come-stains in front, beneath the imagined buttocks of a canee.

'On the contrary, Adelaide,' she purred, 'the gory details are precisely what interest me. And your uniform becomes you admirably.'

She placed her hand on Miss Horsfall's nyloned knee.

'Nylons . . . how wonderfully quaint. I have to make do with silk.'

'Why, thank you, Mrs Gaunt.'

'Habren.'

'I am sure you would like coffee and biscuits, Habren,' Miss Horsfall said, then lifted her telephone and placed her order. 'Perhaps *gory* was the wrong word . . .'

'Shall we say, "painful"?' Habren interrupted. 'Adelaide, I don't think you need keep any secrets from me about the disciplinary regime here, for why else do you think I bought the place?'

'Well, I – you are obviously a successful businesswoman, Habren, and a most striking one. If I didn't know otherwise, I'd swear you were the twin of one of our most . . . *appealing* detainees.'

'May I say that if I resemble this Miss Stark, your own face is slightly familiar. I feel sure we've met before.'

'Hardly. I am only a civil servant and I assume your takeover is for sound financial reasons . . .'

Habren's teeth glinted as she licked them.

'*Corporal punishment*, Adelaide. I'm not a successful businesswoman, I am a successful actress and whore who *married* business: I met my husband Joss as a screen goddesss . . . he is my most adoring fan, a submissive wimp who loves to watch me *done* by other men, then receive a thrashing on the bare for his insolence. I direct and star in *that* sort of film. I trust you aren't shocked.'

Miss Horsfall smiled nervously, then licked her lips.

'A prison governess is unshockable. Besides, insolence is discouraged here at Wrigley Scrubs.'

'By what methods?'

Miss Horsfall gestured at her cane rack.

'We make no secret of our adherence to old-fashioned values, Habren.'

Habren scrutinised the instruments of discipline, and complimented Miss Horsfall on her good taste, which Miss Horsfall received with a winsome smile.

'What if a girl, this Angarad Stark, for example,' said Habren, 'is of perverted tendency and actually takes pleasure in being thrashed?'

'Then we try to thrash her hard enough to dissuade her.'

'Was that the case with Miss Stark?'

'Not quite. She came, ticketed as a submissive pervert, and vehemently denied her true nature, but her time served has taught her to recognise it and accept canings which go beyond the limits of the pleasurable.'

'But it *is* sometimes possible for a submissive pervert to switch and become dominant, given the necessary guidance of the rod?'

'Assuredly, Habren,' said Miss Horsfall, placing her palm on the back of Habren's, still resting a few inches above her stockinged knee, 'and, who knows, perhaps vice versa.'

She placed her own palm on Habren's thigh, revealed beneath her grey mini-skirt and with a peek of lacy pearl-white sussies.

'I do hope you aren't playing games with me,' she murmured.

'*Do* you?' said Habren.

Miss Horsfall blushed, wiped her brow and, in the same gesture, loosened her collar buttons, revealing creamy white breasts swelling beneath her tight bra. There was a scratching at the door and Miss Horsfall bade entrance. The door opened and a slag shuffled in, her ankles enclosed in a wooden hobble bar; she wore only a dirty bra and panties, stained at the gusset and carried a tray of elevenses by a rope held between her teeth. Her wrists were bound together in front of her pubis. She set the tray down on the coffee table by Habren's knees and curtsied to both ladies, before withdrawing backwards. Her skimpy thong panties did not conceal the dark welts of a recent caning to the bare buttocks and haunches.

'The detainee Ingrid Fage was rather naughty, I am afraid,' said Miss Horsfall, pouring coffee. 'She was caught smoking and assigned to servitude as penalty. Do help yourself to a ginger nut, Habren.'

'Servitude!' laughed Habren. 'Not her only penalty, I imagine.'

'There *was* a caning . . .' murmured Miss Horsfall.

'Bare-bum?' said Habren, her teeth like blades, slicing her biscuit. 'This is excellent coffee.'

'Of course – to answer both your question and your compliment.'

Habren began to take off her jacket.

'May I? It's rather hot.'

'Please. You are, from tomorrow, my ow– my superior.'

Habren sat in her white blouse, breasts thrust forward by an uplift scalloped bra allowing the tops of the nipple discs to be seen, and the plums hard, pressing through both satin bra and the sheer voile blouse. She crossed her legs, careless of her skirt's riding up, and giving her hostess a clear view of her skimpily knickered pubis, white sussies and stocking tops. Somehow, another button of Miss Horsfall's uniform shirt came undone, revealing her own, sterner bra cups, her breasts quivering flans, and the faint hillocks of her wide nipples in a state of engorgement. The two ladies sat, gazing, and sipping coffee.

'Let's not beat about the bush, Adelaide,' said Habren. 'You are more than a civil servant. You are a dominatrix of other girls. You have hit on a goldmine: a whipping prison for wayward but basically decent sluts.'

'I'm pleased you should think me a girl, Habren, though I am of a certain age . . . but a goldmine?'

'Rollo Cragg is on the board and, as acquisitions director of Gauntco, will continue to be,' Habren said.

'Dear Rollo! At Gauntco, too,' said Miss Horsfall drily. 'He is a most forceful man . . .'

'Have *you* ever been caned bare-bum, Adelaide?' Habren continued, before swallowing another biscuit, whole.

'*What . . .?*'

'In the past . . . or recently? As your new boss I have been open with you. Gauntco's interest in Wrigley Scrubs is financial – my own, flagellant. Like you, I am a dominatrix, but a recent experience intrigued me. I wonder if switching is truly possible. *Have* you been caned on the bare?'

'I suppose I should take what our American friends call the fifth amendment,' whispered Miss Horsfall.

Habren wiped her mouth of crumbs, smearing her fingers on Miss Horsfall's stockings.

'My question is prettily answered. Lift your skirt, *miss*, lower your panties, and *bare your bottom to me.*'

Miss Horsfall did not reply, save by sighing with a rueful smile. She put down her coffee-cup, wiped her lips on a linen napkin, then rose, with her back to Habren. She bent over the sofa back and rolled up her skirt, showing her white sussies and knickers, over her black nylons. Slowly, she unfastened her garter straps, then rolled down her panties to mid-thigh, parting her bare fesses to show her arse-cleft entire, with the anal pucker spread and the tangle of cunt hair already moistened by juice from her pendant gash flaps. Habren whistled softly: the governess's naked buttocks were seared with a crisscross of bruises from a heavy bare-bum caning, extending to flanks, top bum and underfesse.

'Who did *that*?' Habren asked. 'That bum pucker isn't swollen by piles, she's been royally whopped.'

'Isobel Coker, the new junior warden. She didn't know it was me. I have a ruse . . . only my bottom is displayed for caning, with my head in shadow, and relaying my instructions tape-recorded, as though I am speaking from a distance – with this remote control.'

She displayed the device and pressed keys, which flashed and beeped.

'Now I do recognise you . . . from your arse. Your screen name was Bella Lafesse, wasn't it? The most-caned bum in flagellant pictures, a few years back.'

'May I replace my underthings, Habren . . . or, should I say, Mistress?' said Miss Horsfall with a simper, and Habren agreed; when Miss Horsfall was properly clad, she smiled again.

'Dear Rollo helped to . . . *massage* my curriculum vitae,' she said. 'Wrigley Scrubs was my idea, of course: the perfect, secluded dungeon – literally – for those in high places to indulge their flagellant tastes, whether taking, or dishing out the cane! The beauty of it is, it works. Decent girls, unlucky enough to be caught at mischief, really *do* understand corporal punishment. You'll find that all our wardens, except Miss Coker aforementioned, are former detainees who have opted to serve extra time. They came as subs and my discipline has revealed their true dominant natures. Dominant females are straightforward in their virtuous contempt for the submissive girl, who is a spiteful, manipulative and selfish beast. Why, some subs are *so* sneaky, they pretend to be their opposite!'

The door opened: Althea, Ignoge and Goiswinth burst into the room, falling promptly on the body of Habren and pinioning her to the floor. Ignoge's hand clamped Habren's mouth and stifled her protest, while Althea and Goiswinth ripped off her skirt and blouse, leaving Habren wriggling in her underthings, with Ignoge sitting on her head and the others on her pubis, haunches and ankles. Miss Horsfall rose and seated herself behind her desk.

'The detainee Angarad Stark has, in some fit of delirium, feigned illness and escaped from the infirmary. She has managed to obtain clothing and a motorcar, to present herself with false documents and a truly incredible cock-and-bull story,' she said.

'Bitch!' cried Ignoge, slapping Habren's scarlet face.

'She must experience *peine forte et dure*,' said Miss Horsfall, 'whipped back to sanity! For the moment, rope her on a rail and cane her on the bare to five dozen. Afterwards . . . I have a busy day, preparing for the television people, so continue her chastisement by your own consensus.'

Althea Tite ripped off Habren's knickers, tearing them in half, and sniffed them.

'She's wet, the dirty bitch!' she exclaimed. 'And freshly caned, mum . . .'

'Those are routine cane-marks,' said Miss Horsfall, smiling at Habren, 'and wet knickers at the thought of punishment! So much for your deluded claim to be a domina, my dear Angarad.'

'Why has she got an all-over suntan?' said Goiswinth.

'Some lotion from Oswald,' snapped Ignoge. 'Are we questioning governess's orders?'

Before Habren could shriek, the knickers were wadded in her throat, gagging her. The other girls wheeled a clothes-rail, four feet from the carpet, into place, leaving ample room on all sides; they slung Habren over the rail, bottom up and the rail biting her belly. Ignoge and Goiswinth used their waist ropes to bind the captive's ankles and wrists together, like a calf for the branding, while Althea snapped heavy clamps on her nipples and cunt flaps, fastening them by chains pulled taut to the base of the rail. Habren was helpless to move, her titties and gash stretched by the clamps and the slightest wriggling liable to wrench her tender parts painfully. She squirmed, trembling and sobbing, and clenched her quivering arse-jellies, as three canes were lifted over her bare.

Vip! Vip! Vip!

The three canes lashed her naked buttocks in unison, and Habren squealed, her striped fesses squirming.

'*Mmm!*'

Vip! Vip! Vip!

'*Mmm!*'

Habren's body shook, shuddering in her ropes and clamps, and clenching her croup tight, as deep cane-bites suffused her bare in a mottled pink glow.

'You'll recover your reason much faster, Angarad, if you take your punishment with your usual stoic silence,' Miss Horsfall said, her arms agitated below her desktop.

'*Mmm! Mmm! Mmm!*' squealed Habren, violently shaking her head.

'Of course, you're pretending not to be you. But when you are back in the infirmary, for Miss Maclaren's full treatment, on top of the thrashings that await, I think you'll come to your senses.'

Vip! Vip! Vip!

Each cane lashed Habren's skin in a single weal, on the tender portion of her top buttock; her body jerked, legs and spine shuddering as one.

'*MMM!*'

Miss Horsfall's stroking motions, below her desk, became more vigorous; her breath was harsh and her face a blush.

Vip! Vip! Vip!

As the three canes continued to weal Habren's crimson bare arse-globes, her fesses writhed without pause, the naked skin darkening with deep bruises, and she bucked against her clamps and ropes, stretching her pouch flaps and titties to pale envelopes of flesh; her shrieks of protest became a single, despairing wail.

Vip! Vip! Vip!

'*Mmm . . .*'

Miss Horsfall's skirt rustled, as her feet parted wide beneath her desktop, and her stroking became rapid.

'Of course, when Mrs Gaunt, our new – ah, overseer – arrives tomorrow, we may find all this has been a misunderstanding,' she panted, her hands moving fast between her thighs, and with a tiny seep of liquid dripping down her quivering nylons. 'But, of course, it is invariably a *misunderstanding* that brings girls to us . . .'

The three top strokes chuckled, as they caned Habren's dark blue weals, nearing her tariff of sixty.

'Angarad still pisses herself during a strong beating,' panted Miss Horsfall. 'I *do* hope she's not going to spoil my carpet any more than she has – *look* at her ooze!'

Fifty-seven strokes had been laid; come dripped openly from Habren's swollen red gash flaps on to the carpet.

Vip! Vip! Vip!

The final three cuts took her vertically, straight in the arse-cleft, and slicing both her anus bud and the inner slit of her pouch.

'*MMM!*' Habren screamed, as a jet of yellow piss spat from her writhing cunt, spraying the three caners, to gleam in a steaming pool beneath the flogging rail.

'Ah! Ah! Ah!' gasped Miss Horsfall, her eyes fluttering, and her arms trembling between her thighs. '*Ahh . . .*'

'Should we advise Miss Maclaren, mum?' said Goiswinth. 'About this slut's escape.'

'No, no,' gasped Miss Horsfall. 'Just attend to her further discipline and report. I'd like her to look good for the cameras.'

'With respect, mum,' said Althea, 'you told us to prepare a *soft* scenario for the BBC . . . mild spanking on the panties and suchlike. Angarad Stark will need treatment of more than a few hours and I'm not sure her bum will look – well, very soft.'

Miss Horsfall's glistening wet fingers touched her lips.

'How naughty of me!' she cried. 'How remiss, to forget to tell you – we have a second, *in depth*, televisual documentary tomorrow, by the satellite channel CPTV, serving the more *discerning* public. Mr Marcus Dodd and his delightful wife Bee are coming up from their Teddington studios, along with Miss Tamsin Pollecutt and her friend Will Cragg, manager of Metawear, a subsidiary of our new owners Gauntco, so its director Mr Rollo Cragg informs me. My, we shall all be one flagellant family . . .'

# 13

# Labyrinth

Angarad shivered in the darkness, lit only by the candles held by Amy Patel and Belinda Garce. Her bare breasts were pimpled with cold, the nipples stiff and she kept hoisting her only clothing, a sackcloth dress that billowed around her bare feet, but slipped, exposing the top of her bumcleft: a prison 'shame dress'. Amy laughed.

'Modesty?' she said. 'You might as well go naked. I expect you will, soon.'

'There's nobody in the labyrinth to see you,' said Belinda. 'That's what we're supposed to say.'

'So, now we've told you,' added Amy, 'but you're not supposed to believe us. Remember, it's the *far* door that's open, so you can't stay here. Lots of luck.'

The labyrinth door clanged shut behind the two laughing girls, leaving Angarad alone in the fetid dungeon. She stood still, heart pounding and accustoming her eyes to the darkness. Slowly, the cavern walls began to take gloomy, ghostly shape: the labyrinth was not completely without light. Angarad put out her hands and touched the wall, slimed with damp mould; gingerly, she began to make her way forward, the passage twisting almost at her every step, sometimes so narrow that she had to squeeze, or so low that she must crouch. She let her shame dress slide down her thighs, then her ankles, then stepped out of it and kicked it away. Nude, the trapped girl prowled deeper into her labyrinth. The black shadows grew grey, then to a faint glimmer, until Angarad rounded a corner, after edging forward several minutes, to find the tunnel broadened into an atrium. She halted and drew back behind the rock wall. A cage hung from the cavern's roof, lit by giant slow-burning candles.

Within the cage, the nude figure of Sarah Bunn hung by ropes binding her hair and her clamped nipples, the breasts wrenched upwards, with her wrists, behind her back, tied to her ankles bent behind her. Judon Oates held a rubber cat-o'-nine-tails, which had striped Sarah's bare buttocks to a patchwork of deep crimson welts. Below Sarah's cunt gleamed a pile of her stools, floating in a pond of golden pee. Kneeling before the bound girl was Imogen Tandy, forcing an unskinned branch into her anus, while holding a candle, dripping hot wax on to the girl's exposed clitoris. Her gash was already fattened with hardened wax. Sarah's eyes were closed, her face twisted in an ecstatic smile. Angarad waited for the stroke of the raised whip to fall, yet it did not. She peered, moved into the open and saw that the figures were all wax sculptures. Shuddering, she moved past the cage, into the shadows of the tunnel.

For over half an hour, she made tortuous way forward in the near-blackout, until the shadows began to glimmer once again and she entered a second atrium. Angarad concealed herself but less boldly than before. The cage suspended before her contained the nude bodies of Edra Forge, Belinda Garce and Amy Patel. Angarad strode forward, to confirm that the figures were dummies. Amy's face was contorted in a scream, while she hung suspended in a cross from the cage corners by real hempen ropes, taut on her ankles and wrists. One door of the cage was open, permitting Belinda's wax figurine to flog her with a waxen bullwhip, with Amy's brown back and buttocks, from haunch to underfesse, livid with welts. Edra squatted in the cage before Amy's body and fucked her anally and in cunt with a dildo of black, scaly rubber, like twin serpents, while her teeth fastened on Amy's left nipple, as if to tear it from her breast. Amy's nipples were pierced; from one, hung a copper ring the girth of a fist, which Edra tugged downwards, and the other, ringless, held a lighted cigarette, clamped in Edra's teeth between folds of brown nipple skin, with the simulated ember glowing at Amy's bare nipple. Cunt clamps held the flaps of Amy's gash wide and a pin pierced her swollen, exposed clitoris. Thin chains stretched taut around her buttocks, attaching the cunt apparatus to pins pierced at each lip of her arse bud, so that any clenching of her buttocks under punishment must jerk her nubbin and cunt flaps, with excruciating pain. Belinda and Edra grinned, while Amy's mouth, frozen in a scream, belied her joyful bright eyes.

Angarad plunged once more into darkness and shivered as a new glimmer lightened the tunnel. Her nude body was dripping with sweat, befouled by the mould and fungus that dampened the tunnel walls; her sweat increased, as the atrium ahead seemed to radiate heat as well as light. Within the cage was the naked body of Ghislaine Bassin, cased entirely in hardened wax – a human candle. She hung, suspended by splayed, roped wrists, with her legs bent beneath her, heels held inside her cunt and bum-cleft by twine, binding her ankles and thighs. Her bare buttocks were dark with marks of recent thrashing. All of her, except for her face, was closed in the foot-thick coating of wax, as though it was the live Ghislaine inside, and not wax within wax; her eyes and mouth smiled at Angarad.

The human candle burned with two wicks, the topmost being her tresses coiled in a rope and the second, her luxuriant pube-hair, braided into spikes, extruded from her waxed body and sputtering like fireworks. Fragrant smoke, like the incense she had smelled in Oswald's shop, filled Angarad's nostrils; she panted, wiping sweat from her body. Her hand brushed her own cunt hair, soaked with sweat, then the lips below; they were swollen and Angarad gasped aloud as she touched her clitoris, fully stiffened. A seep of come trickled down her thighs, joining the rivulets of sweat. She squatted and pissed before the caged candle of Ghislaine Bassin, touching her clitoris as she peed, shuddering at the shock of pleasure, then removing her probing hand, but at once brushing it the length of her bum-cleft, to feel her coruscated cane welts adorning her bare croup. Ghislaine's eyes blinked in merriment.

'*No . . .!*' she moaned, hurrying on.

Yet the next display of waxen torment was not far; nor the next and the next. Cage after cage held slags she recognised: wrestling nude in biting contests, the fighters urged on by rubber-clad wardens, with canes poised in mid-air; caned while bound, gagged, branked and hogtied; 'whippled' – the prison practice of whipping on nipples alone; thrashed nude, limbs writhing together, as dog-muzzled slags competed in masturbating contests, with crouching girls, mouths open like sparrows, drinking the come or pee of the girls wanking off; all the faces, whippers or humiliants, bathed in a waxen glow. June Thorbeck, wrists bound and constricted in a rubber punishment corset, crouched before the nude body of Emma Beare, swaddled in ropes of honeysuckle with her cunt wadded in the flowers. June's mouth brimmed with honeysuckle as she chewed Emma free. At each spectacle, Angarad's bare breasts heaved, the nipples hardening; she twined her cunt-hairs in her fingers, but wincing, and slapping her wrist or bum if they strayed to her cunt or clitty.

*Yet Ghislaine had been real . . . hadn't she?*

Two girls hung from the ceiling of their cage, by a single rope wound tightly around their waists. Their arms and legs were bent backwards, with wrists and ankles secured at their spinal nubbins and their cunt basins thrust forward. Apart from the suspending rope, their bodies were woven with tightly knotted cords, biting so hard into naked flesh that the skin was puffy with bruises from rope burn alone. Each girl was impaled by an anal plug of tree bark, peeping from her distended arse bud, and secured by her string embroidery. One girl was small and wiry, the other full-breasted and robust: Ingrid Fage and Clare Cubitt. The girls were inverted, lying on their sides, so that to maintain equilibrium, each girl had to cling with her teeth to the other's cunt flaps. Angarad gasped, pressing her face to the bars of the cage and gazing at the cane-scarred back and wealed arse muscles of Ingrid, whose back was to her, and the erect strawberry nipples of Clare. Both girls' faces were fierce with pleasure. Her eyes blurred by sweat, Angarad did not peer to see if the figures were wax.

'*No . . .!*' she gasped. '*Please, no . . .*'

Her fingers crept to her juicing pouch and, in seconds, she was masturbating hard. She squatted, as though to stool, and pinched her clitty in her fingernails, tears springing from her eyes and her cunt flowing with heavy come. Moaning, she thrust three fingers into her wet pouch, reaming the sides as she frotted her throbbing clitty. Piss dribbled uncontrolled from her gash flaps in spurts until her belly began to heave; she gasped, then squealed. As she looked on the trussed girls cunt-biting, with her own thighs and cunt bush soaking with juice and her clitty pulsing at sopping wet cunt, Angarad orgasmed. The cries of her climax ebbed. She quivered in surprise: in the near distance, there was another woman's cry and a male's grunt of triumphant pleasure. Angarad stood, trembling, and ventured further into the maze: there was nowhere to go except forward, towards a woman screaming.

She was not far. The woman, caged, was bound in a punishment corset of clinging black rubber, with garter straps extending from the base of the garment to mesh rubber stockings, studded with copper pins. Beneath the cage was a brazier, glowing with coals, and inches from her cunt and titties, with a smell of singed hair. Her limbs were full-bound in copper wire, casing her in foetal position, with her wrists and ankles cuffed beneath her thighs and the teats and cunt naked. Pink rubber balls, attached to the cuffs, pressed her cunt basin, as the base of a massive dildo impaling her pouch. The apparatus of cuffs and dildo was roped to the cage's ceiling, so that her body's weight was carried by the shaft in her cunt. A second rope around her belly was slack, but jerked at her haunches' motion: her hips were held by the male who buggered her with fierce, punishing strokes. Her naked buttocks bore the weals of caning; her skull and eyes were closed in a rubber hood, while a copper ball between her teeth pressed down her tongue, gagging her, and fastened around her nape with a rubber thong. Her nipples were pierced and pinned, and likewise her top and bottom lip, each to a nipple, so that her screams wrenched at the nipple flesh and the bouncing of her breasts under buggery jerked her lips over her teeth. The woman was not wax; her tresses flowed, waving like fronds beneath her, and Angarad recognised Miss Horsfall. Numbed, she gazed, while the male grunted, buggering the governess faster and faster. He glanced round.

'You, slut! I knew you'd want a second helping. Right, then! I'll keep my spunk for *your* arsehole . . .'

'No . . .!' wailed Miss Horsfall, as he pulled his monstrous cock, shiny with arse-grease, from the embrace of her anus.

'*No!*' screamed Angarad, running into the darkness of the labyrinth beyond. '*No, Oswald . . .!*'

He lumbered after her, cracking a whip and huffing his leather bellows. Angarad slipped and fell, then rose, bruised, and stumbled on; the laughing male and his whip approaching nearer and nearer.

'More than snout, this time, bitch!' he chuckled. 'Cage and straps and hot metal up your bumhole, before I spunk in you – the *first* time . . . then you can suck me hard again while I thrash your arse purple. That's what you want, you filthy wanking bitch. Isn't it? What *all* bitches want?'

'*No . . . no . . .!*' cried Angarad, her cry shrinking to a sob. 'No, oh *please*, no . . .'

She stumbled again and did not get up, but lay sobbing and exhausted, still giddy from her wanked orgasm.

'I'm coming to whip you . . .' Oswald sang.

Crack!

'I'm coming to strap you . . .'

Crack!

'I'm coming to bugger you blue, girlie . . .'

Crack!

'No . . .' sobbed Angarad, laying her head on the rock floor. 'Please . . . please, Oswald . . .'

The rock shifted under her head and made a squelching sound. She rose to a crouch and got her fingernails around the rim of the slab, managing to prise it up a few inches;

then sobbed in dismay. Beneath the rock was slimy mud. Straining, she raised the rock higher and began to grope. When her hand was elbow deep in slime, her fingers touched the rim of a conduit, or sewer opening. She waggled her hand in the open mouth, her waist's girth. Gulping, she lifted the rock up and slipped her legs into the mud. She dangled her feet until they found the opening, then inserted them, gasping, as her legs slid into the tube up to her thighs, then jammed. She wiggled her feet, managed to lower the rest of her body into the slime. When her head was completely immersed in mud, she replaced the covering rock over her and felt it shake, as Oswald passed overhead. Lungs bursting, she tried to lift the rock again, but could gain no leverage from her slippery foothold. The only way was down. Frantically, she clambered, slithered and fell, immersed in the oily muck, feeling the sides of the shaft undulate; it was curved and warped, seeming to adapt to the contour of her body and allowing her to fall in a sliding embrace, as though sculpted for her own nude body. Suddenly, the sides of the tube vanished and she fell in a pond of slime a few feet deep, with her head above the liquid's surface, breathing air.

She lay, gasping, in the stinking ooze, for some minutes. Starlight penetrated the tiny grotto in which she lay; beyond a chink in the rock, just wide enough for a body to pass, flowed the River Wrigley. Above her head, on a ledge, lay a brass chest, covered in mould and locked with a massively solid brass lock, its opening not lock-shaped but whorled, and for a key more massive than the small chest should warrant. She tried to lift the chest but could not budge it; the box was anchored by brass plates embedded in the rock, a few feet above the river's high water mark. She stuck a finger, then two, into the lock and felt the innards, which were too deep for her fingers, as though half the chest wall accommodated them. Shrugging, she turned away, as the first shaft of dawn penetrated the grotto, then looked back at the tiny plate above the lock. *Property of Sir George Pollecutt, And His True Heirs*, it read. Angarad looked down at her bruised, muddy body and shivered.

'Well, *you're* not going anywhere,' she sighed. 'I wonder if *I* ever shall.'

She squeezed through the chink in the rock, which fitted her body exactly.

*The slightest clothing and I'd be stuck – it seems to be made just for me, naked . . .*

Angarad launched herself into the water, to swim back to her prison.

# 14

# Meat for the Punishment

Smack! Smack! Smack! Despite the protection of thick cotton knickers, worn under flesh-coloured pantyhose, Isobel's bottom clenched as Judon Oates spanked her. Isobel was bent over, with her skirt raised, and touching her toes. Her blond tresses, neatly knotted in a bun, bobbed at each spank. The five other bottom strokes, all in slags' uniforms, stood, watching meekly, with their hands folded at their laps. Imogen Tandy and Amy Patel smiled broadly into the TV cameras.

'Gosh, these knickers are horrid and itchy,' whispered Belinda Garce to Edra Forge.

Smack! Smack! Smack!

'Ouch! Gosh!' said Isobel.

'Be glad it's not you being spanked,' replied Edra.

'I think I'd rather *be* spanked and wear a decent thong, to let some air round my bum,' Belinda said.

'That Max Ogule looks even slimier in the flesh than on TV,' said Sarah Bunn. 'He's positively drooling.'

A middle-aged man with a garish toupee, standing beside Miss Horsfall, spoke to her for the camera.

'Some of our viewers might find this scene a little distressing, Miss Horsfall,' he said. 'Would you care to explain why they shouldn't?'

'Of course,' said Miss Horsfall, smiling for the camera. 'It is no secret that Wrigley Scrubs is run on the lines of a traditional English public school, with a healthy dose of Victorian values. Those include plenty of physical education, spit and polish, and strict adherence to the code of rules, infractions of which are punished, without exception. Normally, a punishment might mean shovelling silt from the riverbed, refusal of exeat or just not getting any jam for tea.'

'Har! Har!' said Max Ogule.

'I should add that, with or without jam, our detainees are fed a minimum of two thousand five hundred calories per day, according to the most modern dietary principles.'

'Har! Har!' said Max Ogule.

'However – and *this* may distress some viewers – on rare occasions, old-fashioned corporal punishment is called for, and given, without hesitation.'

'You mean, spanking, or even caning?' prompted Max Ogule.

'Yes,' said the governess. 'A cane *is* kept polished, but six of the best, taken wearing a flannel nightgown – and *quite optional* – is a rarity. Spanking is the normal method of chastisement, for grave offences. The number of spankings, as you witness here, averages about one per week. This girl, for example, was caught smoking.'

Smack! Smack! Smack!

'Ouch! Ooh, mum!' Isobel cried, dramatically wriggling her bum. 'Gosh, I shan't *ever* smoke again!'

'Girls with an exeat to visit the village are sometimes tempted by village boys with tobacco, or even alcoholic beverages,' Miss Horsfall explained. 'The maximum chastisement is a spanking of thirty smacks, taken on the knickers, and with the spanker's hand not raised above waist level. The deterrent effect of spanking is not so much in the pain caused, which is not very great, but in the shame of the punishment's being witnessed by others.'

Smack! Smack! Smack!

'Well, that's your tariff of two dozen, Coker!' said Judon heartily, and also smiling for the camera. 'Don't be such a silly girl, in future!'

'Ouch!' said Isobel Coker, rubbing her knickered bottom, before replacing her uniform skirt, which she continued to rub. 'I shan't, mum. I was very stupid and I'll never earn a spanking again, promise!'

Max Ogule swivelled to the camera.

'So, there we have it, viewers,' he intoned. 'Wrigley Scrubs prison for young female minor offenders. A regime of strict Victorian discipline, cold showers, physical jerks, cross-country runs and, for naughty girls, no jam for tea – or a spanking! The short, sharp shock, with a recidivism rate of less than two per cent of detainees released. Barbarous, or enlightened? This is Max Ogule, for "Modern Age", returning you to the studio.'

He turned to Miss Horsfall as the camera crew began to dismantle their equipment.

'Super, Miss Horsfall,' he said, 'and, quite sincerely' – turning to the girls – 'I am touched by your genuine appreciation of the care being taken of you.'

'Oh, it's genuine, Mr Ogule,' said Amy Patel, with a curtsy.

'We all feel the same,' said Sarah Bunn. 'Whatever we're here for – shoplifting or mindless vandalism, perhaps – Wrigley Scrubs has taught us our lesson.'

'So gratifying,' said Max Ogule.

'Now, Mr Ogule,' said Miss Horsfall, 'it's time for *your* tea, before your long drive back to London.'

'With jam, or without?' he said, winking at the girls. 'Har! Har!'

'With,' said Miss Horsfall.

Ingrid Fage, in bra and panties, who brought Miss Horsfall the tray of tea things suspended from her teeth, evinced no surprise at the TV personality's presence, or the fact that he was stripped naked, bending over the sofa and receiving a whopping on the bare from Miss Horsfall, skirted but stripped to her bra. Ingrid departed, face down and shuffling backwards, in her wooden hobble. When Miss Horsfall had served the tea and scones, she returned to her work with the rattan.

Vap! Vap! Vap!

'Tight, eh, Max ?' she hissed.

'Yes . . . yes . . .' he groaned. 'Just like old times. Only, in those days, it was *your* arse –'

Vap! Vap! Vap!

'Ouch! That hurt!'

'As it was supposed to. Don't use vulgar language, Max. Just a handful more cuts, then a scrumptious tea.'

'You've certainly changed, Bella, I mean, Miss Horsfall.'

Vap! Vap! Vap!

'We all do. You used to be "Major Rodd"!'

'Don't remind me! Being whopped is less onerous than whopping, and considerably more gratifying . . .'

Vap! Vap! Vap!

' "Don't remind me, *Mistress*"! I dare say you're right. Have you a regular dominatrix in London?'

'Tamsin Pollecutt attends me, Mistress. But she's expensive . . .'

Vap! Vap! Vap!

'*Ooh!*'

'Consider this one on the house, in view of the valuable publicity, Max. You might consider becoming a member of the Pinkarse, on a yearly basis. A number of our tastier girls are adept at thrashing, suitably immodest, and fond of costumes, especially for a reward of extra jam at teatime . . .'

Vap! Vap! Vap!

'*Ouch!*'

'You'll be in the best company, I assure you. The great and the good of England make their way to Wrigley Scrubs, to thrash or be thrashed. Would I lie to you?'

'No, Mistress!'

Vap! Vap! Vap!

'*Ahhh . . .!* I accept! This is most . . .'

Vap! Vap! Vap!

'*Ah! Yes . . .!*'

'Gratifying?' said Miss Horsfall.

'Har! Har!' panted her squirming guest.

The girl, nude but for a bulging brown nappy around her cunt basin, struggled in the ropes from which she hung by her wrists. She was held captive to the ceiling by a ring, round which her long blond tresses were knotted. Her hair supported her whole body weight, unless she pulled up with her forearms, on wrist ropes, to ease the pressure on her mane. Her ankles dangled helplessly, bound by two ropes, looped into rings on the dungeon floor.

'Enough . . . please . . .' she gasped.

Thwap! Thwap! Thwap!

'*Ahhh . . .!*'

Three quirts of rubber thongs lashed her naked back and shoulders, spinning her. Her bare skin was striped with livid purple bruises; above the drooping nappy showed dark blue and purple cane slices on her buttocks. From the nappy oozed a constant dribble of piss and come oil, stained dark brown and with a rancid odour of mushrooms.

'You're a tough bitch, Stark,' said Ignoge, wiping the sweat from her brow. 'But your tariff is a hundred lashes this session, even if you faint. Back gets equal treatment to bum, and you've had your first caning.'

'Please believe me! *I'm Habren Gaunt!*'

Thwap! Thwap! Thwap!

'*AHH!*'

'Not according to the governess. Be reasonable, slut. This is only the Pollecutt room! We haven't taken you to the labyrinth yet, and it's even *worse* than before! And wait till that marsh fungus in your holes *really* starts to rot . . .'

Thwap! Thwap! Thwap!

'We'll depilate your pubes,' said Althea, 'cover your cunt with hot dripping candle wax, let it solidify, then prise it off, in a block; or use plaster of Paris, *or* surgical tape and superglue.'

'*No! Please!*'

'Proud of that cunt bush, eh? There's another way – hung by your wrists and ankles behind your back, over a birthday cake of lighted candles, until your forest is burnt.'

'Oh, my God! This can't be happening . . .!'

'But it is,' said Goiswinth. 'We are *all* females and meat for the punishment. Be happy we don't sew up your cunt flaps with copper wire. After the nappy's full and she pisses out the fungus, perhaps a copper mesh chastity belt? Fill her holes with woodlice and seal them with soap pads of wire wool, to keep the lice at her flesh. Woodlice can live for days, on come and arse grease.'

Thwap! Thwap! Thwap!

'Or a locked chastity belt, cunt packed with marsh fungus and a bush full of pubic crabs,' said Ignoge. 'Surely, you don't want *them*! Just admit who you *are*, bitch! We'll give you a final thrashing, then take you back to surgery.'

All three top strokes had stripped to their loinstrings in the close heat of the Pollecutt room, and their bare breasts bounced as they flogged the trussed Habren. Each punisher held her quirt high, with her other hand pawing aside another's loinstring, to wank her off as they whipped. The room was soundproofed in rubber; around them gleamed racks, branks, tongs, pincers, stocks and flogging-stands, in copper, iron, brass or silver, and none less than three centuries old. Come flowed copiously down the three naked girls' thighs as they masturbated each other.

'I'm in no hurry,' said Goiswinth Moss. 'Having carte blanche with a slag means plenty of wanks . . .'

'I'm not a slag!' Habren sobbed. 'I'm your new boss!'

'Let's break for a rollie,' said Ignoge, her fingers rubbing Goiswinth's clit, with Althea's probing her cunt and Goiswinth masturbating Althea.

All agreed and struggled to roll cigarettes with come-slimed fingers; eventually, all three had damp butts in their mouths and were blowing clouds of smoke over Habren's face and titties.

'Whipping is hard work, slut,' said Ignoge.

'I'm not just some businesswoman!' sobbed Habren, '*I'm a professional dominatrix.*'

She blurted the whole story of her films, and Joss, and Morocco, submissive sluts, and tribesmen huge of tool.

'Thing is, slut, even if all this was true,' Ignoge drawled, 'it wouldn't do you any good. Who runs a prison? Who gives and takes the whoppings? The slags, that's who. They build the labyrinth and even we strokes don't know what's in there. You could order us all whopped but *we do that anyway*, while we wank off. That's why we're here, just like Miss Horsfall, the extreme sub who pretends she's a dom.

We humour her, whop her arse with those corny taped instructions . . . it's all a game! Just like those men in suits who love to be whopped, and pissed on, and stooled on, and to beg for mercy . . . we get two ounces of snout for every session, double if we have to bugger them with strap-ons. The really posh ones insist on that . . .'

Habren stammered that she wished to recruit girls for her films in Morocco. Subs *or* doms . . . and the men with huge, ever-spunking black tools were a reality.

'Imagine,' she said, 'doing your time in the sun, with bare girls' arses to whip all day and huge cocks to spunk in your holes all night!'

The three smoking girls masturbated each other vigorously, moaning, as Habren described a domina's life in a whipping fort. Come flowed from swollen gash flaps as the three wardens ground their cigarette butts on the crotch of Habren's nappy, making it sizzle, then plunged fingers into one another's cunts, and wanked each other off to climax.

'Yes . . .'

'Ah! . . .'

'So good . . .'

'*I wish you'd wank me off*,' blurted Habren. 'God! I . . . *I want to come*.'

Goiswinth grinned and began to rub the crotch of Habren's slimed nappy. Immediately, the trussed woman convulsed; she pissed long and hard, her golden pee mingled with copious come, and her belly flattened, heaving in orgasm.

'Ah! Ah! *Ahh . . .!*' she squealed, panting in harsh gasps. 'God! Oh, *yes* . . .'

'I wish all you say were true,' sighed Ignoge, picking up her whip. 'I'd like to see one of these studs. A good bumming would be more fun than roasting you, stretched on the rack, while we flog your pincered cunt and nipples, you dirty little whore. Which we shall . . .'

Thwap! Thwap! Thwap!

'*Ahh! No! Please!*'

Habren's bare shoulders writhed under the lash of three rubber quirts; yet a powerful new spurt of come flowed down her shuddering bare thighs. Vip! Ignoge delivered a short stroke to the inside of Habren's come-slimed thigh and held the shiny thongs up for her inspection.

'Whoever you are, you came when Goiswinth wanked you and your juice gives you away. You *like* it. You *are* a sub,' she said.

'If you'd only let me get to a telephone . . .!' Habren wailed, her loins jerking. 'I can *send* for my best stud! Put him on the next plane from Marrakesh! His name is Aggar, and his *cock* . . . to die for! If my hands were free . . .!'

The three girls looked at each other.

'Miss Maclaren would let her phone,' said Althea. 'We could take her to surgery, to certify she's fit for the rack, brank and pincers – just to be on the safe side.'

The others murmured agreement.

'Wait,' Habren murmured. 'I've only been flogged seventy-two and . . . and you promised me a full hundred . . .'

The sky was grey and cloudy and a bitter wind blew from the river. Nevertheless, the snow had held off, though a light drizzle threatened.

Crack!

The leather stockwhip lashed the naked shoulders of two staggering cart girls, as they pulled the Vandal cart into the home stretch of the chariot race.

Vip!

A long rattan cane sliced their buttocks, full on the bare. The harnessed and hooved pair already bore the welts of numerous whipmarks, and their nude bodies were puddings of mud, come, piss and tears. Inches behind, the Saracen chariot lumbered, its strapped and harnessed crew red-faced and panting hoarsely as they sobbed and stumbled towards the finishing line, where Miss Horsfall and a group of guests awaited them, cheering. The progress of the two carts was followed by a motorised television crew, their buggy bearing the legend 'CPTV'. Both charioteers were nude, like their crews, and brandished a whip in one arm and a long cane in the other.

'It is so nice to see old friends,' purred Miss Horsfall, sipping champagne, as the Vandal driver leaned over and slashed her opponent's naked, swaying breasts with her cane. 'Goodness! I think the Vandals are going to win.'

Rollo Cragg, Tamsin Pollecutt, Will, Marcus and Bee all clapped as the Saracen driver responded with a canestroke to the Vandal driver's bare bum, throwing her off balance. The Vandal ceased flogging her crew with the stockwhip and lashed her opposing driver instead, right between the thighs, on her open cunt. The Saracen again caned the Vandal's buttocks; the carts veered as the race became a flogging match between drivers. The beslimed cart girls pulled gamely until the Vandal chariot crossed the line, just inches ahead of the Saracen. The two drivers leapt from their vehicles and continued their contest by writhing in the dirt, pummelling, gouging and biting, with slaps and teethmarks to cunts and titties amid snarls and shrieks.

'Good show,' murmured Rollo, blowing cigar smoke.

The Vandal and Saracen teams helped their harnessed friends loose from their straps and rubber corsets, while the drivers fought, slapping, biting and punching, in the mud. Miss Horsfall and her guests deemed the Vandal chariot to have won but the outcome was confused by the Saracen driver, who squatted on her opponent's breasts, with her left foot and head in a thigh-lock, and was clawing the girl's exposed quim, demanding submission. Tamsin Pollecutt settled thc issue: borrowing Miss Horsfall's cane, she stepped into the mud and whipped the topmost fighter savagely across the nipples, toppling her, so that the Vandal driver was now bent over, teeth chewing the Saracen's cunt flaps and clit, while pissing on her face, which dominance was deemed victory for the Vandals.

'I suppose I'm sentimental for the Vandals,' said Tamsin, leaving a smear of black lipstick on her glass as she sipped champagne; she slid open her fur coat and lifted each of her rubber thigh-boots in turn, to allow a barefoot slag, in bra and panties, to lick them clean.

The opening of her fur revealed Tamsin herself, clad in stockings and sussies of fine latex mesh, and a black rubber corset with tightly knotted copper eyelets that made her naked breasts jut high. Her erect nipples were pierced, with copper rings dangling over the studs of her corset.

'There are more things for you to film,' said Miss Horsfall, 'a whole range of penal practices. Shall we proceed to the river for the skin-diving? What a lovely coat, Tamsin. Sable?'

'Not so grand. Submissive girls' pube hair, with the collar and cuffs of my own.'

The party climbed aboard their own chariot, pulled by four nude girls in harness, with two uniformed drivers, Amy Patel and Belinda Garce. Amy and Belinda cracked their whips on bare girl-skin and the carriage moved towards the River Wrigley.

'How convenient, Rollo, that you are a director of SPV, the outgoing franchisee, *and* of Gauntco, the new one,' said Miss Horsfall.

'SPV?' said Rollo. 'Oh, yah . . . Pinkarse. Suppression of loathsome vice in all its female forms.'

'I suppose it's entirely ethical,' added the governess.

'No one has said otherwise,' said Rollo, 'but then, I didn't remind them. What I did do was ride around on railway trains with a mobile phone amid nonentities telling their wives they were on the train, as if they could imaginably be anywhere else. I addressed a nonexistent stockbroker, telling him to buy either SPV stock or Gauntco stock, on a hot tip. Everyone listened, both stocks soared and everyone has made pots of money. I dare say *that's* ethical.'

Five minutes later, they pulled up on the river bank beside a knot of slags, busy beneath a wooden gibbet thirty feet high, and reaching out over the choppy waters. Two slags in bra and panties were hog-tying the wrists and ankles of a girl, clad only in a pink rubber punishment corset, who lay on her back in the mud, her teats and belly squashed by the buttocks of the slags, both girls splattered with mud from the girl's kicking. Her arms and legs were bent upwards over her belly, and pressed over the thighs of the sitter, who slid off her when the roping was complete.

The girl's trussed body formed a diamond shape, with a wooden hobble bar parting her thighs and the spattered slag kicked her, rolling her on her side, so that her spread cunt and buttocks faced the newcomers.

'Carry on,' said Miss Horsfall.

An anal plug of freshly cut, unskinned oak was inserted into the girl's nether hole and a larger plug in her vulva. Her cunt flaps, and both her nipples, were clamped in copper vices, with her mane and pubic forest fixed in similar clamps, all the clamps wrenching her flesh or hair, and tautly hooked above her navel to a copper chain, clipped to her punishment corset. Edra Forge directed a slag, who winched the trussed girl up by the chain, until she was hauled and perched on top of the gibbet by a second slag astride the gibbet's arm, who fastened a rubber cord to each of her body clamps. The rubber cords were piled and coiled in a bow, while the copper chain was unspooled to slack. The slag threw the long end of the bow down to Edra; one pull would release the coil of rubber ropes, sending the girl to plunge towards the water, until her progress was halted by springy rubber, or the longer chain.

'Some girls call this bungee-jumping,' explained Miss Horsfall, licking her teeth, 'but I prefer skin-diving as more ladylike. When her cords are released, the subject can twist, so that the rubber cords jerk her body clamps above water; or she can fall, more painfully, to her chain length, underwater. By skilfully treading water, she may remain under, preventing the rubber from bouncing back and exposing her wet bottom to the girls' canes. The contest is between the girls on shore and the skin diver, who must try and direct her bounce, to spend the maximum time either underwater or aloft, free from canestrokes. Bound, she is of course unable to clutch the gibbet and must drop again. If she cries halt before ten minutes, then she pays a forfeit of a real, dry-bum caning on shore; if she lasts ten minutes, then she may cane her opponents' bottoms. Each cane has a device, like the tachometer of a bicycle: it records each stroke from the movement of the caner's wrist, whether or not it lands. If the skin diver submits, she takes a caning of the largest stroke total of *one* cane but, if she wins, she may cane *each* of her opponents the *total* number of strokes given. This contestant is Ghislaine Bassin and she is *very* good at it.'

'Super game,' said Tamsin.

'I thought of it myself,' said Miss Horsfall.

'Did you test it yourself?' said Tamsin, slyly.

'Why of course!' said Miss Horsfall, adding coyly, 'I mean, I saw that it *was* tested.'

Five girls in bra and panties took position on the muddy shore under the gibbet, while Edra Forge smartly pulled the bow, releasing the bound girl. The rubber cords sprang free, billowing outwards as the girl plunged, head first, plummeting from the gibbet towards the river; she twisted and squirmed, tangling the cords. The copper wire twanged and she jerked to a halt just under the water, emerging in an instant, wet, with a rubber rope wrenching her anal plug. She screamed as five canes lashed her swivelling buttocks, before the rubber cords twanged up again and she squirmed to unravel them before her trussed body cannoned into the gibbet's arm. Bucking, she dropped again, with the cords only halfway untangled, and this time the jerk on her quim clamps made her scream, the cunt ropes twanging tight, followed by the cords on her breast clamps and pubic hair.

Vip! Vip! Vip! Vip! Vip!

Wailing, the girl fought to right herself. Her body spun as the canes slapped her wet titties, cunt flaps and buttocks, and the camera crew cheered, with one camera girl in green wellington boots kneeling to get a close-up of Ghislaine's pain-wracked face and flapping bare titties. Ghislaine rolled and bucked, to soar upwards, before plummeting again, with the cords almost disentangled, and plunging deep into the water; all the rubber cords twanged, save the one fastened on her titties, and the cord that strained most was that on her copper waistband. Miss Horsfall and her guests clapped.

'Clever Ghislaine!' she cried. 'She can stay under for minutes.'

'We have a plain ducking stool at Pinkarse, in Teddington,' murmured Marcus, 'which I shall refine.'

Canes quivered in frustration over the churning water submerging the girl's body; the slags jumped in surprise as Ghislaine rose in a froth out of the water but without ascending to safety. She hung, dangling from her anal plug and her tresses, with her buttocks clenched tight, to hold the arse-dildo inside her. Her face wore an expression of helpless pain as her body spun, to present her attackers with her bare buttocks, wet and spread.

Vip! Vip! Vip! Vip! Vip!

The five canes sliced Ghislaine's buttocks in unison, the caning acquiring a fierce rhythm, as it seemed that Ghislaine, quivering and screaming as her bare bum crimsoned, was powerless to launch herself upwards, away from whopping. Canes sliced her perineum, or full on the cunt flaps and pouch, spinning her, so that the canes could slap her bare breasts. Yet Ghislaine seemed never to stay still, unless it was her full buttocks presented to the canes, at which she stopped threshing; apart from a thorough beating of her croup, most of the canestrokes slipped, or missed. Miss Horsfall consulted her watch.

'Nine minutes and twenty seconds!' she murmured. 'I think Ghislaine's going to make the ten.'

The trussed girl suddenly bounced upwards, to her attackers' cries of dismay, as she opened her mouth and bit into the gibbet, gouging a chunk of wood but holding herself out of harm with her teeth. Canes flailed vainly, inches beneath her dangling bottom; the girls squealed as Ghislaine's pee suddenly sprayed them, hard and hissing, followed by a flurry of pellets, as she stooled copiously over their faces.

'Ten!' cried Miss Horsfall. 'Your canes, please, girls.'

Sheepishly, the caners handed over their instruments, while Ghislaine was released from her bonds.

'Well!' said Miss Horsfall. 'Quite a tally! How many do you think you took, Ghislaine?'

'At least sixty, mum, I'm sure,' panted the naked girl, rubbing her bright crimson bum. 'Look!'

Tamsin ran her fingernails through the ridges of Ghislaine's caned arse.

'Pretty,' she said. 'I'd go with sixty.'

'The tally of strokes is more,' said Miss Horsfall. 'Ninety-four precisely. Which means that each of you slags take that number, on the bare, from Ghislaine.'

'I'd like a go,' said Tamsin.

'Me, too,' said Rollo. 'I think that, for televisual purposes, we should stage a multiple beating: myself, Tamsin, Will and Marcus can join Ghislaine. Five canes, five bottoms.'

The girls bent over in a sullen row, lowering their knickers to their knees, then forced into a crouch, with their titties and faces pushed firmly, one after the other, into the mud by Tamsin's boot. Tamsin herself handed her coat to a cameragirl and, nude but for sussies, corset and stockings, lifted her cane over the first bare bum. Her breasts quivered, with nipples hard and the nipple rings jangling; she patted Ghislaine's bottom, then her breasts and finally the open lips of her slit, as the caned wet girl, slimed with river mud, took position beside her. Ghislaine simpered, clamping Tamsin's fingers between her thighs, the heel of her thumb squashing the dominatrix's swollen clitty, glistening with come.

VIP!

The five canes cracked as one, on the shivering bare croups, which began to clench as their owners squealed.

'*Oh!*'

'*Ah!*'

'*Ouch!*'

'*Mm!*'

'*Uhh!*'

'Ninety-three to go,' panted Miss Horsfall, her thighs and croup trembling and with wetness visible at her cunt basin.

'It's not fair, Marcus!' cried Bee. 'Why can't I take part, too?'

'Ask your mistress,' snapped her husband.

The canes whistled: five bums wealed a vivid pink and squirmed as the girls sobbed in unison.

'*Go* on,' whined Bee. '*Please* . . .'

'You *are* a pain in the arse, you little slut,' said Tamsin. 'Miss Horsfall . . . would it be imposing too much on your hospitality . . . might I be so bold . . .?'

Miss Horsfall lifted her cane.

'I think a birching might be more appropriate for such an appalling show of manners,' said Tamsin. 'Happily, our crew is provided with sheaves. Bee, you slut, crouch with your face in the mud, knickers right off, skirt up and bum bare. If you wouldn't mind, Miss Horsfall . . .'

'Ninety-four, with the birch, on bare?' said Miss Horsfall, the damp at her crotch now gleaming wet. 'I shall be delighted!'

'Thank you so much,' said Tamsin, lifting her cane. 'I fear you are too kind. These submissive sluts are just *too* demanding. Spread your arse cheeks for the tickler, *bitch*!'

'Yes, Mistress,' pouted Bee and sullenly obeyed.

'I agree,' said Miss Horsfall, lifting the sheaf of pickled birch twigs. 'As, I am sure, does Ghislaine Bassin . . .'

'We all hate submissives, mum,' said Ghislaine gravely. 'Dirty tykes!'

Vip!

The five caned bares shivered and squirmed.

Swish!

'Ouch!'

The birch twigs crackled on Bee's exposed and uplifted buttocks, laying a spider's web of tiny pink welts. Her bare bum quivered, clenching under the crackling sheaf of rods, and her sulky face brightened into radiance as her eyes and cunt moistened in harmony.

Swish!

Bee's bare bum jerked; her cunt juiced copiously, with drips of come glistening on her trembling thighs.

'Yes,' she moaned. '*Yes* . . .'

'My, you've certainly put *this* slag through the mangle,' said Miss Maclaren, lighting a rollie and sucking deep smoke. 'But whoever she is, she can't be Angarad Stark. She looks alike but *that* slut is just tidying her things –

she's right as rain after her little bout of snuffles and I've given her a hot eucalyptus enema to make sure. I had to spank her bum, to make her take double tube in her rectum, so she'll walk a bit awkwardly. *Angarad Stark!*'

Angarad appeared at the bathroom door, clutching a towel to her nude body, wiping tears from her eyes and hobbling, while rubbing her stiffly parted arse-cheeks.

'*Please* – surely not *more*, mum?'

Her eyes fell on Habren's smutted and whipped nude body.

'What . . .'

Habren stared.

'So – *that* is Angarad Stark,' she said to her three tormentors, who fidgeted nervously. 'I *am* Habren Gaunt.'

'There's been a misunderstanding, mum,' said Ignoge, curtsying to Miss Maclaren, then to Habren. 'You see –'

'Go about your duties, wardens!' ordered the nurse. 'Misunderstandings are the fault of the misunderstood.'

When Ignoge, Goiswinth and Althea had left, Miss Maclaren invited Habren to explain herself. Habren blurted her story, including her suspicion that she might, somewhere, have a twin. When she had finished, Miss Maclaren smiled and said she supposed that she would have to call Habren 'mum', as her new owner.

'You *are* going to make the phone call, I expect,' she added softly. 'To the male with the tireless black tool . . .'

'Assuredly, Miss Maclaren,' Habren said. 'But there is a more pressing question.'

Her eyes did not leave Angarad's, nor Angarad's hers. Angarad let fall her towel and stood naked before her lookalike. Miss Maclaren inspected both bodies and began to feel and pummel each one, chopping collar-bones, tugging hair, both mane and pubic, pinching belly-buttons, nipples and labia, but ignored by the two girls, lost in each other's gaze. She fired questions – yes, both were foster-children, both of blood group A, both ignorant of their biological parents . . .

'Are we identical twins, mum?' said Angarad.

'Monozygotic, the girl means,' said Habren.

'*I* know what I mean!' Angarad cried.

'I should need a blood sample to see if you have the same haptoglobin,' said Miss Maclaren. 'You have the same blood group and sex, and that's the third thing. You also,' she added drily, 'seem *both* to be submissive sluts.'

Habren opened her mouth to protest but Angarad slapped her nipples, and her protest turned to an '*ooh!*'

'What's haptoglobin?' said both girls in unison.

'It's what carries haemoglobin,' said Miss Maclaren drily. 'However, that test would have to go to a lab. There *is* a practical test that I can do here, if you like.'

'You will please do it,' Habren commanded.

'Very well. It may be rather uncomfortable.'

# 15

# Pollecutt's Box

Angarad and Habren sat opposite each other in surgical chairs with their legs raised on supports and thighs fully parted, to expose genitals and anus. They were strapped at their ankles and mid-thigh. Miss Maclaren told them not to be shocked, then instructed both girls to masturbate. Each looked at the other without a blush and kept their eyes on the other's nude body as she reached to her open quim and began to rub her clitoris. The nurse fastened each anus wide open with a four-pronged surgical speculum that stretched the anal tissue nearly three inches.

'I want your come for a lubricant, as part of the first test,' said Miss Maclaren. 'You are both juicing well.'

Without a word, Angrad and Habren exchanged fingers, each now wanking off the other, with fingers deep inside wet, slimy cunts, copiously dripping come. Both girls sighed, purring, and their bellies began to quiver. Miss Maclaren dipped her fingers in Angarad's bum-cleft, just beneath her dripping cunt, and palmed a portion of fluid, which she soaked in a sponge. She wrapped the sponge around a metal rod and swabbed the inside of Angarad's anus, pushing the swab right to the root, until Angarad's bumhole dripped with her own come. The nurse applied the same procedure to Habren, as both the girls wanked off more and more vigorously and groaned aloud, shifting their buttocks, as their bellies contracted and shuddered. Miss Maclaren lit a bunsen burner and allowed a sheaf of candles to melt into a dish, while she used pincers to hold an oven-glass clyster tube over the flame. The tube was over three inches wide, over a foot long and equipped with a plunger, like a monstrous syringe. When the candle wax was bubbling, she poured it quickly into each tube and, as the girls continued to stare at each other's nude and pulsing bodies, pushed the two tubes into each stretched anus. Both girls screamed and their buttocks and cunts jerked, yet they did not cease their frottage, their fingers now bathed in gushing, slimy cunt juice.

'*Ohh . . .!*'

Miss Maclaren pushed until the tubes had almost disappeared between the girls' squirming buttocks. She pushed the plungers of each tube at once, injecting the cooled but still pliable wax into each girl's anus, and gradually withdrawing the tubes, as the liquid was deposited in the anal chamber.

'*Ahh . . .!*'

'*Ohh . . .!*'

Both girls wriggled, their faces beetroot-red and their tears pouring; yet their fingers continued to masturbate each other's juicing cunts. Their legs kicked, jerking against the rubber straps buckled tightly around their skin and leaving bruises where the thongs bit.

'*Oh! God, mum!*'

'*What the fuck . . . AHH!*'

'*Hold still, both of you!*' rapped the nurse as she withdrew the plungers from the squirming bumholes and unclipped the speculums. 'Now, hold the wax inside until it has solidified.'

The girls wanked off, sobbing, as their cunts flowed with come and their arse puckers tightened, with only tiny dribbles of wax escaping from the anus bud.

'Mm . . .'

'Ahh . . .'

Their shrieks subsided and they began to squirm in earnest, the slippery thighs jerking beneath the wanked cunts, while Miss Maclaren looked at her watch. Several minutes elapsed, while the girls continued their bare-cunt frottage.

'Now,' the nurse said, 'I want you to push, as if stooling, and expel the wax from your holes.'

Both girls strained. A sliver, then a cylinder, of shiny solid wax protruded from each girl's bumhole, growing thicker and deeper as she pushed it into the air. The wax was slimy with arse-grease but curved and hard, spiralling out faster and faster, in the shape of each rectum. Angarad and Habren smiled, wanking off harder, as they stooled their wax likenesses. Miss Maclaren seized each waxwork as it plopped from the girls' bumholes and held them up.

'Identical,' she said.

Habren snatched Angarad's wax rectum and placed it at the lips of her anus, then gripped her own likeness and pushed it two inches into Angarad's bumhole. Each girl pushed her waxen anal form into the other's bumhole, wanking her clitty at the same time. The girls swayed, with cooing gasps, as their cunts poured with come, lathering their pube forests and creaming their inner thighs. The two wax tubes went all the way inside the two bumshafts, which closed over them. Habren and Angarad smiled.

'You fit me, slut,' whispered Angarad, 'perfectly.'

'And *you* fit *me*, bitch,' replied Habren.

Each opened her anus a sliver, to allow a fragment of wax to reappear. Habren fastened Angarad's arse-dildo with her fingernails and manipulated it, thrusting it into her anus like a cock, with Angarad doing the same to her twin. As the girls wanked their cunts, they buggered each other vigorously with the waxen tools. Their moans and gasps grew deeper and the bumholes relaxed and opened more and more, to squeeze the dildos, as their thrusts became harder, the wax shining with arse-grease, until both girls shrieked, convulsing in climax, twisting, to squash nipples and kiss each other on the lips.

'Twin slags,' Angarad gasped.

'Twin sluts,' Habren moaned.

They shrieked as Miss Maclaren plucked the hard wax tools from their bumholes. When the girls were finally freed from their surgical chairs, they went to the showers. Each soaped the other's body in the shower, rinsed, then licked her clean with her tongue. Tongue lingered long at wet cunt, until Miss Maclaren cracked her cane smartly across both pairs of naked fesses.

'I'll make some phone calls and we *may* find out your origins,' Miss Maclaren said, 'but meanwhile, there is a prison to run and it seems that you, Mrs Gaunt, are to run it. Remember that your – ah – *sister* is still serving her sentence.'

'You called *me* a submissive slut,' said Habren.

'Well, your sister has a pink ticket – she undoubtedly has tendencies –'

'Then I must have the same. Submissives are selfish, greedy and demanding, aren't they?'

'Yes,' said Miss Maclaren.

'Then, *she* can be Mrs Habren Gaunt for a while. Let *her* run the prison and deal with Horsfall, while I shall be Angarad Stark.'

Habren pouted and made a threatening *moue.*

'This is a bit irregular –' Miss Maclaren began.

'Would four ounces of snout make it less irregular?' asked Habren.

'Eight,' said Miss Maclaren.

'Six,' said Habren.

'Done,' said Miss Maclaren.

They dressed: Habren in slag's uniform, Angarad in grey shantung silk. On Habren's insistence, Miss Maclaren provided cords, which they looped round their necks, to suspend their waxen dildos between their breasts.

'Now! Angarad, go and wipe the main wardens' toilets clean with your pubic hair, then polish them with your panties, you scruffy little slut!' barked Miss Maclaren.

'Yes, mum,' said Habren Gaunt.

Habren was writhing against the common girls' urinal, an aluminium sluice with bum-dips two feet apart, cleaning the metal with her pubic hair. She wore only her sussies, stockings and top, having shed her knickers and shoes.

'I did enjoy the tug of war,' said Tamsin Pollecutt, as Rollo Cragg escorted her towards the refectory. 'Girls pulling the rubber with their teeth – then that lovely crack as the Saracens let go, and the rubber whopped the Vandals' titties. Shan't be a mo, Rollo, I've just got to pee.'

She ducked into the main toilets but Rollo followed her.

'You won't mind if I watch,' he drawled.

'And what if I do?' said Tamsin, attempting to close her cubicle door, held open by Rollo's knee. 'There's a girl out there!'

'It's only a slag on punishment duty. She's there to obey orders, aren't you, slag?'

'Yes, sir,' Habren answered meekly.

'Then, see nothing.'

'Yes, sir.'

'Pervert,' Tamsin said, giving him her pubic fur coat to hold and squatting to tinkle over the shiny clean porcelain.

Rollo edged inside the cubicle and bolted the door. He kneeled at Tamsin's crotch, sniffing her cunt, as she pissed.

'I *charge* men to do that,' she said in mock outrage.

'Never pay for anything at Pinkarse,' said Rollo.

'What do *you* know? Pinkarse is for females these days. Men are there to serve and suffer.'

'I know more than you, missy. Pinkarse goes back a long way and, when Pollecutt's Box is found, there'll be true reckoning, with the ladies in their rightful place.'

'Piffle! I can tell you *all about* Pollecutt's Box, Rollo . . . but I shan't.'

'I'm glad, for there's something I think you've earned . . .'

'*Rollo! What . . .?*' Tamsin shrieked, as the male wrenched her arse from the toilet seat and, holding her by her wriggling hips, turned her upside down, with her head dangling over the bowl.

Piss sprayed from her cunt, wetting her face and breasts and dribbling down her rubber corset.

'*Let me go, bastard!* I haven't finished! I want to stool!'

'Now it's my turn to say shan't. Unless you tell me what you know about Pollecutt's Box.'

Tamsin was silent, her arse wriggling helplessly in front of Rollo's face; he sank his teeth into her left buttock and bit deeply.

'*Oww!*'

He bit her right fesse, twice, then the left again, leaving livid red bruises.

'*Oh! Fuck you!*'

Rollo lowered Tamsin's head into the toilet bowl, until she gasped, spluttering and twisting, as her face sank in the golden lake of her own piss. He put his foot on her back, pinioning her, and parted his cape. He unbuckled his belt and allowed his trousers to fall, stepping out of them, with his cock already massive. The belt was a double snake of black rubber, with a buckle at both front and back. Unwound, it reassembled into a quirt of four thick thongs. With the clawed end of his little finger, he ripped a jagged ladder in each of her mesh rubber stockings.

'*Oh! You fucking bastard!*' she cried, her shriek turning to a gurgle as he pushed her face under the piss.

'Unladylike language!' Rollo exclaimed. 'From the owner of such a lovely lady's bottom. So tight and fleshy and . . . *whipworthy*. You've had this coming, Tamsin.'

Thwap! Thwap! Thwap!

Tamsin threshed, her bottom clenching and squirming and her head knocking against the toilet bowl, as Rollo's quirt striped her on the bare with twelve vicious and expert weals to mid-fesse. A stream of bubbles floated from Tamsin's mouth to the surface of her pee.

Thwap! Thwap! Thwap!

Twelve new welts crossed the first set; Tamsin's flogged bare buttocks squirmed frantically and Rollo let her come up for air.

'*You fucking –*'

Her head sank below the piss again and there was a gurgling sound as she swallowed.

Thwap! Thwap! Thwap! Thwap!

Two strokes each, to the left and right haunches, raised a puffy mass of bruises on the tender flesh, followed by four strokes to the top bum, and four to the fleshy underfesse, stroking well down her thigh, almost to her stocking tops. Tamsin's long, coltish legs jerked and shuddered, as her bare bum reddened, her feet kicking against the walls of the cubicle. Suddenly, there was a plop, a hiss and a stream of hard dark stools bursting from her anus, to spatter her stockings and Rollo's erect naked cock.

'*Dirty slut!*'

Thwap! Thwap! Thwap!

Each stroke of the quirt the equal of four canestrokes, Rollo took Tamsin's beating to twenty, until a knock on the cubicle door interrupted him.

'Is everything all right, mum?' said Habren. 'May I be of assistance?'

'No!' roared Rollo, slamming the cubicle door open, to reveal Habren kneeling and peeking through a knothole. Habren's hands covered her juicing cunt; she was masturbating as she watched Tamsin whipped on the bare.

Rollo let Tamsin rise and, spluttering, she gazed round.

'Why, Angie!' she cried.

'Yes, mum, it's me, Angarad,' said Habren.

'A peeking bitch merits thrashing!' Rollo cried. 'Wanking herself, too, the slut!'

'Very good, sir. At your pleasure, sir,' said Habren, trembling.

'My, my, Angie!' Tamsin gasped. 'You *are* a true sub . . . *AH!*'.

Thwap! Thwap! Thwap!

Her head once more under her pee, she received a further twelve strokes of the quirt, while Habren held her ankles, on Rollo's orders. Sitting on Tamsin's feet, Habren continued to wank off, obeying Rollo's command to take the glans of his cock between her lips. She engorged his helmet and began to suck, as he continued to flog the threshing Tamsin, while Habren wanked her stiff wet clitty. Her head rose, to plunge again and take Rollo's cock to his balls with the back of her throat.

'*Yes*, slut,' he gasped. 'You filthy fucking whore . . .'

Thwap! Thwap! Thwap!

Tamsin's whipped bare nates were a livid mass of crimson and purple, when Habren groaned and yelped, as her belly contracted, heaving in orgasm, and she pissed herself during spasm, her pee flowing in a fast hissing stream towards the central gutter. Rollo grunted, then began to gasp, as Habren continued to milk his erect cock, and then groaned as creamy spunk jetted around her lips, dribbling on her chin, with her throat convulsing, as she swallowed the larger portion of his sperm. Rollo released Tamsin, who came up gasping and sobbing, her face red.

'Learned your lesson, Tamsin dear?' sneered the male. 'Going to tell all?'

'Yes, Rollo,' Tamsin whimpered. 'Look! The slut's pissed the floor!'

'I'm sorry, mum,' blurted Habren.

'Lick up your mess, bitch!' Tamsin spat, through her sobs.

'At once, mum.'

Habren knelt, presenting her bare, come-slimed thighs and fesses to Rollo and Tamsin, as she licked up the remnants of her piss, then sank to her belly to polish the floor with her pubic bush.

'Take off your blouse and bra, bitch,' Tamsin ordered. 'You can keep that stupid wax amulet, I suppose.'

Habren obeyed; holding her wax amulet in her mouth and crouching, she picked up all of Tamsin's splattered stools, squeezing them between her bare breasts and dropping them into the bowl. Then she polished the stool-slimed toilet floor with her pubic forest. Tamsin ordered her to stand for hosing, and directed a powerful jet of cold water over the shivering girl, soaking the stockings and sussies which were her only modesty. Habren sobbed as the jet thrashed her nipples and cunt, drenching her. Tamsin put aside the hose and rubbed her raw buttocks, with a rueful smile.

'Perhaps I did deserve whopping, Rollo,' she murmured.

'*I'd* say! Never knew a filly that didn't.'

'So I'll *show* you what's in Pollecutt's Box, if . . .'

'Show me! Better and better! If what?'

Tamsin looked at Habren's parted bum-cleft and the thick swollen lips of her piss-flecked juicing gash.

'If I may punish *this* bitch for peeking. It's what you *want*, Angarad, isn't it? What you loved, at Pinkarse . . .'

'At your pleasure, mum,' said Habren.

'No,' spat Tamsin, 'at *yours*. You submissive slut!'

Habren looked at her and smiled, her eyes wide.

'I *am* a submissive slut, mum, and must be caned bare-bum for it. I'm . . . I'm glad you remember me.'

Rollo laughed and slapped his thigh.

'To Miss Horsfall's study, pets,' he said, 'where we can take our time at wench-thrashing. I have a director's key.'

He began to reassemble his rubber quirt until it formed two dog-leashes. Habren took her leash between her teeth and Tamsin, glowering, did the same, after crouching to Rollo's command: her privilege of thrashing the slag depended on her obedience.

'You *are* a rotten bastard,' she hissed as Rollo slapped each bare croup, directing his animals' arse-meat to the governess's room.

'How do you want to take me, mum?' said Habren. 'Over the sofa or crouching? Bare bum, of course, unless you prefer wet knickers.'

'Angie! Drop the "mum" – it's Tamsin.'

'If you please, mum, I'd rather follow prison rules,' Habren replied.

'I'll cane you much harder for that insolence, you luscious young whelp. Best friends – didn't you ever guess it was *your* bum I always wanted – to cane those beautiful bare melons raw? You deserve it – your mouth was *far* too practised, sucking Rollo's filthy tarse . . .'

Both women stood nude, but for sussies and stockings, before Rollo Cragg. Unbidden, Habren positioned herself over the back of the sofa, thighs spread, to show her wet jungle of pubic hair, dangling beneath the swollen wet lips of her already gushing cunt. Tamsin put a hand to her own naked gash, frotting herself to moisture, as she traced the cleft of Habren's trembling buttocks.

'So pure, even in this place,' she murmured, then knelt, to bury her nose in Habren's arse-cleft, nuzzling her anus and tonguing her perineum.

Habren sighed and her buttocks clenched over Tamsin's nose.

'How many is my tariff, mum?' she said.

'Let's say a round fifty, with the rattan,' whispered Tamsin, licking her teeth. 'Yes . . . a beating to the bone, my sweet slut Angie.'

'As you please, mum,' Habren gulped.

Rollo took the heavy rattan from Miss Horsfall's cane rack and handed it to Tamsin.

'You haven't forgotten Pollecutt's Box,' he warned.

Tamsin lifted the rattan over the blond girl's spread bare croup and shook her head.

Vap!

Habren jumped as the wood sprang across her naked buttocks, wealing them dark pink.

Vap!

Her bum clenched and she groaned.

Vap!

Her colt's legs began to shiver and her arse-clenching became a continuous, squirming shudder.

'Gosh, mum . . .' she gasped.

Vap!

'Oh . . .'

'Does it hurt awfully, Angie?' said Tamsin.

Vap!

'*Ah!* I'd never dreamed it could hurt so much!'

'Not even at Pinkarse?'

'No, mum.'

Vap!

'*Ahh . . .!*'

Habren's taut buttocks quivered as the wood striped her fesses crimson, and Tamsin began to wank off as she caned. Her fingers mashed and rubbed her extruded, swollen clitty; rivulets of come streaked her naked thighs. Rollo stood, with cock erect peeping beneath his cape.

Vap!

'*Oh!* Mum . . .! *Oh!*'

Vap!

'I never told you, Angie,' panted Tamsin, 'but I have a whole collection of videos with Habren Dodd, the domina – your absolute lookalike. I'd wank off for hours watching her cane innocent young girls on the bare, but wishing that she was a vile sub and I could flog *her* arse instead. I imagined *her* as *you*, with her magnificent bare bum squirming under my rod . . .'

Vap!

'*AHH!* I'm sorry for blubbing, mum, but *it smarts* . . .'

'I never understood subs, but now that Rollo's thrashed me, I . . . I'm beginning to,' Tamsin gasped, her gasp rising to a shriek as Rollo bared his massive cock and, clutching her by the hips, thrust his helmet into her arse-cleft.

'Then you'll understand this reminder of our deal,' he snarled, ramming his cock two inches into her anus – three, four, and finally, as Tamsin buckled at the knees, wailing, penetrating her anus right to his balls.

'Cane on, my beauty,' he hissed, as he began to bugger Tamsin, his cock sliding in and out of her squirming anus, right to its hilt, and soon shiny with arse-grease.

Vap! Vap! Vap!

'*AH! OHH . . .!*'

Habren danced on tiptoe, her legs and back shuddering in rhythm with to her shivering, clenched bum-globes, darkening to purple under Tamsin's rod. Each lash echoed to the slap of Rollo's hips on Tamsin's own buttocks as he buggered her. Firmly in Rollo's clutch, Tamsin wanked off as she caned Habren's bare, while her nude, quivering body, titties flapping, jerked under buggery.

Vap! Vap! Vap!

Tamsin's caning was as hard as the male's impalement of her own squirming bumhole. As she approached the fiftieth stroke, Rollo began to grunt and, just as the cane poised above the jellied mass of purple bruises that were Habren's bare buttocks, Rollo started his spunk, gasping harshly.

Vap!

'*There* . . .' moaned Tamsin, wanking herself off with both hands, while Rollo's spunk frothed at her anal pucker.

Habren's head drooped, pouring with sweat, over the sofa and she sobbed; her hand clamped her pubis and, as the bugger and his victim both writhed in spasm, Habren's eyes opened and her arm moved in her own wank.

'Yes . . .' Habren gasped. 'Oh . . . *oh!*'

She moaned long and loud, then held up her palm to show Tamsin that it brimmed with come and smiling at the girl who had flogged her.

'Thank you, mum,' said Habren. 'I am your obedient servant.'

'Now, bitch,' wheezed Rollo, '*Pollecutt's Box!*'

'I have its *contents* . . . right here,' said Tamsin, reaching into the pocket of her fur coat and withdrawing a gleaming object of braided leather straps around a central core. 'Angie, be so good as to secure Mr Cragg's person.'

Habren leapt over the sofa and pinioned Rollo, who gaped at two nude and submissive females metamorphosed. Habren held his arms twisted behind his back, forcing him to crouch, while Tamsin buckled the leather strap around her waist and flicked the monstrous cylinder which stood, cock-high between her thighs.

'Yes,' she said, 'a bull's pizzle, sir. The tool of Pinkarse initiates since Sir George's time.'

'No . . . *please* . . .!' gasped Rollo as Tamsin parted the cheeks of his arse, oiling the huge dildo with come from Habren's proffered palm.

'You see, after Sir George whipped his Vandal girls, as he called them, he liked *them* to vandalise *him* . . .!'

'*AHH!*' shrieked Rollo Cragg, as the massive shaft penetrated his anus. 'No! No! God! It hurts! *AHH . . .!*'

Tamsin's arse rammed hard as she vigorously buggered the squirming male, held fast by Habren's armlock.

'Oh, God, *please* . . . I'll do *anything* . . . *Ah! Ah!*'

'I dare say. As if *your* buggery didn't hurt *me*, you fucker! The beauty of Pollecutt's pizzle is that with no cream to spurt, it can fuck you quite raw. When I tire, the girl may have her own revenge, until you'd wish you'd taken a thousand with the cat, rather than be *buggered . . . sir*!'

Habren crouched and smiled as a steaming jet of piss spurted from her cunt, straight into Rollo's flapping jaws. He shrieked, choking and spluttering, as he was forced to swallow her pee. Tamsin's buttocks clenched taut, her hips slapping Rollo's own writhing bum, as she rammed the pizzle to the root of the shuddering male's anus.

'You fucking bitch sluts!' he sobbed. 'Wait until Habren Gaunt gets here! *I'm* the power behind this slut-cage, *I'm* senior director of Gauntco, and she'll have Horsfall cane your arses to ribbons! And . . . and . . . oh, God, *please stop*!'

As she slammed the tool into his arse, Tamsin flicked the peehole of his cock with her cane: the shaft was swelling, rising to full erection.

'Shame to stop, when being buggered by a girl gives you such a *hard-on, sir*,' she spat, as the erect, buggered male sobbed and whimpered.

There were footsteps outside.

'Thank you so much,' said Miss Horsfall, outside the door, 'for your tolerance, Mrs Gaunt. Misunderstandings will happen.'

'I think we understand each other,' said Angarad Stark.

'I'm glad we can show you a caning, given by Miss Coker, to these miscreants,' said Miss Horsfall. 'Caught smoking, in the toilets, and . . . and *masturbating* each other!'

The door opened: there stood the governess with Angarad, dressed in Habren's grey shantung silk; behind them, Isobel Coker, leading Clare Cubitt and Ingrid Fage by two dog-leashes, the girls barefoot, in bra and panties.

'Oh!' said Miss Horsfall. 'I hope we aren't interrupting your television programme, Mr Cragg.'

'Up to mischief, I see, Miss – Stark, isn't it?' said Angie to Habren.

'Yes, mum,' replied Habren. 'I . . . I expect you'll wish to whop me for it.'

Angarad smiled thinly.

'I shall enjoy *watching* you caned – in due course when your crop of welts has faded,' she said. 'How curious that we wear the same necklace – it will be like watching myself caned.'

Her palm cupped Tamsin's croup, stroking the pumping fesses like kittens, as her buggery of Rollo continued, until he gasped, howled and a jet of spunk spurted from his untouched glans. Tamsin withdrew, kicking him in the anus, and he fell to the carpet, sobbing.

'You do bear a striking resemblance to the detainee Angarad Stark, Mrs Gaunt,' said Miss Horsfall to Habren. 'She is normally well-behaved, but television exposure seems to have gone to all our heads, and I can see from her buttocks that she's been recently chastised. As, apparently, has poor Rollo – or was it pleasured, Rollo?'

'The bitch buggered me with . . . with a bull's pizzle from Pollecutt's Box!' cried Rollo, clutching his buggered arse.

'Why, you are mistaken,' said Miss Horsfall. 'Pollecutt's Box remains a legend. It is hidden, containing the title deeds to the entire Wrigley Scrubs estate and village, granted to whomsoever possesses the key to open it.'

'I approve thoroughly of your regime,' said Angarad, 'and promise that under Gauntco's franchise you shall retain your position, Miss Horsfall – in fact, I may well exploit your talents further. Girls in costume shall continue to discipline men in high places, with even greater refinement and gusto. Here, I might suggest, rather than give Miss Coker the bother of chastising these two slags, they should cane each other.'

'Of course, mum . . .' murmured the governess.

Angarad selected a short, whippy yellow cane from Miss Horsfall's rack and ordered Clare to bend over, while Ingrid gave her twenty-one on the bare; then, vice versa. The two girls' faces were a mixture of glee and sullenness, as Clare bared and spread her buttocks for her beating. Ingrid lifted her cane to her full arm's height.

Vip! Vip! Vip!

'*Ohh . . .!*'

The cane whistled as Ingrid lashed Clare's naked arse and Clare grimaced, groaning.

'Hard as you can, Ingrid, or you'll take double Clare's strokes!' said Angarad.

Vip! Vip! Vip!

'*Ahh . . .!*'

Clare's bare bum-pears shook, clenching, as the thin cane striped deep.

Vip! Vip! Vip!

'*Ahh! Bitch!*'

'Thank you, Mrs Gaunt,' said Miss Horsfall. 'I'm quite giddy at the thought of Wrigley Scrubs' being on the BBC.'

'Rollo Cragg isn't from the BBC, though,' said Isobel.

'Neither is Tamsin Pollecutt,' said Angarad.

'Oh! You know each other,' said Miss Horsfall.

'I know Angie Stark,' panted Tamsin to Habren, 'but aren't *you* Habren Dodd, the film "whip queen"?'

'*Who* chastised the detainee Stark?' asked Angarad, staring at her twin's livid, bruised buttocks.

'I did,' blurted Tamsin. 'I've known Angie a long time . . . the slut was in denial, refusing to accept she's a dirty little submissive who craves punishment.'

'Yet *you* don't, Miss Pollecutt?' said Angarad. 'I see from your own bruised fesses . . .'

'That? Rollo tricked me and beat me, the sadistic pig, so I duly punished him,' spat Tamsin, giving Rollo's arse another kick. 'A cry for help, really. It's all men want! Every one a filthy sub . . .'

Vip! Vip! Vip!

'. . . *and* twenty-one!' cried Ingrid.

Clare Cubitt's bare-bum caning was complete.

'You whore!' cried Clare, rising and snatching the cane from Ingrid. 'Your arse'll smart for that . . .'

Her own bum glowed a deep welted crimson, and she jumped, as Ingrid put her tongue out and spanked it with her hand, before spreading her legs and bending over for her own thrashing. The company watched as Ingrid's pert buttocks danced under the stronger girl's cane, slicing her deep in the bum-cleft with uppercuts that whipped her anus bud and moistening cunt flaps.

Vip! Vip! Vip!

'*Ohh!*' cried Ingrid, her buttocks squirming. 'Not *fair*!'

Vip! Vip! Vip!

'*Ah . . . ahh . . . bitch!*'

Angarad and Habren licked their teeth while Tamsin began to rub her pubis; then, putting a thumb to her swollen red clitty, masturbated openly. Ingrid groaned and sobbed throughout her twenty-one stingers, her bare buttocks jerking at the vip! of the cane, crisscrossing her flesh in a careful pattern of welts. By the end of the set, her cunt, like Clare's, seeped come. Habren had her fingers lightly stroking her pouch, with copious come sliming her inner thighs; Miss Horsfall's fingers were at her crotch, her skirt well dampened by her gash fluid, but Angarad pointed at Tamsin.

'I believe Miss Pollecutt is masturbating,' she said. 'Scarcely a good example.'

'Gracious, no,' said Miss Horsfall, blushing.

'If I may be so bold . . .?' murmured Angarad.

'Of course, Mrs Gaunt – as our new director – please . . .'

'The bull's pizzle, please,' said Angarad.

She ordered her twin to stay still while she strapped the huge dildo on her naked cunt basin; Ingrid and Clare held the squirming Tamsin over the sofa, with her bare bottom high and her thighs parted. The pizzle stood massive, with Habren's pubic forest almost obscured.

'You beat this girl viciously, Miss Pollecutt,' Angarad said. 'Now, she may take her revenge.'

'But I *told* you,' Tamsin wailed, 'Angie's a sub! I've known her for ages! She's a filthy, submissive little slut. Fifty with the rattan is *nothing* to an arse like hers . . .!'

'And I thought you were my best friend in all the world,' said Angarad mildly.

'*What?*'

'*I am Angarad Stark*. Habren, here, is my twin. She will now bugger you, *Miss* Pollecutt, until you faint.'

'*No . . . please . . .!*'

Habren mounted the pinioned woman and oiled the pizzle with come gushing from Tamsin's cunt. With one thrust, she had Tamsin impaled on the pizzle, sinking the leather to the root of her anus; she began to bugger the squirming dominatrix, whose face was wet with tears.

'*No! Ah! Oh!* I didn't mean it! You're my best friend, honestly . . .!' she wailed, as the leather dildo slammed into her anus. '*Ahh . . .!*'

Her legs buckled and a steaming jet of piss hissed from her cunt flaps. Isobel Coker unfastened her cane and dealt Rollo a sharp cut on his bare arse.

Vip!

'You, sir!' she ordered. 'Lick up your friend's mess.'

'You can't order me around, bitch!' he snarled.

Vip! Vip! Vip!

'*Oh!*'

'She can,' said Habren, impaling the writhing Tamsin's anus on her arse-greased pizzle, dripping piss, 'and, furthermore, as director of this prison, I command you to lick girl-pee, *and enjoy it.*'

Vip! Vip! Vip!

Sobbing and squirming under Isobel's bare-bum lash, Rollo Cragg began to chew the carpet under Tamsin's cunt, which still dribbled pee mingled with her come-gush. Angarad said Tamsin's buggery must continue until Rollo had licked every drop of her piss from the carpet. The telephone rang and Miss Horsfall answered, passing the receiver to Angarad.

'It is Angarad speaking, Miss Maclaren – my sister is busy. Yes, you may speak to either of us, for we are the same. I see. Thank you.'

'*No . . . no . . . no . . .*' sobbed Tamsin, as Habren's arse jerked above her, slamming the dildo into her bumhole.

'Habren, Miss Maclaren has contacted London,' Angarad said, 'and found that our real name is *Pollecutt.* You are undoubtedly buggering a distant relative.'

'Shall I stop?'

'No.'

'*You bitch!*'

Tamsin's clitoris rubbed against the sofa back with each jolt of her cunt basin, and the trickle of come from her cunt had become a flood. Angarad dipped a finger in the juice and tasted it.

'We all get what we want, Tamsin,' she said. 'Tell me – why was I really sent here? You, Will, Marcus . . . *he* was the only spectator at my sentencing! How many were in on it? You knew I was a Pollecutt, didn't you? What do you *really* want? Tell me or Habren will bugger you till you faint, then *I'll* whip your arse raw.'

Tamsin shook her head, her face crimson and glazed with tears.

'Pollecutt's Box . . .' she mumbled.

'Is *that* what *you* really, secretly want, Mistress Pinkarse? Or do you want to be caned and buggered and peed on, like the submissive slut you really are? Eh?'

'You *bitch*!' Tamsin spat. '*Ah! Ah! . . . You, Angie . . . I wanted to be you!*'

Her belly heaved in orgasm as Angarad's finger touched her swollen clitty, just once. Come streamed down her thighs, puddling the floor, which Rollo's tongue strove to lick clean of Tamsin's fluid under the slicing of Isobel's cane, now at the forty-sixth stroke to his bare arse.

'I thought Isobel was the key,' Rollo whimpered, 'until Tamsin told me about Angarad. The box must be at Wrigley Scrubs. It must be unlocked with the true key, as breaking the lock will release phosphorus, igniting on exposure to air and burning the entire box and contents. Once we have the title deeds . . . we were going to cut you in on it, honestly . . . but we don't even know where the box is . . . Tamsin, that silly cow . . .!'

Vip! Vip! Vip!

'*Ooh!*' Rollo howled.

'Oh, *I* know where the *box* is,' said Angarad, 'and now I know the key.'

# 16

# Vandals

Three girls, stripped to bra and panties, swam in the River Wrigley, past the muddy bank and the bridge to the village, and came to the rocky outcrop where Angarad indicated they should land. She stripped naked and handed her underthings to Habren, then slid, wriggling slowly, through the fissure in the rock. Habren and Isobel followed, the bras and panties left neatly folded on a boulder. They waded through the slime of the cave, until Angarad reached up to a ledge, groping for the box. The girls climbed to hack at the box's encrusted base, until they could lift it down.

'Pollecutt's Box,' Angarad panted.

'But the key?' said Isobel.

'Either of us,' said Angarad, and took Habren's waxen amulet from her neck.

She prodded the prehensile opening of the lock; heard clicks and squeezes and, suddenly, the waxen model of her anus plunged all the way into the box. The lid twitched and disengaged half an inch; with delicate prising, the box opened fully. Inside lay a scroll of parchment, wrapped in oilcloth. Habren unrolled and began to read.

'It's clear enough,' she said with a whoop. 'There's a lot of stuff about ancient peoples of the Sahara, before it was desert, with flagellant goddesses and the globetrotting Vandals – he thinks that the English are all Vandals who landed in Durham two thousand years ago! – but these lands are only *lent* to the crown and whatsoever *females* can open the box, share title to Wrigley Scrubs, village, house, estate, the lot – in perpetuity.'

'I'm so glad – it's awfully sweet, like a fairy-tale – but I don't see why I'm here,' said Isobel.

'Don't you complain you can't find a man big enough for your pouch?' said Angarad.

Isobel blushed.

'Really! Well, yes – but I hardly know Miss Habren . . .'

'You know *me*,' said Angarad. 'You know *us* . . .'

Habren snatched Angarad's amulet from her neck and pressed its whorled tip to the slit of Isobel's pouch. Her thumb found Isobel's clitty and began to wank the girl off.

'What –? Mm . . . I don't understand . . . *mm* . . .'

Isobel's gash began to seep come, rapidly soaking Habren's fingers. She masturbated until Isobel's cunt flaps were writhing, opening and closing like a fishmouth, then plunged the waxen amulet all the way inside the girl's pouch, until only Habren's fingernails were visible.

'Oh, yes!' Isobel cried, now wanking her own clitoris. 'God, yes! It fits perfectly! Oh, I'm going to come . . .'

'Rollo took a wax impression of your cunt,' said Angarad. 'That was to be *your* key, Isobel. You share Wrigley Scrubs with us.'

Isobel's fingers were a blur as she masturbated, with Habren ramming the waxen dildo at her wombneck.

'Oh! Oh! *Yess . . .!*' Isobel sobbed as her cunt gushed come over her fingers, and her titties and belly heaved in orgasm, Habren and Angarad cupping their palms under her gashes to catch her come, with which they rubbed their own wet slits, masturbating rapidly, until their own gasps of orgasm succeeded Isobel's. The three wanked girls embraced, kissing.

'There shall be some changes made,' said Habren. 'Sir George's text tells of the Vandals and their communal punishment days, like festivals. For example, miscreant women had to lie naked, with their breasts in river mud and, when the caner passed, each girl had to immerse her face in the water the whole time of her bare-bum beating. After flogging, they would be hoisted in a net and ducked together. Birched nude at the block, clamped on the rack for flogging on tits and bum . . . or girls wrestling for "sotweed", that's snout, nude, with their pube forests tied together – there are all *sorts* of lovely things in the past.'

Isobel shyly extruded an oilskin pouch from her bum-hole.

'It sounds just like the book of punishments at Wear-bridge! Let's celebrate with a smoke,' she said.

The girls lit up.

'Isobel, I'm so proud of you,' cooed Gemma Cragg. 'You say you designed this labyrinth all by yourself! What a thrilling punishment maze!'

Marcus and Bee nodded their agreement.

'I'm sure I recognise some of my own computer game,' said Will. 'I'm intrigued you are familiar with the great Vandal maze of Oum el Hanch.'

'You should catch up with Rollo,' she said. 'He was in absolute knots of excitement and couldn't wait,' said Isobel. 'After you.'

They stepped before her, inside the labyrinth.

'Of course, if you were girls under chastisement, a gauntlet of molten wax and canes would await you at the far door, which is the only other exit,' she added, stepping back smartly and slamming the door shut on her captives. 'Now, it *is* your only exit,' she cried, above their shrieks.

'They say that stud Aggar has tooled every slag in the prison,' whispered Ingrid Fage to Clare Cubitt. 'I mean, in the bumhole. He has a cock much bigger than Oswald's.'

'Well, he hasn't done *me*,' said Clare crossly.

'Oh . . . I was hoping you might tell. He hasn't done me, either.'

'If that bitch Coker catches you smoking, or wanking, she gives you a choice – strokes or a bumming by the stud.'

'Let's sneak into the strokes' bog and wank off.'

The two girls rouched in a cubicle, alternately dragging smoke from their rollies and blowing it into each other's soaking cunt, as they frotted their clitties. Isobel's footsteps tapped outside.

'Oh! Oh! Wank me harder! Suck my clit! Oh, *yes* . . .!' cried Clare and Ingrid in unison.

Isobel flung the door open.

'Scandalous behaviour!' she blurted. 'You have a choice, ladies –'

'Bumming, please, mum!' chorused the two slags.

Ignoge Brand's face was wet with tears. She lay nude, face down in the mud on the bank of the Wrigley, beside the groaning Goiswinth Moss and Althea Tite, equally nude, and their raised bottoms shivering. Beside them stretched Amy Patel, Belinda Garce and the other bottom strokes. Edra Forge's face was plunged in the river, as her naked bum-flans quivered under the tap-tap-tap of Aggar's cane; bubbles threshed around her head, until she had taken twenty-one strokes and was permitted to raise it. At once, the naked black man fell upon her arse, prising apart her clenched buttocks, oiling his cock with come from her quim, and plunging it into her anus. He clutched her cunt, thumbing her clitty as he buggered her to a squealing orgasm. Without spunking, he rose and it was Sarah Bunn's turn to plunge her head underwater, for a bare-bum caning of twenty-one, or 'a guinea', as Habren had nicknamed it.

'That *cock*,' gasped Goiswinth. 'I'm scared.'

'We're *strokes*, aren't we? I don't see why *we* should take punishment,' wailed Ignoge.

Sarah's bare buttocks writhed, reddening rapidly under the male's cane. When her set was over, she spread her arse-cheeks, already slimed by her spurted come, enabling Aggar to penetrate her anus in a single thrust, and began to masturbate herself, shrieking almost at once in a prolonged climax.

'Don't you?' said Althea Tite.

'There's something bloody good about being elected to parliament,' said Darren Dodd, as Habren led him into the labyrinth. 'The power, the manipulation of others ... bloody socialists don't understand how good it is to make people squirm, know what I mean? That's why Pinkarse is such a delight, I'm really part of the *club*, now. Hey, you remind me of a girl I buggered in London. *She* was a right submissive little slut, like you. Warn you, darling, I'll give you a proper thrashing and all.'

'That's what I'm here for, sir,' said Habren, as she meekly led Darren into the cage. '*You* have *power.* You can chain me up, gag me ... bugger me. *Anything.*'

She took off her bra and panties and, nude, placed her hands in the cuffs dangling from the ceiling. Her frizzy black wig, made of Tamsin Pollecutt's pubic shavings, encased her coiled blond mane.

'Would you rather bind me in rubber or strap me over the flogging horse, sir? There are plenty of candles to drip hot wax on my cunt and titties, and down here we are thoroughly soundproofed, so nobody will hear me scream. I'm *sure* you'll make me scream, sir.'

'*Yeah,*' chuckled Darren. 'I like to make girls scream.'

After he had caned Habren's naked arse an hour, the girl gasped but had not yet screamed. Darren poured with sweat as he flogged her squirming, crimson bum-globes with the heavy rattan, his other hand holding a candle, lit at both ends, over her nipples and cunt. Wax crusted her breasts and belly and glued her cunt forest into a sculpture, like a rock covered in barnacles. The cage door opened and clanged shut. Angarad's blond tresses swirled in front of Darren's face, as Isobel, Ghislaine Bassin and Ignoge Brand pinioned him and released Habren.

'*What the fuck ...?* Let me go, you fucking whores!' he cried as he was stripped, bent over a flogging horse and cuffed at wrists and ankles.

Habren took off her wig and the two twins, naked, stood before him, while Isobel fastened his cock and balls in a leather restrainer and raised a cat-o'-nine-tails.

'*Angie ...?*' he gasped. 'Oh my God ...'

Habren pouted, rubbing her flaming red buttocks.

'So sorry I didn't scream, sir,' she said. 'You wanted a submissive little slut ... perhaps my sister would have suited better.'

'Your *sister*? What do you want?' he blurted.

'Why, Darren, nothing at all,' said Angie. 'Just *you* ...'

Thwap!

The heavy quirt struck the male's trembling bare arse.

Darren screamed.

'I never *dreamed* it could be like this ...' panted Oswald. 'It's so *good.* Oh, fuck me *harder*, Mistress!'

'Gladly,' said Isobel, sweat pouring from her nipples, as she rammed the bull's pizzle between his squirming arse-cheeks. 'For an extra eight ounces of snout ...'

'*Anything* ...'

'I never *dreamed* it could be like this,' gasped Tamsin, as her freshly birched bare arse writhed under Aggar's pumping loins. 'Oh, that cock! Bugger me harder, split me in two, fuck my bumhole till I burst ... give me your spunk, damn you! *Oh*, I'm coming *again* ...!'

Aggar's teeth gleamed briefly and he said nothing.

'Habren, promise me you'll never sleep with anyone else,' whispered Angarad, her lips and nose nuzzling her twin's wet cunt lips.

Their nude bodies were twined in honeysuckle.

'I'll never *sleep* with anyone else,' Habren replied, licking Angarad's anus bud and making her giggle.

'Good night, me.'

'Good night, me.'

Two women, nude but for billowing shame dresses which they had to clutch around their waists with shackled wrists, stumbled from the prison van into the snow. Their bare breasts were stiff and pimpled with cold, and each bore a wooden hobble bar at her ankles, the two bars roped together.

'Prisoners Dummett, Faith and Joule, Constance for delivery,' snapped the accompanying policewoman.

'This is an outrage!' wailed Miss Dummett. 'Shackled, like a common criminal! I demand to speak to Adelaide Horsfall! She assured me that –'

'You can see Miss Horsfall, after her public whipping at teatime,' said Ghislaine Bassin politely.

Her fur coat flapped open over heavy rubber boots, showing her tabard top, rubber corset and luxuriant armpit hair.

'Adelaide? *Whipped?* But – but –'

'There have been some changes,' said Ghislaine. 'Horsfall was caught smoking. By the way, you wouldn't have an ounce of snout on you? I could make your first dustings a bit easier . . .'

'Snout?'

'Tobacco,' said Ghislaine, then, looking at their shabby shame dresses, sighing, 'No, I suppose not.'

She consulted her clipboard and whistled.

'Vile perversity and turpitude in an officer of the crown,' she said.

'Some obsolete statute from the *seventeenth* bloody *century*!' complained former WPC Joule.

Vip!

'*Ah!*'

Ghislaine caned her a stroke across the nipples.

'Apparently, not obsolete,' said Ghislaine, clamping her charges in a neck halter and leading them away. 'You sure you don't have any snout? Not even a half ounce?'

'Smoking is a vile and disgusting practice!' cried Miss Dummett.

Vip!

'*Ah!*'

Her bare breasts quivered under Ghislaine's cane.

'So you don't smoke, eh?' said Ghislaine.

'*Certainly* not!'

'You will.'

'You're *joking*,' said Amy Patel, sluicing her breasts with the shower nozzle. 'The *king* . . .!'

'He wants to visit,' gasped Belinda Garce. 'Says Wrigley Scrubs is the model female nick of the future . . . !'

'Ooh! He's such a *dish*! Do you think he'll want to . . .'
'See everything?'
'Maybe give us a few *lessons* . . .!'
'Well, he might.'
'God! I'm wanking off just *thinking* about it!'
Both girls turned the shower nozzles up to full and directed the jets at their cunts.

'But I don't *want* to be released!' wailed Ghislaine Bassin.
She slapped Habren's face.
'There!' she said. 'I've done something really naughty! That should earn me another six months, at least.'
Habren smiled.
'You're too valuable to release, Ghislaine. I'm simply sending you overseas, to serve your sentence in the desert.'
'But I'd be away from Aggar! He . . . *understands* me!'
'He understands *all* of us girls, Ghislaine. And there are plenty more like him. Watch this video.'
Ghislaine watched for twenty minutes, wanking herself to two climaxes, as whipcracks and groans of nude, buggered girls filled the room.
'One of those girls could be you, Ghislaine,' murmured Habren. 'Truud, whom you see whipped and bummed, with her face hooded and her hands tied by her own silk pantaloons – she and her lover arrived quite out of the blue, and look how she loves it.'
'All right, mum,' Ghislaine said, licking her teeth. 'It's just that . . . I've never been abroad before.'
'Don't think of it as abroad. Think of it as home.'

'Aggar . . . Aggar . . . *Aggar* . . . what are you *doing* to me?' Isobel shrieked. 'Oh, fuck me! It's true . . . there *is* a real man! *Fuck my cunt . . .!*'

Crack!
Habren's bullwhip lashed Adelaide Horsfall's bare shoulders and she winced, drool sliming her chin and her breasts heaving as she strained to pull the cart.

'It doesn't seem fair,' she blurted. 'When Mrs Gaunt said she'd make further use of my talents, I didn't know she meant . . .'

Crack!

'*Ahh!*'

Beside her, Althea Tite shrieked as the whip took her on the bare-bum.

'Shut up and pull, bitch!' hissed Althea.

They drew alongside the rival cart, pulled by the nude Belinda Garce and Amy Patel, both slimed with piss, come and tears, under the lash of Angarad's whip.

'But if we are *all* Vandals, why have tournaments?' gasped Miss Horsfall.

Crack!

'*Ahh . . .!*'

The two carts lumbered across the finishing line and, at once, their nude drivers leapt down into the mud and began to wrestle, biting and gouging each other, until both were mud-caulked and indistinguishable in the bleak northern light. Writhing in the ooze, their slippery contest became an embrace and the two twins gamahuched, while the inhabitants of HMP Wrigley Scrubs wanked off, cheering. Althea churned her fist inside Miss Horsfall's sopping cunt while wanking off her own engorged clitty.

'Oh, yes,' moaned the governess, her cunt squelched with come. '*Yes . . .!*'

'*That's* why , . .' gasped Althea.

'God, that's tight, darling!' groaned Joss Gaunt, writhing in his bondage of rubber cords. 'My balls ache! I haven't had sex for so long . . .'

'Dirty beast!'

Vip!

'Ouch! Oh, darling, if you'll just touch my cock, please . . .'

'You filth!' Habren snapped, tightening his cock harness. 'I've a good mind to leave you in this cage, alone in the labyrinth, for absolutely hours . . .'

'At your pleasure, my sweet.'

'Oh, it's a matter of complete indifference to me, you understand . . . now that you've signed the orders.'

'Yes, of course! No Gauntco supermarkets in – what are they? – Ditton, Wearbridge? – and you're going to fulfil your side, aren't you, my sweet? I flew all the way from Marrakesh, just to feel your cane on my bare! Please say you'll whip me, soon! Thrash me to the bone, my darling!'

'That wasn't the only paper you signed, though,' said Habren. 'Angarad's bail money was a cheque from *Gauntco . . .!*'

'It was in the airmail *Daily Telegraph*, on page three!' wailed Joss. 'She looked so pretty, I felt sorry for her! *Oh!*'

Habren pushed a wad of pink brocade all the way into her husband's anus.

'I *shall* whip you, worm,' she drawled. 'Or someone just *like* me shall . . .'

'But I can't . . .' blurted the girl. 'It wouldn't be right. *I'm* the one who's earned . . .'

'*Be quiet, slut!*' snapped the girl in the rubber punishment corset.

The bare-breasted Miss Horsfall, with her nipples clamped to a rope wedged tightly inside her cunt-cleft, bowed and shuffled backwards out of the room in her wooden ankle hobble.

'*Right*, slut,' the corseted girl continued. 'There'll be no more disobedience! You'll take fifty whops with my cane for *that* insolence and then you *shall* agree to obey my orders! Now, bare your bottom and assume position. Hold her ankles and wrists, if you please, Warden Coker.'

The girl, sobbing, swept up her long mane and bent over, lifting her skirt and lowering her knickers to bare her trembling naked arse-globes. Isobel squatted and obeyed the corseted girl, her towel falling from her naked body. The high-heeled domina strode to the rack of canes, weighed and examined each instrument, then selected a short, whippy little thrasher. She lifted the cane well back from the bare bum and it whistled.

Vip!

The submissive girl's bum-flans shuddered, clenching, as a vivid pink weal striped the bare skin.

'Oh . . .'

Vip!

'Ah . . .!'

Vip! Vip Vip!

'*Ahh . . .!*'

'In future, you will obey, won't you?'

The flogged girl gasped, wordless.

Vip! Vip! Vip!

Her naked arse was turning crimson, the welts overlaying older ones and puffing into deep ridges. Both bare fesses shivered, like jellies.

Vip! Vip! Vip!

The caning went to twenty, then thirty, but still she was silent, save for groans of agony and the slithering of her stockings as her legs jerked and threshed.

'Please, mum,' Isobel said, 'don't be *too* cruel to her.'

'*Flesh is cruel, bitch!*'

Vip! Vip! Vip!

'*Ahh . . .!*'

Come poured from the caned girl's dripping open cunt, the lips swollen and glistening. Isobel released her ankle, and her hand crossed her quivering belly to her own juicing gash, where she fastened the erect clitty between finger and thumb and began to masturbate, her mouth open and tongue poised to lick the come from the flogged girl's pouch flaps.

Vip! Vip! Vip!

'*AHH!*'

'Say you'll obey!'

Vip! Vip! Vip!

The caner's short skirt flew up as her free hand busied itself, masturbating her clitoris and penetrating her pouch inside the soaking wet ribbon of her loinstring. She paused in her caning and thrust one pointed toe inside her victim's flowing cunt, touching and rubbing the clitty. Isobel's tongue touched the sole of the caner's clit-wanking boot, and she wanked off harder as she began to lick the sole while swallowing the flogged girl's copious come.

'Say you'll run this prison as I tell you it should be run!' hissed the domina, masturbating vigorously.

Vip! Vip! Vip!

'*Ahh!* . . . Ohh . . . yes . . .'

'I want to hear it!

'Yes . . . yes . . . oh, *do me* . . . yes . . .'

'I want to hear it, you *submissive* –'

Vip!

'*– little –*'

Vip!

'*– slut!*'

The girl's come flowed from her foot-wanked cunt over the shiny rubber of her caner's boot, diddling her swollen nubbin. The whipped bare buttocks were shading to purple, each bruise writhing and jerking in its own rhythm.

'Wank me off . . . please . . .'

Vip! Vip! Vip!

'*Ahh . . . YES!*'

'*YES!*' cried Isobel Coker, vigorously masturbating her gushing wet slit.

Come gushed from all three girls' wanked cunts, as they began to shudder and squeal in orgasm.

'*Ah! Ah!* Say it!' gasped cane-wielding Habren. 'Say you'll show no mercy to perverted submissive sluts! Say you'll cane them crimson, even your own sister! *Especially* her! Say you'll run this prison as I want you to! Say you'll *dominate!* And your first duty will be to thrash my husband on the bare, *right this minute!* Go on, say it!'

Vip! Vip! Vip!

'*Oh . . .!*'

Vip! Vip! Vip!

'*Oh . . .!*'

'*Say it, you submissive worm!*'

'Yes . . . yes, mum!' sobbed Angarad.

## NEXUS NEW BOOKS

*To be published in November*

### PET TRAINING IN THE PRIVATE HOUSE

Esme Ombreux

£5.99

When Jessica moves from the city to the exclusive Hillingbury estate she fears that she might find life in the suburbs rather dull. But the local shop is owned by the forbiddingly attractive Mrs Morgan, and it stocks a surprisingly wide range of collars, leads and whips. At the Health and Exercise Club Jessica is drawn to Matt, a young man on the staff who, as her personal coach, sets her a strenuous and strict exercise regime. And then one of her neighbours, pretty, blond Mel, sets out to seduce her. As Matt, Mel and Mrs Morgan compete for Jessica's devotion, she discovers the depths of her suppressed desire to be dominated.

ISBN 0 352 33655 2

### SEE THROUGH

Lindsay Gordon

£5.99

In US Air Force intelligence, Frank Defargo was called many things: psychic, clairvoyant or remote-viewer. From secret military installations, he was able to see the activities of many, friend or foe, regardless of distance. But Frank's burnt out, and he finds relief in putting his phenomenal skill to use looking at women in uniform. When his voyeurism is discovered, he's recruited to 'the agency', a mysterious intelligence organisation that monitors sexual subversives – wretched lovers in thrall to 'the Bond', driven to any extreme to find those of their kind. What Frank sees in their bizarre SM punishment rituals makes him understand that his gift is truly both a blessing and a curse.

ISBN 0 352 33656 0

## A TASTE OF AMBER

Penny Birch

£5.99

Expelled from school for spanking a mistress, Amber Oakley finds herself in disgrace and is sent to work on a farm. She quickly discovers that her godfather, Henry Gresham, is far from the respectable country gentleman he appears to be. Introduced to the delights of the strange world of pony-girls, Amber soon knows what she want to be – a pony-girl mistress. Unfortunately for her, many of the people she meets would rather she was at the other end of the reins, particularly Morris Rathwell, a property developer who sees himself as the king of pony-carting. Goaded into a bet with Rathwell, Amber loses, and finds herself in a very different role from the one she had anticipated. Worse still, she finds the experience more enjoyable than she could have imagined. Can she ever hope to fulfil her ambition? A Nexus Classic.

ISBN 0 352 33654 4

*To be published in December*

## VELVET SKIN

Aishling Morgan

£5.99

Henry Truscott, hero of *The Rake* and *Purity*, returns in *Velvet Skin* to continue his habits of indulgence and dissipation. There are ample opportunities in eighteenth-century Devon for an imaginative aristocrat to pursue his perversions. Even so, Henry manages to find himself in trouble – like being caught pony-carting by the local vicar, for example. But the fiendish, rapacious Lewis Stukely, a neighbouring landowner, makes Truscott look like a monk – and Stukely has designs on Suki, Truscott's beguiling servant-girl.

ISBN 0 352 33660 9

## THE BLACK FLAME

Lisette Ashton

£5.99

For private investigator Jo Valentine it is a surveillance operation unlike any other: a coven of witches practising orgiastic pagan ritual; a sadistic preacher intent on extracting penance from every nubile young sinner who falls beneath his cane; and an ongoing feud with her submissive partner. Caught in the midst of this volatile situation, alone, bound and helpless, Jo is subjected to a dark revelation in the pleasures of pain. Tied, teased and tormented, she is immersed in so many sexual excesses that it borders on being a religious experience. The next volume in Lisette Ashton's series of bestselling erotica.

ISBN 0 352 33668 4

## NEXUS BACKLIST

This information is correct at time of printing. For up-to-date information, please visit our website at www.nexus-books.co.uk

All books are priced at £5.99 unless another price is given.

**Nexus books with a contemporary setting**

| | | |
|---|---|---|
| ACCIDENTS WILL HAPPEN | Lucy Golden<br>ISBN 0 352 33596 3 | ☐ |
| ANGEL | Lindsay Gordon<br>ISBN 0 352 33590 4 | ☐ |
| THE BLACK MASQUE | Lisette Ashton<br>ISBN 0 352 33372 3 | ☐ |
| THE BLACK WIDOW | Lisette Ashton<br>ISBN 0 352 33338 3 | ☐ |
| THE BOND | Lindsay Gordon<br>ISBN 0 352 33480 0 | ☐ |
| BROUGHT TO HEEL | Arabella Knight<br>ISBN 0 352 33508 4 | ☐ |
| CANDY IN CAPTIVITY | Arabella Knight<br>ISBN 0 352 33495 9 | ☐ |
| CAPTIVES OF THE PRIVATE HOUSE | Esme Ombreux<br>ISBN 0 352 33619 6 | ☐ |
| DANCE OF SUBMISSION | Lisette Ashton<br>ISBN 0 352 33450 9 | ☐ |
| DARK DELIGHTS | Maria del Rey<br>ISBN 0 352 33276 X | ☐ |
| DARK DESIRES | Maria del Rey<br>ISBN 0 352 33072 4 | ☐ |
| DISCIPLES OF SHAME | Stephanie Calvin<br>ISBN 0 352 33343 X | ☐ |
| DISCIPLINE OF THE PRIVATE HOUSE | Esme Ombreux<br>ISBN 0 352 33459 2 | ☐ |

| | | |
|---|---|---|
| DISCIPLINED SKIN | Wendy Swanscombe<br>ISBN 0 352 33541 6 | ☐ |
| DISPLAYS OF EXPERIENCE | Lucy Golden<br>ISBN 0 352 33505 X | ☐ |
| AN EDUCATION IN THE PRIVATE HOUSE | Esme Ombreux<br>ISBN 0 352 33525 4 | ☐ |
| EMMA'S SECRET DOMINATION | Hilary James<br>ISBN 0 352 33226 3 | ☐ |
| GISELLE | Jean Aveline<br>ISBN 0 352 33440 1 | ☐ |
| GROOMING LUCY | Yvonne Marshall<br>ISBN 0 352 33529 7 | ☐ |
| HEART OF DESIRE | Maria del Rey<br>ISBN 0 352 32900 9 | ☐ |
| HIS MISTRESS'S VOICE | G. C. Scott<br>ISBN 0 352 33425 8 | ☐ |
| HOUSE RULES | G. C. Scott<br>ISBN 0 352 33441 X | ☐ |
| IN FOR A PENNY | Penny Birch<br>ISBN 0 352 33449 5 | ☐ |
| LESSONS IN OBEDIENCE | Lucy Golden<br>ISBN 0 352 33550 5 | ☐ |
| NURSES ENSLAVED | Yolanda Celbridge<br>ISBN 0 352 33601 3 | ☐ |
| ONE WEEK IN THE PRIVATE HOUSE | Esme Ombreux<br>ISBN 0 352 32788 X | ☐ |
| THE ORDER | Nadine Somers<br>ISBN 0 352 33460 6 | ☐ |
| THE PALACE OF EROS | Delver Maddingley<br>ISBN 0 352 32921 1 | ☐ |
| PEEPING AT PAMELA | Yolanda Celbridge<br>ISBN 0 352 33538 6 | ☐ |
| PLAYTHING | Penny Birch<br>ISBN 0 352 33493 2 | ☐ |
| THE PLEASURE CHAMBER | Brigitte Markham<br>ISBN 0 352 33371 5 | ☐ |
| POLICE LADIES | Yolanda Celbridge<br>ISBN 0 352 33489 4 | ☐ |
| SANDRA'S NEW SCHOOL | Yolanda Celbridge<br>ISBN 0 352 33454 1 | ☐ |

| | | |
|---|---|---|
| SKIN SLAVE | Yolanda Celbridge<br>ISBN 0 352 33507 6 | ☐ |
| THE SLAVE AUCTION | Lisette Ashton<br>ISBN 0 352 33481 9 | ☐ |
| SLAVE EXODUS | Jennifer Jane Pope<br>ISBN 0 352 33551 3 | ☐ |
| SLAVE GENESIS | Jennifer Jane Pope<br>ISBN 0 352 33503 3 | ☐ |
| SLAVE SENTENCE | Lisette Ashton<br>ISBN 0 352 33494 0 | ☐ |
| SOLDIER GIRLS | Yolanda Celbridge<br>ISBN 0 352 33586 6 | ☐ |
| THE SUBMISSION GALLERY | Lindsay Gordon<br>ISBN 0 352 33370 7 | ☐ |
| SURRENDER | Laura Bowen<br>ISBN 0 352 33524 6 | ☐ |
| TAKING PAINS TO PLEASE | Arabella Knight<br>ISBN 0 352 33369 3 | ☐ |
| TIE AND TEASE | Penny Birch<br>ISBN 0 352 33591 2 | ☐ |
| TIGHT WHITE COTTON | Penny Birch<br>ISBN 0 352 33537 8 | ☐ |
| THE TORTURE CHAMBER | Lisette Ashton<br>ISBN 0 352 33530 0 | ☐ |
| THE TRAINING OF FALLEN ANGELS | Kendal Grahame<br>ISBN 0 352 33224 7 | ☐ |
| THE YOUNG WIFE | Stephanie Calvin<br>ISBN 0 352 33502 5 | ☐ |
| WHIPPING BOY | G. C. Scott<br>ISBN 0 352 33595 5 | ☐ |

**Nexus books with Ancient and Fantasy settings**

| | | |
|---|---|---|
| CAPTIVE | Aishling Morgan<br>ISBN 0 352 33585 8 | ☐ |
| THE CASTLE OF MALDONA | Yolanda Celbridge<br>ISBN 0 352 33149 6 | ☐ |
| DEEP BLUE | Aishling Morgan<br>ISBN 0 352 33600 5 | ☐ |
| THE FOREST OF BONDAGE | Aran Ashe<br>ISBN 0 352 32803 7 | ☐ |
| MAIDEN | Aishling Morgan | ☐ |

| | | |
|---|---|---|
| | ISBN 0 352 33466 5 | |
| NYMPHS OF DIONYSUS £4.99 | Susan Tinoff ISBN 0 352 33150 X | ☐ |
| THE SLAVE OF LIDIR | Aran Ashe ISBN 0 352 33504 1 | ☐ |
| TIGER, TIGER | Aishling Morgan ISBN 0 352 33455 X | ☐ |
| THE WARRIOR QUEEN | Kendal Grahame ISBN 0 352 33294 8 | ☐ |

**Edwardian, Victorian and older erotica**

| | | |
|---|---|---|
| BEATRICE | Anonymous ISBN 0 352 31326 9 | ☐ |
| CONFESSION OF AN ENGLISH SLAVE | Yolanda Celbridge ISBN 0 352 33433 9 | ☐ |
| DEVON CREAM | Aishling Morgan ISBN 0 352 33488 6 | ☐ |
| THE GOVERNESS AT ST AGATHA'S | Yolanda Celbridge ISBN 0 352 32986 6 | ☐ |
| PURITY | Aishling Morgan ISBN 0 352 33510 6 | ☐ |
| THE TRAINING OF AN ENGLISH GENTLEMAN | Yolanda Celbridge ISBN 0 352 33348 0 | ☐ |

**Samplers and collections**

| | | |
|---|---|---|
| NEW EROTICA 4 | Various ISBN 0 352 33290 5 | ☐ |
| NEW EROTICA 5 | Various ISBN 0 352 33540 8 | ☐ |
| EROTICON 1 | Various ISBN 0 352 33593 9 | ☐ |
| EROTICON 2 | Various ISBN 0 352 33594 7 | ☐ |
| EROTICON 3 | Various ISBN 0 352 33597 1 | ☐ |
| EROTICON 4 | Various ISBN 0 352 33602 1 | ☐ |

**Nexus Classics**

A new imprint dedicated to putting the finest works of erotic fiction back in print.

|  |  | |
|---|---|---|
| AGONY AUNT | G.C. Scott<br>ISBN 0 352 33353 7 | ☐ |
| BOUND TO SERVE | Amanda Ware<br>ISBN 0 352 33457 6 | ☐ |
| BOUND TO SUBMIT | Amanda Ware<br>ISBN 0 352 33451 7 | ☐ |
| CHOOSING LOVERS FOR JUSTINE | Aran Ashe<br>ISBN 0 352 33351 0 | ☐ |
| DIFFERENT STROKES | Sarah Veitch<br>ISBN 0 352 33531 9 | ☐ |
| EDEN UNVEILED | Maria del Rey<br>ISBN 0 352 33542 4 | ☐ |
| THE HANDMAIDENS | Aran Ashe<br>ISBN 0 352 33282 4 | ☐ |
| HIS MISTRESS'S VOICE | G. C. Scott<br>ISBN 0 352 33425 8 | ☐ |
| THE IMAGE | Jean de Berg<br>ISBN 0 352 33350 2 | ☐ |
| THE INSTITUTE | Maria del Rey<br>ISBN 0 352 33352 9 | ☐ |
| LINGERING LESSONS | Sarah Veitch<br>ISBN 0 352 33539 4 | ☐ |
| A MATTER OF POSSESSION | G. C. Scott<br>ISBN 0 352 33468 1 | ☐ |
| OBSESSION | Maria del Rey<br>ISBN 0 352 33375 8 | ☐ |
| THE PLEASURE PRINCIPLE | Maria del Rey<br>ISBN 0 352 33482 7 | ☐ |
| SERVING TIME | Sarah Veitch<br>ISBN 0 352 33509 2 | ☐ |
| SISTERHOOD OF THE INSTITUTE | Maria del Rey<br>ISBN 0 352 33456 8 | ☐ |
| THE TRAINING GROUNDS | Sarah Veitch<br>ISBN 0 352 33526 2 | ☐ |
| UNDERWORLD | Maria del Rey<br>ISBN 0 352 33552 1 | ☐ |

------✂------------------------

Please send me the books I have ticked above.

Name ..................................................................

Address ..................................................................

..................................................................

..................................................................

.................................... Post code ................

Send to: **Cash Sales, Nexus Books, Thames Wharf Studios, Rainville Road, London W6 9HA**

US customers: for prices and details of how to order books for delivery by mail, call 1-800-805-1083.

Please enclose a cheque or postal order, made payable to **Nexus Books Ltd**, to the value of the books you have ordered plus postage and packing costs as follows:

UK and BFPO – £1.00 for the first book, 50p for each subsequent book.

Overseas (including Republic of Ireland) – £2.00 for the first book, £1.00 for each subsequent book.

If you would prefer to pay by VISA, ACCESS/MASTER-CARD, AMEX, DINERS CLUB or SWITCH, please write your card number and expiry date here:

..................................................................

Please allow up to 28 days for delivery.

**Signature** ..................................................................

------✂------------------------